CALL OF THE HEATHER

CALL OF THE HEATHER

Gwen Kirkwood

Severn House Large Print
London & New York

This first large print edition published 2008
in Great Britain and the USA by
SEVERN HOUSE PUBLISHERS of
9-15 High Street, Sutton, Surrey, SM1 1DF.
First world regular print edition published 2007 by
Severn House Publishers, London and New York.

British Library Cataloguing in Publication Data

Kirkwood, Gwen
  Call of the heather. - Large print ed.
  1. Country life - Scotland - Fiction 2. Scotland - Social
  life and customs - Fiction 3. Domestic fiction 4. Large
  type books
  I. Title
  823.9'14[F]

  ISBN-13: 978-0-7278-7728-4

Printed and bound in Great Britain by
MPG Books Ltd, Bodmin, Cornwall.

Acknowledgements

I would like to thank the staff of the Georgetown and Ewart Libraries in Dumfries and Galloway for their support and help with local research.
Also Morag Williams at the Crichton Royal Archive Centre.

THE SKYLARK
by James Hogg

Bird of the wilderness,
Blythesome and cumberless,
Sweet may thy matin be o'er
moorland and lea!
Emblem of happiness,
Blest is thy dwelling-place –
O to abide in the desert with thee!

Wild is thy lay and loud,
Far in the downy cloud,
Love gives it energy, love gave it birth.
Where, on thy dewy wing,
Where art thou journeying?
Thy lay is in heaven, thy love is on earth.

O'er fell and fountain sheen,
O'er moor and mountain green,
O'er the red steamer that heralds the day,
Over the cloudlet dim,
Over the rainbow's rim,
Musical cherub, soar, singing, away!

Then, when the gloaming comes,
Low in the heather blooms,
Sweet will thy welcome and bed of love be!
Emblem of happiness,
Blest is thy dwelling-place –
O to abide in the desert with thee!

One

Andrew and Victoria Pringle stood together on the highest point of Langmune Farm looking across to the distant sparkle of the Solway Firth. Beyond it the purple outline of the Galloway hills was rimmed in gold as the September sun began to sink below the horizon.

Across the burn, high on the other side of the glen, they could see the small white farmhouse of High Bowie nestled against the hill. Andrew smiled.

'That must be young Billy Lennox still playing in the garden, and I believe Maggie is in the doorway. I expect she's calling him in for bed.'

'You have excellent eyesight, Andrew. They are just matchstick figures to me at this distance. It must be lonely for Billy, living at the head of the glen.'

'He's a nice bairn and he seems happy enough any time I see him. It's a long walk on his own, down to Darlonachie to the school.'

'It is, but Maggie says he's inherited his father's stiff upper lip. He doesn't complain. What a glorious autumn day this has been. I expect Maggie and wee Billy are like us,

9

reluctant to end it,' Victoria said with a new awareness of how fragile the simple pleasures in life could be. 'It feels good to be alive. It's hard to believe the world is at war, with young men killing each other. It makes me feel guilty to have so much...' She gestured with a sweep of her arm. 'So much space and beauty, and peace.' A skylark rose and soared into the clear blue of the evening sky, revelling in the vastness of the heavens. Andrew's own heart was filled with a deep appreciation of his surroundings. *Please God let us keep our freedom and our country*, he prayed silently. He rested his chin on the crown of his wife's head, feeling the abundant softness of her hair, listening as she murmured lines from James Hogg's poem.

' "Bird of the wilderness, Blythesome and cumberless".'

Andrew knew the poem. Mr Nelson had taught it to them at Darlonachie village school. He whispered part of the last verse close to her ear, his voice husky now.

'"Then, when the gloaming comes, Low in the heather blooms, Sweet will thy welcome and bed of love be..."'

One finger traced a path down the silky skin of her neck. Victoria leaned into him, loving his warmth and the hard strength of his chest. His free hand rested lightly on her swollen stomach.

'Are you all right?'

'I'm fine. In fact I feel I am the luckiest woman alive tonight. In another few weeks we shall have our second child and every night I thank God for our good fortune.' She shivered involuntarily. 'I couldn't bear it if you have to go to war and leave wee Libby and me. I can't help thinking of all the young men who will be leaving their wives and children to fight. What a waste of human life. I feel so sorry for them all, whichever side they're on.'

'So do I, dearest Vicky.' He sensed she was thinking of her twin brother in Edinburgh. 'But please don't distress yourself.'

'I won't, but I know Mark will volunteer. They're bound to need doctors. It's selfish, but I hope he doesn't join the army.' She twisted within the curve of his arm, turning her face up to his. He lowered his head and sought her mouth in a lingering kiss.

'I love you, Mrs Pringle,' Andrew said gruffly. 'I never tire of calling you my wife, Victoria.'

'And I never tire of hearing you. It doesn't seem three years since we were married. I needed to come up here this evening, just the two of us.' She sighed. 'But I think we should be getting back now in case Libby has wakened and is leading Miss Traill a dance.'

'You're right,' Andrew nodded, smiling as he turned them homeward, 'but I think Miss Traill's dancing days are over.'

'Mmm, but Libby doesn't realize that. She loves to take her hand and toddle round the garden or through the orchard to see the pigs, and Miss Traill can never say no when Libby looks up at her with her beguiling smile.'

'It's those big brown eyes of hers. They're

11

irresistible, like her Mama's.' He grinned, then sobered. 'I don't think Miss Traill will allow Libby to take advantage.'

Miss Traill had been at Langmune longer than either of them. She had come to the farm as a young woman to be housekeeper to Mr Rennie, the previous tenant. Andrew had worked for him since the day he left Darlonachie village school when he was almost fourteen. It never occurred to Andrew that his former employer had recognized his love of the land and his instinctive care of the animals from the beginning. Later, in his increasing frailty, Fraser Rennie had observed and respected Andrew's integrity and high principles. He had made up his mind to recompense his young protégé even before Andrew had risked his life to rescue him and Miss Traill from the fire which had destroyed a large part of Langmune House.

On his death, Mr Rennie had rewarded his housekeeper's care and loyalty by leaving her enough money to live in moderate comfort and maintain her independence if she wished, but to Andrew Pringle he had left his entire stock of cattle, horses and implements, plus a recommendation to the Laird that he should consider him as the next tenant. Miss Traill's leg had been badly broken during the fire and she had gratefully accepted Andrew and Victoria's offer to share their home as long as she desired. They had grown extremely fond of the elderly woman.

Now, as the couple drew nearer the farmyard,

Victoria paused to look down the slope to the three farm cottages. Her eyes were troubled.

'Do you think they will take any of our men to fight this awful war?' she asked. Andrew remained silent, a thoughtful frown creasing his brow. It was a question he had asked himself every day since the meeting he had attended almost a week ago.

The year previously he had joined the local branch of the National Farmers' Union. He still missed the stimulating discussions he had shared with Mr Rennie, so he had sought the company and opinions of other farmers with serious views on farming trends. As a member of the Union he had also made sure Langmune was insured, a step the late Luke Crainby had neglected, which had meant there was no money to restore the farmhouse to its former beauty after the fire. Only the back part now remained standing, narrow and ugly to an onlooker, but to Andrew and Victoria it was their home and they were content – or at least they had been until Mr Chamberlain's announcement three weeks ago, telling the world that Great Britain was at war with Germany.

'Andrew?' Victoria squeezed his arm and repeated her question.

'I don't know, Victoria.' He sighed. 'At the NFU meeting we were warned there would be a limit to the able-bodied men we shall be allowed to employ, even though farming and mining are to be priority occupations. According to Tom McBurnie, the local president, the government

13

had plans drawn up some time ago, even though the Ministry of Food was only set up officially five days after war was declared. He says they're already recruiting girls, some of them from the city, to join the Women's Land Army, and they'll be sending them to replace our young men.'

'City girls? Surely not! How will they manage?'

'I don't know, Vicky.' He put an arm around her shoulders and drew her closer. 'I hope they don't take young Jocky Conley. He's an excellent stocksman. He's keen to know everything about the cows, how they're milking, how I feed them and about the bull and the breeding. His father is a good horseman but he doesn't have Jocky's enquiring mind.'

'What about Jem?' Victoria asked anxiously. Before her marriage to Andrew she had worked at Darlonachie Castle with Jem Wright's wife, Milly. The couple had married in haste and then had come to work at Langmune as herdsman and dairy worker. A few months later they had a baby daughter named Gracie. The following year Milly had given birth to Miriam. A third baby, Sylvie, had been born three months ago. 'I don't know how Milly would cope if Jem had to join the army.'

'Let's hope it doesn't come to that, for all our sakes,' Andrew said. Jem Wright was not the brightest of young men but he was a hard worker. 'The general opinion is that the government has allowed the country to become too depen-

14

dant on imported food. Now they're afraid our merchant ships will be targeted by the German navy in an effort to starve us into surrendering. It will be up to farmers to provide as much food as we can. Officials are drawing up lists of English farms which have lain uncultivated during the depression. A lot of things are going to change in farming with this war, that's for sure.'

Thoughts of the war were temporarily forgotten when Victoria gave birth to a baby boy on October 7th, but just over a week later came a rude awakening. A German submarine had stolen unbelievably close and succeeded in destroying the Royal Oak in its home base of Scapa Flow with the loss of eight hundred men. Then there was a German air raid over the Firth of Forth. The war had suddenly become very real.

On the following Sunday Andrew's parents, Polly and Joe Pringle, made their way up the glen after attending the morning service at Darlonachie Kirk. Victoria had lived with them and their family throughout her teenage years and she loved them dearly. She knew at once that Polly had been crying. She had just finished feeding the baby but she rose to push the kettle on to the fire for a cup of tea. Her heart was heavy. Every family was losing young able-bodied men and the Pringles had four sons. At twenty-six Andrew was the oldest but as a working farmer producing food his labour was considered essential. Twenty-two-year-old Willie worked on a local sheep farm but his employer was elderly and Willie was his main man and therefore also an essential worker, but young George was one of three men on a beef and sheep farm.

'Is it George, Ma?' Andrew asked quietly. 'Has he had his call-up papers?'

'How did you know?' Polly turned startled, tear-drenched eyes to her eldest son.

'He's been expecting them. He's unmarried and he knew Mr Barras wouldn't be allowed to keep three men. He'll be lucky if he keeps the other two. He's young enough to work himself if he wasna so damned lazy.'

'He'll have to now,' Joe Pringle said, pulling hard on his pipe. 'The other young fellow has had word to go for a medical. His wife's only a wee bit of a lassie and they're expecting a bairn.'

'Oor Josh is only a wee bit laddie.' Polly bit back a sob. 'But they've sent him his papers too...'

'Josh?' Andrew and Victoria repeated simultaneously, staring wide-eyed at Joe and Polly.

'The kettle is boiling. I'll make some tea, shall I?' Miss Traill interrupted gently. She knew instinctively that Polly Pringle was going to need some sustenance.

'Yes please,' Victoria said. She laid the baby in his pram and went to hug her, as Polly had so often comforted her. 'Surely they'll not take Josh? Not yet? He's only eighteen.'

16

'He thinks he ought to go,' Polly sniffed, and wiped her eyes. 'He ... he says he'll apply for the RAF. He's done well in his exams, especially in mathematics. Mr Nelson, the school master, says it's young men like Josh they need in the air force.'

Joe moved aside to let Miss Traill pour the tea. 'Have you chosen a name for the wee fellow yet?' he asked in an effort to change the subject.

'We thought we would call him Fraser. That was Mr Rennie's name and he was very good to me,' Andrew said.

'Fraser Joseph Pringle,' Victoria reminded him and saw Joe's eyes brighten and a fleeting smile erase some of the lines on his weathered face. He was head gardener at Darlonachie Castle and spent most of his time outside in all weathers.

'Are you making any changes to the gardens?' Victoria asked, trying to keep the conversation light-hearted.

'One of the lads has gone off already. The other failed his medical. Bad eyesight, I think, or bad ears. I reckon he has both, as well as a thick head,' Joe grumbled. 'Everybody is supposed to grow more vegetables. We'll dig up some o' the grass. Mrs Crainby says we're not to grow them for the local folks. She's going to sell them. You'll have heard she's putting up the rents? She thinks the tenants will be getting loads of money now the government is urging farmers to supply British produce.'

'The only thing we know for sure is income

17

tax is to be raised to seven and six in the pound,' Andrew said.

'It said on the radio the government is going to regulate prices to stop people taking advantage of shortages,' Victoria put in.

'It'll not stop Mistress Crainby frae putting up the rents if she's made up her mind. The new factor is as mean as she is. It's rumoured the estate office is in a real mess since Mr Forsythe left. She thought she could handle the estate herself. She demanded rent twice over from some of the tenants but some havena paid at all. I'll bet Mr Forsythe is pleased he retired when the young laird died.'

'I'll bet he is,' Andrew said with feeling. 'Forsythe still calls in at Home Farm to see Luke Crainby's father though. I've met him there once or twice.'

'Aye, folks say it was Mr Forsythe who suggested Luke Crainby should extend the house at Home Farm so that Sir William could move out o' the castle before the young laird died. He's away frae Mrs Crainby's clutches at Home Farm.'

About a week later Victoria had a phone call from Maggie Lennox who lived across the glen at High Bowie Farm. She sounded upset.

'I'm telephoning from Sir William's house,' she said. 'I'm really worried. Can I come to Langmune in the morning, as soon as I've dropped Billy at school? I need to talk to someone who will understand.'

'All right, Maggie. You sure it will wait until tomorrow?'

'It is urgent, b-but I can't talk now. Sir William is in the sitting room. I don't want to upset him too.'

'I understand. We'll see you tomorrow.' Victoria put the phone down with a puzzled frown. They all knew Doris listened in at the telephone exchange in the village but Maggie had seemed more concerned about upsetting Sir William Crainby. He had lost Luke, his only surviving son, while she had lost the man she loved, the father of her child. Luke Crainby's death had united them and Maggie had grown fond of the old man. There was a growing attachment between six-year-old Billy and his grandfather too. Sir William had bought a pony which he kept at Home Farm, proof that he welcomed his illegitimate grandson.

When Andrew came in for his midday meal Victoria told him of Maggie's proposed visit. 'She seems dreadfully worried about something,' she added.

They were just finishing their meal when a car pulled into the yard. Miss Traill was standing at the sink filling the kettle. 'Why, it's the Bentley Mr Luke used to drive!' she exclaimed. 'The one he was driving the last time he came to Langmune.' She had gone quite pale. 'I think I'll take my afternoon rest in my own room, Victoria. I don't recognize the driver.'

'Shall I bring you in a cup of tea?' Victoria asked.

19

'No thank you, dear.' She frowned. 'He looks a very haughty man.' There was an impatient wrap on the door so she hurried away. Both the baby and Libby had already settled down for their afternoon nap and Victoria hoped the man would not disturb them. She could hear Andrew speaking to him, his voice rising as though in anger.

'You'd better come in and meet my wife.' Andrew led the man into the large room which had sufficed as kitchen and living room since the fire destroyed the main part of the house. Victoria saw him looking around, his lip curling contemptuously, making his moustache bristle like an angry cat. She wanted to laugh but she could see the pulse beating in Andrew's jaw and she knew he was either upset or angry. 'Victoria, this is Mr Ward, the new factor for Darlonachie Estate. He says he has been instructed by Mrs Crainby to serve us with notice to quit Langmune within three months.' Andrew was enunciating each word with exaggerated clarity. Victoria looked at him, her eyes wide and puzzled.

'I'm sure there's no need to trouble your wife with such matters,' Mr Ward snapped impatiently. 'If you're not man enough to handle your own business there's little wonder you're so far behind with your rent.' Victoria gasped and saw Andrew's face go pale, then flush with anger. She moved close to his side, slipping her hand into his, willing him to stay calm in any dealings with such an obnoxious man.

20

'My wife and I are partners in all things, Mister Ward,' Andrew said coldly. 'I think you have made a serious mistake in coming here. We owe no debts to any man or woman. Now I am asking you to leave.'

'Why you impudent young pup, I'll ... I shall...'

'Leave.'

Even Victoria was not sure whether Andrew had issued a command or asked a question.

'I shall not leave until I have delivered this demand for the three years' rent which you owe and a notice to be out of this farm within three months.'

'You can't do that!' Victoria heard herself crying.

'Oh but I can, Mrs Pringle, and I intend to do so. We shall be asking a good rent for this place now the war has started.' He actually sounded pleased about the war. *Obviously he has no sons going away to fight,* Victoria thought bitterly.

'I think you should go back to Mrs Crainby and get your facts sorted out before you come here throwing your weight around,' Andrew said coldly. 'Langmune Farm, the land, the implements and all the stock belong jointly and equally to myself and my wife.'

'Tell me another fairy story,' Ward sneered. Andrew flushed angrily and his blue eyes narrowed.

'Mr Luke Crainby made the change before he died.'

'He couldn't have done. He didn't have time.

And why should he do such a thing for the likes of you? You're dreaming.'

'It is no dream. My wife's father was Luke Crainby's cousin. He wanted to make some recompense for the way she had been treated.'

'Another bastard trying to claim rights that don't exist,' Ward sneered. His eyes glittered coldly. 'Prove it then,' he challenged. Victoria and Andrew looked at each other in dismay. They didn't have any proof. 'As I thought,' he snapped. 'I know all the tricks people try when claiming birthrights under false pretences.'

'They are not false pretences. Mrs Crainby knows that,' Andrew said furiously. 'Now get out of my house before I throw you out.' The man clearly believed Andrew might seize him and fling him out, for he rose quickly, but stopped near the door.

'I shall bring a warrant. I shall evict you, and I shall take your stock in payment of the three years' rent you owe.' He made a swift exit, slamming the door behind him. Andrew and Victoria stared at each other in dismay.

'Luke Crainby didn't give us any deeds, or anything to say the farm belonged to us, did he?' Andrew asked.

'No,' Victoria whispered. 'He was very ill though. He died within a few days of our going to the solicitor, if you remember. Could Mrs Crainby be right?' She looked at Andrew in horror.

Two

Victoria could not sleep that night. She suspected the new factor was the cause of Maggie Lennox's anxiety too. They all knew how spiteful Henrietta Crainby was, and how greedy she was for land and money. Even Luke, her husband, had realized that after their marriage. Victoria knew he had firmly believed his mistress and their son were safe from his wife's treachery at High Bowie Farm. He had transferred Home Farm back to his father's name to keep the older man safe from his daughter-in-law's scheming. Luke Crainby had intended to make sure Victoria and her twin brother Mark had some security too, but had he been too ill to complete the legal documents?

She was white-faced and weary when she followed Andrew to the byre to start the milking early the following morning. She had already lit the fire as she did every day before she went outside. This morning she felt shivery and cold and wished she could stay indoors but she knew it was nerves and lack of sleep that were making her feel ill. She couldn't find the energy to talk as she moved from one cow to the next with her bucket and stool. Andrew was equally quiet.

23

Jem Wright, and Jocky, who also helped with the milking, had also sensed that something was wrong. They got on with the job in silence instead of their usual desultory chat and jokes. As soon as Victoria had finished milking her last cow she always hurried indoors to check up on the children and start the porridge but this morning Miss Traill was already in the kitchen with the porridge boiling.

'Dear Miss Traill, thank you,' Victoria said wearily as she scrubbed her hands. 'But I don't like to see you looking so pale and anxious.' She could hear both Libby and the baby crying. She knew little Fraser had sensed her tension and it seemed to affect her milk. He had not settled well during the night either. 'I'll go and bring the children down,' she said.

'You don't look as though you slept much yourself, Victoria,' Miss Traill commented.

'I didn't, and I suspect Maggie Lennox is coming to talk over the same problem. No wonder she didn't want Sir William to know, or to let Doris listen in at the telephone exchange. I'll bet that horrid man has been hounding her too.'

'Yes, you're probably right,' Miss Traill nodded, her face troubled, 'but he could only do it with Mrs Crainby's authority.'

'Well she always hated me, however much I tried to please when I was cooking at the castle. Her husband preferred Maggie's company to hers, so she has no reason to like her either. This must be her way of seeking revenge. Maggie

24

will be here as soon as she has taken Billy to school but I don't know whether we can give her much comfort.'

Victoria ran up the stairs to get the children and came down more slowly, balancing Libby on one hip and cradling Fraser in her free arm. Halfway across the kitchen she stopped, her eyes widening. Andrew was seating himself at the well-scrubbed table ready for his porridge.

'What's wrong, Victoria?'

'Why didn't we think of it before? Mr Jenkinson said if ever we needed him, we must call on him. He will understand this situation better than anyone. He would tell us if there is anything we can do, even if we do have to pay for his advice.' She set her small chin determinedly. 'We can't let Mrs Crainby put us out of Langmune without a fight. You must telephone and ask for an appointment, Andrew, as soon as his office opens. Maggie will be here by then too.'

'We've nothing to lose.' Andrew sat up, his brain busy. 'In fact, if Maggie Lennox is having the same trouble with Ward, it can't be because Luke Crainby was too ill to complete the transfer in her case. Remember he told us he had put High Bowie Farm into her name as soon as he knew he was seriously ill.'

'Yes, he did say that,' Miss Traill nodded. 'I heard him the day he came to call and he stayed for lunch, just before he died.'

Andrew telephoned the solicitor's office promptly at nine o'clock. His receptionist had not even had time to take her coat off and her

25

voice was cool and brisk.

'Mr Jenkinson is going to Edinburgh on business. He'll be away for three days. I'll make an appointment for his return.'

'But it's urgent,' Andrew said in dismay. 'We think Mrs Lennox needs to see him too.'

'Hold on a moment, please.' He heard the secretary speaking to someone. She came back on the line, her tone more affable. 'Mr Jenkinson says if you can be here in half an hour he will see you before he leaves.'

'We'll be there,' Andrew replied promptly, oblivious to the fact that Victoria was still feeding the baby, Maggie had not yet arrived and he needed to wash and change.

They met Maggie Lennox's old van chugging up the track, and they persuaded her to leave it and jump into the car. She looked as white-faced and haggard as Victoria felt. As they had anticipated, her problem was similar to their own and Ward had bullied and threatened her mercilessly.

When they arrived at the office the secretary showed them into Mr Jenkinson's office.

'Our problem is the same so it will save time if we all see you together,' Andrew said and began to explain about the factor's threats to evict them and claim the back rent. As he talked Mr Jenkinson's face grew grim and his neat features formed a most frightening scowl.

'You have no need to worry,' he said when Andrew finished explaining. 'If Mrs Crainby had any common sense at all she would have checked the estate books, and so would the factor if he had doubts. The farms were officially and legally transferred from the Estate. In the case of Langmune, Luke Crainby signed the documents as soon as I had them completed. He died the following day. I have the deeds safely locked away.' He smiled at the expressions of relief on the three anxious faces. 'Perhaps I should have explained it is customary, and safer, for the deeds to be kept secure, either with a lawyer or at a bank.'

'We thought Mr Crainby must have died before he could sign the documents for Langmune. Even so it has taken Mrs Crainby a long time to look into it,' Andrew said. 'It is three years since he died.'

'Mmm, perhaps she and her new factor are trying to be too clever,' Mr Jenkinson said with some satisfaction. 'She has removed her legal affairs to another firm of solicitors.'

'We didn't know that.'

'Oh yes. She blamed me for advising Luke Crainby to put the estate in trust for their young daughter, Charlotte. In fact it was Luke's own idea, but he was a fair man and he arranged a generous income for his wife. I merely carried out his wishes. However, we must deal with your problems. There is no question of the factor needing to see the deeds. I shall write him a letter. I relish the opportunity to warn him and Mrs Crainby that if they continue their harassment the matter will be brought before the courts. I've heard of the man Ward before. I

27

shall be surprised if he stays very long at Dar-lonachie. He has a reputation for moving on if he has nothing to gain for himself.'

'It is a big relief. Thank you very much for seeing us at such short notice,' Andrew said.

'It is my pleasure,' Mr Jenkinson said with a satisfied nod. 'Yes indeed, I would give much to be a fly on the wall when Mrs Crainby and her factor read my letter.'

Maggie returned with Andrew and Victoria to Langmune to tell Miss Traill their news and to enjoy a cup of Camp coffee.

'Everything is being rationed,' Maggie sighed as she sipped the substitute coffee. 'We shall struggle to get a cup of tea soon according to Mr Ross, the grocer.'

'Of course,' Victoria sighed. 'All those things are imported, and if the ships cannot get through...'

Souter Ward marched up to Darlonachie Castle in a furious temper. Henrietta Crainby was never at her best in the morning and she did not take kindly to being rudely disturbed by her factor. He must learn he was her employee the same as the rest. She kept him waiting, pacing up and down the hall like a caged lion.

'Read this!' he commanded without any pretence of the deference she expected.

'A letter? Surely it could have waited.'

'You've made a fool of me,' he accused. 'Read it. You've made a fool of yourself as well.'

Henrietta scowled at that and snatched the

28

letter, seeing at once it was from Jenkinson, her late husband's solicitor. Her face flushed with anger as she read the letter informing her that two of the farms were no longer part of the Estate. Not only that, her husband had put them in the possession of the two women she most detested: Lachlan – or Mrs Pringle as she was now – and the Lennox woman, his whore, she thought bitterly.

'He was ill,' she muttered. 'I didn't think he had the strength, or the energy, to undertake such business...'

'You should have checked before you gave me instructions to deal ruthlessly with them. And another thing, you didn't tell me that Home Farm no longer supplies butter, milk and eggs and so on to the castle, and to my household. The farm manager tells me it no longer comes under my supervision. Wright, the herdsman, was downright rude.'

'Oh, that...' Henrietta gave a false, high-pitched laugh. 'That's only temporary until the old man dies. Home Farm will revert to my estate then.'

'Are you sure about that? It didn't sound that way to me.'

'Of course I'm sure. You can sack those two men then.'

'The farm could be badly neglected by then if there's only Blake managing it.'

'It will not be for long. Sir William is an old man...'

'I've seen him walking with a stick, but he

29

was playing ball with a young boy too. Who is he, the boy? He's often there.' He knew well enough who Billy Lennox was. He had lost no time in sniffing out the gossip, but he enjoyed rubbing salt into people's wounds and Henrietta Crainby was too haughty for his liking. He was used to women fawning over him. Moreover he was still smarting from the tone of the lawyer's letter and his instruction to make a personal apology to the Pringles and Mrs Lennox for his harassment. There was no way he was going to apologize face to face, but he would have to draft a letter, or a brief note at any rate.

'And what about the other three farmers I'm supposed to evict?' he challenged Mrs Crainby. 'Are you sure they're still part of your estate? And are you sure you have had no rents since your husband died?'

'Of course they are still part of the estate,' Henrietta snapped petulantly. 'There were always some tenants who didn't pay their rents in full. My husband or his factor were always calling on them for payment then settling for what they could afford instead of evicting them. No one has called on them so they haven't paid any rent. Now you must deal with them.'

'Even if it means giving them notice to quit?'

'Of course. Take whatever steps are necessary. I need more income to keep the castle going, and there's your own salary to pay now. You will need to earn it.' She raised her pert little nose in the air and was about to leave. Ward's eyes narrowed and his thin lips tightened but his tone was deceptively smooth.

'Speaking of the castle, have you considered the letter from the government yet? Will you reply, or shall I deal with it?'

'Neither,' Henrietta Crainby said sullenly and her cheeks flushed with anger. 'I told you, we shall ignore it.'

'Then don't say I didn't warn you,' Ward shrugged. 'If the army want to requisition the castle for their own use they will do so, whether you agree or not. I advise you to strike a deal with them and cooperate.'

'You *advise!* You overstep your position, Ward. This is my home.'

'Maybe it is, but that will not stop them. The Air Ministry have taken over a farm belonging to a friend of mine. They moved in and demolished the farmhouse and the buildings. It was his home too. They told him we have to make sacrifices for the good of the country, all of us.' He turned and left her staring after him, her face screwed up with fury.

The Ministry of Food had brought in controls as soon as war was declared. Maximum prices had been fixed for fat cattle, sheep and pigs, as well as for potatoes and sugar; eggs were to be brought under the same legislation. Andrew was more concerned by the order to reduce by a third the consumption of cereals fed to livestock. This would mean trying to feed the cows on hay and turnips with little in the way of cattle cake as a supplement during the winter. The milk yields

31

would certainly drop, which meant the monthly income from milk would fall too. The pigs were even more dependent on bought-in meal.

'I think we shall have to cut back the number of sows,' he said to Victoria.

'Oh, Andrew, we can't do that,' she protested. 'I know the income from the pigs varies terribly depending on supply and demand and bacon imports, but you said the extra money had been a great benefit.'

'It's the only way if we can't buy enough meal to feed them.'

There had been only one sow at Langmune when he and Victoria were first married. They kept two pigs a year to fatten for the house and sold the rest as soon as they were weaned. It had been Victoria's idea to increase the number of sows. She looked after them and the poultry herself. They had brought a necessary addition to the farm's income.

'We shall miss the extra money,' Andrew admitted. 'It has helped us to maintain the fences and the drains the same as Mr Rennie did, and we have a bit set aside for emergencies now. The trouble is the government can't import enough cereal to supply the demand. We have to cut back.'

'But I do everything I can to cheapen the pig feed...'

'I know, but I don't see how else we can reduce the bought-in meal,' Andrew said unhappily. He had known Victoria would be upset. Even before they were married she had been determined to earn money and be a proper partner in every way. He couldn't have had a better wife. She boiled up vegetable peelings and any scraps she could glean from the garden. Two of the sows had rings in their noses and grazed all summer in the orchard, clearing up the fallen apples and pears.

'Perhaps we should let each of the men have a young pig to rear,' Andrew suggested. 'They could use their own scraps and I think they would each get a small allowance of meal. The government are encouraging pig clubs and allotments so that people can grow their own food. We may not be rationed to four ounces of bacon a week but we do have to get a licence to kill a pig now. We're not allowed to kill more than two a year for home consumption.'

'All right,' Victoria agreed reluctantly. 'We'll let the men rear their own instead of supplying them whenever we have a pig for killing.'

'There's another problem too,' Andrew sighed. 'The Ministry of Food has ordered all farmers to plough up at least a tenth more grazing land and produce more home-grown cereals and potatoes. The nation is in desperate need of food.'

'Will that be a big problem? We usually plough one field every year anyway.'

'We do, but it is as much as Jock Conley and his horses can manage. He's not getting any younger and young Jocky has received his call-up papers. He has to go for a medical on Tuesday. We shall miss him badly.'

'He never said anything to me.'

'No. He doesn't want to fight and his mother is terribly upset.'

'No wonder. Couldn't we apply for an exemption? After all, they've already taken Daniel.' The young man had been a general worker and lived with his mother in one of the three Langmune cottages. He had been one of the first to be taken into the army.

'I know. I'm missing Daniel's help more than I expected. His mother has decided to move to her sister's. We shall have a spare cottage, but it's almost impossible to get another able-bodied man. Jocky will be a big loss. He's used to the work and he's so good with animals. Even if Milly had been able to milk she wouldn't have time to do much more than the dairy now she has a young family.'

'And I'm not as free as I was,' Victoria admitted. 'I'm afraid to leave Libby with Miss Traill too often although she's so anxious to help. She's easily tired these days. Wee Fraser is easier for her to manage while he's in his pram.'

'I know.' Andrew sighed. 'We're going to have to make changes, big changes.' He had known Victoria would understand how serious their situation was. She had acquired a good grasp of the running of the farm and the seasonal work as well as the daily routines. 'Unfortunately the government officials don't understand our problems. They have to recruit as many men as possible for the forces and that's all there is to it.'

Three

Christmas came and went almost unnoticed. Andrew's brother, George, was in the army and was expecting to be sent to France at any minute. Josh was in the air force. Victoria's heart was heavy whenever she thought of them. She had lived with Polly and Joe Pringle after the death of her great-grandmother and the boys had been like brothers to her.

She had been nineteen when Doctor Grantly had broken the news that she had a brother of her own: Mark Jacobs was her twin. It had been a terrible shock to learn they had been separated at birth. Mark had been adopted by Colonel and Mrs Jacobs, the doctor's sister and her husband, so he had spent his first ten years in Lancashire. Doctor Peter Grantly and his wife Anna had brought him back to Darlonachie after the death of the doctor's sister. They had cared for him as a well-loved nephew, sending him to Darlonachie village school. There had been some friendly rivalry between them but from the beginning there was an uncanny bond which had strengthened over the years.

Even when Mark moved to Dumfries Academy, and later to Edinburgh University, they had

35

written long letters and seen each other at every opportunity. Now Mark was a doctor and Victoria had a terrible fear he would insist on fighting for his country and using his skills to help his fellow men. He had been engaged to Catriona MacNaught since he was a medical student. Catriona was a nurse and she shared his interest in medicine but Mark was as fiercely independent as Victoria. He had vowed he would not marry until he could support a wife and children and provide a loving home. As an adopted son of Colonel and Mrs Jacobs he had been fortunate but he knew how Victoria had been taunted and cruelly treated by Henrietta Crainby and her ilk.

'We never knew our own parents,' he had once said to Victoria, 'so I shall never do as our father did, even though he did die fighting for his country. He should have waited until he returned.'

Now they were in the midst of another war. What did the future hold for Mark and Catriona? Victoria had been happy to know her twin had found true love, as she had done with Andrew, but Catriona was an only child and she was possessive. Victoria sensed she resented the ties of kinship that bound her and Mark.

Victoria and Andrew listened intently to the news bulletins on the radio and indeed it seemed Mr Chamberlain shared the beliefs of the Glasgow evacuees in believing Britain was safe from Hitler. That was until news came that Holland and Belgium had been overrun by the Nazis with the outrageous excuse that they were being protected from an invasion by the French and British. Now all around the British coast concrete bollards and lookout posts were being built.

On May 10th 1940 Winston Churchill took over as Prime Minister with Clement Atlee as deputy and a coalition government was formed. Victoria's thoughts were on all those she knew who were already fighting for their country – Daniel, the first to go, Jocky Conley, George and Josh, her brothers-in-law. She shuddered, praying Mark would not choose to go too.

'Mr Churchill has promised to tell us the truth,' Miss Traill said, giving them the latest radio news whenever they gathered around the table for a meal. Even Libby seemed subdued by the serious faces of her elders.

The truth when it came from the Prime Minister was that he had nothing to offer the British people but blood, toil, tears and sweat, and his own determination to win the war against the Nazis.

'Not much of a promise, is it?' Andrew said wearily. He was already working from dawn to dusk and longer. He didn't see what more he could give – except his life. Every night he thought of his brothers, George and Josh, and prayed they were safe somewhere.

Towards the end of May the government rushed through an Emergency Powers Act, giving unlimited authority over every person and all the property in the country.

'Men in aircraft factories are to work ten hours a day, seven days a week,' Jock Conley remarked to Andrew when they heard the news. 'Well good luck to the buggers. We do that anyway, even when there is no war.' He had grown bitter since Jocky, his only son, had been taken into the army. They had no idea where he was but on his last short leave he had hinted that he expected to be sent to France. Andrew remained silent. He understood Jock's feelings but took comfort from knowing that however hard they worked at Langmune they always knew there would be an end to each season and task whether it was harvest or hay or lambing, and their lives were not in danger from their work.

Miners were being urged to produce as much coal as humanly possible to supply power to the factories, particularly munitions factories, and news of accidents leaked out despite efforts to keep things quiet. It was vital to keep up the morale of the ordinary British people, as well as to prevent the Germans from hearing of any such disasters. Andrew understood the reasons behind the policies but some of the men with sweeping new powers acted like little Hitlers themselves and caused resentment.

Even while she dreaded it, Victoria had half expected the letter, but when it arrived and she recognized Mark's writing her fingers trembled as she drew out the single sheet. Even without reading it she knew Mark was writing to say he was joining the army. Three days later he arrived at Langmune.

'I couldn't leave without saying goodbye, Victoria. I wanted to see you and Andrew and the children before I go.'

'Did you call on the Grantlys?'

'Yes. It was a brief visit but they understood I needed to see you. They know I shall always be grateful for the loving home and fine education they have given me. I-I hope you don't mind but I have named them as my next of kin. I didn't want you or Catriona to receive a telegram if—'

'Don't even think about it, Mark! You must come back to us safe and sound.'

All too soon it was time to say goodbye. Victoria's heart felt as icy as the waters of the Arctic as he hugged her tightly, then turned his face silently towards the path that would take him away. He had gone only a few yards when he turned back and hugged her again.

'Catriona has always been a little jealous of the close bond between us, Victoria, but I love her very much so I hope you will understand. You will keep in touch with her, won't you?'

'Of course I will,' Victoria promised. 'Remind her about the wee cottage that Luke Crainby left to you. Mrs Grantly and I keep it ready. We're always hoping you will both come and stay at Darlonachie, if only for a few days.'

'Yes,' he sighed. 'There are times when I long for the peace of our wee childhood den and the heather-clad hills where we ran so freely. I'll tell Catriona about the cottage. She would be safer in Darlonachie, away from the city.'

'We thought it was to be used by a family of evacuees but most of them returned home to Glasgow. They said all the talk of war and bombing was phoney.'

Mark's lean face grew grim. 'Hitler will not give up so easily. Take care, Victoria, please take care.' Then with a final hug Mark was gone. Victoria felt as though a little piece of her heart had been torn out and gone with him. That night Andrew held her close and caressed her tenderly. He understood how her heart ached for Mark.

People on the south coast were more aware of what was happening across the narrow strip of water that protected them from the enemy – an enemy that had already invaded France. Back in Scotland Polly and Joe Pringle had no idea that one of their sons was amongst the thousands of British troops trapped on the French coast and surrounded by the German forces, or of the tremendous efforts to rescue them that were being made by fleets of small boats. The first they knew about it was when they received a telegram to say that George was reported missing in France. He was not among the thousands who had been brought back to British shores.

Every evening Victoria or Andrew cycled down to the Pringles' cottage to see whether there was any news and to give what comfort they could.

Victoria received a brief letter from Mark. She understood by now that even personal letters must be circumspect but it was enough to tell her he was working amongst the injured brought ashore from Dunkirk. Jocky Conley was one of them but he was making good progress. Jeannie Conley thanked her over and over again for the news, weeping and smiling in her relief.

'The extra work is proving too much for Jock Conley,' Andrew said, 'and the strain of Jocky being away is affecting him badly. We're all missing his youth and stamina more than we expected. This war is not going to end as quickly as some of the politicians believed. I think the pressures will get worse before things get better. I shall have to make some drastic changes but so long as we win in the end we must do our bit.'

'But what more can we do?' Victoria looked anxiously at Miss Traill's drawn face. She was seventy-six now and she did far more work than she ought to do, to allow Victoria to work outside.

'We must buy a tractor and a plough. I'm certain we shall be ordered to plough up more grassland to satisfy the Ministry of Food. A tractor is so much quicker and it would relieve some of the pressure on Jock Conley. Of course I expect he'll object at first,' he added with a rueful smile.

'Can we afford to buy a tractor?' Victoria asked.

'We shall have to use the money we've set aside. I've been looking into it and we can get a Fordson Standard with spade lugs for a hundred and seventy pounds, plus ten pounds for delivery.'

41

'What are spade lugs?'

'Oh, they're the iron wheels with a series of flat spikes like small spades. They grip well but they churn up the tracks in wet weather. The rubber wheels cost more and I think the spade lugs will grip better if the government makes us plough up some of the steeper fields at the head of the glen.'

'I see. And does it run on petrol?'

'We shall have to apply for coupons. We shall need petrol to start it up then it switches over to paraffin, or TVO as the Americans call it. They are supplying the tractors and machinery on a Lend Lease Scheme. The government will pay when the war is over; meanwhile we buy the tractors and they use the money for making ammunition and aircraft.'

Most of the discussions began at mealtimes around the kitchen table but more often than not Andrew continued mulling over his plans when they were in bed.

'You'll be able to plough if we get a tractor, Victoria,' he chuckled as they snuggled down in each other's arms.

'Mmm, maybe I would if I didn't have two wee rascals to look after. I worry about Miss Traill doing so much. Sometimes I wonder if we should try to get a young maid. There's so many things I could do to help outside but I can't expect her to run after Libby. Even Fraser needs attention now he's nearly walking.'

'I've heard Darlonachie School is taking in children as young as three now,' Andrew said.

'They have a new teacher for the infant class. It's to help with the recent influx of evacuees and for the mothers who want to work. How would you feel about sending Libby?'

'Oh, I don't think I could bear to send her yet, and anyway Fraser would still need watching and he would miss her company.'

'Yes, I suppose you're right. We could certainly use your help outside though.'

'Well you go ahead and order the tractor and we'll see what happens.' Victoria was almost asleep when Andrew remembered another piece of news.

'There were several army men nosing around this afternoon. They said they were looking for a suitable site for tank manoeuvres where they could train the young recruits.'

'Surely they don't want Langmune land?' Victoria was wide awake again instantly.

'No, they agree it's too good for that. They're looking for moorland but they wondered if our track would take them up to High Bowie Moor.'

'Well it doesn't.'

'No, they were disappointed. I think they have their eye on High Bowie's hill land.'

'I think Maggie would have been across to tell us if they'd approached her, don't you?'

'I'm sure she would but they may not have got up there yet. They were talking amongst themselves and it sounded as though they were considering requisitioning the castle for army accommodation and setting up a camp in the grounds.'

'Can they do that? Just take it over, I mean?'

'Apparently Mrs Crainby has refused to co-operate but the way the officer in charge talked he was going ahead anyway.'

'Goodness me. Where will she live?'

'I don't know. After the way she treated you, darling Vicky, I don't care, but if they take over the grounds for an army camp they'll not need a gardener. It's my father I'm worried about. He's aged terribly since they heard George was missing.'

'Yes, it's so awful, not knowing. I daren't think about poor George either but I can't help wondering if he's still alive and if he's been taken prisoner. I don't know which is worse...' She shuddered and Andrew gathered her close to him in the warmth of their big bed.

'Let's think of other things, Victoria,' he whispered. 'I know how lucky I am.' He stroked her gently and gradually she responded to his loving as she always did.

When Victoria awoke the following morning her mind returned to their conversation and she chewed worriedly at her lower lip, as she had always done when she was troubled. Joe and Polly lived in the gardener's cottage at the castle. If Joe lost his job, would he lose his home as well?

As soon as Victoria saw Doctor Grantly's car chugging up the track she felt her heart bump erratically and her blood seemed to turn to ice in her veins. Peter Grantly should have retired by

44

now and today he looked a very old man, his face lined and pale.

'Mark? It's Mark isn't it?' Victoria breathed. Doctor Grantly gripped both her hands, his face was kind, his eyes sad.

'I'm afraid so, Victoria. He – he was killed outright. He was in France, bringing in the wounded.'

'W-will you c-come inside?' Victoria whispered, trying to keep calm when she felt like screaming at the wickedness of the world and the injustice of war.

'No, I'd like to get back to Anna, if you're sure you'll be all right, my dear? She's very upset. We loved Mark, you know, as though he had been our own son.'

'I know, and he loved you too,' Victoria said huskily over the knot of tears in her throat. 'What about Catriona?'

'I telephoned and spoke to her father. I asked him to break the news to her. I thought it was kinder that way.'

'Y-yes, I suppose so. It doesn't seem real, does it?'

'No, it is hard to accept, especially when there can be no funeral. I will call again in a few days, if I may? Perhaps we could hold a memorial service for Mark in Darlonachie Kirk. He has many friends here and they have watched him grow up.'

'Y-yes.' Victoria nodded sadly. She knew Doctor Grantly meant well but she wanted him to go. She wanted to be alone. She wanted to scream and rage and ask God why. *Why?*

Everyone was kind and considerate in the days that followed, and no one was more loving than Andrew, but Victoria had withdrawn into herself. She couldn't help it.

'It will take time, laddie,' Miss Traill said to Andrew. 'Just keep on loving her and give her time to heal. It might be better if Doctor Grantly gets the memorial service arranged. It may help Victoria draw a line under things, so to speak. Help her accept that it has really happened. Perhaps you should call to see him.'

Andrew followed her advice and the service was arranged. Victoria was astonished to see the wee kirk so full and people being so kind, both to her and to the Grantlys, but Catriona was not there. Both Victoria and Anna Grantly had invited her to stay but she had not come.

Maggie Lennox had ignored the order from the Agricultural Executive Committee to plough more land. As far as she was aware the land at High Bowie had never been ploughed. She had only one elderly shepherd and a single team of horses so she didn't think the order applied to her. The largest part of the farm was heather-clad moor land which had proved an attraction to shooting parties before the war, but there were roughly two hundred acres of good in-bye land around the steading and sloping down to the burn. The lower land provided shelter during harsh winters, fresh grass for ewes and young lambs in spring, and fields for hay in summer.

The burn was usually too wide to cross and it often flooded after heavy rains. After a long spell of dry weather it was possible to cross by stepping stones at the narrowest point. This saved a four-mile trip round the track from High Bowie and back up to Langmune, but neither Victoria nor Maggie risked the crossing. They usually cycled if they had reason to visit each other. Petrol was rationed and it was too expensive to use except for essential journeys, so it was a surprise when Maggie's van chugged into the yard at Langmune a fortnight later. It was obvious that Maggie was in a panic. Victoria met her as she came round the corner from the pigsties swinging her empty pails.

'Hello Maggie, you're early on the go this morning. Is anything wrong?'

'Everything!' Maggie wailed. She was not given to dramatizing things as a rule, so Victoria frowned.

'We'd better go in and have a cup of tea then and you can tell me what's up.'

'It's really Andrew I need to talk to. Oh, Victoria, I wish I'd never seen that farm. Luke thought he was doing me a kindness by putting it in my name and making sure Billy and I would always have a home, b-but it doesn't bring in much income by the time I've paid old Arthur. And now I've had a letter saying I'm going to be fined or sent to prison!'

'Prison? Surely there must be some mistake, Maggie. Come on inside. I'll get the whistle and send an SOS to Andrew.' Maggie followed her

47

into the narrow house. Miss Traill took one look and set Libby aside while she put the kettle on the fire to boil. Victoria unhooked the whistle from the hook beside the back door. It was a shrill policeman's whistle but it could be heard from most parts of the farmyard. Victoria gave three loud blasts. 'Andrew will soon come scurrying to the house when he hears that,' she assured Maggie. 'It's our emergency signal. Now tell me, what's all this about fines and prison?'

'I had a letter months ago about ploughing up extra land but we've never ploughed any land at High Bowie. We don't even have a plough...'

Just then Andrew came puffing into the kitchen and stopped short to listen.

'...so I just ignored it. I burnt it I think. Yesterday afternoon two men came to see me. A-and that's what they s-said.' Maggie pulled out her handkerchief and blew hard, struggling to hold back tears. Miss Traill passed her a cup of tea and reached for the precious bowl of sugar. Everyone had stopped taking sugar since the rationing started.

'Put some in, lassie. It will do you good,' she said soothingly.

'What does Sir William say?' Andrew asked.

'I haven't told him. He'll think I'm stupid. I-I can't afford to buy a plough and extra horses or pay someone to come and do it. I j-just can't. We only have the lambs to sell once a year and two or three store beef cattle. There isn't much income. And now the army are going to take over the moor for tank practice.'

'Ah, I wondered about that.' Andrew mused.
'They're talking of coming up our farm track
from the village and then cutting across through
the wee wood on to your land. Tell me, Maggie,
who were the men who came from the
Agricultural Executive Committee?'

She looked up, pushing back her hair distractedly. Victoria felt desperately sorry for her.
Although Maggie was ten years older than
herself she seemed young and vulnerable. She
remembered the name of one of the men.

'I know him. He's in the Farmers' Union. I
heard he's aiming to be County President or
something higher up,' Andrew said. 'Surely
they'll not fine you yet, after only one warning,
Maggie? And I can't believe they would send
you to prison when you have a seven-year-old
boy to care for. Sir William wouldn't allow that.
He's bound to have some influence. The trouble
is we all have to plough some land for cereals,
even if it isn't very suitable. You will have to
write and tell them which fields you intend to
plough and promise to do it without delay.'

'B-but I can't!' Maggie was near to tears. 'I
can't afford to do it and even if I could Arthur
knows nothing about growing corn, or ... or anything except sheep. He should be retired really.
He only stays because Luke asked him to h-help
me.'

'Well we're thinking of buying a tractor to
cope with our extra ploughing,' Andrew said
slowly. 'Maybe we could manage to plough

yours as well. I just wish it was not so far down one track and up the other for vehicles. We could do with a bridge across the burn to reach High Bowie.'

'Maybe the army will make one,' Victoria said, 'if they're bringing their tanks up our track and then cutting across.'

'Their tanks can go anywhere apparently. They'll probably drive straight through the burn,' Andrew muttered disconsolately. 'I told them if they flattened the banks then the fields on both sides would flood in the winter.'

'We could always suggest they make a bridge as compensation and for the good of the land and food production,' Victoria said, her eyes glinting as she quoted from the innumerable leaflets which kept arriving, urging farmers to do their best.

'Oh, Andrew, if only you could deal with it for me?' Maggie pleaded. 'Sometimes I wish Luke had never left the farm to me. I would have been perfectly happy with a wee cottage and keeping house for someone.'

'Victoria and I will talk it over, Maggie, but don't worry, we'll find a solution. Meanwhile I'd advise you to tell Sir William what's happened. Have you heard if they've requisitioned the castle by the way?'

'No! They haven't, have they?'

'I don't know. We've just heard rumours.'

'Oh, why did we have to go to war?' Maggie sighed wearily. 'Now I must let you get on. I'll call in on Sir William on my way home. I've got some things to drop off for him. The house-keeper has not been well for weeks now and one of the maids has joined the ATS. I've been doing the washing and ironing and a bit of cooking.'

'Yes, he said they were having problems the last time I called to see him,' Victoria said. 'It's a bit difficult to be as generous with baking now that we're all rationed.'

'I know.' Maggie smiled. 'He does appreciate the cakes you bake for him though. He often praises your cooking, Victoria.'

Victoria had a sudden thought. 'Would you like to go to the women's meetings in Darlon-achie village, Maggie? I'm thinking of going with Andrew's mother. Women's Rural Institute meetings, they're called. We're supposed to ex-change ideas about cooking and sewing and thrifty ways with the rations.'

'I'd love to go with you but it's impossible. I can't leave Billy, and it's such a long way up to High Bowie on a winter's night.'

When Maggie had gone Miss Traill shook her head. 'The company would have done her good. I think this war and all its rules and regulations are getting her down.'

'I didn't like to tell her,' Andrew said, 'but the Agricultural Executive will take the farm over if Maggie can't comply with the requirements. She would be better renting it out. At least she would get a regular income, so long as she makes a proper lease and gets a decent tenant.'

'Maybe Sir William will have some sugges-tions. I'm pleased he and Maggie get on so well

51

since Luke's death, and he gets a lot of pleasure from young Billy. He has taught him to ride his pony and given him a spaniel of his own.'

'I reckon it's given the old laird a new lease of life,' Andrew agreed.

Four

Victoria was surprised when Sir William Crainby telephoned in person to invite her and Andrew to lunch at Home Farm.

'It is a Saturday so Billy will be home from school and he will be pleased to see your children. Maggie has offered to do the cooking. I have some serious business to discuss with both of you.'

It never occurred to Andrew or Victoria to refuse, although they were now independent of the estate. Sir William Crainby would always be the Laird in their minds and they held him in high regard. Maggie had quickly discovered he never used his position or authority but she respected him as they did.

'He's just like any ordinary, decent person now I've got to know him,' Maggie had said to Victoria. 'Most people would do anything for him simply because they like him and respect him. Mr Blake, the farm manager, and Billy Wright, the herdsman, think the world of him. They have no regrets about leaving the Estate, especially now Mrs Crainby and the new factor are in charge.'

This was a special occasion so Andrew used

some of the meagre petrol ration and drove his family to Home Farm promptly at twelve thirty. It was a beautiful big house, though nothing like the castle, even with the library and a conservatory extension which Luke had added for his father. As soon as the meal was over Billy lead Libby into the garden to play hide and seek and baby Fraser settled down for a nap.

'I have a proposition to make to both of you,' Sir William said, getting to the point of their visit. 'I would like Maggie and her son to move into Home Farm to live with me. I need someone to run my household and it will be nearer for Billy to cycle to school. It would make me very happy to know they were living under my roof.'

Victoria gave Maggie a startled look, wondering how she felt about this.

'Yes, Victoria, it is the whim of a selfish old man.' He chuckled and Victoria blushed. 'But never fear, I shall see Maggie is well recompensed for her friendship and her help.' He smiled at her and Maggie's expression was full of affection. 'Maggie is reluctant to ask any more favours of you, Andrew, but I know you have both been good friends to her and Billy since Luke's death. Farming High Bowie is proving too much of a struggle for her with all the wartime regulations.'

'I can understand that, Sir,' Andrew nodded. 'What would you like us to do?'

'I hear you are purchasing a tractor to deal with the additional ploughing and cultivations at Langmune?'

'Yes, we expect it to be delivered in ten days' time.'

'You have probably heard the army is taking over the High Bowie moor for tank training? Would you consider renting the remainder of Maggie's land and running the two farms together?' Andrew and Victoria looked at each other. 'You can take your time to discuss it if you wish and let us know.' Sir William said.

'Andrew has already said he thinks the best solution for Maggie would be to rent out the land until after the war,' Victoria said, 'but he never thought of renting it himself, did you?'

'No-o,' Andrew said slowly, but his mind was racing. 'No, I never thought of that. Whatever happens I do think a proper lease should be drawn up to protect Maggie from unscrupulous tenants who don't pay the rent. Although the government has capped our prices, at least they have fixed a minimum price as well, so it should be easier to budget. The only thing we can't control is the weather and with extra acres I think shortage of labour might be a problem during the hay and harvest times...'

'If it wouldn't be too much of a burden,' Maggie said, 'I would prefer it if you two would take over the tenancy.'

'I don't think we could take over all your sheep without the hill land,' Andrew demurred, 'especially if we have to plough some of the lower fields.'

'That's all right,' Maggie smiled. 'Arthur is ready to retire and move in with his sister down at Annan. I shall sell the sheep.'

'Then I think we should give it a try,' Victoria said eagerly. 'The government would surely allow us to employ another man with the extra acres. What do you think, Andrew?'

'Ye-es,' he nodded, frowning. 'Yes, we must give it a try,' he added with more certainty. 'If we could persuade the army to build a bridge across the burn it would make a tremendous difference for moving machinery, and carting home hay and grain.'

'That's a splendid idea, my boy. It would make a better route for the tanks, and for all concerned,' Sir William said, 'and Billy could cycle to school that way. It would cut off quite a corner for him. Leave it with me. I know the Colonel pretty well.' It was clear Sir William felt a great deal of affection for his grandson. Victoria wondered how Mrs Crainby would feel about Maggie and her son moving into Home Farm.

'If you get a proper lease drawn up we'll sign it as soon as possible,' Andrew said. 'Then I will have a word with the man I know on the War Agriculture Committee. I'll explain about the changes and guarantee to have the required acreage ploughed for next spring. We can't do more than that. I think they will accept it.'

Maggie heaved a huge sigh of relief and Sir William smiled at her. 'I told you it would all work out, my dear. Luke could not have foreseen another war and the changes it would bring. Now,' he turned to Andrew, 'I would be obliged if you would take a walk over Home

56

Farm with Mr Blake and give him your opinion on the additional land they are asking us to plough.'

'I canna do that,' Andrew gasped. 'Mr Blake would soon send me off with a flea in my ear. He was managing Home Farm when I was a laddie at the school.'

'It was his suggestion,' Sir William said calmly, but his blue eyes were glinting with amusement and his bushy eyebrows twitched. 'He said he would wait for you at the byre. He thinks we should invest in a tractor and he wants your advice. This is a young man's world now, Andrew, with machines being invented for everything. Even when the war is over it will never be the same again, whoever wins. Your youngest brother is in the air force, I hear?'

'He is, Sir,' Andrew nodded. 'He seems to have no fear of the aeroplanes or of flying through the night.'

'Is there any further news of young George?'

'None, Sir. It is a great worry to all of us, but especially my parents. Now, if you'll excuse me I had better meet up with Mr Blake. Perhaps he will show me the new milking machine you have installed? I can't imagine how it can milk cows but if the labour situation gets any worse we shall all have to consider new ways, even for milking cows.'

'And I had better see what Libby is up to,' Victoria added.

'She's having a good time with Billy and his dog,' Maggie chuckled. 'Come through to the kitchen and you can watch them through the window.'

'I shall retire to the library until Andrew returns,' Sir William announced. He paused to look down at Fraser, curled up in his blanket on the settee and sound asleep. 'He is a fine wee fellow, Victoria.'

Maggie led the way to the kitchen where a young maid had almost finished washing-up. 'You can take the rest of the afternoon off, Lucy, when you've finished that.'

'Oh, thank you, Mrs Lennox,' the girl smiled shyly. 'Our Lily is home on leave frae the ATS and she's to go back tomorrow.'

'Then you must spend some time with her,' Maggie nodded. 'Has Mary decided what she's going to do yet?'

'She's thinking about joining the land army but Ma doesn't want her to go away like our Lily.'

Victoria had been looking around the big kitchen while Maggie talked. It was laid out as a typical Scottish farmhouse kitchen with a larder, scullery and washhouse leading off at one side of the back door, which led to the yard and kitchen garden. There the similarity ended. The usual black-leaded range had been replaced by one of the new cookers which was stoked with coke and never went out, keeping the kitchen warm both night and day. It had four oven doors in cream enamel and two big round lids on top, covering the hot plates where pans and soup and kettles were set to boil. Victoria was drawn to it like a magnet, tracing the raised name 'Aga' with her forefinger.

'Lovely, isn't it?' Maggie smiled. 'I can't say I shall be sorry to leave my old range for this gem, and it cooks beautifully, and it airs off the washing on the pulley up above.' She raised her eyes to the ceiling.

'What's that at the side with more doors?'

'That's the water boiler. We're never short of hot water with that but it does guzzle fuel so we let it go out at night except in winter.' It occurred to Victoria that Maggie must spend quite a lot of time here already since she was so familiar with everything.

Lucy wiped the draining boards and set the cloths to dry before leaving them alone.

'Is Lucy's father the ploughman here? Mary Hardie's wee sister?' Victoria asked.

'Yes, she's a good wee worker.'

'I went to school with Mary but Lucy was quite young then.'

'Mary has had a tough time. She was engaged to a boy from Annan but he died at Dunkirk. She worked in a bakery in the town but the younger women are being called up for one of the services or to work in the munitions factories.'

'We used to tease Mary and say she was Hardy by name and hardy by nature. I must ask Andrew if we could give her a job as a land girl. We're missing young Jocky Conley terribly.' She glanced out of the window and smiled, watching Libby and Billy romping together. Although Billy was seven he seemed to be

59

remarkably patient with three-year-old Libby and her efforts to catch the ball. 'He's a lovely boy, Maggie. You must be very proud.'

'I am, and his grandfather has been so kind to both of us, but he's wonderful the way he talks to Billy and tells him about the trees and plants, the fields and animals. He knows such a lot and he's so patient.'

'He always was,' Victoria sighed. 'He taught me a lot and he always let me read books from his library at the castle, until...' She grimaced. 'Until Mrs Crainby and her mother came along and said I must be kept in my place as a servant.'

'I can imagine that from what I've heard of her,' Maggie said. 'I hope I never need to come into contact with her. Meeting her factor was bad enough. He was so nasty.'

'Never mind, Maggie, you'll not need to worry about that any more, and I'd loved to have seen his face when he read the letter from the lawyer.'

'Mummy, Mummy, can I take Libby to see Tommy and can I give her a ride?' Billy asked eagerly, running into the kitchen, closely followed by Libby.

'We'll come with you to see the pony but Libby is too small to ride Tommy,' Maggie said firmly.

'If Grandfather does get the army to make a bridge and a road through the wood, can I go to Langmune to play with Libby and to see the new tractor? Libby says her daddy will give us a ride on it.'

'We'll see. We may never get a bridge and you are never to cross the burn yourself, Billy,' Maggie warned.

'It's a pity it is such a long way around,' Victoria sighed. 'I expect it will take years before they make a bridge, even if the army agrees.'

The war was going badly and Britain was fighting alone. The Pringles had learned that George had been shot dead while trying to make his way back to Britain after being sheltered and nursed by a French family after Dunkirk. Many felt it could only be a matter of time before the whole country must surrender against the might of the German army on land, the Luftwaffe, which rained bombs from above, and the U-boats that were bent on ruling the seas which had protected Britain's shores for generations.

Victoria was wrong about the time it would take the army to construct a bridge. True to his word, Sir William had contacted the Colonel in charge. Two of his men had arrived to consult with Andrew and the following day men, trucks and steel girders had arrived. Two days later a substantial bridge had been built, following Andrew's advice to keep it well above the flood level. A week later half a dozen tanks churned the roadsides into muddy tracks as they trundled up on to High Bowie Moor, flattening the purple heather to a dirty brown.

'Where will all the wild birds live, Mummy?' Billy asked Maggie, his blue eyes full of concern.

'We must hope they find another moor where they can live in peace.'

Andrew and Jock Conley had joined forces with two men from Home Farm and their dogs to round up Maggie's sheep flock. They had penned them in the low meadow until they could be removed by lorry to the market.

Even with the additional acres to plough and sow, Andrew knew there was little hope of getting the extra man he needed. He decided to take Victoria's advice and ask for Mary Hardy to be allocated to him through the Women's Land Army. Much to his surprise they sent Mary, and they also sent another young woman from Manchester named Trudy Turnbull. Mary lived near enough to live with her family and cycle to work but Trudy had to be accommodated in the farmhouse. It soon became clear that she was terrified of cows and had very little idea what farming involved. Although the government was urging farmers to grow more and more cereals and potatoes, milk was still badly needed too, not only for the children to drink but also to make butter and cheese which had mainly been imported previously. Andrew was willing to do his bit and plough the additional acres but he knew the high rainfall of the south of Scotland made Langmune far more suited to grass, and therefore milk production, so this remained the most important part of his farming business. He tried to explain this to Trudy but her fear of sitting beside a cow was very real. It was a fear which Jem Wright's wife, Milly, shared.

'What have I done to get two women who refuse to do the most essential job on the farm?' Andrew raged in frustration, while Trudy bit her lip and tried to hold back tears.

'She is very good with the children,' Victoria intervened. 'If Trudy will take care of them I will continue to help with the milking,' she suggested. 'And Mary is a good milker already.'

'She will need to be. You two will probably end up milking most of the cows when the rest of us are struggling to get the harvest in.'

If Trudy had been offered a job as a maid in a humble farmhouse she would probably have refused before the war, considering it beneath the daughter of a headmaster in a large Manchester secondary school, but that is what she became now. Her help was a great relief to Victoria as it meant Miss Traill could give advice without having to do work for which she was no longer fit. So they fell into a routine where Victoria and Mary milked the cows along with Jem, while Milly carried the pails of milk to the dairy as usual. Andrew was relieved when Trudy quickly learned to drive the new tractor, swinging the starting handle with cheerful gusto.

Mary Hardy could turn her hand to most things and she proved a godsend with so much extra work to be done. Victoria sensed she worked hard and hoped to fall into bed each night, too tired to think of the death of her fiancé, or the future that lay ahead for her. She was not the happy-go-lucky girl Victoria remembered from their school days.

* * *

Back at Darlonachie Castle Henrietta Crainby couldn't believe her ears when the army arrived to take over.

'Mrs Crainby, you were notified that the castle and the grounds were to be requisitioned for use by the army.'

'Oh that! I ignored it. This is my home. Anyway the government is always sending out notifications. Why don't they just get on with fighting the Germans?'

'That is what we are trying to do,' Major Armstrong said with some exasperation. 'We expect the cooperation of every man, woman and child if we are to stand any chance of winning this war. If you think this is bad, imagine how you will feel if the Germans take over your precious castle and set you to scrubbing the floors for them – or worse.' He thought Mrs Crainby was about to explode as she drew herself up, an ugly red staining her sallow skin, but he had no time to waste. All the soldiers they could muster were badly needed and most of the remaining recruits were little more than schoolboys now and in need of training and discipline. 'I shall give you four days to remove yourself and your family. You may keep two of the attics for storing your goods if you wish, though we cannot be responsible for anything you choose to leave behind.' He turned on his heel and strode back to his waiting jeep.

Henrietta Crainby lost no time in taking out her ill temper on her factor.

64

'I did warn you,' Soutar Ward responded coolly. 'Presumably you want all the men I can spare to move furniture now? Are you going to live in the Dower House? It needs a few renovations but—'

'Dower House! It's a ruin.' Henrietta scowled at him, but it finally began to dawn on her that she really had to leave the castle and she would get no sympathy from Ward. 'It's a ruin, I tell you!'

'It's not so bad. We could have had it ready if you had given the order.'

'I'm not living there,' she repeated. Her eyes narrowed. 'Of course! We shall move to Home Farm. My late husband spent plenty of money improving it. It must be very comfortable now and I can't imagine that stupid old man can last much longer. We shall simply move in a little earlier than expected. I shall drive over to make arrangements now. Meanwhile you must arrange for the furniture to be stored in the attics.'

Mr Ward watched her flounce away with a mocking smile on his thin lips. He had heard rumours that her late husband's mistress was already living at Home Farm, and contrary to her belief it didn't look as though Sir William Crainby would need a coffin for a long time yet.

It was difficult to know who was the most surprised when Henrietta Crainby rapped impatiently on the door at Home Farm a little while later and Maggie Lennox opened it, an enquiring smile curving her generous mouth. The smile died instantly.

'May I help you?' she asked coolly, recovering first. Henrietta gaped at her a few seconds longer.

'No, you may not. I demand to see Sir William, my father-in-law.' Without waiting for an invitation she swept past Maggie and into the hall.

'Is that Victoria, Maggie? Send her in, my dear. I have a fine copy—'

'It is not Victoria.' Henrietta followed his voice and found herself in a pleasant book-lined room. Sir William was seated in a large leather chair in front of the fire, a thick book in his hands.

'Henrietta?' The book snapped shut. He laid it on a side table and rose to his feet, a frown creasing his high forehead, his blue eyes penetrating. Henrietta stared at him. He looked fit and well, far better than he had when he had lived at the castle. She scowled.

'The army have requisitioned the castle. They are making a camp for soldiers. We shall make this our home from now on. Charlotte will need a room to herself, as well as a school room and a bedroom for her governess. I shall need—'

'My dear Henrietta, the house is already occupied, and I do not recall inviting you, or your young daughter, to share my home.' Sir William's bushy eyebrows had risen and his blue eyes were sharp as flints.

'There is no need to invite us. It is only a matter of time before this house will belong to me anyway, so...'

'Henrietta!' Sir William's voice was fierce. 'There are plenty of houses on the Estate. I am surprised it has taken you so long to move out of the castle anyway. The Dower House is perfectly adequate for you and Charlotte.'

'Charlotte is your granddaughter! How can you expect...?'

'Is she? Strange then that I have not seen her since her father's death, don't you think?' Henrietta couldn't fail to recognize that cold steel in his voice, or see the derision on his face. 'I believe Mrs Lennox and her son would find this house a little overcrowded if you were to move in here with us.' He said it calmly, beginning to enjoy the discomfiture of his haughty daughter-in-law.

'Mrs Lennox? That woman has wormed her way in here?'

'This is her home, and Billy's too. Shall I ask her to show you out or can you find your own way?' He sat down in his chair again and lifted the book. Henrietta gaped, her mouth opening and shutting like a stranded fish, but no words came. Sir William did not raise his eyes as he calmly opened the book and pretended to read. Henrietta spun on her heel and strode out of the room and out of the house, slamming the door behind her. Sir William chuckled, turned his book the right way up, then set it aside. He went to find Maggie.

Five

The first person Mrs Crainby saw when she returned from Home Farm was Joe Pringle. He was chuckling at some quip made by one of the estate workers Mr Ward had brought to the castle to help move the furniture. Henrietta was still seething from her encounter with her father-in-law. It didn't matter that Joe Pringle had never displeased her or that his smile hid the grief he would always feel for the death of his son. His crime was to have Victoria Lachlan for a daughter-in-law. In Henrietta's present fury it was enough. She detested the kitchen maid who had become Mrs Andrew Pringle, joint owner of Langmune Farm.

She had always been one of Sir William's favourite people, even before it was discovered she was the illegitimate granddaughter of his sister, and of Henrietta's stepfather. That discovery had been a pill she had found hard to swallow. Luke, her own husband, had always had affection for Victoria Lachlan. He had gone behind her back to make sure she and Maggie Lennox were legal owners of property which should have remained part of the Estate and under her control. Both women were still find-

68

ing favour with Sir William Crainby, but he had the effrontery to tell her there was no place for Henrietta or her daughter at Home Farm. Jealous fury boiled in her. She marched up to Joe Pringle.

'Pringle, you are no longer needed here.'

'No, Ma'am. I understand. Mr Ward has informed us the army are taking over the castle and the grounds,' Joe acknowledged politely, his face expressing sympathy towards her.

'Then I hope he has also told you to get out of your cottage by the end of the week.' She almost spat the words, unaware that the factor had appeared and was standing on the castle steps behind her. He ran down them now, his eyes wide and angry. He had seen the colour drain from Joe Pringle's ruddy cheeks.

'I certainly did not tell Pringle any such thing. The Estate has no need of his cottage, and he can turn his hand to many things, including fencing. I've seen the way he built the garden wall too, and the excellent job he made of laying the hedge around the orchard. The estate can't afford to lose a man with—'

'When I want your opinion I shall ask for it,' Henrietta interrupted rudely. 'Bring the keys to Garden Cottage to me by the end of the week.' She glared at Joe and then at her factor and swept past them without another word.

'Something's biting her!' the other estate worker growled. Joe Pringle was well known and well liked by most of the men.

'Yes, and I can guess what it is,' Ward said.

'She expected to move into Home Farm and take over there.'

'What? With Mistress Lennox living there?' the man gasped. 'And her wee laddie ... My, but that would make the feathers fly.'

'I don't think she was aware that Mrs Lennox had moved into Home Farm to live,' Ward said. 'Now I expect we shall have to prepare the Dower House,' he added dryly. 'We could have done it a month ago if she had listened. The garden there is a wilderness. She'll need you there, Pringle. When she's calmed down a bit I'll talk to her about the cottage...'

'No,' Joe said firmly. His face was still pale with shock but he had his pride. 'If I'm to leave I'll go now, right away. I'll go and tell Polly we have to move out.'

'But you can't do that, man!' Ward was dismayed. 'I told you a month ago there'd be plenty of work for you whatever happened. Most of the younger men have been called up for the services. And anyway, where would you live? Where will you go?'

'There's always a way,' Joe said flatly. 'The Lord will provide.' He moved past the factor and made his way home to Polly and the cottage where they had spent all their married life. His shoulders were bowed. He and Polly had both been born on the Estate. All his life he had worked for the Crainbys, and to leave like this...

'The army are taking over,' he announced flatly when he entered the cottage and saw Polly staring at him with round, questioning eyes.

'Well, it's only what we expected when the rumours went round a month ago,' she nodded. Joe's face was pale and she looked at him more closely. 'The factor said there would be other work for you. Has he changed his mind, Joe?'

'There would be work, but Mistress Crainby has taken a dislike to me. God knows what I can have done to displease her.'

'Nothing, very likely,' Polly muttered. 'Remember she was always like that with Victoria, even though she was little more than a bairn and slaving away in the kitchens, doing her best to please everybody. Folks like Mrs Crainby don't need a reason to be nasty, Joe. Take no notice.'

'I can't do that, lassie.' Joe took her hand and pulled her down on to the old box bed beside him. 'We've to get out o' here, leave our wee cottage, by the end o' the week, Polly.' He sounded tired and defeated.

'Leave here? Are you sure she said that, Joe?'

'Aye.' He dropped his head on to his chest. Polly kept hold of his hand and covered it with her other one, drawing it up to her chest and resting her chin on their clasped hands.

'We'll manage, Joe. Something will turn up. I'll make us a cup of tea, shall I?'

'Please. Have we any sugar ration left?'

'Of course I'll put sugar in. Don't worry, dear Joe.' Polly's mind was already turning to a conversation she had had with Victoria soon after they had heard George was dead. She had said she wished they could have come to live in the cottage at Langmune but she understood Joe had

71

to stay near his work. She made the tea and added two teaspoons of sugar to Joe's. He looked exhausted. She sat beside him again.

'Joe? I can manage without the cottage, and I can manage without your wages, but oh, Joe, I canna manage without you.' Her voice shook. 'So long as we have each other we'll get by.'

'Aye, we'll get by somehow,' Joe said, but without conviction.

'You look exhausted.'

'I feel ... drained,' he admitted. 'It was the shock – and the viciousness in her tone. Even Ward, the factor, seemed staggered.'

'Well, drink your tea and have a lie down for a bit. I'm going out for a wee while but I'll not be long, then we'll talk things through. We're not short o' money. I've always put a bit by and then we have the money Josh would have had to pay for his education.'

'He'll still need it when he comes home. *If* he comes home,' he added almost under his breath.'

'He will. Oh, he will. The good Lord couldna take two of our laddies. We'll cross that bridge if we come to it. Now you settle down and have a wee rest.'

Polly hurried down to the telephone box in the village to telephone Langmune, hoping desperately that Victoria would be in at this time of day. In fact it was Victoria who answered the phone. Polly lost no time in telling her what Mrs Crainby had done and she didn't care if Doris was still listening in at the exchange after she

72

had put her through. If she was Polly knew she would probably give her extra time for her money.

'This is my fault,' Victoria gasped. 'It's because I'm part of your family. I never did know why she hated me so much but it's unforgivable of her to take it out on Andrew's father. How can she be so spiteful? Especially when the factor says there is plenty of other work and he doesn't need the Garden Cottage anyway...'

'She's just a jealous bitch,' Polly said vehemently. 'I don't care about the house. It's Joe I'm worried about. It's the shock of losing his job like that.'

'We'll come down after we finish milking the cows,' Victoria promised. 'We'll work something out. We have an empty cottage and you know how pleased I would be if you were nearer.'

'I know, lassie.' Polly sighed. 'But Joe's such a proud man. He'll never accept charity, not even from his own son.'

'Please don't say that,' Victoria pleaded, her voice trembling. 'I can never repay the debt I owe you both. You took me in when I had no family or home or money. I long to do something in return.'

'You owe us nothing, lassie,' Polly said gruffly. 'You have brought us more joy than we dared to hope and you've made Andrew the happiest man on God's earth.'

'Speaking of Andrew, he hasn't had time to come and tell you his news yet. He's now the tenant of High Bowie Farm, officially, with a lease and everything legal. And he has reached an agreement with the Agricultural Executive Committee about ploughing extra land on Langmune so we can leave the High Bowie land in pasture, at least for the next year. It does mean there will be a lot more work though. He had hoped to be allocated an extra man but they expect him to manage with two land girls. I'm certain Andrew would welcome his father's help.'

'Do you think so, Victoria?' Polly asked doubtfully. 'You know Joe has never done anything but gardening.'

'But he's so versatile, and he's good with his hands. I just know Andrew will be grateful for his help. I'll get the children to bed early and ask Trudy to look after them. We'll come down as soon as we can.'

'Ah, Victoria, ye're a good lassie. I feel better already. I'll get back home and tell Joe. I've never seen him so downcast.'

'Mrs Crainby is a nasty woman,' Victoria said, feeling far more hurt on Joe's behalf than she had ever felt for herself.

It was not easy for Andrew to convince Joe how much his help would be appreciated at Langmune Farm.

'I'm not a charity case either, Father,' Andrew said firmly. 'We'll make it a proper business arrangement and if you work for us we'll pay you as we would have done anyone else. As it

74

happens you can have a choice of houses. The farmhouse at High Bowie is empty now that Maggie and young Billy have moved to Darlonachie Home Farm permanently.'

'I wouldn't like to live up there,' Polly said promptly. 'It's too isolated and too far from the village. Besides,' she looked sheepishly at Joe, 'I'm looking forward to being nearer my grandchildren and seeing them every day.'

'Are you, Polly?' Joe asked. 'You mean you'll be happy to move?'

'Aye, well to be honest, I shall, Joe, though I'd stay here for ever if it had suited you.'

'Well, well,' he sighed. 'Maybe some things do work out for the best after all.' He looked at Victoria and Andrew sitting close together on the old sofa. They looked so happy in spite of all their hard work, and they had a couple of fine children. He drew out his pipe for the first time since he had arrived home earlier in the day. 'You're right, lass,' he smiled at Polly, 'it does not matter where we live so long as it's home and we're both in it, eh?'

'Oh, Joe.' Polly hugged him thankfully.

'We'll bring the horse and cart down on Saturday then, Father,' Andrew said. 'I'd like to throw the key to this place in her sour face. I thank God Luke saw through her nasty nature and tied everything up securely for Victoria and me. She would have made our life hell if she could have done.'

'Yours and Mrs Lennox's,' Joe nodded. 'Maybe Sir William's too.'

75

* * *

It was astonishing how quickly most people adapted to the changes that had been thrust upon them. At Langmune it seemed as though Joe and Polly Pringle had lived in the end cottage for ever by the time the 1943 harvest came around. Joe knew nothing about farming but he did know about vegetables and he knew that working men needed good food. In the spring of 1942 he had advised Andrew to set aside a few rows of his potato field for his own family and his workers.

'When the field is ploughed and cultivated it will be easy enough to plant a couple of rows of Kerr's Pink potatoes for ourselves, and some carrots, beetroot, and cabbage,' he had said. 'There'll be no disease where they've never been grown before. If your workers appreciate them they'll not mind helping to gather them in. The bairns can help too. It'll be good for them.'

The German U-boats were destroying ship after ship, both British and American, and as the food rationing became more severe they were all grateful for the fresh vegetables. Meat was scarce and Victoria devised all kinds of recipes to spin it out, utilizing the vegetables and sauces, dried eggs and grating the meagre ration of dry strong cheese when there was no meat at all. Only Milly refused to help, saying she was too busy now she had four daughters to care for, but the children enjoyed being in the fields, helping to harvest vegetables.

Joe had a large garden at the cottage and he

76

also cultivated the farm garden, growing peas and beans and salad crops, as well as sprouts and leeks for winter, and Jem and the Conleys followed his example and advice. Everyone had a patch of rhubarb but Joe helped them grow strawberries and raspberries and blackcurrants as well. He pruned the fruit trees and plucked the fruit when it was ripe so they all had plums and pears and apples. There were extra rations of sugar for the jam-making season and most people were learning to manage without sugar in their tea, saving it for special treats.

'I've learned a lot about growing crops from you, Father,' Andrew admitted as they surveyed a field of oats which was ready for the binder. 'I see why it pays to rotate the crops in different fields so we don't build up pests and disease in the soil.'

'Aye, well, it's more important than ever now nobody is allowed to leave the fields fallow for a season. A field without a crop could be cultivated to kill off the weeds,' Joe nodded. 'Working the fields of potatoes and turnips does the same job if you tend them well.'

'Mmm, I suppose farming is only gardening on a larger scale,' Andrew mused, surprised at his father's knowledge and perception. 'The cows are milking better too when they graze the young leys we've grown after corn. We never considered ploughing up and renewing grass on a regular rotation before. The better grass helps compensate now the animal concentrates are so severely rationed.'

'I expect applying the lime has helped,' Joe nodded, drawing contentedly on his pipe as he leaned on the gate beside his eldest son. 'Somebody in the government must have had a bit of gumption when they decided to subsidize the price of ground limestone to persuade farmers to apply it. What is it they say? "A farm without lime is not worth a dime" or something like that.'

'Some of the farmers in the south are experimenting with putting fresh grass into pits to make silage instead of hay.' Andrew sighed. 'British farmers are producing more than we've ever done before, but still it's not enough. It's worrying the way the war is dragging on. Every night when I hear the aeroplanes going over I wonder where Josh is and whether he's safe.'

'I know, laddie.' Joe's eyes held a sad, faraway look for a moment but he shrugged away the melancholy. 'There's no wonder wee Libby is scared to go to sleep at night. Does she still look under her bed to see if the Germans are hiding there?'

'She does. She's deadly serious about it since that young madam frightened them at school.' Andrew pursed his lips.

'You mean young Charlotte Crainby? The Crainbys always had a governess until they went to boarding school. I was surprised to hear her mother had sent her to the village school.'

'Some folks say she didn't want to go away to school, others reckon her mother grudged the money for school fees. She's supposed to be spending hundreds of pounds making the Dower House more posh than Home Farm. I don't know how she gets furnishings of any kind. We can't buy anything without coupons, not even a sheet for wee Fraser's bed. Did you see Barbour's are advertising adhesive safety nets for the windows at one shilling and threepence a yard?'

'Please God we shall never get bombs in this area,' Joe muttered. 'As for Mrs Crainby, I've heard she's not averse to using the black market, or bullying and bartering with produce from the farm whenever she can get her hands on it. She seems to think she's above the law.' Joe bit hard on the stem of his pipe.

'Well I wish it was all over,' Andrew sighed. 'Apparently they've massacred Clydebank, and it was too close for comfort when they dropped a bomb on Gretna.'

'Aye, that's made everybody more careful about the blackout.' Joe frowned. He knew how Andrew had struggled to black out the windows along the ridge of the byre roof. A number of farmers had been in trouble for windows left unpainted in farm buildings, or broken panes allowing light to show. 'But we do have hope, laddie, even if it has cost a terrible price.'

'You mean the Japanese bombing Pearl Harbor?'

'Aye. It has brought America in on our side. I can't see Hitler winning the war now.'

'I hope you're right, Father.' Andrew turned his thoughts to the field waiting to be harvested.

He would need to set the binder cutting corn tomorrow. He was glad he'd paid for the machine to be converted so that the tractor could pull it instead of Jock and the horses. They would need everyone in the field for stooking the sheaves.

'There's always a good side to things if we can see it,' Joe went on, almost to himself. 'I never expected to find satisfaction in my life after Mrs Crainby banished me frae Darlonachie Estate, and my garden, but I've enjoyed working at High Bowie, helping you put things in order, laddie.'

'You've certainly made an excellent job of laying the hedges, Father. Those you did the first winter you were here have grown and thickened beautifully. They're stock-proof and damned near sheep-proof. Sheep seem to find the smallest hole and they always squeeze through. Before you know it the whole flock has followed.'

'Aye well it's the best we can do when wire is so scarce. You were lucky the army wanted to rent the farmhouse for their training officers.'

'That has suited everyone. I'm glad they keep their training tanks up on the moor now they do their maintenance at the farm steading. They're so wide they make a hell of a mess churning up the farm track when they travel. Young Billy is eager to see them close at hand though,' Andrew grinned. 'He can't wait for them to come down off the moor. He waves to the jeeps every morning as they transport the trainee soldiers from the castle. We haven't seen so many of them lately though.'

'I imagine there can't be many left to train, except for the lads who are leaving school.'

'Are you two going to stand out there blethering all night?' Andrew and Joe turned, smiling at the sound of Willie's voice. 'It's nearly time I was getting back.'

'Hi Willie, we were just coming in to say hello.' Andrew grinned at his brother. They had all missed George and still grieved over his death, but it had hit Willie hardest. There had been just eleven months between them and they had always done everything together, even down to getting the belt at school. Since Polly and Joe had moved to Langmune, Willie boarded at the farm where he had worked as shepherd since he left school, but he always came home once a week to see his family, bringing his washing and asking for news of Josh. Sometimes he brought a roast of lamb when his boss had killed a sheep for his own use. Whether it was slaughtered legally or not, Polly dare not ask. There were many new regulations, licences and inspections to make sure farmers were producing as much as possible and not exceeding their allowances or dealing on the black market.

They were more fortunate than the people living in the towns, especially those without a garden or an allotment – people like Catriona MacNaught. Victoria had thought she and Catriona might be able to offer each other comfort after Mark's death. She had invited her to live in Mark's cottage at Darlonachie until the war was

81

over, but Catriona had surprised everyone. The first Christmas card after Mark's death stated baldly that she had married a colleague of Mark's. Polly knew how hurt Victoria had been. The only communication between them now was a card at Christmas.

Willie came home every weekend. He enjoyed his mother's Sunday lunches, in spite of the rationing, but recently he had begun to come on Saturdays. Polly's maternal instinct was working overtime. Mary Hardie cycled home in the same direction when the milking was finished on a Saturday evening, but Mary didn't come to work on Sunday afternoons. She usually spent them at home with her family. Polly sighed, remembering the plump, laughing schoolgirl Mary Hardie used to be. It seemed as though some inner light had been switched off since her fiancée was killed. She worked terribly hard and never grumbled but there were shadows in her eyes and she had lost weight. War affected so many lives.

Victoria worried about Mary too. As the herdsman's wife, Milly was supposed to do the dairy work but she and Jem had recently had another baby, a little boy named Jimmy. Mary had taken on the daily scrubbing and steaming of churns and pails and the rest of the dairy utensils, in addition to her own work. She did an excellent job but Victoria was afraid she was working too hard. Since the birth Milly didn't seem to be regaining her usual spirits. She was irritable and depressed and she seemed constantly tired. She blamed the war. She had never been a good cook and she was a poor organizer, as Victoria remembered from their time together in the castle kitchens. Every week she got in a muddle with her coupons, usually blaming the butcher, baker or grocer, rather than herself. The wages had risen to three pounds five shillings for the men who worked fifty-four hours a week and Jem earned the full wage, but Milly was missing the two pounds eight shillings she had earned and seemed unable to budget.

'She flares into a temper when I try to help her,' Jem confided to Victoria anxiously. 'I don't know what to do.'

Everyone did their best to help. Victoria and Polly often took her a pot of nourishing broth and Jeannie Conley helped amuse the two younger girls who were not yet at school.

Victoria wanted everyone to be as happy as she and Andrew were. When Polly and Joe had moved up to the cottage at Langmune she had worried about Polly more than Joe. She had eventually persuaded her to buy a bicycle.

'I don't want you to miss the company, or your friends in the village,' she had said anxiously. 'You could come to the WRI with Maggie and me.'

'I'm over fifty,' Polly protested. 'I'm too old for a bike – and what's the WRI anyway?'

'The Women's Rural Institute. You would enjoy it.'

Despite her protests, Polly tried Victoria's bicycle. After some precarious wobbles, a great many laughs and a lot of practice around the yard she had conquered the dreaded machine. Now she looked forward to her evening at Darlonachie village hall once a month. Maggie Lennox cycled over the bridge and along the new track through the wood to the cottages and the three women went to the village together. Victoria tried to persuade Milly to join them.

'Mary comes with us sometimes,' she said. 'You would enjoy it, Milly, and you might get some ideas for you and the children.'

'Humph, Mary only goes because you give her a meal first.'

'She goes because she enjoys the meetings,' Victoria said patiently, 'and talking to people. 'She wouldn't have time to go home for her supper first.'

'Well it's all right for some folk. I have five bairns to look after,' Milly said sullenly.

'Jem would look after them once a month. He would like you to go out sometimes.'

'You've been talking about me! You've been talking to Jem.' Milly flew into such a temper that Victoria was alarmed. It was impossible to help Milly in her present moods.

Victoria had rapidly become known for her cooking skills and her ability to turn the meagre rations into a tasty pie or stew. She was invited to talk at other meetings but it worried Andrew if she went out alone at nights. Sometimes she persuaded Trudy to accompany her. Maggie was always willing to go but she didn't like to leave Billy with his grandfather too often, even though he was usually in bed and asleep. Sir William was growing frail and shaky now. Sometimes Polly offered to have Billy to stay overnight and go to school with Libby as usual. He enjoyed hearing Joe's stories about Darlonachie and Andrew was happier if Victoria had Maggie for company when the meetings were in village halls further away.

Although she enjoyed taking part in all the meetings, Victoria was puzzled when she received an official letter.

'Oh my!' she exclaimed in astonishment. 'One of the members has told her husband about my talk at her WRI. He is some sort of official. This letter is to ask if I will give talks to other women's groups during the day on how to cook and how to make the best of food rations.'

'Where?' Andrew asked at once. 'When?'

'Goodness me! They want to pay me if I will do it. And they're offering me extra petrol coupons for travelling.'

Andrew chewed his lower lip and said nothing. He had always known Victoria was a fine cook. Her grandmother had trained her well and she enjoyed it. His mother had always said she was born to it.

'These people have no idea how much work there is to do on a farm,' she chuckled, and set the letter aside. 'I'll reply tonight. Right now I need to feed the hens and get this young man into his warm clothes to come with me.' She drew Fraser away from the breakfast table and hugged him. He was four years old and a sturdy, healthy boy who loved to follow her around outside. This was just as well because Miss Traill was over eighty now and increasingly unsteady on her feet. Victoria never left her alone with the mischievous little boy.

'I always knew you deserved something better, Victoria,' Andrew said that night when they were in bed. 'I expect Mother would look after Fraser if you want to go.'

'The money would have been useful,' Victoria admitted. 'We could have bought one of those cookers like Maggie has. Then the kitchen would always be warm when we get up in the morning.'

'Maybe we could afford one anyway,' Andrew began, but Victoria's chuckle cut him short. She leaned over and kissed him.

'I was only teasing about the money. I wouldn't think of going anywhere when we all have so much work to do. It's not just Fraser either, it would worry me if I had to leave Miss Traill alone for most of the day. She's very frail and I know her bad leg often gives her pain, but she never complains.'

'I think we're all holding you back, Victoria. It would prove to Mrs Crainby what a skilful cook and housewife you are. I don't want you to be unhappy.'

'I don't care tuppence for Mrs Crainby's opinion. I only care about you. Do you think I'm unhappy?' she whispered, while her fingers danced lightly over his chest, moving lower and lower. He groaned softly and rolled towards her,

86

seizing her in his arms.

'I'm the luckiest man alive,' he murmured against the silky skin of her breast.

Six

Billy Lennox had a naturally happy nature and he was popular at school. Some of the children had lost their fathers in the war and many were away in the services, so no one bothered to ask about his father. At home Billy had Grandfather Crainby. Although he did not play football or other games he knew a lot of interesting things and Billy was never bored in his company. Grandfather had given him his dog and his pony too. He met Libby at her grandparents' cottage and they cycled to school together every morning. He was content.

Polly had grown very fond of him and saved sweets from her ration for him and Libby whenever she could. Libby, who had never shown fear of anything, had become unusually nervous about cycling down the track to the village on her own, so Victoria was grateful to Billy. She knew her small daughter felt safe in his company and he was always patient, even though Libby sometimes found it difficult to keep up with him on her small cycle.

'Charlotte Crainby tried to frighten the younger children,' Billy told his mother, 'that's why Libby is frightened of the Germans.'

'Well, you take care of Libby. I expect Charlotte is only teasing,' Maggie said. 'Or perhaps that's what her mother says to her.' She felt sure the child must have some good in her. Luke had been such a kind and thoughtful man and he had detested his wife's jealousy and spite. But Maggie was less sanguine when she heard why Billy had been kept in after school, especially since it meant Libby had had to cycle home alone.

Mr Nelson would have been retired had it not been for the war and a shortage of teachers. He had been allocated two young assistant teachers to help with the influx of evacuees. Miss Macrae had recently moved to the area from Inverness. Charlotte Crainby was uncooperative the first day she was teaching the older children. Miss Macrae suspected she was lazy. She had set the class a poem to learn. When it was Charlotte's turn to say hers she made a poor effort, but Billy recited his perfectly, although he was a year younger.

'Teacher's pet!' Charlotte hissed.

'Will you try again, Charlotte? Recite the poem about the baby seeds, please.' Miss Macrae's voice was firm. She had met children like Charlotte before, usually spoiled brats, or unloved and craving attention. 'Billy will say it with you to help you along,' she said encouragingly. Glaring furiously, Charlotte moved to Billy's side.

'"Little brown brother, oh little brown brother, are you awake in the dark?"'

Two of the boys began to titter and whisper.

'Eh, that's right! He is your brother,' one of them said, loud enough for Charlotte to hear. Her face grew red with anger.

'He is not!' she said loudly, glaring at Drew Tomkins, then turning to Billy with a look of disdain. 'His mother is a servant.' She quoted Henrietta Crainby's words and sneering tone perfectly.

'Charlotte!' Miss Macrae shouted from the other side of the classroom. 'You are keeping the class from their break. Stop muttering. Now get on with your poem.'

'I'm not saying it! It's a stupid poem anyway. He's not my brother, he's not, he's not!' she yelled loudly, becoming more hysterical as Drew Tomkins and his friend persisted with their whispered taunts.

'I wouldna want you for a sister anyway,' Billy retaliated indignantly. 'Nobody would!'

'But she *is* your sister!' Drew Tomkins insisted. 'Did ye no ken?' he asked, relishing the trouble he was stirring. Charlotte flew at him, her fists clenched. Billy pulled her back, but she turned and slapped him across the face. For a moment he was stunned, then he slapped her back. Drew Tomkins was all set to enjoy a fight if Miss Macrae had not come storming across the classroom.

The result was that Drew, Charlotte and Billy were kept behind after school and ordered to write out the poem four times in their best handwriting.

Later Miss Macrae told Mr Nelson of the unexpected rumpus that had appeared to blow up out of nothing. She was surprised and embarrassed when the headmaster explained that the two children did indeed share the same father.

'To be frank, Miss Macrae, I knew there would be trouble when Mrs Crainby decided to send her daughter to the village school, and I wish she had not done so. She is a year older than Billy so she should be moving on next summer, but whether Mrs Crainby will send her to a private school or to Dumfries I don't know. It is not our problem. Billy is an exceptionally bright boy, is he not?'

'He is, and normally it is a pleasure to teach him. He has knowledge of a wide range of subjects, not usually covered in primary school.'

'He lives with his mother and his grandfather, Sir William Crainby, and I suspect the old man has enjoyed passing on his own knowledge of nature, and history.'

The incident passed and seemed relatively harmless, but as they were leaving school Charlotte couldn't resist jeering at Billy.

'My mama says you're a bastard.' Neither she nor Billy knew what it meant but Charlotte knew from her mother's sneering tone that it was not a compliment. Billy did not respond but he went home and sought the word in one of his grandfather's dictionaries. Maggie found him in the library and asked what was puzzling him. Her heart sank when he began to ask about his father. She had dreaded having to give him an explanation and hoped he would wait until he was old enough to understand the complications of loving someone, even when that person belonged to another. But Billy was persistent. Why was their name not the same as his father's? Why didn't they marry? Had his father preferred Charlotte Crainby to him? Had he loved her mother more than his? Maggie knew her answers did not satisfy him but she believed she had distracted his attention with other things.

Billy had a natural thirst for knowledge, which his grandfather had encouraged, and he was intelligent and quick to learn. His school work progressed but deep inside him there were doubts. Later, when Maggie looked back, she recalled that afternoon and realized it had marked the beginning of subtle changes in her son. He had become more introspective, sometimes moody, less confident and less trusting too.

Victoria was always glad she had refused the invitation to talk to the women's groups during the day, much as she would have loved to do it. It was a cold Monday morning in November and it had taken her longer than usual to hang the washing in the orchard. Fraser was happy to play in the grass while she worked. Miss Traill always insisted on peeling the vegetables in preparation for the midday meal as soon as breakfast was cleared away. It had taken a lot of persuasion to get her to sit down at the table and rest her bad leg while she worked. When Victoria and Fraser returned to the kitchen Miss Traill was sitting at the table as usual, the peeling knife in one hand. Her head was leaning against the back of the wooden Windsor chair, tilted to the side, a faint smile curving her mouth. At first Victoria thought she was having a little nap, as she often did now. Then she realized her old friend would never waken again. She felt cold all over. Fraser was talking in a loud whisper, trying not to disturb her. Victoria bent down in front of him and whispered too.

'Daddy is working in the dairy, Fraser. Will you go and tell him Miss Traill is sleeping and Mummy needs him? Ask him to take you to stay with Granny Pringle first. She will play games with you and she will not mind if you make a noise.' His eyes lit up and he marched importantly out of the door and across the yard. Victoria telephoned Doctor Grantly with a heavy heart. He advised them to contact Mr Jenkinson, the solicitor, to ask whether Miss Traill had stipulated the arrangements for her funeral. She had told Andrew more than once that she would rely on him to carry out her wishes as he had done for their former employer, Mr Rennie.

'Miss Traill wants a private funeral,' Mr Jenkinson said. 'She is to be laid to rest in the little plot of land she acquired next to Mr Rennie.'

The house seemed empty without her. Many times Victoria turned to exchange a comment or pass on a piece of news, only to find the empty wooden armchair beside the table. She had a hollow feeling whenever she realized Miss Traill would never again offer her wisdom or her unexpected quips of dry humour.

As well as her funeral arrangements she had also left a letter for Victoria with the solicitor. Moreover she had bequeathed to her everything still in her possession. Victoria couldn't stem the tears as she read the kindly words of gratitude.

'We did so little...'

'You gave her a home and affection. You made her a part of your family,' Mr Jenkinson said gently. 'She told me more than once how grateful she was to both of you. Now that everything is settled you will receive nearly three thousand pounds between you. I believe she has already stated in her letter to you, Mrs Pringle, that the first thing she wants you to do is install an Aga cooker, like the one Mrs Lennox has at Home Farm. She told me she hoped you would think of her whenever you use it and she knows that will be often.'

'I-I can't believe it,' Victoria gasped. 'I didn't know she had heard of such things.'

'She told me she had asked Mrs Lennox all about it. Apart from the cooking she said it would save you having to kindle the fire every morning before you went out to the milking, and the children would be safer when she was not there to keep an eye on them.' His eyes twinkled. 'She was very firm about her wishes.'

'She was thrifty too,' Andrew said. 'It's hard to believe she had so much money.'

'Remember she inherited the money from Mr Rennie's life insurance, and she had saved all her life for her old age. As it happened she said her wants were few and you two had given her more than money could buy. So, my advice is take it and put it to good use. If it will make life a little easier for both of you, Miss Traill will consider it has been worthwhile.

By the end of the year a new scheme had been introduced in which a ballot would be held to draft one in every ten men to work in the mines instead of being sent into the services. There were mixed feelings about the system but it was the idea of the Minister of Labour, Ernest Bevin, who had worked in the mines himself and believed mixing the classes would be good for democracy.

'I suppose there's no use having soldiers and airmen if there isn't enough coal to fuel the ammunitions factories,' Andrew said thoughtfully. 'But I can't imagine some of the men wanting to get their hands dirty down a mine. To be honest I wouldn't like working in the bowels of the earth in the darkness.'

'I think the government are just doing their best to make sure everybody does their bit for the country,' Victoria said.

'You mean like asking all the women to work, unless they're too tied up with young children?' Andrew gave a wry grin. 'It's folk like Mrs Crainby they're getting at, or ought to be. I heard she's been roped in for rolling bandages.'

'I suppose there are people who think every-one should work but them,' Victoria sighed. 'Milly says she wishes she could escape from her house and work in a factory with other women. I think she is making Jem's life a mis-ery. She's so unreasonable sometimes. Even if the children do keep her busy at least she has a home and enough to eat. Some of the poor people in the cities have neither, and many of them have lost their families as well.'

Seven

The war raged on and the Japanese were advancing in Burma but nonetheless the spring of 1944 brought hope to Britain.

'Surely the government would not be making plans for free health care for everybody if they didn't think the end of the war was in sight?' Victoria said. Although she still listened avidly to the news on the radio she liked to study the weekly newspaper too. 'And they are planning more education and secondary schools. Libby and Fraser will have to stay at school until they're fifteen.' She shuddered as memories came flooding back to her. 'I'm glad it was not like that for us. I needed to earn my living. They might have put me in a workhouse...'

'Ah, Victoria, you know my mother and father would never have allowed that,' Andrew said. 'They would have given you a home with us whether you could work or not.'

'Yes, they were always kind to me.' She grinned and gave him a hug. 'They even gave me their wee spoiled boy for my husband.'

'I was never spoiled!' Andrew began indignantly, until he saw the laughter in her eyes. 'You'll pay for that tonight, my girl,' he said softly. 'What is Josh saying in his letter, and where is he?'

'You know he never says very much. He explained the letters are censored. But he says they are getting the machines he talked about when he was home just before Christmas.'

'That will be the aeroplanes with jet engines,' Andrew nodded. 'I think Josh really hates seeing all the destruction and dropping hundreds of bombs on innocent people, even if they are the enemy.'

'He mentions a new medicine called penicillin. He says it works like a miracle on infected wounds.'

'I suppose even war brings out some good things, though sometimes it's hard to believe that.'

'When I write back I'll ask if he's seen one of the new prefabricated houses, and if it's true a few men can erect one in hours.' She laughed aloud. 'He'll never believe how long it has taken to get my Aga cooker and install it.'

'That wouldn't be considered an essential,' Andrew chuckled. 'In fact we were lucky to get one at all, but I must admit it is a great improvement. The new milking machine will be installed and ready to use by next week too. Miss Traill has certainly made our lives a lot easier. I hope she knows how much we appreciate it.'

'So do I,' Victoria agreed fervently. 'I just wish Milly was showing signs of getting back to normal. When I told her about the milking machine and how much easier it will be for Jem, as well as for us, she just shrugged and muttered that no one made *her* life any easier.'

'Milly's health is a worry.' Andrew nodded, frowning thoughtfully. 'Her moods and angry outbursts are getting Jem down. I think she needs to see the doctor.'

'I'll see if I can persuade her,' Victoria said. 'Surely things must improve soon for everybody. It says in the paper they plan to make half a million prefabricated houses for families who have lost their homes in the bombing, and for the soldiers when they return home, so they must think the war is coming to an end.'

'I don't know how we'd have managed without the Americans though,' Andrew mused. 'By the way, the army are moving their tanks away from High Bowie next week and the officers are moving out of the house. We shall have to look for a shepherd and see if we can get lime and seed to improve the moor where the tanks have churned up the ground.'

Billy, Libby and Milly's two oldest girls had just passed the Pringles' cottage on their way home from school when they saw the tanks coming down from the hill.

'I'm going back to where the tracks join to watch them pass!' Billy yelled in excitement and dropped his bike on to the roadside and ran down the lane. Gracie and Miriam followed with Libby running behind. They clambered up the narrow grassy bank beside the road and ducked under the pole which had sufficed as a gate since the government had collected all the iron railings and gates to smelt for weapons.

'We'll be safe here,' Billy said. 'The tanks are wider than the track but we're in the field so they can't touch us up here. We shall see them close up.'

'They look huge,' Libby said nervously. 'They don't have any Germans in them, do they, Billy?' She edged nearer to him and he took her hand and squeezed it reassuringly, giving her his lopsided smile.

''Course they don't have Germans, stupid,' Grace Wright snapped.

'There's no need to be horrid to her,' Miriam said. 'Oh look, Sylvie and Joan are looking for mushrooms in the field with Mam. She's carrying wee Jimmy.' She waved eagerly. Sylvie waved back and began to run towards them. The children's attention was riveted on the huge lumbering machine as it ground slowly by them. None of them noticed Sylvie, running as fast as her four-year-old legs allowed. She had almost reached them when she slithered on to her bottom in the damp grass and rolled down on to the track below. The driver of the second tank had no chance of seeing her, or of stopping in time if he had. The children stared in horror. Libby hid her face in her hands, afraid to look. Grace and Miriam screamed. Billy was waving frantically at the tank, shouting as loudly as he could, even though he knew the driver would never hear. The driver of the last tank sensed something was wrong when he saw their distress. He drew to a halt and climbed out, just as Milly came panting up with the howling baby in her arms, leaving Joan toddling some way behind. Her face went white when she realized what had happened.

'It's your fault!' she screamed hysterically at Billy. 'You killed her! You shouldn't have brought them here. It's...'

'It was an accident, missus.' The driver of the tank tried to calm her. 'It had nothing to do with the laddie.'

'It did, it did! He's to blame. It was his fault, I tell you! He's a bloody Crainby, that's what he is. They don't care about folks like us.' She began to sob loudly. Billy's face was white and he was shaking badly but he didn't cry. His blue eyes were dark and round with shock. Why didn't they lift her up? How tiny she looked lying on the track. He began to duck under the pole.

'No, no, laddie, stay here,' the driver said quietly. 'It's no place for you.' His own face was white and strained as he looked around for help, afraid to loosen his grip on the hysterical mother. It was a relief to see Joe and Polly and Mrs Conley hurrying from their cottages.

Polly immediately took charge of the children and ushered them up to the farmhouse, as far away from the scene, and Milly, as possible. Billy couldn't stop shaking. Libby whimpered softly, hiding her face against Victoria's skirt. Grace was almost as hysterical as her mother and Polly had to shake her to make her listen. Miriam was weeping with real grief for her younger sister. They all knew they had done nothing wrong, but Milly's outburst made them all feel responsible.

Billy was ten years old and he knew he would never forget this day as long as he lived. Milly Wright's accusations seemed burned into his brain. He was sorry. Sorry. Sorry. But he couldn't cry like the girls. He couldn't speak. The words wouldn't come.

Victoria took one look at him and telephoned for Maggie and for Doctor Grantly.

Although Jem grieved for his little girl he was even more worried about his wife and his remaining children. Milly had not been coping for a long time and Sylvie's death had brought things to a head. Jem admitted they had no money to pay for the funeral. Andrew dealt with it and Victoria told Doctor Grantly about Milly's condition even before the accident. He prescribed medication.

'It could take a long time before she recovers completely. Meanwhile she needs complete rest,' he advised, his expression grim. 'I don't want to have her admitted to the Crichton if it can be avoided.'

None of them wanted Milly sent to the local mental hospital, however good its reputation. Surprisingly it was Jem's mother who gave most support, although Milly had always given the impression they didn't get on. For the first few weeks she came and stayed while Milly seemed to sleep almost continuously. Doctor Grantly said that was a good thing and he would reduce her medication when he felt she was more able to deal with life. Milly's mother came once a week to 'clean through'. It fell to Victoria and Polly to provide food for Jem and the children whenever they could and Mrs Conley helped with baby Jimmy and Joan while the two older girls were at school.

'I canna tell you how grateful I am to Andrew,' Jem said to Victoria a few weeks later. 'I've needed a lot of time off. I thought he might tell me we had to move on and look for another job, and that would have made Milly worse than ever.'

'Of course it would, Jem. We all want to see her back to normal. Anyway it has made a tremendous difference to the milking now we have the milking machine. Thank goodness Mary has learned how to put the units on to the cows so quickly. Two of us can manage now so long as we have someone to carry the milk to the dairy.'

She didn't tell him the government wanted more and more milk.

It was a great relief and there were joyous celebrations all over the country when peace was finally declared, though many of the British soldiers had been drafted to Malaya where the war against the Japanese continued.

Josh said it would be a long time before the country was restored to normal. Land and crops in Europe had been devastated and people were starving. In Britain food supplies were scarce and the regulations increased instead of relaxing. The government responded by guaranteeing prices for essential commodities. Children under five years old were allocated tokens for a ration of milk at a cheaper rate. The pressure on farmers increased and grants were given for ploughing old pasture land, and subsidies were offered to help buy extra fertilizer. There was a desperate need to increase production. It was a well guarded secret that the Germans had been close to starving the British people into submission.

At Home Farm Maggie Lennox heard reports of Milly's illness. She was sympathetic but she was also angry. Slowly, bit by bit, and from various sources, she had begun to realize Milly blamed Billy for Sylvie's death. No wonder he had nightmares in which he sobbed that he was not to blame. He didn't seem able to shake off the spectre of wee Sylvie. It haunted his dreams. Although the nightmares gradually became less frequent Billy was no longer the merry, outgoing boy he had been, but he did pass the exam to go to Dumfries Academy. Maggie knew that was due in part to his grandfather's continuing interest and encouragement and she appreciated Sir William's guidance.

It was a blow when the old man caught a bout of influenza the following winter. In spite of Doctor Grantly's skill and her careful nursing it turned into pneumonia.

'I know I don't have to tell you how serious this is for a man of his age, Mrs Lennox,' the doctor said gravely.

There was nothing anyone could do. Sir William Crainby died in the late afternoon. Billy considered himself too old to shed tears, but the old man had been the father he had never known, the grandfather who loved and encouraged him, and a true friend and teacher. Maggie listened helplessly when Billy grieved in the privacy of his bedroom.

Sir William had retained his family's solicitor so it was Mr Jenkinson who handled all the arrangements for the funeral and he called to see Maggie to discuss the details.

'It was Sir William's wish, Mrs Lennox – no not his wish, it was his command...' He broke off to give her a wry smile, but Maggie was too tense to return it as she clasped her hands tightly together. 'He gave instructions that you and your son were to sit at the front of the church, with your friends, Mr and Mrs Pringle—'

'B-but Mrs Crainby ... Surely...'

'Sir William said if she attended she should be shown to the front seat at the other side of the pulpit. It would be best if you and Mr and Mrs Pringle could arrive early, perhaps? It would avoid a certain ... er ... awkwardness...'

'Well, y-yes, if that is your instructions.'

'It is. I imagine Mrs Crainby will want to make her entrance last, possibly with her daughter. I know most of Sir William's contemporaries have passed on but I am sure there will be a big turnout. He was a popular Laird in his day.'

Maggie nodded numbly. She had known this

day must come but she felt totally bereft, far worse than she had felt for her husband, or even for Luke, whom she had loved so tenderly. It would mean a tremendous upheaval in their lives; she was not sure she could face moving back up to High Bowie to live. It would be more difficult for Billy cycling down to Darlonachie to catch the bus for school too.

Victoria cycled over later that evening to see whether there was anything she could do to help. 'Will you need baking for the tea afterwards, Maggie?' She knew how awkward this was for her friend in the circumstances, especially when Mrs Crainby was so hostile.

'No.' Maggie shook her head. 'Mr Jenkinson is arranging everything. He said it was not usual but he felt it was better if the funeral tea was held on neutral ground so he has arranged for refreshments in the new hotel which opened last year. All the tenants will be invited to attend if they wish.'

'He's a good man, Mr Jenkinson,' Victoria said with warm approval. 'Mind you, I wouldn't like him for an enemy. I think he could be very fierce.'

'Mmm, I know what you mean. He says Sir William requested you and Andrew to sit with Billy and me in the front seat at the church, in the Crainbys' own pew. He wants us to be there early.'

'Whew! What will Mrs Crainby say to that?'

'She will not be pleased, that's for sure,' Maggie said unhappily. 'You will be with me, won't you, Victoria? Sometimes I feel so alone ... Billy is just a child yet and he's been so upset, although he tries to hide it.'

'He's a fine boy, Maggie. Sir William recognized that. He's always welcome at Langmune. You know Andrew will do his best to help if you have any problems.'

'Thank you,' Maggie whispered, but she was frowning.

'Has he got over the horror of the tank?'

'I don't think he'll ever forget it,' Maggie said slowly. 'The nightmare still comes back occasionally, especially if he's upset. It's as though there's a coiled wire inside of him and he's holding it in. One day I fear it may just explode. Och, I expect that sounds foolish, but my instinct tells me he's not the happy boy he used to be and he does brood about things. This will not help. He really loved his grandfather. In spite of their ages they had a lot in common.'

Mrs Crainby's displeasure at being relegated to the opposite side of the church was plain to everyone. She refused to attend the funeral tea.

'You will return with me to the Dower House for the reading of the will,' she said to Mr Jenkinson. 'We shall discuss Home Farm and the eviction of the present occupants.' Even the elderly solicitor was startled. He frowned but Henrietta was too busy with her own thoughts to notice.

'Mrs Crainby, Sir William did leave a will. You may hear the details if you present yourself at my office at eleven thirty tomorrow.' Without waiting for a reply he strode away, leaving Henrietta gasping with anger.

She had every intention of keeping Home Farm in her name, quite disconnected from her daughter's trust. She resented Luke's precautions over Charlotte's inheritance. They seriously curtailed her spending in spite of the fiddling she contrived over expenses which were entered into the estate's accounts as maintenance or repairs for the farms. She could not accept Luke had taken the precautions for her own good, as well as their daughter's. Like her mother she was a spendthrift and her husband had soon realized that fact. Mr Jenkinson had been the Crainby family's solicitor but she had changed to another firm for her affairs. Mr Jenkinson's firm was still Charlotte's trustee, however, and she could not change that. Henrietta detested him. She longed for his impending retirement. She needed additional income in spite of the yearly allowance Luke had settled on her, and her need was growing desperate as bills mounted up. The old man's death had come just in time. All she needed now was to get her hands on Home Farm. It had always been the best farm on the estate.

Farm prices had stabilized during the war and Soutar Ward, her factor, had steadily increased rents, but she had squandered the additional income even before it came in, a cause of many disagreements between them. Consequently the farms, which were to be Charlotte's inheritance, were becoming increasingly neglected. Four of the best tenants had given notice and moved away.

As arranged Mr Jenkinson arrived at Home Farm promptly at nine thirty the morning after the funeral. Maggie had barely slept. She dreaded telling Billy they would have to move. She felt jaded as she opened the door and showed Mr Jenkinson into Sir William's library.

He saw how troubled she looked and he began without preamble.

'Mrs Lennox, I think it would ease your mind to know that Sir William has left this house and the Home Farm in trust for your son, William Crainby Lennox, with a proviso that it is to be your home for as long as you wish to live with him—'

'That can't be true!' Maggie jerked upright in her seat.

'I assure you it is. Sir William made his wishes very clear some time ago. He has also left you a small annuity for your own use. There are one or two small bequests to Mr Blake, who has been his farm manager for many years, and to Mr Forsythe, who was factor for the estate, plus a couple of others.'

'I-I can't believe it...' Maggie stammered. 'All this...' She looked wonderingly around the lovely room. 'For Billy ... We shall not have to move then?'

'No, you will not need to move out, Mrs Lennox,' Mr Jenkinson smiled. 'Make an appointment to see me at my office in a week or so. We shall go over the details then.'

'I-I can't believe it ... Mrs Crainby? Her daughter?'

'They were well provided for by Luke Crainby.' He smiled wryly. 'Don't worry, Mrs Lennox. I shall deal with Mrs Crainby.'

'She – she doesn't know?'

'Not yet, but you can relax. If there is any unpleasantness I shall deal with it. It was clear to me that Sir William enjoyed the company of your son. He had suffered more losses than most during his lifetime and he deserved the joy and brightness his grandson brought to his declining years. You looked after him well and he appreciated your care.'

'B-but he paid me. He was always generous to both of us. I ... we never expected...'

The solicitor rose to his feet and patted her shoulder. 'I must be going now, I have another appointment.'

'Will you take a cup of tea first?' Maggie got to her feet too. Mr Jenkinson smiled and declined her offer.

'Maybe next time I call on you. I'd better be on my way.'

Maggie showed him out then returned to her chair, clasping her hands tightly together. She couldn't believe Sir William had left this lovely house, as well as the farm, to her son. She sent up a silent prayer of gratitude and hoped he knew.

* * *

Later, Henrietta Crainby faced Mr Jenkinson across his wide mahogany desk. Shock and fury had brought her to her feet.

'You can't be serious!' she hissed.

'I am perfectly serious. Those are the terms of Sir William Crainby's will.'

'You are telling me that my husband transferred the title deeds for Home Farm back to his father?'

'He did. He reversed the ownership as soon as he knew he was seriously ill.'

'This is your doing! You—'

'My dear Mrs Crainby, I merely carry out the wishes of my clients,' Mr Jenkinson said mildly, but he couldn't help comparing the demeanour of Henrietta Crainby with that of the woman he had just left at Home Farm.

'Even if Luke did give the farm back to his father, Sir William Crainby would never leave it to ... to Luke's bastard.'

'He has left the house and land in trust for William Crainby Lennox, exactly as it is stated in the will I already read to you.'

Henrietta was speechless with rage. 'I shall contest the will...'

'I would not advise it, Mrs Crainby,' Mr Jenkinson interrupted coolly. 'Everything has been done legally, both by your late husband and by his father.'

'He was senile! He must have been. This is your doing! You are responsible. You advised him what to do. You have done this in spite because I took the Estate business away from your firm...'

'I merely carry out the wishes of my clients, madam. They make their own decisions. As for being senile, Sir William arranged the trust for his grandson some time ago. Even if he had not he was still in perfect control of all his faculties to the end of his days.'

'I don't believe you! You...'

'You would if you had been in the habit of visiting him. I should point out that he derived a great deal of unexpected pleasure from the company of his grandson. On the other hand I believe he rarely saw his granddaughter.' He watched Henrietta's face flush a dull red and then turn white with anger. 'Now I have another appointment. If you will excuse me...' He moved round his desk and held open the door. Henrietta had no option but to walk through it, seething with anger, and all of it now focussed on Maggie Lennox. She would contest the will, she promised herself. She would sue. She would go to the highest court in the land and Maggie Lennox's name would be mud.

Eight

It was three years since the government had introduced a tax on wages. It was called pay as you earn and the regulations showed no signs of being relaxed since the war ended. Victoria had taken on what she had expected to be a temporary chore but instead it was increasing every year. Even her eggs had to be accounted for.

'We're expected to keep detailed records of everything we buy and sell,' Andrew said. 'They were discussing it at one of the NFU meetings. One man kept saying he had never made a profit so he didn't pay any tax. If one farmer is continually different to others in the same area the government officials inspect his records to see if they're genuine.'

'What if they are genuine and the officials didn't believe it?'

'Don't worry,' Andrew grinned. 'You're managing fine. Anyway I have more important things to do outside than write down lots of numbers.'

'That's all very well but I didn't expect to have so many records to keep.'

'You were always good at school, and you're far too honest to cheat. I have faith in you,

113

Victoria.' He sighed. 'I know keeping all those records is a bore when you'd rather be rearing more chickens, but it seems to be part of the changing world since the war. I think we should buy another chicken brooder and buy all the chicks from a hatchery as day-olds. That would save you some time.'

'It wouldn't be as satisfying though. I love to see the hens teaching their chicks how to scavenge, or collecting them all underneath her to keep them warm. Anyway, you may know I wouldn't cheat, but supposing I need to prove it?' Victoria demanded shortly, chewing her new pen in agitation.

'Hey, don't waste that pen. It cost me a fortune.' He didn't tell his thrifty wife he had paid two pounds fifteen and sixpence for it.

'I wouldn't like to damage it,' Victoria said, examining it closely where her teeth had gripped. 'It's marvellous. It never needs dipped in ink and it doesn't make blots or smudge. Mr Biro must be a very clever man to invent it.'

'Mmm.' Andrew nodded sceptically. 'We'll wait and see. I can't believe such a wee thing can write two hundred thousand words without refilling.'

'It's doing a good job so far. Look at all the pages of numbers I've written. When are you going down to see Maggie about High Bowie by the way? She is definitely meaning to sell it. Do you really want to buy it from her?'

'Aah,' Andrew said. 'I nearly forgot. I have some news for you, but we need to discuss things, Victoria. You must tell me the truth if you don't like my suggestion.'

'Have you ever known me to do anything else?' Victoria asked wryly. 'But you've made me curious. What's the news?'

'We'll walk to the top of the hill, then we'll not be overheard. Can you ask Trudy to keep an eye on the children?'

'Yes. We shall miss her when she leaves, won't we? All the land girls are going home. There's supposed to be a million men demobbed by the end of the year and there's not much of 1946 left.'

'Aye, it's a funny old world,' Andrew sighed. He looked pensive and Victoria knew he was thinking of George and Mark, who would never return. She put her hand on his arm. He smiled down at her, knowing she had read his mind and shared his thoughts. 'Fifty-five million people dead,' he muttered, 'and people desperate for food, and we call it victory.'

A little while later they walked side by side up the track leading to the higher fields of Langmune. Andrew reached for her hand and squeezed it, smiling at her.

'Langmune,' he murmured pensively. 'The land of the long moon. Mr Rennie used to say it meant "for eternity". I hope that's what it means for us and our children. I'd hate to give it up.'

'Is there any reason why we should?' Victoria frowned. 'What news do you have, Andrew? Do tell me. Is it bad news?'

'Oh no. Good news, I reckon. Willie and Mary

115

have decided to get married.' Andrew grinned.

'Oh, it is good news! I'm so pleased for them. Your mother and father will be happy too...'

'They don't know yet. Willie only told me this afternoon. For a couple of thirty-year-olds they act as shyly as a pair of teenagers.'

'I hope you didn't tease them?'

'Me? As though I would do such a thing...' He looked innocently up at the sky, but he couldn't prevent a grin spreading over his tanned lean face.

'You did! Poor Mary. It's taken them so long to get to this stage even though we could all see what a good match they were for each other. Willie would understand better than anyone how Mary needed time to grieve. They have both lost people they loved with this horrid war.'

'Most families have known sorrow. They went to school together so they know each other well enough. I think they'll make a good marriage.' Andrew frowned. 'The problem is Willie has worked for old Mr Butterworth since he left the school but the old man's giving up the tenancy next spring. He says he's getting too old to farm and the factor keeps putting up the rent and never doing any repairs. Willie says the house roof has been leaking for two years, and the sheds are falling down around their ears. They've done as much as Butterworth can afford with temporary repairs but Willie reckons the whole place needs a major overhaul. Most of the farms on the estate are the same apparently but the factor keeps saying there's no spare

116

money.'

'So? Are you thinking of offering Willie work at High Bowie?'

'I thought about it as soon as he mentioned leaving the Butterworths. We would need a shepherd. But he and Mary have plans of their own. They want to rent a sheep farm and set up on their own. Willie doesn't know Maggie plans to sell High Bowie, or that we were thinking of buying it from her.' As they reached the grassy bank in the shelter of some trees, his expression grew serious and vaguely troubled. 'He doesn't think they would consider him as a tenant anyway but he doesn't really want Mrs Crainby for his landlord either.'

'I don't blame him,' Victoria said with feeling.

'He asked if we would consider giving up the tenancy of High Bowie and whether Maggie would consider him and Mary as tenants instead.'

'So, what did you say?'

'I didn't know what to say. I wanted to hear *what* you think?'

'I see...' Victoria chewed her lower lip. 'We were so lucky with Mr Rennie and Luke. They gave us our chance in life. I'd like to see Willie and Mary have a go, but Maggie has set her heart on selling High Bowie. She plans to use the money to send Billy to university because Sir William thought he ought to broaden his horizons before he takes over Home Farm. Billy has other ideas, she says. In any case Maggie intends to use some of the money to modernize

Home Farm now she has a new manager. She says it will be an investment for Billy's future.'

'I think she's probably right about that, within reason.' Andrew frowned. Then he went on slowly. 'We've always decided things together, Victoria, so please be honest with me over this. I don't want you to think I'm doing it because Willie is my brother and I'm favouring him.'

'I don't think I can persuade Maggie to keep High—'

'No, I know that. Maggie has enough problems with Billy. His grandfather's death was hard enough on him without all the unpleasantness Mrs Crainby is causing.'

'The awful publicity during the court case was hard enough to bear but the way Mrs Crainby has dragged it out and exaggerated things to the newspapers is terrible.' Victoria shuddered.

'I agree with Maggie; it will be good for Billy to get away from the area as soon as he's old enough to go to agricultural college. It will give him time to grow up and get things into perspective, as well as benefiting from some practical farming experience on top of his education. I agree with the laddie on that score.'

'So what had you in mind for Willie?' Victoria asked.

'Suppose we go ahead and buy High Bowie as we had planned? Then we could rent it to Willie and Mary.' He saw Victoria frown and went on hurriedly, 'They would have to pay a proper rent, of course, to help us repay the money we shall be borrowing from the bank, but they are

118

expecting to do that anyway. Willie says they've both been saving up for a long time. They have enough to buy a decent-sized flock of sheep, a good pair of horses, a couple of house cows, a sow or two and some hens. Willie already has a pair of good collie dogs to work the sheep on the High Bowie moor land. They have thought it through. Willie knows how much we pay Maggie for rent at present. They were hoping we would help out if they need to borrow any machines, such as the hay mower and a roller, things like that, until they get established. They seem to have it all worked out.' Andrew sighed and rubbed his temple. 'Willie is so enthusiastic. I hadn't the heart to tell him Maggie intends to sell.'

'I suppose we would need to buy breeding sheep to restock the hill now it is recovering after the tanks,' Victoria said slowly. 'We had only budgeted for buying the land.'

'Mmm, Willie knows more about hill flocks than I do anyway. We would need to employ a shepherd.'

'I'd love to see Willie and Mary make a success,' Victoria said. 'They're both hard workers – not a bit like Milly. They take care of their money. But you've forgotten one thing.'

'What's that?' Andrew asked, spreading his overcoat in the shelter of the hedge and drawing her down beside him. 'What have I forgotten?

'The Pringle pride. Do you think Willie will want you for his landlord, especially when he realizes we have had to borrow some of the

119

money to buy High Bowie, and that we'll be using Langmune as security? He'll think we're doing it as a favour.'

'You're right, I hadn't thought of that. Willie does have a hellish lot of pride. I think that's why it's taken him so long to ask Mary to marry him. He wanted to provide everything himself, but she's as keen to have a farm of their own as he is and they're not getting any younger.'

'I suppose we could ask Maggie to continue acting as though she's still the landlord?' Victoria mused. 'We would need to keep the purchase of High Bowie a secret between the three of us. The solicitor would have to deal with the purchase, of course, but Mr Jenkinson is moving to Inverness soon to stay with his daughter.'

'You mean they would pay the rent to Maggie, and she would pay it into our bank?'

'Yes. I'm sure we could trust her to do that, don't you?'

'We shall need to see whether she's agreeable first though, before we say anything to Willie and Mary. I hope it never leaks out that we're their landlords. Willie would blow his top.'

'Will you mind giving up the tenancy of High Bowie? And are you sure the bank will still loan us the money if we are not farming it ourselves?'

'I reckon land is one of the safest assets. There'll never be any more of it. That's one thing the government can't manufacture. I believe it will be a good investment. Everything depends on Willie paying the rent on time. I suppose we shall have to tell Mr McNeill our plans too if he's arranging the bank loan.'

'I think Willie and Mary know what they'll be taking on,' Victoria said firmly. 'Anyway, we shall not need to borrow as much money when we don't need to buy sheep to re-stock.'

'That's true. I've been thinking though...'

'Oh yes? And what other plans to build an empire have you dreamed up now, Andrew Pringle?' Victoria teased.

'Well there's other ways of expanding.' He smiled ruefully. 'Och, you know I don't like to stand still, Victoria, and we have two children of our own growing up. Libby is convinced she should be a farmer too. Anyway the government are granting subsidies for chemical fertilizers so we can produce better yields of cereals, or more grass. I've read some good articles recently on treating our grassland as a crop with better seeds and proper cultivation, rather than depending on the grace of God and not producing anything for half the year. In Wales they're breeding varieties of grass to get better yields and more palatability, as well as a longer season for grazing. We have a big advantage for growing grass in our climate. I think we could keep more cows at Langmune if I manage it efficiently. We shall still have to grow our cereal allocation to comply with the government regulations but I know more about cows than I do about hill farming. Since Willie mentioned his own plans, and I've had time to consider, I think we should concentrate on what we do best. We already have

121

the milking machine. All we need now is a bigger byre to keep more cows.'

'A-ah,' Victoria sighed. 'I should have guessed. Well I agree so long as you remember more cows mean more calves.'

'Of course it does, which means we can build up our numbers gradually, without having to spend precious capital buying from someone else, as we would have done to get a sheep flock...'

'You're missing the point, Andrew! It also means more calves to rear, meaning more work for me.'

'But I thought you liked rearing the young calves?'

'I do, but not when we have so many in one shed that they nearly knock me down whenever they hear the rattle of milk pails.' She chuckled and aimed a playful fist at his chest. 'You, Andrew Pringle, know nothing about wee calves slavering all over you and butting each other out of the way, spilling the milk all over the place, including over me. I'm just reminding you we need more sheds to put calves in if we keep more cows, so just include that in your budget.'

'Yes, ma'am.' Andrew grinned wickedly and gave a mock salute. She retaliated with another aim at his ribs but he caught her wrist and drew her closer, silencing her words and her laughter with a long kiss.

It was some time later when Victoria sat up, trying to smooth down her hair and brush wisps of dried grass and twigs from her clothes.

'Have we reached a decision about High Bowie, then?' she asked with a smile, looking down into her husband's lean face. Andrew lay gazing up into the crisp blue of the December sky, one arm under his head. 'You don't look like a responsible married man of thirty-three lying there,' she teased.

'I don't feel it either. I hope Willie is as happy as I am in his marriage,' he said huskily, and reached towards Victoria again. She scrambled hastily away.

'Come on, lazy bones, it's too cold to stay out here any longer. We have a nice warm house to go to. Anyway Trudy will be wondering where we've got to. I shall miss her help, and Mary's, when they leave us.'

'I thought Jocky Conley would have been demobbed by now. His father says he's looking forward to coming back to work at Langmune.' Andrew jumped to his feet and dusted himself down, making sure he was respectable again, before he retrieved his overcoat. 'I don't think Milly will ever return to work in the dairy though, so I suggest we look for a maid to do the dairy work and to help you with the poultry.'

'I'll ask around in the village. When she's not at school Libby is a good wee helper with the calves, although she's not ten yet.'

'She seems to be doing well at school too, according to her reports.'

'Yes, she's determined to pass the exam to go to the Academy. I suspect she's determined to do everything at least as well as Billy Lennox.

There's a bit of rivalry between them now they're growing up.' Victoria smiled. Her daughter had a very determined streak once she made her mind up, but it was not a bad thing to have a strong character.

Mary had counted her pennies all her life and as she and Willie planned their wedding she considered the expense.

'Even if food was not still rationed, I wouldn't expect Mother and Father to make us an elaborate wedding,' she said. 'They've worked hard all their lives and they're too old now to make sacrifices for us. If there's any money to spare I'd rather spend it making a comfortable home at High Bowie. Do you mind not having a do?' She looked anxiously up at Willie. Their love and respect for each other had grown steadily and Mary felt she was well blessed to be marrying such a kind and loving man.

'Eh, my lassie, as long as we get married and spend the rest of our lives together, I don't care how we do it.'

Mary smiled in relief and hugged his arm. Willie didn't go in for fancy talk but when he called her his lassie he made her feel young and cherished. Her sister, Lily, was newly home from the ATS and she considered Willie boring because he discussed farming with their father instead of responding to her flirtatious quips. She watched the slow smile light his craggy features as he squeezed her hand in response and her heart filled with love and gratitude. Maybe they did have their feet firmly on the ground but she was thankful Willie was genuine and sincere. Never in a million years could she act like Lily with her painted nails and scarlet lips. Even her hair was a different colour to what it had been when she first left home, but Willie was unimpressed by her appearance, much to Lily's chagrin.

Lily was not used to men ignoring her and she had no intention of being upstaged by her elder, plainer sister. She vowed to win Willie's admiration at the first opportunity, not that he was the type of man she would ever consider marrying. Even Lucy, the baby of the family, was already married and expecting a baby. Mary was nearly thirty and Lily had thought she would never marry so the wedding made her realize the years were passing and she was still unattached in spite of the many young men who had appeared to enjoy her favours.

When it came to wedding plans Mary and Willie had reckoned without Victoria's generosity. She and Polly had been saving sugar rations and dried fruit for months to make a cake.

'We're not having one of those cardboard pretend wedding cakes, all covered in white chalk,' Victoria said firmly. 'Even if it is small it will be a proper fruit cake.'

'We'll likely need tae use some semolina and almond essence for the almond paste,' Polly said doubtfully.

'We'll make the best meal we can manage for

Mary and Willie,' Victoria vowed. 'They deserve it. We'll clear as much out of the kitchen as we can and make a long table in the middle. I still have Granny's best linen sheets. We'll use one of them for a tablecloth.'

'Joe has promised he'll have some early salads for us by then,' Polly said, 'and I've still plenty of pickles and chutney left.'

'That's splendid. I've set aside one of the hams so I'll cook it to eat cold, as well as a couple of young cockerels.'

'You're a kind lassie, Victoria,' Polly said. 'You always were a wee gem.'

'Och, it's the least we can do.' Victoria smiled affectionately at her mother-in-law. 'Besides, you know I enjoy it. If only the rationing would end. The fighting may be over but we're still suffering the effects of war.'

'I'll bake fresh bread early that morning,' Polly volunteered. 'Maybe you'll make some drop scones. You're better with the griddle than I am but I'm saving my last pot of strawberry jam – and maybe there'll be a wee bit o' cream?'

'Of course, and a trifle. I've been saving a tin of fruit for a special occasion. It's a pity Josh has no word of being demobbed.'

'I reckon he's in no hurry. He'll miss the company of the other young air-force men. He's promised to be here in good time for the wedding though. He's pleased Willie wants him for his best man.'

'Not half as pleased as Libby is to be bridesmaid,' Victoria chuckled. 'She says you're making her the prettiest dress she's ever seen.'

'We-el now, the bairn hasna seen many pretty clothes since the war began. Josh managed to get me a parcel of parachute silk so I've made her a petticoat to match and it's a full skirt so she keeps swirling around. Miss Phipps managed to get me some dark blue ribbon to tone with Mary's suit so I've made a narrow velvet sash and wee bows down the front. I was a bit surprised Mary didn't ask Lily to be an attendant too, but I'm glad she didn't. She always wants to be centre stage. This is Mary's day and I've enjoyed having a wee girl to sew for at long last. I don't know whether Mary and Willie will give us any grandchildren.'

Victoria looked affectionately at Polly, the woman who had taken her in and loved her when she was a thirteen-year-old homeless waif. There would always be a bond between them.

'You really do love children, don't you?' she said softly.

'Aye, I do, I always have.'

'Well you're going to have at least one more grandchild to keep you entertained.' Victoria chuckled at her stunned expression. 'Don't tell anyone until after the wedding. We don't want to overshadow Mary and Willie's day.'

'Ah, lassie, that's wonderful news. We thought you were putting on a bit o' weight, Joe and me, but I never dreamed ... Are you keeping well? Are you pleased about it? When will it be?' She hugged Victoria warmly.

'Not until the end of the summer. We're both

127

pleased now we've got over the shock. Fraser will be nearly eight. It's a big gap, but we still have the pram and the cot.'

'I do hope Fraser will not be jealous.'

'I don't think he will. He's a good-natured laddie.'

'I pray this wee one never sees a war,' Polly said fervently.

Nine

William Pringle and Mary Jane Hardie were married in Darlonachie Kirk in the third week of May 1947. Mary had chosen a serviceable two-piece suit in royal blue with a matching hat, trimmed with net. Willie thought she looked beautiful with the spray of spring flowers pinned to her jacket.

Lily had bought one of the new-look suits and a pair of high-heeled strappy shoes. She had intended to outshine her sister, but there was an aura of happiness about the bride that gave her a radiance impossible to buy in a bottle. It made Lily all the more determined to gain attention and she flirted outrageously with Andrew and Willie, but it was Josh who received most of her attention. She remembered him vaguely from their school days at Darlonachie, and he was the only eligible man around. . He was tall with an attractive smile and a sparkle in his blue eyes which he seemed to reserve for Victoria. Lily mistook the deep affection and witty camaraderie between the two for sexual attraction, the only kind of relationship she understood between men and women. She lost no time in telling Josh he shouldn't be wasting his time on a married woman, especially when there were attractive single women available. She gave him one of her coquettish glances with much fluttering of eyelashes. She was affronted when he threw back his head and roared with laughter.

'Flirt with Victoria? Why, she's my second mother. She's always loved me, haven't you, sweet sister?'

'Of course I have, Josh dear.' Victoria grinned back at him and everybody chuckled. Lily felt foolish and for the first time she almost envied Mary being married into the warm and friendly Pringle family. Her own parents seemed much older, especially now her father was crippled with rheumatism, and her mother appeared to have shrunk every time Lily had seen her in recent years. She had no idea how much they had depended on Mary for help, or that her eldest sister was relieved to know she intended staying with them. She was looking for work in the area, or at least that had been her plan. She had forgotten how dull she had found Darlonachie. It was even worse now that she'd had a taste of the bright lights and the social life in the forces.

Libby enjoyed pirouetting around the kitchen and out into the garden to show off her pretty bridesmaid's dress. She was quite unselfconscious as she coaxed Billy into the garden to dance with her. He hesitated at first. He was fourteen now and tall for his age. He looked smart in his first tailor-made suit with long trousers and he considered himself almost a man. But he and Libby had always been good friends and he obligingly admired the pretty picture she made as she swirled around in front of him.

Maggie breathed a sigh of relief as she watched them go. She was finding it harder to know how to deal with Billy's unpredictable moods these days. Polly had told her it was because he was a teenager and he would grow out of it, but her mother's instinct told her his personality had begun to change from the day Milly accused him of being responsible for Sylvie's death. His moods had become even worse since the court case which Henrietta had insisted on bringing in her pursuit of Home Farm.

Billy didn't need to analyse his feelings. He had become acutely aware of other people's reactions towards him, and Libby was one of the few who treated him as she had always done – as her friend. In her eyes he was just a person – not Luke Crainby's bastard son, or worse, the boy who had cheated his half sister, Charlotte Crainby, out of her inheritance. He had loved his grandfather and enjoyed his company and the knowledge he had imparted so readily to a boy's eager ears. He bitterly resented Mrs Crainby's public assertion that he had ingratiated himself with an old man in order to get his hands on Home Farm. It spoiled all the joy he had shared with his grandfather as they had planned and dreamed together for the future.

His mother had done her best to hide the

131

newspaper reports from him but he had seen most of them anyway. Some of his fellow pupils had delighted in showing him a report in one of the sensational national newspapers. It described how his mother's first marriage had not been consummated and how she had then ensnared the local laird and tried to entice him away from his wife and daughter. They had delved into details like the registration of his birth and the inclusion of the name Crainby, and the fact that Luke Crainby had admitted paternity.

'There was no question of "admitting" anything,' Maggie had declared indignantly, but there had been tears in her eyes and her shoulders slumped dejectedly. 'Luke was proud to claim you as his son. Henrietta Crainby refused to have him near her or to bear any more of his children. And Sir William delighted in your company, Billy. He treated you as his grandson in every way.'

Billy knew it was the truth but he still hated the gossip and the taunts. He couldn't wait to get away from the snide remarks from some of the people he had believed were his friends. He knew people whispered behind his back. His mother knew it too. She had stopped going to the women's meetings, and she rarely left the farm except on business or to visit at Langmune.

The whole experience had shaken Billy's self-esteem but he was too proud to let any of them see. Instead he hid his feelings behind a moody silence and a stern, almost sullen, set to his young features. His expression warned people not to approach him with their sly tales or their questions. Once or twice he had been involved in fights at school but he knew he didn't deserve a reputation for being a wild boy, which some of the parents had attached to him.

Today at Willie and Mary's wedding, for the first time in what seemed like years, he was amongst friends who liked him, and people who respected his mother. So he went with Libby to the garden and for a short time they enjoyed the innocence of childhood once more.

There was no doubt that Mary and Willie were happy and well suited to each other. Their first big task after the wedding was to shear their new flock of sheep and check them all for injuries and foot rot. The flock was new to High Bowie and needed more diligent herding until they learned the boundaries, but Willie was a good shepherd and he had a pair of intelligent working collie dogs to help him.

Mary was happy putting their new home in order, washing and scrubbing, making new curtains and distempering the walls. She had bought fifty point-of-lay pullets and Willie and his father had made a new wooden hut for them, and Joe had offered to build another hut. She intended to keep more hens as soon as she was sure she could sell all the eggs to the local egg-packing firm. As soon as the fowls were in full lay the manager had agreed to send his van round by High Bowie to collect them once a week, provided they were clean and fresh and

none of them were chipped. Mary was determined they would be first class.

Although the sheep would be their main
source of income they would only have the wool
to sell in their first year at High Bowie. It would
be the following spring before they had any
lambs and late summer before they had any to
sell. So Mary planned to have a regular supply
of eggs for most of the year so they would have
a small amount of money coming in each week.
There wouldn't be many eggs in winter, however, so they had bought two sows and they
planned to have some young pigs to sell during
the leaner months. Andrew had given them a
cow for the house to start them off with milk and
butter. They would need to buy another when
Violet went dry but that was for their own use
and would not bring in any money.

They had planned carefully and in the beginning all went well. They had waited a long time
for marriage and they found great joy and satisfaction in their union, as well as in working
together with a common aim. They both loved
children, and only nine weeks after their wedding Mary was delighted to find she was expecting a baby. She suffered badly from morning
sickness, and not just in the mornings. She went
over to see Victoria to share her news and ask if
she had any advice.

'You look blooming, Victoria,' Mary said as
she greeted her friend and sister-in-law. 'The
baby must be due soon.'

'Just a few more weeks.' Victoria nodded

happily. 'You're looking a bit peaky though, Mary. I hope you're not working too hard getting everything into order?'

Mary shook her head and confided her secret. 'I feel so tired and there's so much to do,' she said. 'Willie is wonderfully considerate but he can't do everything and I had so many plans. How long will it be before I feel all right again?'

'The first three months are the worst,' Victoria said slowly, but Mary did look dreadfully pale and there were blue shadows beneath her eyes. 'Perhaps you should see Doctor Grantly, or his new assistant doctor? He may have some better advice.'

'I hoped I wouldn't need to see a doctor at all,' Mary muttered. 'It's bad enough having to have a midwife for the birth. I suppose I thought I'd just have babies like the cows have their calves. I never thought I could feel this bad. The very smell of cooking makes my stomach turn inside out.'

'Oh dear, Mary, I'm so sorry. Are you going to tell Willie's mother? I know she will be concerned for you and she may have some suggestions, but she will be delighted that you are giving her another grandchild. Do you want a boy or a girl?'

'We don't care, so long as it's all right. Will you tell Ma Pringle? You two get on so well. I don't intend to tell my family until I have to...'

Mary had not reckoned on having regular Sunday visits from Lily, nor her sister's sharp eyes

135

and barbed tongue. Lily was bored with her work in an ironmonger's, she considered the social life to be non-existent and she made everyone around her pay for her discontent.

'If I stay at home Ma thinks I should do the ironing or make the tea, or some other chore, so I thought I may as well come and keep you company.'

'Oh, Lily!' Mary said in exasperation. The last thing she needed was her sister's constant grumbling. 'I always did the ironing when I was living at home. You know Mother's back aches when she has to stand for long. Anyway, Ma and Pa never have much to iron these days, with no Sunday shirts and collars to starch now Pa has stopped going to the Kirk every week.'

Lily looked sullen. It was her own clothes that made up the bulk of the ironing. She had expected everything to be the same as it had been before she went away, when her mother had done everything about the house. She had been astonished when her father had insisted, albeit gently, that they needed her to pay for her keep. She hadn't expected to help with the chores as well.

'It's your fault, Mary,' she snapped suddenly. 'Just because you had nothing better to do than help mother with the housework she thinks I should do the same.'

'Nothing better to do? We worked jolly hard, probably a lot harder than you did in the ATS. Surely you realize our parents are getting old? The war has taken its toll, and since Pa had to give up working he seems to have become an old man. Mother worries about him.'

'Well that's not my concern ... A-ah, here comes Willie.' She turned eagerly towards her brother-in-law but if he noticed her fluttering lashes and provocative glances he gave no indication. All of his attention was on Mary. He was anxious about her being so sick. He wouldn't mind Lily coming to visit but she seemed to expect Mary to make her tea and clear away and wash up, while she sat and preened, or stretched her legs to show off her best silk stockings. He had started going off with the dogs whenever she arrived on a Sunday afternoon. Sometimes he went up the hill to make an extra check on his sheep; sometimes he crossed the glen to talk to Andrew or to see whether his parents had news of Josh, who was as busy as ever helping with the Allied airlift to Berlin and the effort to foil the Soviet blockade.

He felt bad about leaving Mary but Lily was her sister so he couldn't afford to lose his temper and tell her exactly what he thought of her. He knew she wanted him to fall for her feminine charms but Mary was the one he loved. His own mother had taken to baking a batch of bread every week and sending it over with Andrew. Victoria often sent Libby on her bicycle if she had made a stew or baked a meat and potato pie, thinking it might save Mary a little time and work, but Lily did nothing but stir up trouble.

On 8th September 1947 Victoria gave birth to a baby boy. Mary couldn't wait to see him and immediately after lunch on the Sunday she and Willie walked over to Langmune, both of them aware that Lily would be furious to find an empty house.

'She just expects I shall be there, ready to wait on her whenever she likes,' Mary said. Willie glanced at her and grinned, but he offered no comment. He didn't like family squabbles and he certainly didn't want to cause trouble for Mary with her own family.

'Oh, he's adorable,' Mary exclaimed in delight as she looked down at the sleeping infant cocooned in his new white shawl and lying in his crib. 'Maybe I'll think it's worth all this sickness when I can hold my own baby in my arms,' she said softly, offering Willie her gentle smile.

'We thought of calling him George,' Victoria said, 'but we thought if you have a boy, Willie, you would probably want to call him George.'

'Aye, well we had thought about it if we have a boy, but we'll take what we get and be happy. Don't let that prevent you, Victoria, but what about your own brother, Mark?'

'I'm suggesting we give him both names,' Andrew said, 'but I want to call him Lachlan after Victoria.'

'Lachlan Mark George Pringle,' Willie repeated. 'That's a big mouthful for a wee fellow.' He smiled down at his tiny nephew.

'Libby likes it,' Andrew said, 'but Fraser says he'll call him Lachie.'

'I expect he will too, and then it will stick,' Victoria said. 'But what's in a name? We're just

138

so lucky to have all three of them and be a complete family. So many children will never know their fathers.'

'That's true. So, wee fellow, you're Lachie Pringle from now on,' Willie grinned, watching the baby curling and uncurling his tiny fist and longing for his own child to be born.

'Can I make tea for Uncle Willie and Aunt Mary?' Libby asked eagerly.

'You certainly can, Libby.' Victoria smiled gratefully at her young daughter. 'She's going to be a great help I think.' She lowered her voice. 'She has been baking scones all on her own, and a gingerbread loaf, so be sure to tell her how good they are, Willie. She values your opinion, you know.'

Some time later Willie told Victoria she had every reason to be proud of Libby. 'She'll soon be as good at cooking as her mother, and that's saying something.'

'Mmm, that's just what Maggie said when she came yesterday. Billy didn't say anything but he ate three scones so he must have enjoyed them. He said he hoped it would be a boy because he had made him a wee truck in his woodwork class. He's finished it off beautifully and varnished it too.'

'The laddie has more than brains then if he can use his hands well,' Willie said approvingly.

It was late afternoon before Mary and Willie left Langmune and when they arrived home it was evident Lily had been to visit as usual. She had cut a large piece from an apple pie and left

139

the remainder on the table, as well as one of Mary's best china plates and her used cup and saucer.

'It's a good job Snowy or the dogs didn't get in,' Mary grimaced. 'She could have put the pie back in the pantry, even if she couldn't be bothered to wash her own dirty cup.'

'Mmm,' Willie said. 'I'm glad I chose the right sister.' He put an arm around her and kissed her cheek. 'I'll feed the pigs and collect the eggs while you have a rest after walking all the way to Langmune and back.'

'To tell the truth, Willie, I feel better than I ever do after sitting around all Sunday afternoon listening to Lily's whines and criticism. In fact I enjoyed it, and I loved the baby. I can't wait for ours to be born.'

'We've a long wait until March m'dear, but I'm glad you're not exhausted. We should go out every Sunday afternoon when the weather is good.' He looked down into her eyes, his own glinting with humour, one brow quirked upwards waiting for her reaction.

'You mean you wouldn't miss Lily's visits any more than I would?'

'I wouldn't miss them at all, sweetheart, but she's your sister and—'

'She thinks you look forward to seeing her. She says you must get tired of only seeing a jaded pregnant woman every day.'

'Well, we know how wrong she is, don't we, Mary?' Willie said gruffly and turned her to face him, tilting her chin with a gentle finger as he

140

bent his head to kiss her mouth. It was a long kiss, satisfying to them both, and Mary gave a deep sigh when he released her.

'I'm so lucky, Willie. I had begun to wonder if you wished you had a more attractive wife, especially just now when I feel so tired all the time. Even my hair is beginning to lose its curl, yet Victoria looked positively blooming while she was expecting.'

'Ma says all women are different and sometimes the sex of the baby makes a difference too. I'll bet she's glad I didn't get Lily for a wife,' he chuckled. 'She says she couldn't have got me a better match if she'd chosen you herself.'

'Did she really say that?'

'She did. I was telling her I'm worried about you being sick so often. She says I must do something about it and take you to see Doctor Grantly. He might give you a tonic.'

Reluctantly Mary agreed to go down to Darlonachie in their old van to hear what the doctor had to say. Contrary to her expectations he did not tell her that pregnancy was a perfectly natural event and nothing to worry about. He examined her thoroughly and told her she was anaemic, which would probably make her tired. He gave her a few hints to help the sickness and asked her to come once a month. His manner was pleasant and his tone cheerful so Mary did not notice his thoughtful frown or the concern in his eyes as he showed her out.

Ten

Victoria was relieved and delighted by Libby's eagerness to help with her baby brother and her determination to learn to cook.

'This is delicious beef stew, Libby,' Andrew said truthfully when he tasted her first attempt.

'Mother told me what to do while she was feeding Lachie.'

'I did,' Victoria smiled, 'but you did it all yourself, even peeling the vegetables and making the gravy.'

'Did you make an extra pot for Uncle Willie?' Andrew asked.

'No. Can I make one this afternoon, Mum? Have we enough meat?' she asked eagerly. 'I can remember what to do, and I promise I'll be careful.'

So Libby started a regular Saturday cooking session and cycled over to High Bowie every week with something she had made. Mary welcomed her warmly. She appreciated both the food and Libby's cheerful chatter.

When it came to Christmas Lily declared it was Mary's duty to invite her and their elderly parents to High Bowie for Christmas dinner but Willie intervened.

'Mary isna well. You can see that for yourself. You live with them; you make the dinner for your parents.' Lily glared sullenly, watching with narrowed eyes as he exchanged an affectionate smile with her sister. How could he look at her like that? Mary looked puffed up and ugly. Lily left early that day.

'Don't worry, Willie. You were right,' Victoria assured him when he ruefully confessed to interfering in his wife's family. 'Mary has more than enough to do without running after Lily. Normally she would stick up for herself with Lily, but it's hard when you feel weary and out of sorts. Mary will be pleased you made the decision for her.'

'I hope so. Mr and Mrs Hardie are decent, kindly folk, but I can't stick Lily.'

'Your mother has the best solution. I have the biggest kitchen so she has offered to come up here and help with Lachie and prepare the vegetables. If you and Mary come here Lily can't argue with that. After all we're her family as well now.'

'You're a good lass, Victoria,' he said with feeling.

'I'm hardly a lass any more, Willie,' she chuckled. 'Not with three children.'

Christmas turned out to be a happy affair at Langmune with Josh home on leave. Maggie and Billy Lennox came over, as well as Mary and Willie.

Lachie was a contented, smiling baby and Mary cuddled him happily while Victoria,

Maggie and Libby cleared away the meal and washed the dishes. It was much later, after Willie and Mary had gone home, that Polly voiced her fears to Victoria.

'Mary has a full three months to go before the baby's due, but did you see how puffy her face and hands are?'

'Yes,' Victoria nodded, gnawing anxiously on her lower lip. 'Did Willie tell you Doctor Grantly has advised Mary to have the baby in hospital?'

'I didn't know that. Did he say why?'

'We-ell, he told Mary it was because the weather might be bad. No one would be able to get up the glen to High Bowie if we have as much snow as we did last March. If you remember we had to take the milk across the fields with the tractor and meet the milk lorry at the village.'

'Well I suppose it could happen,' Polly frowned. 'But you think he has other reasons?'

'I think he's concerned about her. She looks so ... so bloated. She's not fat. And Lily doesn't help when she keeps telling her she looks a mess,' Victoria muttered balefully.

'She's a spiteful bitch, that Lily!' Polly said. 'I hear she's changed her job again. If you ask me she's bone lazy. She's working in the chemist's now and I'll bet she tries out all the rouges and powders. Her face is always thick with stuff.'

Libby sat very quiet, listening to her mother and grandmother and hoping they wouldn't remember she was still in the kitchen, but Billy

144

came searching for her to join in a new game called Monopoly that Fraser had received for Christmas.

It was the beginning of March when Doctor Grantly urged Mary to go into the cottage hospital where she could rest and have medical attention, although he would have preferred her to go into the maternity hospital at Dumfries. Mary was reluctant to leave her home but she finally consented to go so that Doctor Grantly could be present if he was needed.

'She has such faith in me,' Peter Grantly said to his wife, 'and I'm terribly afraid I may have to let her down.'

'You can only do your best, my dear, and trust in a doctor is a great help.'

'I've always thought so too,' he sighed, 'but I'm not so young any more. I can't bear the thought of telling Mary she has lost her baby after all she has come through during the past eight months.' He shuddered suddenly and buried his face in his hands. 'It will be even more intolerable if I have to tell Willie Pringle I have lost his wife.'

'You think Mary's condition is as serious as that?' Anna Grantly asked in dismay. She had been a nurse herself once and her husband often confided in her when he was anxious.

'I suspect her kidneys are affected and the sooner the baby is born the better. They might have considered operating to remove the baby if Mary had consented to go to Dumfries. Willie says he understands – and I believe he does in a way. He's used to dealing with birth and death with his animals, but it's a different thing when it comes to the person who means more than anything in the world to you – and that's how Willie feels about Mary. He has already told me if it comes to a choice between the baby's life and his wife's I have to save Mary.'

'Willie said that?'

'He did. He waylaid me about three weeks ago on my way down the glen. He knows things are not normal. The thing is, Anna...' He twisted his hands together in agitation.

'I can guess what you're thinking, dearest Peter. You're remembering the night Victoria and Mark were born and their mother died. But that was completely different...'

'The end was the same. I failed to save the life of a young mother.'

'The circumstances were completely different. Elizabeth Lachlan was little more than a child herself and she was carrying twins, and there was nothing normal about their conception or the pregnancy. You said yourself you felt she didn't want to live.' Anna grasped her husband's arm tightly. 'Mary Pringle does want to live. It's not like you to be so down about a case and you have delivered more babies than most of the doctors in the hospital will ever see. Now come on, Peter. Think positively. Think about Willie and Mary.'

'Yes, Anna.' Doctor Grantly gave a wan smile. 'You're right as always. What should I do

146

without you? We're all in God's hands at the end of the day. Even so I can't help wishing He had spared Mark and that he was here with us now, with his youth and up-to-date knowledge.'

'Even if Mark had been spared in that horrible war I don't think he would have returned to Darlonachie. Catriona would have kept him in Edinburgh. If I'm honest I always felt she was a bit too possessive. She wanted to keep him away from us from the beginning, and especially from Victoria. I think she was jealous of the bond those two shared.'

'Mmm, she certainly hasn't made any effort to keep in touch since Mark was killed,' Doctor Grantly mused. Anna was pleased to have found a topic to take his mind off Mary Pringle, at least for now.

Willie drove Mary to the cottage hospital and saw her tucked up into bed by a motherly midwife. Although the baby was not due for at least three weeks Willie felt he ought to warn Mary's parents that she was in the hospital. In his heart he knew that anything could happen and the Pringles were too old for shocks. Moreover the village grapevine was always efficient with bad news so it was better if he called and explained in person.

High Bowie seemed a lonely, isolated place when Willie returned alone to the silence of the farm at the head of the glen. For the first time he considered how Maggie Lennox must have felt as a young widow, living there alone. Perhaps she could be excused for welcoming the company of Luke Crainby, the young Laird of Darlonachie. It was a sin for them to have had a child when Luke Crainby already had a wife and daughter of his own, but in that moment Willie would have given anything to have Mary's warm and loving arms around him, with or without a wedding ring and licence. He ate a solitary lunch of bread and cheese then he whistled his dogs and went off up the hill to check on the sheep.

The days were getting a little longer now but there was a lot to do with lambing approaching. He would have the pigs and poultry to look after and the two house cows to milk now that Mary was not here. He knew the doctor was right. She was too conscientious to rest when there was work to be done.

As he toiled up the heathery hillside Willie was oblivious to the land he loved. He prayed as he had never prayed before that Mary would come through this alive. He stopped and stared over the expanse of moor land. His two collies, Dan and Jess, prostrated themselves at his feet, waiting patiently for their master's command. They seemed to sense his melancholy mood. He turned slowly and looked back and across the glen. Langmune was just several white dots in the distance. He relaxed a little, knowing his mother and Victoria would visit Mary in the hospital if they could. They would probably bake him some fresh bread and cook him a bit of meat now and then. He would leave his ration book with his mother until Mary returned home, he decided.

Willie was a diligent shepherd and he spent some time out on the hill, catching a lame ewe and paring its foot, checking another which was lying alone. He knew instinctively she was going to lamb early and would lose her lambs, and possibly the ewe would die too. Sheep were like that but he had done his best for them. He knew it was part of a shepherd's lot and had to be accepted. This would be his first crop of lambs – his and Mary's. They had planned and saved, dreaming of running a farm of their own. Now he would give it up like a shot if it meant Mary would be all right. He had a niggling worry they wouldn't be able to find the next payment for the rent anyway. Mary's health had prevented them from keeping as many pigs and hens as they had planned. The lambs were not even born yet, and it would be months before they were fattened and ready for sale.

It was late afternoon before Willie returned to the small farm steading and it was dark by the time he had fed the hens, collected the eggs, fed the pigs and milked the two cows. Violet was almost dry now, in readiness for her next calf, but Rosy, the young cow he had bought only three weeks ago, had produced a fine heifer calf and she was full of milk. He decided he would go straight over to his parents' cottage and take some of the milk with him. He knew his mother would find him a bowl of broth or some bacon and eggs.

Later that night, as he climbed the narrow stairs to bed, Willie gave a huge yawn. He had stayed longer than he had intended with his parents and it had been a stressful day. The flame on his candle flickered uncertainly in the draught from the landing window. His bedroom door was ajar and he pushed it open with his shoulder. At first he thought his imagination was playing tricks. Had he lost his senses? Mary? How had she got back home? His heart lurched with fear. He raised his candle higher. Then he saw it was not Mary in his bed. It was the face of her sister Lily leering at him.

'God! What the hell are you playing at?' Lily still had all that stuff she wore on her eyelashes and she was batting them up and down. Her mouth was bright red and she had a smile like a cat who has stolen the cream. Willie took a deep breath as his heartbeat steadied. She had given him a fright. Anger surfaced in him. He knew well enough what she wanted: she had been flaunting herself ever since she knew Mary was expecting. He had seen women like her before. It would serve her damn right if she got it. Even as he set the candlestick on the tallboy she stretched her arms above the blankets, deliberately exposing her breasts. He guessed she was probably naked. She had been waiting for him. His mouth tightened.

'What d'ye think ye're doing?'

'I've come to look after you while Mary's in the hospital. You'll be ready for a real woman to cuddle, eh, Willie? I'll bet you havena touched

150

Mary since you gave her the bairn. Poor you. Who'd have thought she'd have turned out such a sickly soul. But never mind...' She held out her arms towards him, showing off her body, naked to the waist – and beyond. She lifted the bed-clothes invitingly. 'Get undressed and jump in beside me. I'll soon warm you up. I'll show you what it's like to have a real woman in your bed.' For a moment Willie stared as she lifted one white leg and pointed her toes towards him, giving her feline smile. His mouth curled in revulsion.

'Get dressed. Get out o' my bed. Awa' home with ye!'

'Dearest Willie, don't be like that,' she purred. 'I can't go home now. It's dark out there. I told you. I've come to look after you. I've given up my job for you.'

'You've what! You can't have done...'

'I have. As soon as Ma told me I telephoned Mr Craiker and told him he could stuff his job in the chemist's shop. You need me more than he does. Mary could die and—'

'Don't say that! Don't even think it! I don't want you here, d'ye hear me?'

'I can't go home in the dark,' she pleaded in her little-girl voice. Willie sighed. He was dead-ly tired. He lifted the candlestick again.

'I'll sleep downstairs tonight. As soon as it's light I want you out of here and I don't want you back again. Not ever!'

'But I only came to please you, Willie,' Lily wheedled like a child after a lollipop.

151

'Please me! You never wanted to please anyone except yourself. You're a slut. Mary is worth ten women like you.' His voice shook with emotion and he turned and slammed the door behind him. His candle flickered and died with the sudden draught but Willie groped his way blindly down the stairs. There were other bedrooms at High Bowie but they would be cold and damp and he wanted to get as far away from Lily Hardie as he could.

The kitchen fire was out, but still warm. He threw on some wood and then some peat until it was going again. For a long while he sat with his head in his hands, his thoughts on Mary. He felt sick at heart and right now he felt he could murder that sister of hers. If Mary ever heard she had spent the night in their bed ... He shuddered. He must have dozed because the next time he looked at the clock on the mantelpiece it was five o'clock. He rose stiffly, lit a lantern and made his way to the yard to feed the pigs and milk Rosy. Instead of going back to the house he decided to walk across the glen, back to Langmune. Andrew and Victoria would be in the byre, milking by now. He would tell them what had happened. Maybe he could have his breakfast with them and perhaps Lily would have gone by the time he returned.

As soon as he entered the byre at Langmune Andrew and Victoria moved towards him, their eyes full of concern.

'Mary?' Victoria whispered.

'I think she's all right. She's in the hospital. I

told Ma last night. She was going to tell you both this morning.' He told them about finding Mary's sister in his bed when he arrived home. As one they moved to the relative quiet of the dairy, leaving Jocky Conley to change the milking machines to the next batch of cows.

Victoria's eyes narrowed as Willie recounted his confrontation with Lily Hardie.

'You must tell Mary what she did before Lily tells her and makes a mountain of her tale,' Victoria said, guessing at the damage Lily could cause, especially when Willie had spurned her offer.

'I can't do that! Lily's her sister. Anyway I don't want Mary to be worried any more than she is already.'

'We'll talk about it later. Go to the house, Willie,' Victoria said more gently. 'You look exhausted. Have a good wash in the scullery and I'll be up soon to make you some breakfast. We'll decide what to do then.'

Willie didn't need any persuading. He was tired and hungry and he felt he would never be warm again. He was worried sick about Mary.

Victoria watched him go. 'I'll come back to the byre in a minute, Andrew. There's something I want to do.'

Andrew raised his eyebrows at his wife's determined look. He knew she was hatching a plan. He shrugged in acceptance. Victoria would tell him later.

Polly was just beginning to light the fire at her cottage when Victoria hurried in. She lost no time in telling Willie's version of things at High Bowie.

'But Willie was here last night. He had his supper with us and it was bedtime when he left...'

'And Lily was waiting for him – in her sister's bed!' Victoria repeated. 'If Mary hears her side of things she'll never believe Willie didn't want her there – not when Mary is so ... so...'

'I know, lassie. Mary has no conceit of herself at the best o' times and she'll think any red-blooded man would succumb to Lily's so-called charms. You do believe Willie then?'

'Of course I do! Don't you?'

'Aye, though he wouldn't be the first in the circumstances...'

'I know it's a lot to ask but I wondered if you'd consider going over there now and – and sort of pretending you and Willie's father had already planned to stay at High Bowie until Mary gets home. I know it's a long walk but I'm sure Lily Hardie will not be out of bed for ages yet. If she sees you in the kitchen she'll feel a bit silly – or at least I would.'

'You wouldna do such a thing though, Victoria. But I ken what ye mean and it would serve her right. In fact,' Polly said, entering into Victoria's plan with enthusiasm, 'she might even think we've been there all night. If I get there soon enough I could rumple up the bed in the downstairs bedroom and leave the door ajar. She'll think we returned to High Bowie with Willie last night.' Her lined face broke into a smile and she hugged Victoria. 'She wouldna dare spin Mary a yarn then. The lassie doesna deserve an evil sister like Lily. I'll just give Joe a shout. We'll both get over to High Bowie right away. I'll make his breakfast there.'

'I'll give Willie some breakfast and he might even have a nap. He looks worried to death.'

'Aye, he is. But we'll watch out for him between us, lassie. Lily Hardie wouldna reckon on him turning his back on her, even less that he would tell you. She doesna have a brain like yours either, Victoria. It will take more than her wiles to cause a rift in the Pringle family, eh?'

'I do hope so. Mary and Willie have enough worries. I'll try to visit Mary at the hospital this afternoon if I'm allowed in, and if I can take Lachie with me. He will sleep in the clothes basket in the back of the car if I wrap him in a blanket.'

At midday Andrew came into the house for his lunch, a wide grin on his face. 'I've just come back from High Bowie. Mother says I'm to tell you your plan worked better than you could have dreamed. Lily was so flustered at seeing them there when she went into the kitchen and smelled bacon cooking that she gathered up her clothes and left without even waiting for a cup of tea. Willie is going to bring Mother up to the cottage in the van this afternoon to collect some clothes for her and Father. They are going to stay there until Mary gets home. Father will help with the poultry and Willie will be better with company. He said you could tell Mary he is going in to see her this evening.'

Victoria didn't trust Lily not to twist things around to save her face or to cause Mary heartbreak. She made the whole episode sound like a huge joke at Lily's expense. At first Mary stared in dismay, but she knew Willie would never have mentioned it to anyone if he had succumbed to temptation. He would have felt too guilty. They ended up reminiscing about their schooldays and the visiting time passed quickly. On the way out one of the staff waylaid Victoria.

'I heard you laughing with Mrs Pringle.' She smiled. 'Your visit will have done her more good than any medicine. She is not used to being idle. Her fingers are too swollen even for knitting.'

'Yes,' Victoria said slowly. 'I noticed.' She chewed her lower lip. 'We are all praying for Mary and a safe delivery of the baby.' Lachie began to squirm and the nurse stroked his head with a gentle finger. 'He's getting hungry. I'd better get home. Please ask Matron to telephone, whatever hour of the day or night, if Mary needs anything.'

Four days later Willie called in on Mary's parents to tell them her condition was much the same and she was bored with waiting. Then he went on his way, making a detour to Langmune.

'Lily has left home,' he said as soon as he stepped inside the house. 'Mr and Mrs Hardie don't seem sorry either. She's gone back to Birmingham to stay with a friend from her army days, and the woman's brother. She's going to look for work down there.'

'Well I can't say I'm sorry,' Victoria said.

'That's exactly what young Lucy said.' Willie nodded. 'She was visiting the Hardies when I called in. She's a lovely lass, with lovely bairns.' He sighed. 'It will break Mary's heart if our baby doesn't survive. That's what I really called to tell you. Doctor Grantly is going to bring on the birth if he can.'

'Does he...? I mean...'

'Mary is fretting about the cost of her stay in the hospital and the doctor's visits. I've tried to tell her we'll find the money, even if it means I have to give up the farm and get a job.'

'Oh, Willie, don't talk like that,' Victoria said in dismay, even though she knew she and Andrew depended on Willie's rent, via Maggie, to pay the bank loan they had taken out to buy High Bowie. *Thank goodness Willie knows nothing of that,* she thought. 'The government are supposed to be bringing in free health care soon,' she said instead. 'It's a pity it hadn't come sooner for Mary's sake.'

'Aye, but it's not the money Doctor Grantly is thinking of. He says it's too dangerous for Mary. He daren't risk leaving it any longer. If he can't induce the baby at the cottage hospital she will have to go to Dumfries, but he hasn't told her that yet.'

Eleven

'So you're to get an OBE today,' the brisk younger nurse announced as she entered Mary's room on Monday morning. Mary looked at her blankly. 'You don't know?' She grimaced, which did nothing to soothe Mary's frazzled nerves. 'Oil, bath, enema. We try that to set the baby off.'

Mary submitted to what she considered such humiliating and embarrassing procedures. Later in the day Doctor Grantly looked in to see her. She was clean and exhausted but there was no sign of labour beginning. Mary was relieved to see Willie that evening but she couldn't keep back her tears as she told him all that had happened and without any results.

'What do you think they'll do next?' she asked fearfully.

'I-I don't know, love. I will go over to Langmune first thing in the morning and telephone Doctor Grantly to ask what's going on. If he tells me anything new I'll come in and tell you.'

Mary was restless during the night and all the next day but there was still no sign of the baby coming. It was a relief to see the older midwife was back on duty on Tuesday evening.

'Call me Jeannie,' she said, taking Mary's hand and giving it a squeeze. 'They tell me this baby is not cooperating, eh?'

'No. I've got the most awful backache from doing nothing but lie around. I want to get up and go for a walk but the other nurse said I couldn't.'

'Just wait until I've checked up on the other patients. We only have two in tonight so we're not busy. Then I'll come back and examine you and if everything is all right we'll go for a walk together, just round about the hospital though, not outside.'

'I don't care where we go so long as I can get up.'

'Aye, I remember what it was like having my first one,' Jeannie nodded in sympathy.

That night Mary dozed but only fitfully and by four in the morning the backache was excruciating. Jeannie brought her a cup of tea. When she had drunk it she examined Mary again and suggested a warm bath and a harder bed.

'A bath? In the middle of the night? Will there be hot water?'

'Och, bless ye, ma lamb, we always have hot water here. We never know when we're going to need it. Anyway I have time to help you just now. Later there'll be the morning routines before the other nurses take over.'

'You've been very good. I wish you were here all the time,' Mary sighed. 'I don't like the other nurse much.'

'Hazel you mean? She can be a bit sharp.

159

She's not had any bairns of her own yet, you see. She'll learn.' Jeannie nodded. 'Anyway I'll have a word with Matron. I reckon she'll keep an eye on you today. You're one of Doctor Grantly's special patients.' Jeannie didn't mention that the baby was slowly moving down, or that she had an uneasy feeling there were going to be complications.

Back at High Bowie a few early lambs had been born and Willie was glad to have his parents staying to help with all the odd jobs and to make a hot meal in the middle of the day. He was worried sick about Mary. She looked strained and tired and he was terribly afraid Doctor Grantly would have her moved to Dumfries hospital.

True to her word the matron looked in on Mary several times that day and in the late afternoon Doctor Grantly came in to see her. His face was grave as he ushered Matron out in front of him.

'Tomorrow morning I will arrange for an ambulance to move Mrs Pringle to Dumfries. The baby is in the breach position and it is time it was born if we're to save the mother.'

'I understand, Doctor,' Matron nodded gravely. She told Jeannie what the doctor had said when she came on night duty with another young nurse. Jeannie frowned.

'Poor soul. She's been a lovely patient and she never grumbles like some of them do with a lot less cause. We daren't give her another enema, dare we?'

'Better not. It might damage the baby. Encourage her to eat plenty of fruit though. I've been doing that all day but it hasn't had much effect.'

Jeannie accompanied Mary for another walk when everything was quiet and her other patients were settled for the night. She didn't believe nature intended all that lying around any more than Mary did herself. Afterwards she suggested having a nice relaxing bath again, and during this Mary felt an urgent desire to go to the toilet. Jeannie was at her side in a flash.

'I think we'd better get you dried and straight into bed now,' she said anxiously. 'I think the baby is on his way.'

'Why do you think it's a boy?'

'Only boys cause their poor mothers this much trouble.' Mary began to chuckle then bit her lip as a sharp pain convulsed her. Jeannie knew she couldn't expect much help from the other young nurse. It was after midnight. Should she call Doctor Grantly? She wondered anxiously. An hour later the pains were coming regularly and Jeannie put through a call to Darlonachie. Peter Grantly was immediately alert.

'You did right to telephone, Jeannie. I need to be there. I'll come at once. Get everything ready and sterilized, will you? It will be a forceps delivery unless the baby has turned at the last minute.'

'It hasna, Doctor.'

The other staff had come on duty. Outside the

pale March sun was shining but Jeannie was still standing beside the bed. She didn't want to leave until Mary had regained consciousness. It had been a long night and a difficult birth. It would take her patient a long time to get over it but at least she was alive and Doctor Grantly thought she stood a good chance of surviving now the birth was over. The doctor had telephoned somebody with a message for Mary's husband and he was expected soon. Matron brought her a cup of tea and some buttered toast.

'You've had a long hard night, Jeannie. You ought to go home now.'

'No. I'd like to see Mary come round. I-I want to be with her. I want to warn her...'

Matron nodded, and went to check on her other patients.

As soon as Willie saw Doctor Grantly he asked urgently, 'Mary? Will she be all right?'

'She will live. It was a difficult birth and it will take her some time to recover, but you have a baby daughter...'

'The baby is alive?' Willie asked incredulously. He sank on to a chair and hid his head in his hands. 'The Lord be praised.'

'I should warn you it was a forceps delivery. The baby is marked. It may distress Mary when she sees her...'

'We shall love her just the same.'

'Most of the marks will fade in time. Your baby daughter is a survivor, Willie. It was touch and go but there she is ... Listen.' A smile spread over Doctor Grantly's face at the sound of a baby bawling it's head off.

'That's our baby?' Willie asked in awe.

'Yes. She has a fine pair of lungs. She weighed eight pounds three ounces. Aah, here comes Nurse now. She will bring the baby for you to see. Jeannie, shouldn't you be away home by now?'

'I should, Doctor, but so should you.' She beamed broadly. 'Mrs Pringle has come round. I want to see her face and be with her when she first sees her baby. It was a good night's work, wasn't it?'

'It was indeed, and a better outcome than I had dared to hope. You are a good midwife, Jeannie.'

'Thank you, Doctor,' Jeannie smiled widely. 'We had a good doctor though, and an excellent patient. There were no hysterics, Mr Pringle. Your wife did everything we asked of her. The tenth of March will be your lucky day from now on.'

'She would be pleased you were there,' Willie smiled gratefully. 'She trusted you. I-I don't know how to thank you and Doctor Grantly.'

'We're just glad to have both Mary and her baby alive and well. Er ... that is, as well as we can expect in the circumstances. She will need a lot of care and good nourishment for the next three months at least. It would be better if she could stay here for a few weeks until she regains her strength and until the baby has recovered from her stormy passage into the world.'

* * *

Although she had a baby brother of her own, Libby couldn't wait for Victoria to take her to see her new cousin in the hospital. Mary was delighted to see them both.

'What will you call her, Auntie Mary?'

'Willie would like to call her Mary. Although his mother gets called Polly he says she was christened Mary. We think we might call her Wilhelmina Mary...' For a moment Mary's face clouded and her eyes swam with unshed tears. She gulped. 'Doctor Grantly says I shouldna have any more babies if I value my life, s-so Wilhelmina is the nearest I can think of to William.' Victoria thought it was a large mouthful for such a tiny tot but Mary added, 'I expect we shall soon find a shortened version for a pet name but she will have to learn how to spell it for school. Poor wee lamb.' She looked affectionately at Libby, standing by the crib, stroking the tiny fist with a gentle finger. 'I know Libby is a bit young but Willie and I wondered if she could be a godmother. She has been such a great help to us. Would you like to do it, Libby? What do you think, Victoria?'

'We-ell, Libby will not be eleven until July. She's a bit young to make promises,' Victoria said. She saw the disappointment on Mary's face and added swiftly, 'On the other hand, perhaps it's a good idea to have a young godmother. She will watch over her as she grows up.'

'Oh, yes please!' Libby pleaded. 'I would love to do it. Shall I get to hold her at the kirk?'

'Yes, of course you will,' Mary smiled. 'I

thought I might ask Lucy too. She's good with her own children. It will not be for a while.' She shuffled uncomfortably, easing her position.

Victoria nodded. 'I think it's time we were leaving now, if I can tear Libby away. You need all the rest you can get.'

'I must get home soon. I'm worried about the cost of being in hospital so long.'

'It's a pity Mr Bevan didn't brought his free health care in a bit quicker. It will all be free before the end of the year.'

Willie arranged to have the pig killed a bit earlier than usual so that his mother and father could deal with it before Mary came home with the baby. There was a lot of work involved in dealing with the offal and Willie was pleased to get the bacon and ham cured in the cellar before the lambing really got going.

Polly rendered the fat and made potted meat and a large pork pie ready for Mary coming home. She put them in the coolest part of the cellar but she wished there had been some way of preserving the liver and kidney. On the day Willie was to bring Mary and the baby home she baked a large batch of bread and scones and a fruit cake with some dried fruit Victoria had let her have. Willie's young cow was milking well so she had made butter and used some of it to make a batch of shortbread as well.

Mary was grateful and tearful when she got back to her own home at last. Polly had never found her a demonstrative girl so she was sur-

165

prised when Mary hugged her just as Victoria would have done, and wept on her shoulder.

'I-I'm j-just so happy to be home, and I'm so grateful for all you have done for us.'

'Eh, lassie, you deserve anything we can do to help. Look at the fine wee grandbairn you've given Joe and me,' Polly said huskily, her own throat thick with unexpected tears.

'I hope you will come over to see her whenever you can be bothered,' Mary said.

'Aye, we will that,' Joe said, gently rocking the cradle he had helped Willie to make. 'In fact I'm thinking of coming over to look after the pigs and hens until Willie finishes lambing, if ye dinna mind, lassie?'

'We dinna want to impose,' Polly added quickly, 'but Doctor Grantly says ye must take time and get your health back and not be getting a chill on your kidneys in the cold March winds.'

'Everyone has been so considerate, I feel I'm wrapped in cotton wool,' Mary laughed happily. 'We shall be very glad of any help you can give us,' she added.

'Aye, we shall that,' Willie nodded, grinning from ear to ear as he looked down at his sleeping daughter.

Twelve

Maggie had forgotten the rent for High Bowie would be due until she saw Willie looking embarrassed and ill at ease, unconsciously twisting his cap. He was under the impression she still owned his farm, of course, so he had come to her as his landlord. They all knew how hard this first year must have been for him and Mary and she guessed he wanted to delay the rent payment. She wished with all her heart she could grant his request and reassure him. She had only got to know Willie in recent years and she liked both him and Mary.

'We – we think we shall have the money by the end of July,' he said awkwardly, lifting his troubled blue gaze to hers. 'Things havena turned out as we planned, and...'

'I understand, Willie. You've had a rotten start to married life and for your first year as a farmer on your own.' But she knew Andrew and Victoria had taken out a loan to buy High Bowie and they had pledged Langmune as security. They depended on the rent to make repayments to the bank, but Willie was unaware of this. 'Give me a d-day to think about it, Willie? ' she said falteringly. 'I – I'll let you know.' She knew she would have to consult Andrew and Victoria. There was little wonder Willie and Mary had gone off their target, she thought when he had gone. It must have cost them dearly paying for Mary's care and medical attention, but at least she was alive. Once she regained her health and they were able to increase the pigs and poultry, as they had planned originally, things would surely improve. Willie would have his first crop of lambs to sell in the autumn. Maggie wished she had enough spare money in the bank to pay the rent on Willie's behalf so that Andrew need never know his brother was in trouble.

Some of the money she had received for the sale of High Bowie had been needed to pay for legal advice when Henrietta Crainby tried to contest Sir William's will and the trust he had set up for Billy. The case had dragged on interminably from one hearing to another, finally ending up in the High Court. It had cost more than she had anticipated, even though the trust had been upheld in the end. Mrs Crainby was responsible for the main costs. Two more of the farms had been sold on the northern boundary of the Darlonachie Estate and rumour had it they were to cover the legal costs, although Luke had left the land in Trust for his daughter, Charlotte, who was a year older than Billy.

Maggie shuddered. The publicity in the newspapers had cost her far more than any monetary burden. There was nothing she could have done to stop the horrible things that had been printed about her and Luke. She suspected many of them had been prompted by Henrietta, setting herself up as the innocent and wronged young wife. Every angle, every report seemed aimed at debasing the loving relationship she had shared with Billy's father. It had been portrayed as a sordid affair with her as the guilty temptress. She had not been able to prevent Billy reading the newspapers. His young mind had been poisoned by the concocted details and she feared the effects had gone too deep for her to repair. He refused to listen to her explanations, her pleas for understanding. He was too young to comprehend the love, the passions, and the destructive jealousies of the adult world. She doubted whether he would ever recover from the mockery and bullying he had endured as a result of Henrietta Crainby's greed and malice.

Billy had made up his mind to escape from Darlonachie as soon as he had gained his school certificate the following year. He would be sixteen by then. He intended moving to another part of the country to gain the practical experience he would require before he would be accepted for a place at an agricultural college, and even for that he was determined to apply to one of the English colleges. When his grandfather was alive, and even afterwards, he had spent all his spare time at the farm. It vexed Maggie that he never went near the place now. He seemed to have no interest in his inheritance. Maggie would have been shocked and angry had she known of the taunts and snide comments their new farm manager had uttered within Billy's hearing after reading the newspaper reports.

Instead she felt increasingly disheartened by her son's indifference. Before his death Sir William had discussed the need to modernize the dairy premises and consequently she had acted on his suggestions and spent the rest of the money from the sale of High Bowie to make Home Farm a place of which Billy could be proud. A modern byre had been built with concrete stalls for the cows down either side and a broad walkway down the centre. It was light and airy and healthier for the animals and more easily cleaned than the old wooden stalls. There was a new dairy conveniently at one end, with a washroom to house the steam chest for cleaning the new milking units, as well as a steam stool to sterilize the churns. Adjacent to the byre a shed had been erected with calf pens and two special isolation boxes for sick animals.

She had listened attentively to the ideas of Ezra Riddel, the young manager who had taken the place of Mr Blake, but she felt he was too new, and relatively inexperienced, to be in sole charge of such major expenditure. She had been disappointed by his sulky manner when she told him she intended seeking several opinions and estimates. She had discussed all his suggestions with Andrew. Many of them were good ideas but they were costly so she had taken Andrew's advice and engaged a local architect who specialized in dairy buildings and understood the new Scottish regulations for dairy hygiene.

She knew Ezra Riddel resented not being given sole charge of the expenditure and the plans.

Following the final summing up of the court case, with a repetition of the sordid reports in the local papers, she had also become aware of a familiarity in her farm manager's manner. His attitude made her uncomfortable but she had no idea he had the same effect on Billy.

Billy felt more and more like an intruder around Home Farm and so he spent his spare time walking over the peaks above High Bowie, apparently preferring the wild isolation of the heather moors to the company of his peers. Sometimes he ran into Willie herding his sheep on the hill. He began to respect Willie's knowledge of the hills and his sheep and the working of his dogs. He had a simple philosophy and honesty which Billy found reassuring in his own confusing and uncertain world. The two of them had many a pleasant conversation and shared the artless pleasures of watching a partridge with her brood running behind her, or listening to the plaintive 'pee-wit, pee-wit' cry as a lapwing circled over their heads when they inadvertently came upon her nest on the bare ground in the middle of a field. Sometimes they saw a merlin but the only bird Willie detested was the carrion crow.

'Corbies we aye call them,' he said, shaking his head emphatically. 'I shoot the devils if I see them hanging around the steading. They'd snatch up a young chick before your eyes. Up here on the hill I've seen the eyes picked out of a sickly ewe long before she's dead, aye, and even from a healthy one if she happens to get couped on her back.'

'Why do they lie on their backs? I mean, why don't they just roll over when they see the corbie coming at them?'

'They would if they could but sometimes they're heavy in lamb, or maybe it's near shearing time and their fleeces are so thick and springy they canna roll back on to their feet. The corbies dinna miss a chance, especially if they have a brood to feed. Their beaks are sharp and strong and they'll tear a newborn lamb to bits if it's a weakly one and the mother canna protect it.'

Willie enjoyed the boy's company just as much as Billy appreciated the older man's forthright manner. If there were things Willie didn't know he was not afraid to say so, but he seemed unaware of the wealth of knowledge he had acquired over the years. Billy had missed his grandfather more than anyone realized and he frequently sought Willie's uncomplicated views on aspects of the countryside and on the changes he was contemplating in his life. Willie never tried to influence him. If he had an opinion he stated it simply and truthfully. Billy sensed he understood his charged emotions and uncertainties. He knew, as everyone now knew, the gossip about his parents. He had probably always known, but unlike Ezra Riddel he never made sarcastic remarks or offered judgement, and for that Billy was grateful.

*　*　*

Maggie had not looked forward to telling Andrew his brother was unable to pay the rent on time but she went over to Langmune to give him the news in person. As soon as Andrew saw her troubled expression he guessed the reason for her visit.

'We half expected this with Mary being so ill,' he said. 'It's not your problem, Maggie. Come on in. We're just having a cup of tea after lunch.'

Victoria greeted her warmly, as she always did. 'It must have cost quite a lot for Mary to have the baby in hospital, and to stay there beforehand,' she remarked as she poured another cup of tea. 'But at least Mary and the baby have both survived and that's worth more than money. Anyway, we've been setting aside as much as we can ourselves in case of something like this.'

'Mmm, but it's not enough to pay the instalment on our bank loan,' Andrew said anxiously. 'I shall have to make an appointment to see Mr MacNeil. He'll not be happy to hear we're falling behind so soon.'

'I'm so sorry,' Maggie said.

'There's no reason for you to be sorry, Maggie,' Andrew said quickly. 'I wouldn't have involved you at all, but I know how proud Willie is. He would hate to think I'm his landlord, and even more so when he can't pay the rent. I know what it would cost him to come begging to you for more time. Anyway, how's Billy getting on?' he asked, deliberately changing the subject from

173

the problems of his own family. 'Is he still determined to move away from this area for his practical training? I would have taken him on myself if he doesn't want to work at Home Farm.'

'He doesn't talk much at all these days,' Maggie sighed, 'but he's made up his mind to move away. At times like this he reminds me of my own father. I was only seventeen when he died but I remember him being very stubborn. And he would have condemned Luke and me just as Billy has done.'

'Oh, Maggie!' Victoria said in sympathy. 'Billy is too young to understand how men and women feel for each other. One day he will, then he'll be sorry he's made you so unhappy. Besides,' she added grimly, 'anyone who knew Mrs Crainby would never blame Luke for finding comfort with someone as kind and loving as you.'

'It's nice of you to say so, Victoria,' Maggie grimaced, 'but in Billy's eyes I'm a sinful woman and he thinks he's tainted with my sin because he's illegitimate. It makes no difference to him that his grandfather could forgive me and accept him as his grandson...'

'He did more than that, Maggie. Sir William had great affection and respect for you. He asked you to share his home. He would never have put Home Farm in trust for Billy if he hadn't trusted you and admired your courage.'

'I tried to talk to Billy about everything but he just clams up and doesn't want to know. He says we have nothing to discuss and he's not sure he'll ever take over at Home Farm now he knows how he inherited it.'

'He'll need time to come to terms with life,' Andrew nodded. 'Perhaps it would be best if he moves away for a while. We must help him find a good farm where he will learn modern methods and get plenty of experience. Things are changing rapidly since the war. Shall I ask some of the Farmers' Union officials if they have any suggestions? Some of them attend meetings in London so they meet up with farmers from all over the country. Do you know if he has a particular interest, like dairying, or arable, or sheep and beef farming?'

'He doesn't discuss it with me. A gulf has grown between us. Shall I ask him to come over and see you?'

'You do that, Maggie. We'll do what we can, so try not to worry.'

Billy worked hard at school and he had done well in his examinations at Dumfries Academy. Some of his teachers were disappointed by his stubborn refusal to stay on and go to university. He felt he was permanently under a cloud for displeasing somebody or other. So in July 1949 William Crainby Lennox left Darlonachie and travelled by train to a large farm in Yorkshire where he intended to work for a year before attending agricultural college.

'He's a hard worker so I think you need have no fears for him, Maggie,' Andrew said in an attempt to comfort the boy's mother.

'I suppose so,' Maggie sniffed, struggling to hold back the tears. Her house seemed empty without Billy. 'Willie and Mary seem to be doing all right now, don't you think?' she said, changing the subject.

'Yes,' Victoria nodded. 'Now they have paid their rent in full it has meant we can pay off a bit more of the bank loan than we had expected. We're in Mr MacNeil's good books again. To tell the truth we wondered whether Mary would regain her former health after having kidney problems, but she seems fine. She's got a lot more poultry now and they're going to have geese to sell at Christmas. As for Willie, he's as happy as can be with his wife and wee Mimi, as he calls Wilhelmina. You wouldn't think he used to go out to the dances at every opportunity when he was younger.'

'He was never as good at the dancing as George, though,' Andrew said. 'But the pair of them used to cycle for miles, especially if Jimmy Shand was playing.' Andrew's thoughts returned to Billy. 'Libby says Billy has taken his pony up to High Bowie for Mimi. She'll have to grow a bit before she can ride him.'

'He's too old for much riding now,' Maggie said. 'Billy knows he'll not live much longer but he didn't seem to want to leave him in Ezra Riddel's care. He said Willie would see he didn't suffer, and Mimi will love him. He's round as a barrel but Mary says Willie holds her on his back while Libby leads her round the garden.'

'Yes, Libby says she loves it, even though her wee legs are so short they just stick out at the sides.'

'I think leaving Tommy was the only thing that bothered Billy about going away,' Maggie said ruefully.

'Don't worry, he'll see things differently when he's a man,' Victoria comforted. 'Don't blame yourself. I've always felt he never got over seeing Sylvie crushed beneath that tank. It was unforgivable of Milly, blaming him and screaming at him. He was only a boy and Milly should have been looking after her children.'

'Mmm, maybe. He had nightmares on and off for a long time afterwards. He may still have them for all I know but he keeps such things to himself now. How is Milly these days?'

'Moody and idle,' Andrew replied before Victoria could open her mouth. 'But Jem is a good herdsman so he makes up for her, and young Grace will be leaving school next year and she's a handy lassie. She would like to help with the dairy and work in the house for Victoria. We think we might give her a try, don't we?'

'We may as well,' Victoria nodded. 'There's plenty of work for her. Libby is doing well at school so we're hoping she will stay on and gain her school certificate. I'd like her to have a career, maybe even go in for teaching. She loves the farm and the animals but with two brothers there will be no future for her here. Anyway she spends most of her spare time at High Bowie since Mimi was born.' She laughed. 'No one

177

would think she had a wee brother of her own.'

'I expect it makes a change having a little girl.' Maggie sighed. 'We don't know how our children will grow up, do we? Billy was such a happy little boy. I would never have believed he would become so moody and unreliable.'

'Oh, Maggie, Billy isn't unreliable!'

'Unpredictable then. He's cocky and arrogant one minute, or grim and silent, and the next he's so uncertain and sensitive I believe he'd burst into tears if he hadn't learned to control his emotions so well. I know he's not happy within himself and that's what troubles me. He's never been away f-from h-home before.'

'I'm sure he'll get on fine, Maggie,' Victoria comforted.

Willie missed his occasional chats with Billy more than he had expected. Once he had learned something he didn't forget and during the early summer he had saved the lives of two good ewes. He was an observant lad and his keen young eyes had spotted the ewes on their back, struggling with their legs in the air. He had gone out of his way to get them back on to their feet.

Libby missed Billy's company too. Although he was older and they seldom talked while they were at the Academy they travelled together on the bus and cycled along the track. He was always willing to lend her his books if she had a lot of homework, and sometimes he had even discussed his own essays with her, claiming she had more imagination and better English than he had.

In the spring of the following year Andrew came home from the market wearing a troubled frown.

'What's wrong? Did you get a poor price for your heifer?' Victoria asked.'

'No, the trade was good. I was early in the ring for once so I went through to the other ring to see how the sheep were selling.' He frowned and rubbed his brow. 'Do you remember Maggie telling us the income from the sheep at Home Farm was down quite a lot last year, and according to Ezra Riddell it looked like being just as bad this year?'

'Yes, I do. She wondered if they ought to get rid of the sheep and concentrate on the milk cows but her manager persuaded her it was bad to put all their eggs in one basket. I think she had discussed the sheep with Willie. He couldn't understand why the income was down when it had been a good lambing. He said Home Farm lambs were on good land and they nearly always got top prices.'

'Yes, he said the same to me. He reckoned Darlonachie Suffolks were some of the best commercial sheep in the county when Mr Blake was managing Home Farm.' He frowned and rubbed his brow. 'I'm beginning to wonder whether that young manager of hers can be trusted.'

'Ezra Riddel you mean?' Victoria's eyes

widened. 'What makes you think that?'

'He was selling three good Suffolk ewes with lambs at foot today. He didn't sell them in the name of Darlonachie Trust, or Lennox, nor in his own name, but he was standing beside the auctioneer as the vendor. I recognized the man who bought them so I quizzed him a bit. He believed the sheep were from a Mr Lewis. He said he bought a few from the same man last year and they had done well.'

'You're sure it was Ezra Riddell?'

'Of course I am, and I'm certain they were Home Farm ewes. I suspect Riddel was selling them on the sly. I don't know whether he would cash the cheque at the market or pay it into an account in the name of Lewis. But I'm almost sure he's pocketing the money himself. If he is, and if he can do that with a few ewes, how do we know what else he sells without Maggie's knowledge?'

'Mmm ... If that's what he's up to there's no wonder he can afford his shiny leather boots and tailor-made suits.'

'He does rather fancy himself as a gentleman since he came to Home Farm, doesn't he? I remember Maggie saying he was sullen when she wouldn't agree to him handling the plans and estimates for the new buildings.'

'Yes, and he had wanted to take over the accounts but Maggie had been doing them for Sir William while Mr Blake was farm manager, so she decided to continue doing them to keep herself in touch.'

180

'These sheep wouldn't go through the Home Farm books if they were sold under another name. He could easily tell Maggie they had lost a few ewes at lambing time. Everybody loses some. She'd be none the wiser if he sold them and pocketed the money.'

'But surely the shepherd would know?'

'Bert Smith retired soon after the new manager came. As far as I know Ezra Riddell didn't replace him. He told Maggie he and the other men could manage the sheep between them so long as they got help at shearing time.'

'Maggie has enough worries just now. She's still missing Billy.'

'I agree. Anyway we need proof before we mention anything that might upset her. Willie knows most of the sheep farmers for miles around from the days when he went to the sheep-dog trialling and he often attended the market in place of old Butterworth. He knows how to keep his mouth shut. I'll see if he has any suggestions before we worry Maggie'

Thirteen

Several days later Andrew made a point of going across the glen to talk to Willie. He didn't want to arouse suspicion if Riddel was innocent, but he couldn't bear swindlers and it would be easy enough to cheat Maggie. In Victoria's case she knew all the animals on Langmune and she would have known immediately if any were missing, or if there were more deaths than usual, but Maggie had never been in the habit of working outside at Home Farm. Sir William had trusted the men who worked for him but he had also known what was going on when Mr Blake was manager. Mary's father had been head stableman and Bert Smith was shepherd, but they were all retired now. There had been a number of changes since Ezra Riddel took over, but they had seemed necessary at the time.

Willie listened while Andrew confided in him. 'I wouldna like to do Riddel an injustice, or worry Maggie unnecessarily,' he concluded.

Willie had taken to smoking a pipe like their father and he drew it out now and tamped in the tobacco, taking his time to digest Andrew's story. 'It's strange you should come with such a tale,' he said at last. 'We went down to visit

Mary's parents last Sunday. Mr Hardie is bothered with his chest again. He hasna been out much lately so some of his old cronies pop in for a chat. Bert Smith had called during the week. He doesna like young Riddel; reckons he's not to be trusted. He didna say why. You know what old Bert's like. He always stopped halfway through a tale. Mary's father was telling me about it because Mr Blake had expressed a similar opinion a few weeks ago so he was wondering if there could be any truth in Bert's insinuations.'

'Well I'd have more faith in Mr Blake's opinion than Bert's. Did Mr Hardie tell you what had made him mention Riddel?'

'Aye. Mr Blake had bumped into a man from one of the smallholdings down at Gretna. He said he'd bought two young dairy heifers from Home Farm and he was well pleased with them. They were just ready for putting with the bull. Apparently it had never been Home Farm policy to sell stock at that age. Mr Blake had always kept them until they had had a calf then the best could be selected for the Home Farm herd for breeding. The others were sold in the market as in-milk heifers.'

'That sounds right to me,' Andrew said. 'It's what we do at Langmune. Calved heifers usually bring a decent price, especially when the Cheshire dairy farmers are looking for replacements.'

'Mr Blake wasna suggesting there was anything dishonest going on,' Willie added carefully, 'but he did wonder why the stirks had been sold privately. He thought it must be a change in policy to cut out the market commission.'

'It makes you wonder though.' Andrew frowned.

'I didn't think much about it when Mary's father was rambling on. You know what it's like when old cronies get together. A new manager with different ideas was sure to come in for criticism. Darlonachie hadn't seen many incomers for generations until the war. Anyway, come on in for a cup of tea. Mary says they've increased the tea ration to three quarters of a pound this time. It's surprising what the women hear from the delivery vans and the butcher, the baker, the candlestick maker.' Willie grinned. 'Ye ken what I mean. They're travelling round the countryside everyday delivering groceries and stuff. They always hear the news and Mary willna gossip if we tell her.'

But Mary was too busy looking after Mimi to think much about Ezra Riddel until six weeks later. Ted Tweedie asked her if she would like to buy a leg of spring lamb for a Sunday treat. His parents owned the butcher's shop in the village and the small abattoir behind it. Ted was reputed to possess the strength of Samson and he could manoeuvre the van along the country roads and in the farmyards better than his father, but he was a bit slow witted. He made the deliveries to the more remote customers but his father didn't encourage him to handle money. Instead customers settled their accounts at the shop once a quarter. Mr Tweedie knew them all and he selected only those he could trust to register with him for their meat ration.

'A leg of spring lamb,' Mary laughed now. 'That's something we all dream about, Ted.'

'I'm serious. Look.' Ted reached under the back shelf of the van and drew out a small leg of lamb. 'Or there's the shoulder if you prefer?'

'But I haven't enough meat coupons for anything like that. Didn't your father tell you?'

'Faither doesna ken about this. You'll get your ration o' sausages and mince as usual.'

'You mean it's on the black market, Ted! Or was it a dead lamb you've butchered yourself?' she asked suspiciously.

'Aw, Mistress Pringle, as though I'd sell ye a dead yin!' Ted gave his charmingly boyish grin and Mary couldn't help but smile back at him. 'It's the best lamb you'll get. You should know. Your father would have many a one like this when he worked at Home Farm.'

'Home Farm?' Mary said slowly. 'I didn't think we could slaughter our own sheep without a permit. Did Mrs Lennox really send it?'

'Naw, not Mrs Lennox. The manager at Home Farm. He says he's got too many lambs this year and Mrs Lennox doesna need them all. He says she and her brat got more than they deserve just for going tae bed...' He frowned uncertainly, clearly repeating what Riddel had said but without understanding the implication.

'I see,' Mary said quietly. 'Tell me, Ted, what

185

does your father say about you selling lamb for Mr Riddel?'

'Oh, Father doesna ken. Ye'd need to pay me cash. I'm to sell the lamb joints for Mr Riddel then he said he would give me some pocket money to spend at the pub with ma friends. Ma doesna let me have money for beer, see.'

'Your mother and father do what they think is best for you, Ted,' Mary said firmly. 'I think you should tell them about Mr Riddel's proposition.'

'Prop ... proper what?'

'Just tell your father Mr Riddel offered you some spring lambs to sell on his van. You wouldn't like him to get into trouble with the Ministry of Food inspectors, would you? That's what will happen if you use his van to sell Mr Riddel's black-market lambs.' She looked at the young man and sighed. It was clear he didn't understand. 'I'll take my rations please. That will have to do for today, thank you, Ted.'

He looked disappointed. 'Mr Riddel said people would snatch my hand off for a good roast o' lamb.'

'Does he know you only deliver to the out-lying farms and cottages?'

'Aye, he said I shouldna take it to the villages.'

'Mmm, I wonder why,' Mary mused under her breath. She accepted her rations and gave Ted a smile. He couldn't help being so gullible. 'Just be sure and tell your father about it, Ted. Don't get him into trouble.'

When Willie came in for his supper that evening Mary told him about Ted Tweedie's offer of spring lamb off ration.

'Sounds like black market to me, and if Riddel is involved Andrew could be right about him swindling Maggie. Ted Tweedie would be too simple to ask questions.'

Willie passed on this bit of information to Andrew.

'I'm convinced now that Ezra Riddel isna trustworthy,' Andrew told Victoria. 'We still have no proof but don't you think we ought to put Maggie on her guard? After all we promised Luke Crainby we would help her if we could.'

'I'll invite her for lunch next Sunday,' Victoria agreed. 'It will be easier to talk things over. She will be very disappointed. I know Ezra Riddel had excellent references and it was the Agricultural Consultants who interviewed all the applicants and selected him on her behalf.'

'Well maybe she would do better to interview the next lot herself.'

Maggie drove up to Langmune before Victoria had had time to issue the invitation to lunch and it was obvious she was upset.

'I've had a visit from Mr Tweedie, the butcher,' she announced before she had even had time to sit down. 'He accused me of selling fat lambs on the black market and involving his son Ted with delivering them with his van. He was furious.'

'Oh, Maggie.' Victoria pulled her to a chair and sat her down. 'What did you say?'

'I told him I'd never heard such nonsense, of course, b-but he didn't believe me. He said Ted

187

told him the lamb came from Home Farm. In the end I went with him to his house to confront Ted. His wife was there too. Mrs Tweedie managed to get Ted to tell us exactly what had happened. We think Ezra Riddel must have butchered some of the lambs himself and tried to sell them through Ted without my knowledge, though I'm still not sure Mr Tweedie believes me. Just imagine the trouble we would be in if the Ministry of Food found out. They might send us to gaol.' She bit back a sob. 'If only Billy had stayed at home where he belongs...'

'But Billy is happy where he is and he's done well to get a place at the Cirencester College in the autumn.'

'Oh, I know, and I'm pleased for him, b-but if he had been here, working at Home Farm, as he should have been...' She sounded angry.

'How did Mr Tweedie find out?' Victoria interrupted softly.

'One of the customers refused to buy the lamb. She told Ted he would get his father into trouble if he sold it from the van. She said he must tell his father.'

'That would be Mary,' Victoria nodded. 'Willie came over to tell us. We were going to tell you we suspected Ezra Riddel was a swindler, Maggie, but we have no proof, at least none that would stand up in court.'

'Court?' Maggie shuddered. 'No!' She stared up at Victoria, her face blanching. 'I couldn't face any more lawyers and legal proceedings, a-and newspapers and g-gossip.' She shook her head wildly.

Andrew had come in and he was standing quietly in the doorway, listening to the conversation, his mouth tight. Now he came forward and took Maggie's restless hands in his.

'We wanted to have proof before we worried you. Are you convinced Riddel is on the fiddle?'

'I am now that my eyes have been opened. There's other things which didn't quite add up. I never thought of him deliberately cheating though. I'd begun to think he must be a poor manager, or a bad stockman, losing too many animals.'

'Well if you're convinced he's dishonest, and if you don't want to take him to court, I think there's enough evidence to frighten him. It should be simple enough for you to get rid of him.' Andrew proceeded to tell her of their suspicions with the ewes and stirks while Victoria plied her with a cup of strong tea.

'I don't see how it can be simple,' Maggie said, pushing back her greying hair distractedly.

'Tell him several things have been brought to your notice. Just hint at a couple of them to begin with, enough to let him know you've discovered what he's been up to. If he denies it tell him you have witnesses and you are dismissing him from the farm immediately and he must be out of his cottage within seven days otherwise you have no option but to call in the police.'

'The police? B-but...'

'I know you don't want to involve the police, Maggie, but Riddel doesn't know that. I'm fairly certain he'll not call your bluff if he's as guilty as we suspect.'

'But will he leave the farm immediately?'

'He must. Don't give him an opportunity to steal anything else. I'll come back with you now if you need some moral support.'

'N-no. Thank you, Andrew, but I think I have to do this on my own. B-but maybe I should have one of the other men nearby in case he turns nasty.' Maggie shuddered.

'I think you'll feel better when you have dealt with him,' Andrew said and squeezed her shoulder encouragingly. 'But phone straight away if you want me to come over. Now I'll go and get on with some work. We'll help all we can, Maggie, until you get fixed up with another manager. And I'm sure Mr Blake would supervise the men even though he's no longer fit to work himself.'

'Y-yes, he was always so trustworthy.' She sighed.

'Choose your own manager this time, Maggie,' Andrew called from the back door. 'You have to deal with them, so you're the best judge.'

Maggie's manner appeared cool and calm when she faced Ezra Riddel later that afternoon. She had taken trouble to brush her hair into a smooth bob and had dressed in her second-best navy costume and her leather shoes with heels. It was all a façade to give her confidence and hide her nerves. Her stomach was churning horribly as

190

she made her way to the farm office. She had asked Sam King to wait on the bench outside. He was in his forties and the only man left who had not been engaged by Riddel. He was in charge of the tractors, which were rapidly replacing horses for field work at Home Farm. Mr Blake had engaged him shortly before he retired and he was quiet and reliable.

As it happened she need not have worried. Riddel already knew something had gone wrong with his plans to sell butchered lambs through Ted Tweedie and he was realizing how efficient the country grapevine was at passing on news. Consequently he was edgy, wondering whether Maggie Lennox had heard a rumour already, and what she would do about it. Instant dismissal did not enter his mind.

'You couldn't rely on anything Ted Tweedie said.' He gave her an oily smile. 'He's a halfwit. I'll tell you what –' he lowered his voice as though humouring a child – 'we could go round the flock together and count the lambs. You would enjoy that ... er ... Mistress Lennox.' Ever since the newspaper reports about her relation-ship with Luke had appeared he had avoided addressing her if he could. Maggie had seen mockery in his eyes and arrogance in his man-ner. She gave a snort of contempt and looked him in the eye.

'Anyone with any decency would not try to take advantage of a halfwit.' She held his gaze coldly. 'Unfortunately there have been too many incidents when you have stolen and sold stock

191

and pocketed the money yourself. The people who are witnesses to your swindling are not halfwits.' Her knees shook as she delivered the final ultimatum. 'I shall not hesitate to give their names to the police unless you leave Home Farm immediately and vacate your house within a week.'

'Now wait a minute! You can't do that! I-I...' he blustered, then he looked sullen and his eyes narrowed, his mouth curled unpleasantly. 'Why shouldn't I line my own pockets when I get the chance? It's what you did with your whoring. You—'

Maggie took a swift step and opened the door. Her eyes glittered with anger, all nerves forgotten.

'Come in here, Sam, please. Riddel has been dismissed for stealing.' She looked back at Riddel. 'Do you want to leave of your own free will or shall I ask Sam to bring the police?'

'Why you – you...'

Maggie turned her back on him and looked at Sam's shocked face. 'Sam, perhaps you would deliver a warning to the rest of the farm staff. Tell them they can expect instant dismissal if any of them are found to be aiding Mr Ezra Riddel.'

'Yes, ma'am, I'll do that.' There was a light in his eyes and Maggie knew he had no sympathy for Riddel.'

'You can't do this!' Riddel snarled behind her. 'You can't manage this place without me.'

'On the contrary, Home Farm will be better

without you.' Maggie deliberately unhooked the key for the office, stood back to see him out, then locked the door behind him. 'Now go. Sam, perhaps you would call to see me at the house when you have finished work. I will let you know how things will be managed from now on. Ask Arthur Williams, the new herdsman, to come too please. You may tell the rest of the men they will be treated fairly so long as they behave honourably.'

'Yes, ma'am.' Sam nodded and stood at her side until Riddel disappeared down the road towards his house. Maggie's legs were shaking as she made her way back to the farmhouse and flung herself into the wooden chair beside the Aga. She felt exhausted but triumphant. She hadn't realized what a relief it would be to see the end of Riddel. Her only worry now was whether he would seek revenge before he left. Would he damage the buildings, set fire to the barn? But no, that would be too obvious. He would be suspected immediately. But there were other, more devious ways of taking revenge. He might harm the animals or contaminate the milk so that it was rejected, or poison the drinking water. She shivered and wished she did not feel so alone. She wished Billy would come home. He was young but she would have welcomed his company and his alert mind. Part of her felt a spurt of anger; she had suffered so much worry over his inheritance while he didn't seem to care about it at all.

Fourteen

A couple of hours later, once she had recovered from the confrontation, Maggie telephoned Victoria.

'Andrew was right. I didn't need to go into detail. He would have argued but he realized I knew more than he had expected. I must thank you both – and Willie.'

'There's no need, Maggie. Andrew said he would come over as soon as milking is finished. There's a few things he wants to discuss with you.'

'Oh, Victoria, I would be so relieved. I expect you think I'm paranoid but I've always felt Riddel could be vengeful if he didn't get his own way. I keep wondering what he might do.'

'We think you're wise to be on your guard until he has left the district. That's what Andrew wanted to talk to you about. Would you agree to him bringing Mr Blake? He knows Home Farm like the back of his hand and there's a lot of work to organize at this time of year, with the sheep shearing and the turnip hoeing. It will be hay time before we know where we are.'

'I shall be grateful for any suggestions from Andrew.'

That evening Andrew and Mr Blake, along with Sam King and the herdsman, Arthur Williams, assembled in the Home Farm kitchen.

'Ted Waldie and his lad have decided to leave when Riddel goes,' Sam told Maggie anxiously. 'They reckon they'll be out o' the house by the end o' the week.'

'I see,' Maggie nodded. 'Thank you for telling me, Sam. No doubt they will come to collect their wages. I shall see them then.' Arthur Williams was the only one Maggie was uncertain about as he had not been there very long. She need not have worried.

'My missus an' me were thinking o' moving on again, Mistress Lennox, but if you're sure Mr Riddel willna be coming back, we'd like to stay.'

'I see,' Maggie frowned. 'Didn't you get on with Riddel?'

'Somebody's been taking a couple o' gallons o' milk every night. I thought ye'd be blaming me but I only take the two quarts I'm allowed, same as the rest o' the workers. I mentioned it to Mr Riddel. He said I was imagining things. My missus thinks he was taking it himself. She reckons he took the cream off the cans. We thought he must make butter.'

'Well I have already decided the dairy door must be locked at night until Riddel has gone. Here is one of the keys. I shall hold you responsible if you allow anyone in.'

'Ah, Mistress, that suits me fine.'

'That explains why we have been receiving

warnings about the low butterfat quality from the Milk Board.' She didn't tell Williams that Riddel had blamed him. 'That will be all, except to say if you have any problems you must come directly to me until I engage another manager.'

'If I might interrupt...?' Andrew stepped forward. 'Mr Blake is willing to supervise the men if that would help?'

'It would be a great help,' Maggie said with relief. 'Thank you.' She smiled at the elderly manager. 'In that case, Arthur, you may come to me or to Mr Blake. He was manager here for many years until he retired.'

The man nodded, grinned all round and departed.

'I reckon most o' the folks round here will be pleased Riddel has gone,' Sam King said with feeling. 'Did you want me for anything else, Mistress Lennox? Only I'm booked to play in the darts team at the Dusty Miller.'

'That's all right, Sam. You already know Mr Blake but please tell the other men they are to take their orders from him for the present.'

'I'll do that. Good night everybody.'

'I wish I were twenty years younger,' Mr Blake sighed, watching the young tractor driver depart with a jaunty step. 'He's a decent fellow, Sam.'

'We didn't want to alarm you, Maggie,' Andrew said, 'but you've obviously considered Riddel might get up to some tricks. We spoke to Bert Smith on the way here. He is willing to come and spend the night in the stables with his

196

collie dogs until Riddel gets away. The dogs will soon alert him if there's anyone prowling around.'

'Well I am a bit apprehensive, but is it fair, or necessary, to ask Bert to stay up all night?'

'He often stayed up all night at lambing time,' Mr Blake said, 'and he offered to do it. We don't like scoundrels in Darlonachie, Mistress Lennox. You'll come to no harm with Bert and his dogs around.'

'You're all very kind,' Maggie said gratefully.

'In that case I'll call and tell him on my way home. Would it be convenient for us to meet in the farm office, about ten o'clock each morning? That's what I used to do when Sir William took over Home Farm again.'

'Yes, I'd like that,' Maggie said. Riddel had not wanted her anywhere near the farm if he could avoid it.

'Er ... there is just one thing,' Mr Blake said diffidently. 'I have a nephew. A good lad he is, been farming all his life. He doesna have any bits o' paper, like Mr Riddel, but he's had plenty o' experience and he's a hard worker. I think he would make a good manager for ye if ye want to consider him? Of course, he would need to give a couple of months' notice if you hired him. He's under manager at Croston Estate.'

Maggie looked at Andrew and saw him nod. 'It would be good to have someone who has been personally recommended,' she said slowly. 'I don't know about the bits of paper.'

'I haven't any of them to my name either,'

Andrew chuckled, 'and neither has Mr Blake, but we've managed all right so far.'

'Yes, you have! Mr Riddel had plenty of paper qualifications. Presumably your nephew has experience in mixed farming, Mr Blake?'

'Oh aye. He's my sister's laddie. His name's Fergus Dunlop. His family have worked on farms as far back as he can go, on both sides, but he's a bright laddie. He's always learning something new and reading the farming papers to keep up with the changes.'

'Perhaps you could ask your nephew if he would be interested, Mr Blake? If he is, we must arrange an interview. Will you come over too, Andrew? You would know what questions to ask.' Again Maggie felt dreadfully alone and she wished Billy was not so determined to stay away from Darlonachie. He seemed to have settled well in Yorkshire. He was enjoying the work and he had joined a young farmers' club with his boss's son. Apparently the two of them sang together at some of the concerts and Billy was learning to play the trumpet in the local brass band. He had never shown an interest in anything musical when he was at home. She wanted him to be happy, of course she did, but he was the only family she had and she missed him dreadfully.

Fergus Dunlop proved to be a hard-working and capable man and Maggie felt happier about Home Farm, and more in control of her life, than she had felt since Sir William's death. Mr Blake no longer felt excluded as he had when Riddel took over. He often came for a walk across the fields which had been so familiar, sometimes passing on bits of information gleaned from his years of experience to his nephew. Sometimes he called to see Maggie, regaling her with the local gossip and partaking of a welcome cup of tea before returning home. He missed his old friend Dod Hardie.

Mary's father had died in his sleep at the end of the summer. Willie had suggested they should offer her mother a home with them at High Bowie, though he dreaded the thought of being pestered by Lily again if she came to visit her mother. In the end Mrs Hardie decided to live with Lucy, her youngest daughter, so that she could be nearer the village and her old friends.

In the autumn Billy Lennox started his two-year course at agricultural college. Although he would never have admitted it, he felt homesick and out of his depth during those first few weeks. He missed the friends he had made in Yorkshire and he wrote long letters to Libby telling her about his new life and hoping she would reply, giving him news of the glen. Libby obliged willingly. She missed Billy's companionship and she looked forward to hearing from him. He never mentioned his uncertainties. He made it all sound so exciting and interesting to Libby. She was doing well at the Academy but she still spent a lot of her spare time with Willie and Mary and her baby cousin Mimi at High Bowie, or helping her mother rear the young calves at Langmune. She loved animals and children.

Victoria had a secret dream that her daughter would go to college and train to be a teacher. It had been the ambition of her Uncle Josh before the war took him away. Since his discharge from the air force he had enrolled at university as a mature student. He enjoyed studying and he was doing extremely well. She wanted her daughter to have opportunities that she and Andrew had never had, even though they had done well at school – not that either of them had any regrets. They were happy together at Langmune. Life had treated them kindly in the end. Mark, her twin, had had all the opportunities of a fine education. He had had so many ambitions to heal the sick, and now he was dead – a young life wasted, just like thousands of others.

Victoria felt a deep sense of loss whenever she thought of Mark. They had had such a short time to get used to being brother and sister. It saddened her to think of Catriona, the girl he had loved. She obviously had no desire to keep in touch, not even with the Grantlys, who had been so kind and generous to Mark. They had all been astonished when she married an old friend, another doctor, so soon after Mark's death. Since then a Christmas card was the only communication between them. The first year there was the addition of a baby boy named Peter, then several Christmases later there was a little girl. Now there were three children but Victoria had never seen them, not even in a photograph.

Several times she had written asking if Catriona and her family would like to spend a holiday in the little cottage in Darlonachie. The cottage had been Mark's, given to him by Luke Crainby shortly before he died. Catriona had never even seen it. It seemed she wanted to sever all connection with Mark.

Victoria loved Andrew dearly, and Polly and Joe had treated her as their own daughter since she was thirteen, but she knew there would always be an empty, hollow feeling of deep loss when she thought of Mark. There had been a bond between them almost from the day they met at Darlonachie village school, long before they knew they were brother and sister.

Mark had never loved anyone but Catriona so there had been no need for her to be so possessive, but from their first meeting Victoria had sensed she resented Mark having a twin sister. She had been jealous of the bond between them. Sometimes Victoria felt he had had a premonition that he would not survive the war. She knew he didn't want Catriona to be a grieving widow, or worse, burdened with a crippled ex-soldier for her husband. He had understood the duties and the dangers for a doctor in uniform, so he had refused to marry until the war was over. Had he been right? Would Catriona have been friendlier if she had been her sister-in-law? She would never know.

'Why are you looking so sad, Victoria?' Andrew asked, coming upon her unexpectedly. She had been feeding the hens in one of the huts near the burn and Andrew had cut across the corner of the hayfield to join her. Sometimes he wondered how he would survive if anything happened to Victoria, he loved her with such intensity. She turned now and smiled at him.

'I'm not really sad, but I was thinking about Mark, and about Catriona. She couldn't really have loved him as much as I thought she did or she would never have married so soon after he was killed – and surely she would have come to visit sometimes. After all I was his twin sister.'

'Perhaps she felt guilty and couldn't face us,' Andrew murmured and put his arm around her shoulders, drawing her to him and kissing her upturned face. 'I know you still miss Mark, but you do have me and our children. We're your very own family now, Victoria.'

'Oh yes, I know.' She smiled at him. 'And you know I wouldn't be without you and our children for the world, but just sometimes memories of Mark spring into my mind unbidden and I think I shall always regret all those years when we were so close and we didn't know we were twins. It makes me sad. But, Andrew, speaking of the children...'

'Yes? What plot are you hatching now?'

'I wondered about inviting Josh to tea next time he comes to stay with your parents. I thought he might encourage Libby to go in for teaching.'

'Mmm.' Andrew frowned doubtfully. 'I think Libby has enough of you in her to make up her own mind when the time comes.'

'It bothers me when she pays so much attention to Billy's letters and the course he is doing at agricultural college. There's no future for Victoria in doing something like that, not when we have two sons to make into farmers.'

'Fraser and Lachie may not want to be farmers.'

'You'll be very disappointed if they don't, won't you?'

'Of course I would, and so would you after all the hard work we've put into Langmune, but I would never want them to farm against their will to please us,' he added warningly.

'No of course not, but I'm sure they'll want to farm. They love animals and helping with the hay and harvesting the corn.'

'They do, but so does Libby, and she knows more about the cows and their breeding than either of them, and she recognizes their calves too.'

'I know.' Victoria frowned and thrust out her chin. 'But there's no future for a girl in farming. We must encourage her to have a career. It will be a big enough struggle helping both of the boys to start out in farms.'

'Yes I know, and we shall have to give them both the same chance. Sometimes I wish we had never bought High Bowie. We could have bought one of the other farms from the Darlonachie Estate and then we should have had one for each of our laddies.'

'Oh, Andrew, you don't really regret helping Willie and Mary, do you?'

'No, not really, but we didn't know we were going to have another son when we bought High Bowie. They both work damned hard and they dote on wee Mimi. No, I don't regret it and we've plenty of time before Lachie grows up. While the government continues with guaranteed prices we can plan for the future. We have paid off more of the loan than I expected.' He gave Victoria a hug. 'I expect that's because I have a thrifty wife.'

'Everyone has had to be thrifty with the rationing of food and clothes. I'm sure the government will continue the guarantees until we can do without rationing. Do you really think the rest of the Darlonachie farms will be sold?'

'Mrs Crainby seems to do as she pleases since Mr Jenkinson died and the new lawyer took over. If half the rumours are true there'll be no farms left in the trust for Charlotte Crainby to inherit by the time she's twenty-five.'

'She'll be eighteen now, a year older than Billy.'

'A lot can happen in seven years and I'll bet her mother has made sure she has taken all she can get her hands on.'

'Even Henrietta Crainby wouldn't cheat her own daughter, surely? On the other hand maybe she can't help spending. It was common knowledge that her mother frittered away all of Sir Joshua's money, so maybe Henrietta is the same, but I thought Luke Crainby put the estate in trust for Charlotte, so it's not really hers to spend.'

'As Charlotte's mother I expect she's the main trustee so she'll probably find a reason to get her hands on it. Time will tell – and anyway it's not our problem, thank goodness. Maybe the lassie realizes what her mother is like. Mr Blake spoke to her in the village post office when she was home at Easter. He reckons she's growing more like her father since she's been away from her mother's influence for so long. She told him she was starting training to be an infant teacher soon.'

'A teacher?' Victoria echoed incredulously. 'She must be very different from her mother then.'

Fifteen

Both Maggie and Libby looked forward to Billy's return to Darlonachie during the holidays but although he came for Christmas and again at Easter he spent more time with Willie on the High Bowie moor than he spent at Home Farm. Libby didn't mind because she was often at High Bowie herself when she was not helping her mother with calves or hens. She loved looking after Mimi and Mary appreciated her help. Sometimes Willie brought Billy into the house to join them for the midday meal or afternoon tea if Libby was there. They often walked part of the way home together. He answered her eager questions willingly and told her about his life as a student.

'I am going back to work on the farm in Yorkshire for most of the summer holidays,' he said the day before he returned to college at the end of the Easter holiday. He was too preoccupied with the well-loved landscape to see Libby's disappointment.

'I think I should enjoy going to Agricultural College,' she said.

Billy turned and stared at her. 'Why would you want to do that? I thought you were going to teach children.'

'I never said that!'

'Well you're very good with Mimi. You're only fourteen, but it's what your mother thinks you're going to do. She told my mother so. I think you'd make a good teacher, Libby. Mimi adores you, and so does that wee scamp of a brother.'

'I love them too, but it doesn't mean I want to spend my life teaching. I'd like to go to an agricultural college, but I want to learn more about dairy farming and cows than you seem to do.'

'Our course is general agriculture, a bit of everything. You'd have to choose a college where they teach you about dairying. I know there's one in Devon, and Lancashire I think. There's also the one in Ayrshire of course. You would have to work for a year on a farm first, before you went. It's one of the conditions. They like practical people. Mr Butler is a good farmer and I'm pleased I had him to show me the ropes before I started college. Your father made enquiries and one of the NFU men recommended him, you know. A lot of the chaps are older than me and they've done a lot more science, but I've nearly caught up with them. Some of them don't care whether they pass their exams or not. Most of them are going to family farms or estates. They think they're young gentlemen. They don't intend to dirty their hands but I'm looking forward to going back to Yorkshire when I finish at college.'

'Oh, Billy, you're not!' Libby stopped in her tracks and stared up at him. He was eighteen now and a lot taller than she was. 'Your mother is expecting you to come back and look after Home Farm when you finish at college.'

'Why ever would I do that? I enjoy being in Yorkshire. I've made some good friends there and I've still a lot to learn. She has a good manager now. Thank God she got rid of Riddel.'

'You never liked him much, did you?'

'I hated him!' Billy spoke vehemently. 'He was a sly, jealous weasel of a man and he had a spiteful tongue.' His face had a shuttered look. 'I soon learned to keep out of his way.'

'But that's exactly what he wanted, don't you see?'

'Maybe it was. I was too young to stand up to him anyway, and for all I know some of the things he said could be true.' He kicked a stone viciously and his mouth was set, his eyes narrowed. Then he lifted his head and stared into the distance at the moor land rising above them as far as the eye could see. The sheep were mere dots here and there. He looked down at her again and his face softened. 'You were the only one who didn't criticize. Now I don't care because I've found people who like me for myself and they don't care who my father was or what my mother did. I don't need to talk about them.'

Young as she was, Libby detected an underlying bitterness in him and a fierce determination to stay away from Darlonachie and its gossip. 'Your mother will be terribly disappointed,' she said earnestly. 'She misses you. So do I,' she added and then blushed and turned away so that he wouldn't see.

In the summer of 1952 Billy left college with a diploma in agriculture. In spite of his mother's pleading he knew he was not ready to return to Darlonachie. Maybe he would never return. There was a place and a welcome for him at the farm in Yorkshire where he had done his pre-college practical work. His friendship with Mick, his boss's only son, had strengthened despite his two years away at college. He enjoyed the variety of the work, with the beef and sheep, corn and potatoes and sugar beet, but he was also looking forward to joining the village brass band again and to singing in the young farmers' concert with Mick. Most of all he was his own person: William Lennox, not the bastard son of the local laird who had inherited a farm he didn't deserve.

'You're not learning anything about dairy farming, and Home Farm depends on the dairy herd,' Maggie protested, interrupting his thoughts.

'Give me time, Mother!' He swallowed his irritation and guilt with an effort. 'Mr Butler understands that so he's arranged for me to spend six months with his brother-in-law. He has a big dairy herd, and he's changed from Ayrshire cattle to pedigree Friesians.' He gave her a glimpse of his old mischievous smile. 'And he has a pretty young daughter.'

Maggie didn't return his smile, or ask any questions. She had begun to wonder whether Billy would ever return to Darlonachie. He seemed to have no interest in Home Farm, in fact whenever she mentioned inheritance his mouth tightened and he changed the subject. She began to ask herself why she bothered to carry on with the farm. She would be fifty next year and sometimes she felt twice her age. Victoria and Andrew were the only close friends she had. They visited each other regularly and she was grateful for their friendship. She had lots of acquaintances but it was not the same as having Billy at home, living in the house, enjoying the meals she cooked. She even missed his dirty washing and making his bed each day.

Every week she wrote to him giving him news of Home Farm but she felt she had little else to say that would interest him. He replied regularly but the letters were often scrappy and she guessed they were more a duty than a pleasure. She knew Libby wrote to him regularly and gave him all the local news and Victoria had mentioned the long letters she received in return. Her life seemed so depressing, living alone in the big farmhouse which she had once thought so lovely. She felt tired and lacking her old enthusiasm for the simple pleasures she had always enjoyed – a walk on a crisp frosty morning, the sight of a litter of new puppies, or a dew-spangled spiderweb. Everything seemed an effort and she didn't have the energy to cope.

* * *

Mimi started at the village school in Darlon-achie after Easter. Libby had taught her to write her name in large round letters and she knew all the letters of the alphabet and already recognized some simple words. Willie doted on his small curly-haired daughter with her wide smile and sparkling blue eyes. He insisted she was too small to walk the three miles to the village alone. Mary laughed and teased him.

'Willie Pringle, that child can wind you round her wee finger. We all walked miles to school as soon as we were the age to go.'

'Aye.' His eyes clouded momentarily. 'But I had George for company, and there was always Andrew looking out for us.'

'Aye, and hard work it was for him, if I remember. You and George were always up to mischief and getting into trouble.' Her eyes sparkled up at him. He hugged her close.

'I'm glad to see your old spirits have returned, Mary. I really thought I was going to lose you when Mimi was born. I would never have stayed here if anything had happened to you.'

'Well nothing did, and I'm fine.'

'Aye you're really blooming, bonnier by the day ye are.'

'Is that so, Willie?' Mary eyed him with a spark of humour. 'Or are ye trying to get round me for something?'

'I mean it,' he chuckled, 'of course I do. But ... er ... well I did think we should drive Mimi down to the village until she's a bit older.'

Mimi Pringle had all of her parents' independent spirit and it was not long before she was meeting Lachie where the High Bowie track joined the new bridge on to the Langmune road.

'When I learn to ride a bicycle will you buy one for me?' she asked her father. 'Lachie is learning already and he's going to get Fraser's old bicycle when he's six.'

'Of course we'll get you a bicycle, ma bairn,' Willie said fondly. 'What do you say, Mary?'

'Yes, all right. Old Mr Crabbe still has the cycle shop. We'll ask him to look out for one for a special wee girl.' Mary beamed at her. 'If we get one in the summer holidays, Daddy will teach you to ride.' She laughed up at Willie. 'That's a father's job. No shirking mind!'

At Langmune, Libby had taught Lachie his letters too and he was good at counting. Victoria had noticed how patient her daughter was with her young brother and small cousin and she was convinced Libby was born to be a teacher.

The maternal dream looked like coming true when Libby reached sixteen and gained an excellent school certificate at Dumfries Academy, so it was a shock when her only daughter declared she had no intention of staying at school to get a higher school certificate and nor did she intend to become a teacher.

'I want to work here, at Langmune. I want to learn everything, not just how to milk or feed the calves and hens. I want to drive a tractor and learn to plough, and everything else. Then I shall go to college like Billy but I shall study

212

dairy farming.'

Victoria stared at her in dismay. She looked at Andrew, expecting him to tell Libby such an idea was impossible. But Andrew said nothing.

'Tell her, Andrew, there's no future for a girl in farming. She would be wasting her ability.' Andrew raised one eyebrow and did his best not to smile. Libby saw the irony of it and pounced.

'Farming is your life, Mother. You're happy here.'

'That's different. They're our own animals. It's our future, and our children's future, and...'

'The work is just the same. It's what I want to do.'

'You don't understand, Libby. You have a good brain and you can have a career. Your father and I never had that opportunity. Anyway it will be a big enough struggle getting Fraser and Lachie into farms now we have two sons.'

'Fraser could have a career then. He does well enough at school. He doesn't know half as much about the animals as I do, does he, Dad?'

'No-o,' Andrew said, reluctant to be drawn into this debate. He could see both sides of the argument. 'We'll discuss it later.' He scraped his chair back and made for the door.

'There's nothing to discuss,' Victoria insisted. 'We can't make three of them into farmers.'

Andrew heard but he closed the door behind him, causing Victoria to purse her lips in frustration.

'I didn't say I wanted you to set me up in a farm,' Libby argued, 'but I don't see why you

213

should do that for my brothers if you don't want to do it for me.'

'There's no future for you in farming, Libby. What will you do when you finish at college? Come home and work here? Expect us to pay you a wage?'

'Well why not, if I earn it?'

'Your father and I are not going to live for ever. What happens if your brothers get married and take over Langmune? Will you want to be a paid servant for them and their wives?' Libby scowled and Victoria sighed heavily. 'I only want what is best for you, dear,' she said more gently. 'I want you to have a career and be able to earn your own living, a good living. There's a scarcity of teachers since the war, and you're so good with children.'

'I don't want to be a teacher!' Libby hurried outside, near to tears and unwilling to let her mother see. It hurt to know her parents thought more of Fraser and Lachie than they did of her, and neither of them worked as hard as she did.

She wrote to Billy and poured out her problems. She asked him for particulars of the agricultural colleges that accepted women students. She would send for a prospectus from the ones he had recommended for dairying. She would convince her father she had made up her mind. Her mouth set in a determined line.

Lying in bed that evening, unable to sleep, Libby heard the voices of her parents and she guessed they were discussing her future.

'She's been telling us for a long time this is

what she wanted to do,' Andrew said, trying to be patient, 'and you know she can be as stubborn as her lovely mama,' he added with a smile in his voice. His hand moved to caress Victoria's stomach. She pushed it away.

'I expected you to support me in this, Andrew. You know teaching would be a good career for any girl and Libby has the brains for it.'

'I know she does, but if it would make her unhappy ... I love the land and the animals. They're in my blood. Even if my parents had been wealthy I don't think I would have wanted to do anything different with my life.'

'Yes, but you were lucky that Fraser Rennie was so generous to you. We were both lucky...'

'But we had to work hard and make our own decisions first. We had to strive for what we wanted. Things don't just happen. Anyway, look at Josh. He wanted to be a teacher all his life but now he's going to be a lecturer and train students how to teach.'

'Well that's near enough the same thing, surely. I know!' Victoria exclaimed. 'I'll get Josh to talk to Libby. He thinks the world of her. He'll soon persuade her how sensible it would be.'

'If you say so,' Andrew sighed. In his heart he felt Libby had already made up her mind, and their daughter was made of stern stuff. She had all of their determination in her blood. He knew Victoria was right too; teaching would be a better future for her. He kissed his wife gently and settled down to sleep.

However much Victoria and Willie loved their

respective daughters, however carefully they planned for them, or wanted the best in life for them, fate had a nasty habit of interfering and dealing cruel blows when least expected.

Sixteen

The Sunday School outing was in July and both Lachie and Mimi were desperate to go. Willie was reluctant to allow his wee angel to go to the seaside without her mother to watch over her and Mary was needed to help him get the hay in while the weather held. At Langmune Libby felt there was an uneasy atmosphere between herself and her mother for the first time in her life. She did not know her parents had reached a truce regarding her future.

Andrew had agreed to give Libby as much hard and difficult work as he would have done with any other worker. If she was still determined to go to agricultural college at the end of the long summer holiday Victoria would accept defeat. It was Mary who asked if Libby could be spared to take both the children to the outing since she had no time to go herself. Libby agreed to accompany the two youngsters although she would have preferred to stay at home and prove she was as able as anyone else when it came to haymaking all day.

All of the children were excited about travelling on a bus to the seashore. They were to have a picnic and play ball games and perhaps paddle in the rock pools if the day was warm. Libby felt a little out of place with some of the mothers and the two middle-aged Sunday School teachers but there was one younger teacher, Helen Wriggley, who was only a few years older than herself. The two chatted amicably on the bus journey. Helen worked as a shorthand typist in an office in the town and lived with her parents and elder brother on the other side of Darlonachie. During their conversation Libby discovered she had been in the same year at school as William Lennox.

'We have always called him Billy,' Libby laughed.

'He was a lot cleverer than our group. Most of us thought he would be head boy but he left quite suddenly. Some of his friends said it was because of all that stuff in the papers about his family. Boys in the year above teased him terribly. People can be so cruel,' she said sadly.

'Yes, they can. I'll tell Billy I met you when I write to him. He'll be twenty-one next year and his mother is already planning to give him a coming-of-age party. She's really hoping he will meet up with old friends again and come back to stay in Darlonachie but I don't think he plans to return, at least not yet. He's enjoying living in Yorkshire,' she added, unaware of the wistful note in her voice.

They were too busy keeping an eye on the children and joining in the games to chat much during the afternoon. Three young children who were on holiday from Manchester lingered hopefully on the edge of the group, and in the way of children they were soon joining in the games. When it came to the picnic the teachers divided up the food to include the three pale-faced waifs. Just before they said goodbye and climbed on the bus the teachers gathered all the children together and encouraged them to sing a favourite hymn, 'There's a friend for little children, above the bright blue sky'. Nearly all the children looked up at the sky as though expecting to see God and His angels smiling down at them.

It was a fleeting incident but it lingered in Libby's memory for the rest of her life whenever she looked back to that day. She and Helen were almost as sleepy as the children on the journey home. There had been several minor accidents with children falling into pools and needing to be dried off. Mimi had been one of them but Mary had sent spare clothes, much to Libby's relief, although she had thought it was a bit of a fuss at the time.

About ten days later Mimi woke up feeling ill and out of sorts, complaining of a stiff neck and a sore throat. Mary gave her a drink of hot milk and tucked her up on the kitchen chair with a plaid rug while she got on with her work. Willie needed help to load the hay on to the carts after dinner and Mimi usually enjoyed going with them and riding home on top of the load of sweet-smelling hay. Today she grew more fretful as time went on.

'The bairn has a temperature by the looks o'

her,' Willie said when he came in for his dinner. 'Do you think we should send for the doctor?'

'Och, I expect it's just some childish ailment,' Mary said, hiding her own anxiety, knowing Willie worried enough for two when it came to Mimi or herself, yet he never worried about his own health.

'I'll wrap her in the rug and she can ride to the field on the cart. She might sleep under the hedge while we load up the hay.' She felt torn in two. It was vital to get the hay in while it was dry, and yet she didn't want to neglect Mimi.

'She's better where we can keep an eye on her,' Willie agreed.

Next morning, after a very restless night, it was obvious that Mimi was worse. Willie drove over to Langmune and asked Victoria to telephone for the doctor.

'We must get the phone in at our place,' he said irritably. 'I'll enquire what it would cost.'

'No problem, Willie,' Victoria said cheerfully. 'The doctor is coming out right away. Tell Mimi I hope she'll soon be better. I haven't heard of measles or mumps going around but I suppose these things have to start somewhere.'

It was Doctor Grantly's new assistant who arrived at High Bowie. Mary frowned. She had faith in Doctor Grantly but she knew he must be getting near to retiring. Doctor Ritchie was very thorough and when Mimi complained about her bones aching he didn't laugh – in fact Mary thought he looked alarmed, especially when Mimi told him her left leg was worst and her right hand felt funny.'

'Could it be rheumatic fever, Doctor?' she asked worriedly.

'I don't think so, Mrs Pringle,' he replied slowly, thoughtfully. 'Just give her a small amount of aspirin for the pain and plenty of drinks.'

'You mean you dinna ken what's wrong with the bairn?' Willie asked with unusual brusqueness. All his instincts told him his beloved Mimi had more than a childish ailment but he didn't know what.

'I'm sorry, Mr Pringle, it is too soon to say and I don't want to worry you unnecessarily. I would like to discuss Mimi's symptoms with Doctor Grantly. One of us will return later in the day to have another look at her.'

'Ye'll come back? Today? All the way up here?' Willie didn't know whether to be relieved or even more worried.

Doctor Grantly came bumping up the track in his old car soon after lunch. He examined Mimi and asked her questions, as Doctor Ritchie had done, but she was flushed and her head ached and she began to cry. He turned to Mary, his face grave.

'Doctor Ritchie is an excellent man,' he said, drawing her to the door out of Mimi's hearing. Willie had seen the doctor's car and came hurrying across the yard. 'I might not have picked this up so soon had he not put it into my head,' he went on, looking gravely from one to the other.

'What is it, Doctor? What d'ye think is wrong

221

with the bairn?'

'We suspect it may be Poliomyelitis, or infantile paralysis, as it is often called. I must admit Mimi to hospital without delay—'

'P-polio! But people die with that, don't they, Doctor Grantly?' Mary whimpered, and clasped Willie's arm, fearing her legs might give way. The colour had drained from his face too.

'Poliomyelitis,' he whispered. 'Oh God, help us.'

'Mimi is normally a healthy, well-nourished child. She tells me she can still swallow without too much difficulty, and her breathing isn't badly affected so far. That is the danger so it is essential we get her admitted to Park Head right away.'

'You're not sending her to the Infirmary?'

'But that's the fever hospital...'

'Yes. We can't risk spreading infection'

The ensuing weeks were a waking nightmare for Mary and Willie and to all those who cared for them.

Libby went around in silence, pale-faced. She blamed herself. She had heard children could catch polio while swimming and she had let Mimi fall in the water. Victoria tried to reassure her. Two young women as well as a little boy who had been on the outing had also been admitted to the same isolation hospital. His parents feared he would need to be put into an iron lung to help him to breathe.

Mary and Willie felt each day was a lifetime,

but the days stretched into weeks and then a month. There was no word of their precious child getting well enough to come home. Then Doctor Ritchie gave them the news that she was to be moved from the fever hospital to the Grove, a convalescent home on the outskirts of Dumfries.

'Will that cost a lot?' Willie asked, doing rapid mental calculations about what he could sell.

'No, it is all part of the National Health Service,' Doctor Ritchie assured them, 'so please don't worry about that. The main thing is to do what we can to give Mimi the best possible chance of recovery.'

At High Bowie the work had to be done and the animals cared for. They were all glad to have Libby's help. Sometimes she accompanied Mary to visit Mimi; sometimes she went over to High Bowie to help Willie with the work to let Mary spend more time with Mimi.

'We must be thankful Libby is well and strong,' Andrew said to Victoria one night as he held her close in his arms. 'Doctor Grantly said she could have been infected just as easily as Mimi. We must accept her decision and let her be happy in whatever she chooses to do. She has proved she can work hard and use her initiative. Life can be so short, and it can be so cruel.'

'You know she thinks she is to blame for Mimi getting polio?' Victoria said. 'I'd do anything now to bring back her smile and the colour to her cheeks. She is going with me to visit Mimi tomorrow, to give Mary and Willie a break.'

223

Doctor Grantly was visiting at the convalescent home when Victoria and Libby arrived.

'I know we must all be thankful that Mimi hasn't needed an iron lung,' Victoria said, 'but do you know how badly she will be affected, or when she will be allowed home?'

'I fear she will probably need to wear a calliper on her left leg to help her to get around.' Libby gasped and stared at him in horror. Doctor Grantly looked at her. 'Your aunt and uncle know and they have accepted it.' He looked at Victoria. 'Did they not tell you?'

'Yes, we knew it was a possibility,' she nodded, 'but we didn't tell Libby. She blames herself for Mimi's illness because she fell in the water on the Sunday School picnic.'

'You were on the Sunday School outing, Elizabeth? Did you meet a young woman called Helen Wriggley?'

'Yes, we sat together on the bus.'

'I see.' His face was grave, his voice low and full of regret. 'She also contracted polio. She died ten days ago.'

'Oh no! No...' Libby stared at him in disbelief. 'Th-that's not possible. She was so healthy, so happy. She was so patient and good with the children...' Her voice quavered.

'I'm afraid it is true, my dear. So you see, Elizabeth, Mimi's illness has nothing to do with you. It could have been you too. We must be thankful Mimi is alive. She's a fighter. It is true her left leg seems to be affected, and her right arm lacks the power of her left one, but Doctor

Ritchie is a great believer in the treatment devised by Sister Elizabeth Kenny.'

'Does she work here?'

'No. She was a nurse during the Great War. She came from the Australian Outback. She often had to treat patients with polio there without any help. She believed it was essential to stimulate the unaffected muscles with massage instead of keeping the patients in bed all the time. Her ideas met with a great deal of opposition from doctors, and many still oppose them, but she travelled to America during a serious epidemic of poliomyelitis and her methods have been widely adopted there. According to Doctor Ritchie several Kenny clinics have been established over there now. Unfortunately she died last year.'

'Yes,' Victoria said slowly, 'I can see it would make sense not to allow the muscles to waste away, but I can imagine how difficult it must be if the affected limbs prevent the patients from walking, or even moving very much without help.'

'Doctor Ritchie is keeping a close eye on wee Mimi. They've become great friends. I suspect he will be a regular visitor at High Bowie when she gets home and he will pass on plenty of advice about her treatment. I think you will be a great help to her too, Elizabeth. Doctor Ritchie says she adores you and she will need a great deal of encouragement from those she trusts. Sometimes it will be hard to persuade her to persevere with her exercises. Now, I have kept you from her long enough...'

Libby and her mother walked together across the grounds towards the large house which had become a convalescent home.

'Fate has a strange way of working,' Victoria mused. 'It seems we shall all be glad of your help in the months before you start at the agricultural college.'

'You mean you've accepted my decision, Mother? You – you're not angry with me any more?'

'I was never angry, Libby. Just disappointed,' Victoria said softly, looking at her daughter's shining eyes and the relief on her face. 'I know you have a lot of ability and I thought I knew best what your future ought to be. When I think of that poor young woman...' She shuddered. 'You might not have been here at all. I thank God for our blessings. We are all in His hands.'

It was Christmas before Mimi was allowed home and only then on the understanding that she must return two days after Christmas when the doctors would decide whether she should be fitted with a calliper to help her learn to move around unaided. Everyone was determined to make it the happiest Christmas possible for her.

'She is so small and so brave,' Libby wrote to Billy. Throughout her young cousin's illness she had poured out her guilt and anxiety in her letters. He had done his best to reassure her that she was not responsible for Mimi's illness, but only Doctor Grantly had been able to convince her.

'It's like learning to write and to colour in pictures all over again,' Libby chuckled when she realized Mimi's right hand didn't have the strength to grip the pencil. 'See, Mimi, you are much better at using your left hand than I am.'

Mimi giggled at Libby's exaggerated effort to write her name, but in truth Libby didn't find it easy to write legibly with the wrong hand and her heart ached for her young cousin. It seemed as though her thumb and first finger were useless but her other three fingers could grip a little.

Once Christmas was past and Mimi had returned to the hospital Mary and Willie realized how much their only child's disability was going to affect their own lives. They had bought her a small bicycle in July but she would never learn to ride it now. It was too far and too rough for her to walk to school and back again every day, even if Doctor Ritchie was right in saying she would learn to walk unaided eventually.

'One of us will have to drive her to school and collect her again in the afternoon,' Willie said.

'I've been thinking about it,' Mary said and nodded. 'She will need a lot of help for a long time with things like dressing and bathing. I've been thinking I should get rid of the pigs so that I shall have more time for Mimi.'

'I've been wondering if we should give up the farm altogether,' Willie said despondently. 'We've saved a bit. We could rent a cottage in the village, or maybe get one of the new prefabricated houses on the outskirts. It would be near enough for Mimi to get to school herself eventually. You know how independent she likes to be, even now.'

'Oh, Willie,' Mary said in distress. 'You dreamed so long of farming your own place. You would hate to move to the village. What would you do for work?'

'My happiness is nothing compared to Mimi's,' Willie sighed. 'She's never known what it is to enjoy the freedom and games we enjoyed as bairns, and now she never will. As for work, I expect there's something I could do. I could try for a job on one of the delivery vans. Surely the rationing can't last much longer, and then there'll be more vans travelling around the countryside with groceries and bread and meat.'

'We'll not do anything in a rush,' Mary said. She knew Willie would give his life for their small daughter and she loved him all the more for that, but she didn't want him to give up everything he had dreamed of. They had done better with the farm during the last three years, once she had regained her own health and things had settled down, or so they had thought until Mimi's illness.

Victoria came over with some marmalade she had made and they told her what they were considering.

'Oh, don't give up High Bowie yet, Willie. We'll all help out with taking the children to school. Libby can drive the tractor and next year she'll learn to drive the car.'

'Libby is a grand lassie,' Willie said warmly, 'but she'll not be here. She has her own life to lead.'

'She'll be here until the autumn and our new David Brown tractor has a bench seat for two. Let's see how things go.'

'Ye've aye been good to us, you and Andrew,' Willie said wearily. 'I don't want to give up High Bowie but we have to do what's best for Mimi. She'll never have a proper life – I mean like going to dances or getting married and having bairnies of her own.'

'Oh, Willie, you mustn't look at it like that. Mimi has survived. She's a great wee character with a lot of courage. We don't know what the future holds for any of us, or what new cures might be found by the time she grows up. Look at the wonderful way penicillin has helped people recover from wounds and suchlike since it was discovered during the war. Even tuberculosis doesn't always mean a death sentence these days, as it did a few years ago.'

Andrew said much the same when he and Willie discussed the future. 'Victoria's right. If you still want to leave High Bowie in a year's time that's fine. You'll have given things a trial. After all Mimi loves the farm and the animals as much as you do.'

'I suppose you're right,' Willie sighed. 'We'll wait a wee while.'

Seventeen

Billy came home to Darlonachie for a week at Easter. Libby had confided all her feelings of guilt in her letters to him, and told him of every tiny improvement in Mimi's condition. He had done his best to comfort and reassure her, but he was surprised at the change in her. She was no longer the schoolgirl he had known all his life. She had the air of a capable and determined young woman and it was a shock to see her in the company of the new doctor, bending over Mimi together as they discussed the massage and movements which would help strengthen the little girl's muscles.

He remembered Libby had mentioned that Doctor Steve Ritchie was the new assistant to Doctor Grantly but she had not said he was so young. Billy thought he must be in his late twenties, only four or five years older than him. In one of her letters his mother had mentioned the new doctor was an eligible bachelor but he hadn't paid much attention. Now he looked at the man's dark head so close to Libby's.

'You would make an excellent nurse, Elizabeth,' Doctor Ritchie said as he watched Libby following his instructions. It was a sunny afternoon and warm for early spring so they were all out in the garden at High Bowie. 'Have you thought about what I said?'

'Yes,' Libby smiled up at him, at ease in his company since he visited Mimi whenever he had a few hours to spare. He seemed to have adopted her as his special protégée. 'It is easy to do things for Mimi. I've known her since she was a baby and we all love her – don't we, poppet?' Mimi nodded, giving a wide grin. She had lost one front tooth and Billy had to smile at her impish look. 'It would be different caring for strangers and I don't think I would want to work inside all the time. I'm an outdoor girl.'

'Yes she is,' Billy heard himself saying. 'She always has been.' He didn't know why he sounded so belligerent. 'Farming is in her blood.' Doctor Ritchie looked up at him in surprise.

'Mmm, it's a pity. Good nurses are badly needed. You'll be Mrs Lennox's son? She was looking forward to you coming home at Easter.'

'You know my mother?' Billy frowned.

'Yes, didn't she tell you?'

'Has she been to the surgery?'

'I think you had better ask her that yourself.'

'I see.' Billy's mouth tightened. 'Patient confidentiality, is that what you call it?' Billy hadn't paid much attention to his mother's appearance although she was considerably thinner than she used to be. He hadn't noticed the bluish tinge that had replaced the healthy pink in her cheeks or that her eyes were strained

231

and edged with fine lines.

Doctor Ritchie straightened and looked Billy in the eye briefly before turning back to Mimi with a smile and ruffling her curls. 'I shall have to be getting along now but I shall be back to see you another day, young lady. We have to get you walking without the need of a calliper.'

'Oh, Doctor, won't you join us for a meal?' Mary said, wiping her hands on her apron as she hurried from the kitchen. 'Willie will be in from the hill soon.'

'Thanks, Mrs Pringle, but I'd better not. Mrs Telfer will have left a meal in the oven for me.' He smiled. 'I mustn't offend her or she might leave me to starve another day.' Billy listened and remembered his mother had said the new doctor was living at Rose Cottage, the small house only a few hundred yards from Doctor's Grantly's surgery.

'It's so good of you to give up your free afternoon and come all the way up here to see Mimi,' Mary said gratefully.

'Ah, but Mimi is a special wee girl and she's responding better than we dared to hope, what with Elizabeth here to help her with the exercises. You're going back to school after the Easter holidays I hear, Mimi?'

'Yes, I am,' Mimi lisped slightly through the gap in her teeth. 'Libby says I can write as good with this hand,' she held up a chubby fist, 'as I could with that one.' She looked down at the hand which lay curled on her lap. A shadow darkened Doctor Ritchie's eyes. Her right arm was not totally paralysed but it would never regain its former strength, in spite of his and Elizabeth's efforts.

Billy was shocked at the effect Mimi's illness had had on her parents. Mary's shining brown hair had turned almost white. Willie's ruddy face was lined and drawn and there was a sadness in his eyes instead of the serenity Billy had so often envied as he watched Willie gaze into the distance across the hills and glens below High Bowie. Both he and Libby stayed at High Bowie for the evening meal. Mary had cooked the week's ration of sausages and made a leek and cheese bake topped with creamy mashed potatoes. Billy picked Mimi up from her chair. He pretended to let her drop, making her giggle, wanting him to do it again. She was as light a feather. She would never be able to walk to school. He remembered what a long road it had seemed to him when he had lived at High Bowie and he had always had a sturdy pair of legs. He had been glad when they moved to Home Farm. He had loved being there when his grandfather was alive and he had been innocent and ignorant of the gossip.

'It's a pity Tommy is too old for much riding these days,' he mused, almost to himself. 'He would have carried you to school, Mimi, and he would never have made you fall off.'

'Would the teacher let him in to school, like Mary and her little lamb in the nursery rhyme?'

'I'm afraid not.' He grinned down at her. 'I expect somebody would have let him graze in their orchard, but he might have eaten all the apples and then you'd be in trouble,' he chuckled. 'Better stick to riding on the tractor with Libby, eh?' He changed the subject. Tommy was too old anyway and Mimi would need a pony that was utterly reliable.

'But I could have a little ride on Tommy, couldn't I, Billy? He's not too old for a wee ride, is he?'

'Of course not, if your daddy agrees and if Libby will hold you on while I lead him.'

'Tomorrow then? When Libby comes back to do my legs?'

'Mimi, it's a date. Shake on it, partner!' He held out a hand and Mimi slapped it with her little fist. Billy winked at her and she chuckled with delight. He looked across at Libby. 'That OK with you?'

'Yes,' she nodded, 'so long as Uncle Willie agrees.'

'I don't see why not if it's what she wants. I'll agree to anything that makes ma bairn happy.'

Later, when Mary had taken Mimi up to bed, Willie looked at Billy.

'Maybe it wouldn't be such a daft idea to get the bairn a pony. I know she's not ready for that yet, but she may be next year.'

'It would need to be a very quiet pony, and utterly reliable,' Billy said doubtfully. 'Tommy was not always quiet when he was younger, but Grandfather taught me how to handle him.'

'Well maybe you could teach Mimi. It would give her a wee bit of independence. She gets in

234

a temper and then we have tears when she can't do things herself. She gets frustrated. If we could get one quiet enough we'd soon find some grazing in the village, or her Aunt Lucy would stable it.'

'We'll see how she gets on with Tommy tomorrow,' Billy said cautiously. 'It might be worth considering when she's a bit older.'

'Aye, I think it might,' Willie nodded, looking brighter and more hopeful than Libby had seen him for a long time. 'It's a pity ye're not staying for a month, Billy. I'm starting the lambing soon. I could just have done with a fit young fellow to help.'

'Sorry, Willie, I've got a job.' Billy smiled but Libby saw there was a tension about him and she guessed his mother had been trying to persuade him to return to the glen too.

Every evening when she had finished her day's work Libby went to High Bowie to massage and exercise Mimi's muscles. Sometimes she thought the power was returning to the little girl's right arm, but at other times she felt as hopeless and frustrated as Mimi did herself. Every evening Billy was there and together they saddled Tommy and gave Mimi a ride. By the end of the week she could sit confidently in the saddle with only the lightest touch from Libby. Billy showed her how he would normally hold the reins, then together they devised a way for her to hold them in one hand and by twisting it she could exert enough pressure to show a biddable pony which way she wanted him to go.

'I'm going back to Yorkshire tomorrow,' Billy said to Libby on his last evening. 'I can't believe how quickly the week has gone this time.'

'Perhaps that's because you've been doing something worthwhile; for Mimi, I mean,' she added quickly.

'And I've had good company.' He grinned at her. 'Seriously though it has been easy to show Mimi what to do on Tommy but he's too old now to take her to school and back every day and there's not many ponies reliable enough for a child with Mimi's problems. She's a brave wee thing but it would be terrible if she fell off. She couldn't get back on herself. In fact she'll not be able to mount or dismount so it's quite impossible.'

'Lachie will be there. He would help her dismount. He's got a bicycle to ride to school now but he could ride beside her, and there's her other cousins, Lucy's children, to help once she reaches the village.'

'Will you keep putting her on Tommy when I'm not here then?'

'Yes, if that's what she wants. It may seem a daft idea getting a pony to take her to school but Uncle Willie has even considered giving up High Bowie and living in the village for Mimi's sake. He might do that yet if it all proves too much for them.'

'That would be a pity. He loves shepherding and he loves the hills.'

'I know. They both love the life up here, but they love Mimi even more. I shall be going to college in September so I can't help with taking Mimi to school then.'

'Has your mother accepted your decision then, Libby?'

'Yes, she has. She said seeing Mimi crippled like this, and knowing it could have been me, helped her get things into perspective.'

'I wish my mother would see things that way,' Billy muttered gloomily. 'I can just imagine all the old gossip starting up again if I came home and took over Home Farm.'

'You can't blame Aunt Maggie for thinking that's your place. Whatever people say, it is your inheritance. No one influenced Sir William. He loved you and he respected your mother. Do you plan to stay away forever because of the gossips?' she asked with asperity.

'Don't talk like that, Libby! I believed you were the one person I could rely on to understand and see my point of view.' His tone was sharp and Libby flushed but she stood her ground.

'Does this mean you'll never return to Darlonachie then?'

'Never is a long time. How should I know?' he said irritably.

'I think it's time you stopped thinking only about yourself, William Lennox,' Libby snapped, losing patience. 'Your mother may have a good farm manager with Fergus Dunlop but the responsibility is still hers. She has all the decisions to make when it comes to money and repairs and paying tax and increasing wages and

... and, oh, the thousand and one things that have to be done. You're so wrapped up in your own feelings I don't suppose you've considered that she has no one to confide in or consult and she's doing her very best for you.' It was not often Libby lost her temper. She had enjoyed Billy's company all week and she didn't realize it was her own disappointment that made her so sharp and outspoken as she stomped away from him down the track to Langmune.

'Wait, Libby! Hey!'

But she tossed her head and kept on walking, vowing she wouldn't humour him, or feel sympathy for him just because he had no father to guide him. Her own mother had had no parents at all but she hadn't made a mess of her life, or made other people miserable. Granny Pringle had told her often about the hard time she'd had as a young girl in the kitchens at Darlonachie Castle, how hard she had worked with her courage and determination.

A letter from Billy arrived soon after he returned to Yorkshire and there was nothing in it to indicate he had taken her criticism seriously. He was full of his friends and how much he was enjoying the variety of the work and how much he still had to learn. Libby pursed her lips. She was missing his company more than she would admit even to herself, but she was determined not to answer promptly as she had always done.

Less than a week later another letter arrived from Billy. It was breakfast time when the post-man came. Her father scanned the usual bills and government missives and discussed them with her mother as Libby opened her own letter with a small smile of satisfaction. The smile soon fled. She gasped aloud. Billy had not forgotten her outburst after all, although he had pretended to pay no attention in his first letter. Now his anger was all too plain. Indignant colour rushed to her cheeks as she read on. Just because she had not replied as promptly as usual he was accusing her of sulking. He demanded to know who gave her the authority to lecture him, but then the blood leached from her face at the accusations that followed. She pushed her chair back and hurried upstairs to her bedroom to finish the letter in private.

It is obvious to everyone that you are flattered by the new doctor's attention. Does he enjoy your doe-eyed glance upon him, and your lips, parted so invitingly, so temptingly close? It is clear that he admires you and no doubt he has designs on you. Does he know you are not yet seventeen? Has he any idea how innocent you are? Or how your parents have sheltered and protected you from the real world? You have no right to lecture me when you have no experience of the realities of life. I did not expect you to add to the cruel tongues which abound in Darlon-achie and the glen. Have a care, Libby. If the good doctor has his way with you before he moves on to greater things you may experience the cruelty yourself.

I'm deeply disappointed by your sulky silence,

but I shall manage without your letters, just as I can manage without your lectures on how to run my life. I shall have left this address by the time you receive this letter. I am moving to broaden my experience in dairy farming. So you see I am not wasting my time on selfish pleasures as you seem to imagine.

There was little more and there was no new address so Libby could only assume he no longer wanted to receive her letters. Part of her was furious at his pompous tone, but a greater part of her was mortified that Billy should think she tried to attract Doctor Ritchie's admiration. She had believed they were a team, working together to improve Mimi's young life in any way they could. She had always regarded him in a professional capacity, as a doctor, but suppose he thought the same way Billy did? She dropped the letter to her lap and clasped her burning cheeks with cold hands.

Whenever possible after that Libby avoided being at High Bowie when she thought Doctor Ritchie might be there, but she could not, and would not neglect Mimi. Uncle Willie and Aunt Mary had more work than they could manage. Libby knew how much they appreciated the time she spent with Mimi, not only massaging her limbs, but helping her catch up with her lessons, and supervising her riding Tommy. It had become the little girl's greatest delight to sit up high on the pony's back and to guide him where she wanted to go around the farmyard and a short way down the track.

Victoria noticed that Billy's letters had stopped arriving and that Libby no longer left her weekly letter for the postman to take away. She mentioned this to Maggie one day when she went down to see her at Home Farm.

'They're both growing up,' Maggie sighed. 'Billy will be twenty-one soon. He is working on another farm for six months and he did mention the farmer had a pretty daughter. Maybe she is jealous of him receiving letters from a girl back home.'

'Possessive, you mean? Like Catriona was with Mark. She knew I was his sister, his twin sister, but she still resented me.'

'But she had no reason to resent you, Victoria.'

'We know that. I would never have stood in the way of Mark's happiness, or tried to influence him, but Catriona always put up an invisible barrier. Even when we knew Mark had been killed and we were both hurting so much she could neither give, nor accept comfort.'

'You still miss him, don't you, Victoria?' Maggie said sadly.

'I suppose I always shall, and I shall always regret the time we could have spent together.' Victoria summoned a smile. 'But I didn't come down here to moan. I came to see how you're keeping. I hate to see you so pale and tired.'

'I think that's something I have to accept.' Maggie shrugged. 'I can't buy a new heart so I shall have to make do with this old thing for as long as it keeps going.'

'Has Doctor Ritchie no suggestions?'

'Oh, he has prescribed some pills and he tells me to rest regularly and not get anxious or tense.' She gave Victoria a wry smile. 'You and Andrew know that's easier said than done in farming.'

'Still no word of Billy coming back to take over?'

'No. He's agreed to come home for the week-end for his birthday though. He's bringing Mick Butler and a couple of other friends, but he doesn't want a proper coming–of-age party. He's so bitter.' Maggie's eyes filled with tears but she brushed them away impatiently. 'He says coming-of-age parties are for real lairds, not for the laird's bastard. I don't think he'll ever forgive me.'

'Gossip can be so cruel,' Victoria said with feeling. 'And everything happened at a sensitive age for Billy. If he'd been an adult he would have understood better, and if he'd been a toddler he would never have heard the gossip. He will understand one day, Maggie. I'm sure he will, when he falls in love himself. Love can be so wonderful, but it can be painful too when you're plagued by choices and uncertainties.'

'Well at least he's now bringing his friends home so I suppose that's a start. He and Mick really enjoyed coming up for the Highland Show in June and they only came because it was held at Dumfries. Anyway his birthday is near enough Lockerbie Show so he says I can arrange a dinner party for a few close friends but they are spending the next day at the show and going to the dance at night. He seems to have got quite involved with the Young Farmers' movement since he went to Yorkshire.'

'Well that's not a bad thing. Her Majesty, Queen Elizabeth, the Queen Mother, spent some time in the marquee for the girls' competition when she visited in June and I believe the Scottish Association are to receive a generous grant for leadership training, and another towards bursaries to assist a few worthy members to travel to the Commonwealth. The movement had barely become established when the war started so it's good that the young people who are growing up now will have a brighter future.'

'I know you're right, Victoria, but Billy already has a bright future. His grandfather did his best to ensure that – if only he would see it.'

Eighteen

Maggie was a good cook and she had done her best to make a memorable meal for Billy and his friends from Yorkshire. When she had made a rare telephone call to ask if she should invite any of the boys he knew at school he had replied brusquely.

'There's none of them I want to see. Ask the neighbours you like if you must make a formal meal.'

So Maggie asked Andrew and Victoria and their family and Willie and Mary with little Mimi. After some hesitation she also invited Fergus Dunlop, the Home Farm manager, and his wife.

The food was excellent and Victoria had baked a birthday cake and decorated it beautifully, thankful that icing sugar was freely available now that rationing had ended. At more than four shillings a pound for butter it had rationed itself and most people were trying out margarine as a substitute but Maggie had not skimped on anything for Billy and his friends. In spite of all her efforts the atmosphere was strained. Fergus Dunlop was ill at ease in Billy's company and Billy either didn't notice or simply made no effort to engage him in conversation about Home Farm. That was left to Andrew and Willie. It was the first time Libby and Billy had been together since their stormy exchange and there was a tension between them. This did not prevent his friends from teasing her and flirting openly, becoming even more outrageous when they saw Billy scowl. Only with Mimi did he seem at ease and it would have taken a harder heart than Billy's to resist the little girl's wide smile and sparkling eyes, not to mention the courage with which she accepted her lame leg.

'Shall we collect you for the show tomorrow?' Mick asked Libby as everyone prepared to leave.

'Oh ... er ... no thank you.' Libby's gaze moved beyond him to Billy's set face. 'I think Father will give me a lift in. I need to be there early to get my exhibits arranged in the Young Farmers' tent, ready for the judging, you know.'

'Ah, so you're not just a pretty face then,' Mick teased. 'No wonder Billy didn't tell us about you. He always keeps the prettiest girls to himself. It's his Scottish accent. They all fall for him.' He pulled a comically sad face. 'Pete and Jim and I don't stand a chance.' Libby glanced at Billy but he didn't meet her eyes; his old familiar grin had been missing all evening. Fergus Dunlop and his wife had made an excuse to leave soon after the meal but the tension in Billy had not lessened.

'Tha's a silly bugger, William Lennox, does tha' know that!' Mick demanded in his broad

Yorkshire accent. He was sharing Billy's bedroom and he barely waited until the door was
closed.

'What d'you mean?' Billy scowled.

'You have a farm here waiting for you, your
ma's a lovely woman, and then there's that lass
of yours—'

'What lass?' Billy's mouth tightened and his
eyes narrowed.

'It was Libby who used to write the letters
every week, wasn't it? Even Ma noticed they'd
stopped coming and you'd stopped writing to
her. What's wrong with yer?'

'Libby's just a schoolgirl,' Billy scoffed.

'School girl, my arse,' Mick retorted rudely.
'She told me she'll be seventeen soon, and she's
going away to college. Somebody else'll snap
her up if you don't watch out. Come to think
on't I wouldn't mind snatching her from under
yer toffee nose meself if I didn't live so far
away.'

'I'm not a toffee-nosed...' Billy began indignantly.

'O-oh! So you are listening then, when you're
not putting on that stone face? I mean it, Billy, I
quite fancy—'

'Let's get to bed and thank the Lord that's
over. Why Mother had to make such a fuss I
don't know.'

'Because she cares about you, you big nit, and
because you're all she's got...'

'Don't remind me!' Billy said darkly. Mick
was one of the few people Billy had confided in

about his family and the reason he wanted to get away from everything and everyone that was familiar.

'All right, all right, keep yer 'air on. We'll get to bed but I 'ope you'll be more cheerful tomorrow. We are going to the dance after the show, aren't we? How's about asking Libby to go with us?'

'You can ask her if you want.' Billy shrugged. 'I'll borrow Mother's car and drive Pete and Jim.'

Libby saw Billy and his pals several times in the distance, laughing and joking together and teasing some of the local girls around the Young Farmers' tent. She had won several prizes for home baking but she was determined not to go near while they were hanging around. She hated Billy when he was gruff and tense as he had been last night. On the other hand she had no intention of staying away from the dance just because he and his friends planned to go. She wished she had her driving licence now. She usually cycled down with Milly's daughters, Grace and Miriam. Recently Fraser had started going to some of the meetings with them but he was too young for the dance. She had just finished making a new dress so they would have to beg her father to give them a lift if they wanted to arrive looking glamorous.

'I would really love a new dress for the show dance, Granny,' she had said, looking into Polly's lined face with a beguiling smile. Both her grandparents had aged alarmingly since

Mimi's illness.

'Och, and it wouldna have anything to do with Billy Lennox coming home and bringing his fine friends, would it?'

'Of course not,' Libby denied too swiftly, and felt her cheeks flush.

'My old fingers are getting stiff, lassie, but I'll help you cut it out and pin the tucks and seams for you. Your mother was always better with the treadle sewing machine than me anyway, and I hear you're not so bad yourself.'

'Well I'd like to have a go if you'll help me with the fitting. Do you like the style?'

'I do. You've lost weight since you've been working at home and spending all your free time helping Mimi.' She looked fondly at Libby. 'We're all grateful, Willie especially. He says you make her exercises seem like fun and you've helped the wee soul feel as normal as everybody else.' She scrutinized the dress pattern again. 'Aye the narrow waist and full skirt will be grand for the dancing and that turquoise colour will bring out the chestnut lights in your bonnie hair. It seems fairer since you've been working in the fields so much. Your grandfather was telling Andrew he is giving you too much hard work, what with hoeing turnips and helping with the hay, as well as working with the cows.'

'Oh but I enjoy it all, Granny. Anyway, Dad says I should know what's involved if I'm still determined to go to agricultural college.' She gave a mischievous smile which wrenched at

Polly's heart for a moment because it reminded her of George as a boy. 'I think Mum hoped I would find the work too hard and change my mind,' Libby said.

'Aye, lassie, I think you're right, but they'll be thankful if you're healthy and happy.'

So they had cut out the dress together and Libby was pleased with it. She was not going to let Billy's angry moods spoil her evening.

'Billy's friends are calling to pick you up for the dance tonight,' her mother announced as soon as she got home from the show in the late afternoon.

'But we can't all get in. Miriam and Grace need a lift too. I can't leave them behind.'

'That's all right. It was the boy called Mick who phoned. He said he would fix things up. Billy will take Pete and Jim in his mother's car. He'll come for you girls himself. He's a bit of a charmer that one,' Victoria smiled. 'He asked if I couldn't come along to make up the numbers.' She chuckled. 'The cheek of the laddie. I told him my dancing days were long past and he would soon find a fourth girl when he got to the dance.' She looked shrewdly at Libby. 'He said he was making sure of his girl before he got there.' She raised her eyebrows questioningly at Libby. 'Maggie says he's quite a wealthy lad. His father owns the farm and he's an only son.'

'Mother?' Libby's eyes widened. 'You're not wanting to marry me off, are you?'

Victoria hesitated for a moment, then she hugged Libby. 'No, of course not. We don't want to lose you for a long time yet, and even when we do have to let you go I hope you'll settle near us. Yorkshire would be too far away and money isna everything. Look for a kind man like your father, lassie. We shall miss you when you go to college.'

'But I shall be home for the holidays, Mum.' She returned her mother's hug. 'But I shall miss all of you, even Fraser and his teasing, and I hate the thought of not seeing Mimi for a whole term.'

'I expect you'll soon settle in and forget about us,' Victoria said briskly. 'I've never lived away from Darlonachie so I don't know what it would be like. You must enjoy yourself while you can.'

'Mmm, well the first thing I'd better do is bring the cows in from the field and get on with the milking. I want to have a bath and wash my hair before the dance.'

The evening was a happy affair with members of visiting Young Farmers clubs adding to the melee. Libby was never short of a partner but Billy had not asked her to dance, although she had danced with Mick several times already. She saw Mick having a quick word with one of the accordionists in the band and shortly after the compere announced there had been a request for a song from William Lennox. Would he come to the stage please? Billy glared across at Mick but someone set up a chant and he had little option but to comply.

'I'm amazed!' Libby whispered to Mick at the end of the Lincolnshire Poacher. At Billy's behest everyone had joined in the chorus with gusto and there were calls for another song. 'We've never heard Billy sing before. What a lovely rich voice he has.'

'Our local bandmaster thinks he has a natural ear.' He grinned. 'Whatever that means.'

Libby didn't answer. She was listening to the words of the song. 'I'd crowns resign to call thee mine, sweet lass of Richmond Hill.' She wondered whether Billy had a special girl in Yorkshire.

The door of the hall opened quietly and to Libby's surprise Doctor Steve Ritchie made a late entrance. He had probably been on call but he was dressed for dancing and he looked a little diffident as he looked around the crowded room. Libby met his eye and he smiled warmly. She lifted her hand in a brief salute and he came to join her group. She sensed his relief. Although he was older and always confident and assured in his professional capacity this was an unfamiliar setting for him and Libby felt some sympathy. From the stage Billy had noted the exchange and he frowned as he jumped from the platform and strode towards them, just as Doctor Ritchie invited Libby to dance and swept her expertly on to the floor.

'I expect you feel a bit peckish if you've been working late. June Appleby is through the back dealing with the refreshments,' Libby said, glancing up at him with a mischievous smile.

251

'I'll take you through if you like?'

Steve Ritchie gasped softly. His eyebrows rose and he shook his head despairingly. 'Should I assume the Darlonachie grapevine has been working overtime where I'm concerned, Elizabeth?'

Libby's brown eyes twinkled. Although she was not yet seventeen she was perfectly at ease when surrounded by familiar faces but she sensed the young doctor was as vulnerable as anyone else when it came to personal relationships.

'Maybe,' she teased. 'Anyway June is very popular and a good organizer. This is her last year in the Young Farmers and we shall miss her.' The music ended and Steve Ritchie seized Libby's hand.

'Lead on then, Elizabeth. I'm more convinced than ever you would make an excellent nurse. You're both observant and understanding.'

Billy had been dancing but he saw Libby leave the hall with the doctor and he was surprised at his own feeling of unease. Libby was so friendly but she was still young and innocent. Surely a man in Doctor Ritchie's position wouldn't dare take advantage?

'Come on, old man,' Mick nudged him. 'You look as though you've lost a sixpence and found a penny. How about asking those two lasses over there to dance? Do you know them?'

'I was at school with the wee dark-haired one. You ask her, I'll ask the other one.' He knew his attention was distracted until he saw Libby returning to the hall. She was alone.

'It will be coming up for the last dance soon,' his partner said hopefully, wondering if he would offer to see her home.

'Is it that time already?' Billy made his mind up and as soon as the music stopped he made a beeline for Libby.

'You haven't danced with me yet tonight,' he said.

'You haven't asked me!' Libby retorted indignantly.

'Well I'm asking you now.'

'Oh? Is that what you call asking?'

'Oh, come on, Libby.' He took her hand and drew her on to the floor. She felt she ought to resist but she wanted to dance with Billy. She realized she had been waiting subconsciously for him all evening. Watching them, Mick sucked in his cheeks and winked at Billy.

'Don't forget I'm having the last dance and taking her home,' he called.

'Like hell you are,' Billy muttered. Libby was close enough to hear. 'I thought this was the last dance anyway,' he added.

'Not quite.' She knew Billy had manoeuvred their steps to end up as far away from Mick and his friends as possible when the dance ended and he kept a firm grip on her arm.

'We may as well stay together for this one,' he said.

'You're so charming, the way you ask,' Libby said dryly.

'Aren't I just,' Billy murmured. 'There's no

use beating about the bush when I know what I want.' His arm tightened as the music began for the last selection.

'But it doesn't mean to say it's what I want,' Libby said.

'Come on, Libby, we've known each other too long to have any pretence between us. I'll see you home.'

'But Mick brought us, Grace and Miriam and me. He's expecting to take us all home.'

'I know, and drop you off last no doubt.' He nodded sagely.

'Well, what's wrong in that? I thought Mick was your best friend?'

'He is. I know him well – too well,' he added darkly. 'I can guess what he has in mind. Sweet sixteen and never been kissed. That's what he believes and he would like to remedy that.'

Libby was glad the lights had dimmed when she felt her cheeks flush. Billy was a good dancer and she gave herself up to the pleasure of the music and the strength of his arms, but it had been a very long day and she struggled to stifle a yawn.

'Tired?' Billy asked softly. 'Or bored?'

Libby smiled up at him. 'Whatever else you might be, Billy Lennox, you're never boring.'

'Thank the Lord for that small mercy then.'

'I do wish you weren't so bitter and brittle,' Libby sighed.

Billy was silent for a while, but the words seemed to be drawn out against his will. 'To tell the truth I'm a bit worried about Mother. She looks so tired and she doesn't seem to have any energy.' He swore softly. 'I must be mad, spending the last dance of the evening with a lovely girl in my arms, and I talk about my worries.'

'That's what friends are for, Billy. We've all been a bit concerned about Aunt Maggie but she brushes her ailments aside most of the time, even with my mother.'

'I'm glad we're still friends then,' he said softly and laid his cheek against her hair as the music gradually came to an end.

Billy and his friends waited outside the hall while the girls collected their coats but as soon as they appeared he grabbed Libby's arm.

'I'll see Libby home. You can take the rest in your car, Mick.'

'But that's crazy!' Mick protested. 'I brought the lasses so I'll take them home. There's no point in taking two cars up to Langmune.'

'Mick's right, Billy,' Libby said.

'No, he isn't. We've things to talk about.' He ushered her towards his car and opened the door.

'You could at least give Libby a choice,' Mick said. 'You come with me, love. Old Mick will look after you.'

'Get in,' Billy insisted. Libby raised her eyes heavenwards.

'He was always bossy. You might at least ask what I want...' But Billy slammed the door shut and hurried round to the driver's side.

'I'll see you in the morning, Mick.' He grinned triumphantly. Mick watched them draw away, shaking his head.

'I thought they'd fallen out when Libby stopped writing to him. He was like a bear with a sore head for months.'

'Oh, he's always looked after Libby like a big brother,' Grace assured him nonchalantly, 'and their parents are friends. I expect he's protecting her from you lot.' She grinned.

'Big brother, ugh?' Mick scoffed. 'I'm not so sure that's the way he feels about young Elizabeth Pringle considering the scowls he sent my way every time I danced with her.' He gave a wicked chuckle. 'Of course he probably doesn't know what's biting him yet. Our Billy's a mixed-up kid. Half the girls in our club in Yorkshire have fallen for him.'

'Are ye meaning love is blind, or whatever it is they say?' Grace shrugged. 'I dinna ken about Billy but I reckon Libby's a bit young for love yet. She's looking forward to going to college soon. I'll bet she'll enjoy herself then. I know I would.'

'Come on love, jump in. We can enjoy ourselves without going to college, can't we boys?' Laughingly they all crammed into the car and set off towards Langmune in Billy's wake.

'D'you folks in Yorkshire call everybody love?' Miriam asked. 'Even when you're mad at them?'

'I suppose we do,' Pete chuckled. 'I never thought about it before, Miriam love.'

Billy drew the car to a halt outside the house at Langmune. 'It's a good job the blackout is over.

I think I see a chink of light from your kitchen window, Libby.'

'Yes,' she sighed, 'I told Mum there was no need to wait up but I expect she has.'

'She's probably dozing in front of the Aga. Just stay to talk a wee while.' He looked up at the sky. It was almost a full moon. 'It's a lovely night. We should get a fine day for travelling back tomorrow.' He stretched his long legs and slid his arm along the back of the seats but he made no effort to embrace her and Libby was glad. She was not ready for things like that yet. Sometimes she wondered whether she ever would be. 'I've missed getting all the news from you, Libby. I hope we can be friends again. Maybe you'll send me a letter now and again when you get to college? Tell me how you're doing and what your course is like?'

'Of course I will, if you're interested. I didn't think you were...'

'Well I am,' Billy said firmly. 'I remember I was terribly homesick for the first few weeks when I first went to college,' he mused.

'Were you, Billy? I didn't think you'd ever been homesick in your life.'

'Well I don't know whether I was homesick exactly but I remember everything was strange and I missed Mick and the friends I'd made in Yorkshire and I missed the chats with your Uncle Willie, and our walks over the hill.' He grinned. 'And I missed you.' He turned to look at her. 'So send me your address and I'll write to you.' He frowned thoughtfully. 'I never really thought of Charlotte Crainby as my family but I suppose she is really, even if we are almost strangers. She is my half-sister whether we like what our father did or not. Do you ever see her around?'

'No. I hardly know her. She went to boarding school in England at the time you moved to the Academy in Dumfries. She doesn't come back to Darlonachie very often but there were rumours that she was ill with tuberculosis and she had gone to Switzerland. Other people said she had gone to a finishing school there.' Libby hesitated for a moment then she added in a rush, 'You know, I don't suppose she liked all that stuff in the papers about her father any more than you did. It was bound to affect her too.'

'Well it was her mother who caused it all and supplied the fodder for the scandal.' Billy sounded indignant.

'I know. My mother says she was always a nasty woman. It wasn't Charlotte's fault. Mr Ross, who has the grocer's shop in Darlonachie, says she's turned into a really nice girl and she reminds him of her father. He never liked Mrs Crainby. Miss Phipps said much the same to Mum, and Doctor Grantly must have had a long talk with her on one of her visits home because he said she was turning out just like her father and he felt sorry for her having to live with Henrietta Crainby and it was just as well she had to return to Switzerland. He's too professional to discuss a patient's affairs but Mum got the impression that she was staying in a clinic there.'

'Sounds as though she may have tuberculosis then,' Billy mused.

'When Littleburn Farm was sold last year Mrs Crainby put word around that the money was needed to pay for her daughter's stay in Switzerland but everybody in Darlonachie says she's just extravagant.' Libby hesitated.

Billy was watching her intently. 'Go on, tell me what you were going to say,' he prompted with a note of his old irritation. 'I'm sure it can't be any worse than all that gossip in the papers.'

'Why do you always think everything affects you, Billy?' Libby sighed heavily. 'There's a whole world out there which goes along very well without a thought for you, or me. I was going to tell you about my father's plans. You're going back to Yorkshire tomorrow, I suppose, so you're not likely to tell anyone in Darlonachie, least of all Mrs Crainby.'

'You can be sure about that,' Billy said darkly.

'The remaining farms on Darlonachie Estate are all up for sale. Rumour has it that the castle is to be demolished to save paying rates, but the land and the gardens will be to sell, everything except the house Mrs Crainby lives in and the gardens and paddock belonging to it.'

'Surely not!' Billy was shocked. 'I thought the land was in trust for her daughter, though I suppose Charlotte will have no authority to make decisions yet. If it's the same as the trust for Home Farm she'll not be able to take over the estate, either to keep it or sell it, until she's twenty-five.'

Libby stared at Billy but his face looked strange and shadowy in the moonlight. A shiver passed over her. Is that what he was waiting for? Was he planning to sell Home Farm as soon as it came into his possession? Is that why he hadn't returned to the glen? Was he never coming back here to live?

Nineteen

'So, Libby? What were you going to tell me about your father?'

'Och, if you're not intending to return you'll not be interested in what's happening around here.' Libby's voice was sharp.

'I'm always interested to hear what your family are doing.'

'Mmm. Well, Father is going to try and buy Throstlebrae Farm. It lies alongside the bottom end of Langmune and faces the south-west, but he is hoping to do it through a solicitor. He thinks if Mrs Crainby hears he is interested she'll sell it to anyone else but him, even at a lower price.'

'I don't understand how she is allowed to do what she wants, even if she is Charlotte's mother and her main trustee. Surely my father would appoint a solicitor as trustee as well, especially when he knew Henrietta was a spend-thrift.'

'I think he did but the man who took over from Mr Jenkinson seems to go along with whatever she suggests. My father says she probably convinces him that Charlotte needs the money more than the land. Father has got a solicitor in

Dumfries to do the negotiating. He hopes Mrs Crainby will not realize he is the purchaser until the final papers are signed.'

'Langmune must be paying very well if your father can afford to buy another farm.'

'Not that well. My parents are borrowing the money from the bank and Langmune will be used as security again. Mother thinks it is a big gamble. They could lose everything if things go badly, but Father thinks he'll never get another chance as good as this. Throstlebrae is so well situated and convenient to Langmune, and all the estate farms are to be sold together, mainly to the existing tenants. He says it's a case of supply and demand and the quantity of land will never increase. He reckons it will be safe so long as he can work and make the repayments and the interest to the bank.'

'I see. Well neither Mrs Crainby nor her daughter are interested in making money from farming their land so maybe the money will be more use. I did hear rumours that the trustees were not maintaining the farms very well.'

'That's true. They don't do any repairs at all and the farms are becoming run down.'

'Is Throstlebrae Farm in a poor state of repair then?

'Yes, it will need a lot of improvements but Father thinks the government will continue to guarantee prices to food producers until Britain and Europe recover from the effects of the war and food becomes plentiful again. He says the country can't afford to have continual demands for wage increases so the government are trying to keep the price of food low by controlling supplies and guaranteeing prices to the farmers for the essentials.'

'Well that's true enough. Mick's father keeps increasing his yields of wheat every year but the Ministry still want more so he gets subsidies for fertilizer and lime. He rears a lot of bullocks though so we get plenty of manure as well. He's a good farmer, but different to the farmers in this area. It's good experience for me,' he added earnestly, or was that a defensive note? Libby wondered. She sighed.

'Well I hope the politicians don't change their minds all of a sudden. Father is hoping he will pay off the bank loan for Throstlebrae in twenty years and by then Fraser and Lachie will be ready for a farm each.'

'And what about you, Libby? You're as keen on the farm as your brothers, maybe even keener.'

'You know very well farmers only consider their sons when it comes to setting them up in farms of their own ... Anyway it's late, past my bedtime.'

'So it is.' Billy turned towards her and clasped her chin, scanning her face in the moonlight. 'Sweet sixteen and never been kissed,' he murmured softly. Libby opened her mouth to protest but he bent his head and covered it with his own. It was not a passionate kiss but it was enough to cause an unfamiliar clenching of her muscles and a yearning for more. She sensed it was a questioning, exploring kiss for Billy. He lifted his head and his fingers trailed gently down her cheek. 'Good night, little Libby. Don't forget to write to me sometimes when you get to college.'

'All right,' she said huskily and hurried towards the house, knowing her cheeks were burning and her heart was beating faster than usual. She hoped her mother would be asleep in the chair and not wanting to ask questions tonight. She wanted to hurry to the privacy of her room and hug herself. She would have denied it but Billy was right, it was her first real kiss.

At the end of September, with the harvest safely in, Libby packed her trunk for college. There was the requisite green dairy dresses, white aprons and caps, to be worn when making butter and cheese, the wellingtons, cream milking coat and cap for milking, and the white coats for the chemistry and bacteriology laboratories. In addition she had to take her own sheets and pillowcases and towels as well as her usual clothes.

'Are you sure you've got everything?' Victoria asked as Libby closed and locked the trunk ready to be sent by train. A few days later she followed on the train herself to start her new life at college.

Everything was so new and strange and there were so many rules. The girl students were in a hostel set apart from the main lecture rooms and the accommodation for the men students. The matron made it very plain that the two were never to mix, lights were to be out by ten o'clock and students must be prompt at meal times. Beds must be made before breakfast and turned up to air every Monday until midday; the sheets and towels must be changed and put out for the laundry once a fortnight. She would personally inspect rooms regularly.

During the first few weeks Libby felt like running away several times. She was dreadfully homesick. She wrote regularly to her parents and she tried to keep her letters cheerful. She had resolved she would not resume a regular correspondence with Billy but after a particularly discouraging week she found it oddly comforting to write to her old childhood friend. She was surprised and delighted when he replied almost immediately. He reminded her again how homesick he had been and somehow Libby felt better.

There were only ten girls studying the same course as her but there were more than twice as many male students. There were plenty of other girls around the college studying for diplomas in horticulture and poultry. Gradually they got to know each other. Her own group were a friendly bunch with the exception of one girl named Hilda. She was quiet and studious and didn't seem inclined to be sociable. She had a permanently watchful air, listening intently to conversations but never joining in, yet she was almost insistent when it came to answering questions and joining in discussions with lecturers. She was two years older than Libby and had studied chemistry at a more advanced level. Libby was struggling to catch up but Hilda showed no inclination to help her. On the other hand she did not come from a farming background so she found some of the lectures difficult to understand. She badgered Libby and two of her friends for explanations.

'She's a taker, but never a giver that one,' Libby's friend, Alma, declared darkly. 'Have you noticed how she demands the lecturers' attention and tries to make a favourable impression?'

''Course we've noticed. She'd trample the rest of us into the tattie field if she could,' Alice Armstrong chuckled. 'Her daddy is a member of parliament and before that he was some kind of big wig in finance. I can't imagine why she wants to study dairying.'

'Probably fancies herself managing some big estate and marrying the owner,' Alma said dryly.

Libby looked forward to her mother's weekly letters. Victoria was a good correspondent and she'd guessed Libby was missing everybody.

'It seems unlikely that we shall be able to buy Throstlebrae Farm after all,' she wrote at the end of November. 'All the farms have been withdrawn.'

The sale of Darlonachie Estate was not as straightforward as Henrietta Crainby had anticipated. Not for the first time she cursed her late husband for putting everything in trust for Charlotte and leaving her, his wife, with an annual income. She considered it a pittance, although it would have kept half the families in Darlonachie in food and clothes.

Charlotte had changed when she went away to boarding school, but it was nothing to the more recent metamorphosis that had occurred during her sojourn in the Swiss clinic where she was recovering from tuberculosis.

When money had been required for her daughter's education, and even more so when her life had seemed in danger, Henrietta had had no difficulty persuading Mr Whyte it was in Charlotte's interest to sell some of the farms in the trust to buy the best care available. She would never admit it suited her to send her daughter as far away as possible when the tuberculosis was diagnosed. She abhorred illness, and more so if there was the slightest risk to her own health. Neither would she have acknowledged that the bulk of the money so far had gone to provide her own home comforts, not to mention extravagant clothes and visits to London and abroad. She had enjoyed more than a little flutter in the casinos of Monte Carlo when she was supposed to be visiting the Swiss clinic. None of her activities had brought Henrietta either friends or contentment. Happiness was not a word she understood and frustration caused her to seek release in alcohol.

Months passed while one legal point after another prevented the sale of the remaining farms. Henrietta's money supply dwindled and debts piled higher. Charlotte was making an excellent recovery and the solicitor felt, belatedly, that her interests should be protected. Like Andrew Pringle he believed land was a solid and secure asset. He tried to explain this to Mrs Crainby but without success.

When the summer of 1954 came round Libby could scarcely believe she had completed her first year at college and was halfway through her course. There was a wide variety of interesting subjects, but the microbiology lectures were totally absorbing. It seemed incredible that anything so small could cause such destruction, and even death. It was hard to believe an anthrax spore could lie hidden in the soil for a hundred years then cause the death of one of her father's cattle without warning. The microscope opened up a whole new world to her.

Meanwhile Charlotte Crainby had reached a decision about her own future. She wanted to become a teacher. The idea that her daughter wanted to work, insisted on earning her own living, was preposterous to Henrietta. Not only did she want to teach young children, she wanted to teach those who were ill or in some way deprived of ordinary education by their disabilities. Henrietta declared the idea outrageous.

'You would be no more than a governess, less than that even.'

'No, Mother. I aim to be a great deal better than the governesses you employed to teach me,' Charlotte stated firmly. 'I was less equipped for school than the poorest child on the estate, and yet you sent me to the same school as them.'

'That's nonsense. It was that old teacher who was stupid.'

'No, Mr Nelson was far from stupid. Anyway I am twenty-two years old and it is irrelevant whether you approve or not. I have been for an interview. I am to start at a training college near Glasgow in the autumn.' Charlotte smiled to herself and wondered what her mother would say if she knew one of the men who had interviewed her was the youngest son of her father's gardener, Joe Pringle. He hadn't known her, of course. She often used her middle name of Laine since all the horrid publicity appeared in the newspapers. Laine had been her paternal grandmother's maiden name and Charlotte rather liked it. In Switzerland the nurses at the clinic had called her Lottie Laine and she had liked that even better.

She had been incredibly nervous at the interview, aware that the standard of her education was lower than many of the other applicants, in spite of her time at boarding school. She knew now it had been a very mediocre school, no doubt due to her mother's scrimping so that she could spend the money on herself. Teachers were in demand since the war so the standards of entry had been lowered, which was fortunate for her. One of the older interviewers had been stern and abrupt and she was sure he did not consider her good enough, but Mr Pringle had smiled kindly and put her at her ease, encouraging her to talk of her aspirations to teach sick children. He had seemed genuinely interested and she was doubly glad she had not used the name Crainby. She barely remembered her father and she hoped he would forgive her for denying his name. Of course she would have to use it on any official documents, so Mr Pringle would find out her true identity then.

But Josh had no reason to connect the pale, delicate-looking young woman with the Crainby family. He had been more intrigued by her desire to teach sick children and when he realized she had recently recovered from the dreaded tuberculosis he understood her desire and considered it a worthy calling. He thought of his young niece, Mimi. Just because she was a cripple it didn't mean she was not capable of learning, or that she did not need education. Indeed it was possible she would need it more than other girls. It was unlikely that she would marry, so she would need to earn her living. Physically she would never be as strong and agile as other young women, so all the more reason to give her every opportunity to learn.

Josh almost missed his train that Friday afternoon so he was panting as he hauled himself into the carriage just in time. When he recovered his breath and composed himself he sat back in his seat to survey his fellow passengers. He was surprised to see the pale features of Miss Charlotte Laine in the same compartment. He tried to draw her into conversation. She answered his questions politely but she did not ask any of her own. There was something about her that intrigued him. He attributed her reticence to the fact that she would soon be one of his students and she was mindful of his position of authority. Even so he felt oddly disappointed when she left the train at Dumfries while he continued on to Annan where he would catch a bus to Darlonachie. A brisk walk from the village would take him to his parents' cottage in time for a hearty supper.

Josh had never lacked female company. He had a friendly personality and his tall slim figure and RAF uniform had added to his attraction. Normally he was not easily distracted by young women but he found himself haunted by the pale, almost luminous face of Charlotte Laine. He reminded himself that she would soon be just another of his students, even if she was a little older than the rest.

Libby returned home for the long summer holiday. She worked at Langmune, revelling in the freedom from Matron's rules and happy to be home. Even Fraser seemed pleased to have her there in spite of the usual sibling rivalry, and Lachlan followed her around like a lost sheep. She had missed her younger brother more than she had realized. She visited Mimi often at High Bowie and Lachie usually accompanied her.

Twice during the summer Billy returned from Yorkshire but his visits were disappointingly brief and he never repeated the kiss. On his second visit to the glen he confided that he had been offered a job as under manager on a fairly large estate a few miles from the farm where Mick lived.

'It's a good opportunity,' he said abruptly. 'I'm going up to High Bowie this afternoon. I might talk it over with your Uncle Willie if I get a chance.'

'Uncle Willie? What has it to do with him?' Libby asked in surprise.

'Why nothing, I suppose, but he's a man and he usually gives sound advice.' He shrugged in the way she hated. 'You may have noticed I don't have too many men in my family to discuss things. I never had a father to talk things over with, so I don't know what he would have wanted.' The bleakness was back in his voice, the brittleness in his manner. Libby wanted to tell him he was luckier than many who had lost their fathers during the war. His father had tried to provide for him and he didn't seem to appreciate that at all. She didn't want to argue with him again so she remained silent. He strode away.

Willie and Billy had climbed almost to the highest point of High Bowie before Billy finally began to talk about the job he had been offered. Willie turned to him in surprise.

'Surely if ye're ready to manage an estate ye're ready to take over Home Farm, Billy?'

'I wouldn't be managing exactly. As under manager I shall be working with, and supervising the men and liaising between them and

272

the manager.'

'But surely you could do that at Home Farm?'

'You mean work under Fergus?'

'Oh no, you'll be Fergus's boss if you're coming back for good.'

'Fergus wouldn't like that after being in charge. He'll not want to give up for years yet. He's been a good man for my mother, but I don't think we should agree very well and I don't want to upset things. There's been enough trouble and gossip surrounding my family as it is.'

'Why wouldn't you and Fergus agree? He's not a bad fellow and you've done what your Grandfather Crainby advised – been away, worked for a boss, learned about different ways of farming.'

'That's it exactly. Fergus is a good worker, I know that, but ... but he's never moved on. He doesna want anything to change, Willie.'

'Surely you could make changes gradually? He'd come round, wouldn't he?'

'I'm not so sure.'

'What sort of changes d'ye have in mind anyway, laddie?' Willie pulled out his pipe and prepared to light up.

'Oh, nothing major, at least not yet, not until I see the farm is paying. But there's some things need to change. Yesterday, for instance, I saw Fergus putting the bull into the yard to serve a cow. He's a good bull, well bred. I know that,' Billy said emphatically, 'but he's a bloody bad-tempered bull and he'd go for you if he got a chance, and he's old. They've used him enough. It's time they got rid of him. I don't know how Fergus manages him on his own. I went to help get the bull in and it was not easy, even with two of us and a pitchfork each.'

'What did Fergus say?'

'He laughed, not cocky or anything. That's not his nature. He's a nice fellow doing his best to please my mother and keep the place running. It would be easier if he was an arrogant so and so.' Billy gave a wry smile. 'Anyway I suggested we get a bull pen built, like the one at Langmune.'

'Aye, Andrew made a good job of that and I know it's eased Victoria's mind. She didn't like him working with the bull on his own.'

'No, well that's another thing. I told Fergus he should always have one of the other men there to help him and it would be a good thing to replace the bull before he did any damage.'

'Did he agree?'

'No. He said he'd worked with animals all his life and none had beaten him yet. It's all in the handling of 'em, he said, and I'd soon learn that men weren't always available when the cow was ready to stand to the bull. I told him that was all the more reason to get a bull pen built, and until that could be done he should use one of the younger bulls and send that one for slaughter.'

'That seems fair enough.'

'Not to Fergus. He said a bull pen was just a waste of money and there was no need for one. He brushed the whole thing aside and more or less told me it was college boy's talk.'

'I see.' Willie frowned thoughtfully.

'I mentioned it to Mother. She said she had already told Fergus never to let the bull out if he was on his own. She has heard him roaring and pawing the ground on previous occasions. But of course she doesn't want to quarrel with Fergus over that and she said I should just leave things as they are. I didn't argue with her. She looks so tired and drained most of the time I hadn't the heart to upset her. But don't you see, even if I came home, that's just how things would be? I'd probably be so frustrated I'd end up having a row with Fergus. Then Mother would be really upset.'

'Mmm, it's difficult.' Willie frowned thoughtfully. 'I can't really help ye, laddie. I see your point of view, but I don't think your mother is keeping as well as she ought to be and I'd like to see you coming back to Darlonachie.'

They moved on, walking in companionable silence. They were descending the hill when Billy spoke again.

'Do you think Libby will return to Darlonachie next year, when she's finished at college?'

'I don't know, laddie.' Willie looked at him. 'I certainly hope she will. Mimi misses her. She thinks there's nobody like her cousin, Libby. She was fair heartbroken when Tommy died. Libby had her on him every day when she was at home. I'll bet she shed a few tears as well when she got Mary's letter with Mimi's drawing of Tommy.'

'We should look out for another pony if it

275

gives Mimi so much pleasure. It would have to be quiet but the exercise must be good for her I suppose. Maybe Libby will come back to Darlonachie if she can find a suitable job in the area.' He stopped and looked Willie in the eye. 'Thanks for listening to me. I've decided what I'll do. I shall take the under manager's job but I'll tell them it is on a year's trial. Maybe if I learn something about managing men I shall feel able to come back to Home Farm and manage the men there, including Fergus, without offending him.' He gave a wry grin, but he felt better for reaching a decision.

'Oh aye, a year's trial, eh?' Willie said dryly, his eyes twinkling, 'And that wouldna have anything to do with whether Libby comes back in a year's time, eh?'

'Of course not,' Billy denied a bit too quickly and Willie chuckled.

Libby felt the summer vacation had flown by but she knew what to expect now and she had made some good friends so she felt more enthusiastic as she prepared to return to college. During the first year the foundations had been laid for all the subjects and she was looking forward to applying the chemistry and the bacteriology.

'You don't just learn about making rations for the different classes of stock then?' Andrew asked with interest.

'Oh no, but you can tell Mum –' she grinned mischievously – 'we do have to be pretty good

276

at maths to work out the percentages of proteins and starches and roughage in different crops and cereals. We have to balance them and cost them too.'

'Mmm, well we haven't had any choice since the war but all that should come in useful now that cereals and fishmeal are becoming more plentiful. You'll be able to advise me.'

'You would find the bacteriology interesting too, Dad. I think you should send Fraser to college,' she grinned, catching her brother's eye, 'then he would see how important it is to wash his hands occasionally.' She ducked as Fraser threw a cushion at her head. 'It's true. We were amazed when we put a hair on a sterile plate of agar and saw the bugs grow, and the same with our fingerprints. Every one of the bacteria which gets into the milk will multiply every twenty minutes unless the temperature of the milk is really cold. So, little brother, that's why Dad keeps telling you to take care in the dairy. We learn about the different kinds of mastitis as well, and the bacteria which cause other illnesses in humans and animals. We have to learn to identify them under the microscope this term before we can pass our final exam.'

'You sound as though you're enjoying that side of things as much as the farming aspect,' Andrew said.

'We have a really good lecturer, Miss Cuttle, who is so enthusiastic she makes most of us want to know more. Of course we have practical things as well. We take turns at getting up in the mornings to milk the cows, or feed pigs or calves. We have a rota and do each task for a week. We all make butter and cheese once a week so we need the chemistry and the bacteriology for that side of dairying too. Two of the boys want to be creamery managers eventually but they all have to do two years' national service before they can get a job.'

'What about accounts?' Victoria asked. 'I would like somebody to relieve me of that chore.' She looked pointedly at Andrew but he gave her his usual heart-stopping grin.

'You make such an excellent job, m'dear. Do you learn how to do accounts, Libby?'

'Yes, and costing different enterprises. We have finished the course for now but we have to pass an exam in the finals. We do economics this year. "Land, labour and capital",' she chanted, 'they're the three limiting factors to expansion in farming.'

'Is that right?' Andrew frowned, considering it. 'I suppose it is. Well it doesn't look as though we're going to get the chance to buy more land near Langmune. Everybody seems to think the solicitor who is trustee has called a halt to prevent Mrs Crainby selling off any more of her daughter's inheritance.'

'Throstlebrae will be to sell one day,' Victoria said. 'It's common knowledge Darlonachie Estate is run down. Mrs Crainby has dismissed the factor. No repairs have been done for years, according to the farmers' wives who come to the WRI meetings. It will give us more time to build up some capital. As for the labour, we're rearing our own if these two boys ever learn to be tidy workers.' She raised an eyebrow at Fraser.

'Aw, Ma, don't you start on me,' he pleaded, giving the limpid smile which always twisted Victoria's heart. It reminded her of the way Mark used to smile when they were exploring together behind Darlonachie Castle in the school holidays. She was unaware that she had the same beguiling smile as her twin. She sighed now. It all seemed such a long time ago.

'Victoria?' Andrew prompted. 'You were miles away.'

'Was I? Sorry.'

'Thinking about Mark?' he asked softly. 'I can always tell.'

Charlotte Crainby was looking forward to starting at college. She had returned from Switzerland to spend three weeks with her mother before she embarked on her teacher-training course. It had been exceedingly grim. When her mother was not in a drunken stupor she nagged constantly. She was unable to accept that Charlotte was now twenty-three and had a mind of her own.

'It will cost money to keep you in Glasgow,' Henrietta whined.

'It will cost money to keep me wherever I live until I have some training and can earn my own living,' Charlotte said reasonably, or at least she thought she was being reasonable until her mother flew into an uncontrollable rage. The

279

gist of it seemed to be that her mother was not only short of money but that she was also in debt to all and sundry. Charlotte was tempted to tell her to stop spending so much money on drink. Not only would she be better off but she would have a clearer head for sorting out their affairs. She sighed and held her tongue, as she had learned to do years ago when her nanny had been dismissed suddenly and there was no one to shield her.

'Your allowance will be due at the end of the month and the rents will be coming in at the end of November,' she said soothingly. Henrietta made a rude snort and muttered a string of oaths. Charlotte looked up at the ceiling for divine inspiration. She had no idea how to handle her mother when she was in one of her alcohol-induced depressions. 'I don't mind if you need to use some of the cash from the rents, Mother, especially now you have dispensed with a factor and you're doing the estate work yourself. Will there be many repairs needed this time?'

'Repairs! You're as bad as your bloody father. That's all he thought about, what the bloody tenants needed. He never considered what I needed.'

'I was thinking of other things, Mother. I would like some of the money from my trust fund to rent a flat. Most of the students will be younger than I am and I know I shall need to work hard to keep up. I ... er ... I thought if I had a flat I might stay there some of the weekends if you don't mind.' Charlotte knew she could never cope with returning home every weekend with her mother flying into a temper or in an alcoholic daze.

Henrietta's eyes narrowed. It irked her having Charlotte under her feet, watching her, just as Luke used to do. She never quite knew whether their blue eyes registered pity or contempt. She pushed herself away from the heap of crumpled cushions and sat up.

'I'll tell that bloody solicitor you need the money for lodgings. He'll have to get it one way or another. He always says your welfare is a priority, that you must be taken care of.'

'I don't need taken care of, Mother. I only want to rent a flat and have a space of my own,' Charlotte said, exasperated.

'Leave it to me,' Henrietta said more brightly. She would tell the solicitor Charlotte wanted enough money to buy a flat. She could use the money herself and pay the rent every month, at least in the beginning. After that it would just have to become another addition to her list of creditors. Neither her daughter nor the miserable little lawyer need know the truth.

Twenty

Libby did well in her exams at Christmas and even better at Easter. She never mentioned her success in her letters to Billy but it was generally expected, both by her fellow students and the lecturers, that she would gain her diploma with flying colours and win some of the prizes for students who excel in their particular year. Ever since she arrived at college, Hilda Aspinall had set her sights on outshining the rest of her group. During the first year she had succeeded but much of the second-year work was new. It was all applied to the production of milk and farming, the manufacture of dairy products, plus the science affecting such things as quality or health or deterioration. She was gradually falling behind. Libby worked hard too but she was a popular student, always willing to help, swap duties, or fill in when someone needed a favour. She joined in the social evenings, especially the dances, but Hilda rarely joined in anything.

'Did you see her face when the results went up?' Alice chuckled at the end of the Easter term. Her bedroom was next to Libby's and they had been friends almost from the beginning. She made no secret of her dislike for Hilda. 'Matron favours her,' she had declared early on when they discovered the MP's daughter had been allocated the bedroom on the other side of Libby's. It was the best since it was at the end of the corridor and had a window looking out on to the grounds and the playing fields, instead of a view of the roof of the annex and the dustbins like the rest of the girls' bedrooms. Hilda was also next to the fire escape and she policed it well. None of the girls risked coming in that way after lights out if they had failed to gain a late pass. This required special permission from Matron and it always involved a stern interrogation, unless your name was Hilda Aspinall. Her parents only lived twenty miles away and sometimes she was allowed to visit during term time if they were holding one of their prestigious dinner parties. She never invited any of the other students to accompany her.

Libby had accepted the regulations as part of her new life at college but there were constant grumbles about Matron being too strict from those who had lived away from home during their pre-college farming year. They had tasted freedom and regarded most of Miss Fanshaw's rules as petty.

Alice turned to Libby with a grin as they studied the results before leaving to catch their respective trains for the Easter vacation.

'She was really meaning to beat you this time, Libby, that's why she didn't come to the end of term dance. She was swotting up for the crops exam.'

'I can't see that it matters so long as we all get our Diplomas.' Libby shrugged. 'They are what count and most of us seem likely to pass.'

Charlotte was finding her course at teacher-training college a stiff challenge but she was determined to work hard and she was managing to hold her own. She needed time and peace to study and it had been a relief when she found a small flat not too far from the college. Twice when she had travelled home for the weekend she had seen Josh on the same train. She guessed he spent a lot of his weekends with his parents. She couldn't remember much about the Pringles because her mother had never allowed her to mix with anyone who worked on the estate.

'Your father mixed too freely with labourers and their brats,' she had sneered. 'No daughter of mine will mix with such people.' Then without warning she had dismissed the governess and sent her to the village school where most of the children had some connection with the estate or the village. She had been the odd one out, unwilling or unable to mix naturally, and dismayed to find the children of her own age all knew far more than she did. Even now Charlotte shook her head at her mother's illogical actions.

Billy arrived home unexpectedly for Easter weekend and Victoria invited him and Maggie to Langmune for Sunday lunch. Willie and Mary came too with Mimi, but Joe and Polly elected to stay at home.

'Joe likes a wee rest after his dinner,' Polly said. 'He tires easily these days. You're a good lassie, Victoria, inviting us all.'

'You know you're the only family I have, or need,' Victoria smiled, 'and you're always welcome. Josh too if he wants to come.'

'I'll tell him. He'll probably take a walk up to see you all in the afternoon.' She frowned. 'We had a bit of an argument the last time he was home.'

'You and Josh? I can't believe it.' Victoria stared at Polly's lined face. Joe wasn't the only one who had aged recently.

'One of his students is Mrs Crainby's daughter. She's older than the others. It was true about her having tuberculosis. She spent a long time in a clinic in Sweden, or was it Switzerland Josh said? It doesn't matter anyway. Josh is giving her extra help to catch up.' Polly pursed her lips disapprovingly. 'He reckons he didn't know she was a Crainby at first because she calls herself Charlotte Laine these days. That was her grandmother's maiden name, you know.'

'No, I didn't know that, but why would she pretend?'

'I dinna ken,' Polly shrugged her thin shoulders huffily. 'Josh only discovered when he was looking through the student files to fill in reports.'

'Didn't he ask her?' Victoria asked curiously.

'He said he hadn't had the right opportunity to

approach the subject yet,' Polly enunciated clearly, imitating Josh. 'But you know how soft-hearted Josh is. He'd help a snake if it was in trouble, and that's just what they are, Henrietta Crainby and her daughter, venomous.'

'Maybe the girl is more like her father?' Victoria suggested tentatively, knowing how bitter Polly was regarding Henrietta Crainby and anyone belonging to her. 'Mr Ross, the grocer, said she had grown into a pleasant young lady.'

'I'm surprised you can say anything good about a girl with a mother like Henrietta Crainby. She treated you abominably and you were little more than a bairn. Cruel she was. I shall never forgive her.'

'They're not worth getting upset about,' Victoria said gently and put an arm around her mother-in-law's bent shoulders. Polly seemed to be shrinking, she thought with dismay. Both of Andrew's parents were growing old and frail. 'Please don't worry about Mrs Crainby on my account. Luke Crainby more than made up for her with his generosity over Langmune. Andrew and I will always be grateful to him. As for Josh, he's seen more of life than most of us so I'm sure he'll not be easily duped.'

There was no opportunity at Easter for Libby and Billy to spend time alone together.

'I have to return tomorrow,' he explained, 'even though it is Easter Monday. Now that I'm a manager I have to set a good example.' He grinned.

'Eh, laddie, you dinna look old enough to be managing a button box, let alone an estate,' Willie teased.

'How do you like your new job, Billy?' Andrew asked and the men fell to discussing farming and its changing patterns.

Just before the Easter vacation was over Libby saw an advertisement in the local paper for a job in a new laboratory which was being built at one of the local creameries.

'Do you think they'd consider me? Do you think I'd have enough experience? Do you think they would think I'm too young?' she asked excitedly.

'You'll never know if you don't try,' Victoria smiled.

'It would be ideal, lassie,' Andrew said with enthusiasm. 'You would have a job and still be able to live at home.'

'And no doubt get roped in to lend a hand.' Victoria nodded sagely. 'There's no harm in asking though, Libby, but you haven't got much time before you return to college.'

'Why not telephone and explain your situation?' Andrew urged.

Libby followed her father's advice and was eventually put through to the creamery manager, a Mr Whittaker. He asked a few questions and explained that the advertisement would be appearing in the national press over the next two weeks so he would be unable to make a decision until all the applications were in but he could see her the day before she returned to college if she cared to come for an interview.

'He didn't sound very enthusiastic,' Libby said nervously.

'I expect they're advertising now to get the pick of the students who will be leaving college this summer.' Andrew nodded. 'Just show him how enthusiastic you are. After all you said the building will not be finished and equipped until the end of August. Not all the students will be able to wait so long for a job, but you'll be living at home here and you can help out with the hay and harvest.'

'Oh yes?' Libby grinned and hugged her father. 'I think you just want me for your part-time slave.'

'A very pretty slave though, isn't she, Victoria?'

'Of course she is.' Her mother smiled at them both. 'Your father always knew how to get his own way with compliments. We shall have to wait and see how you get on at the interview, dear. You can't expect to be successful every time and this is your first interview, and you may not even want the job when you hear more.'

'Maybe not,' Libby said thoughtfully, 'but now that I've seen it I think it would be ideal to have a job I like and still be able to stay at home.'

Almost from the moment she entered his office she realized Mr Whittaker was not really interested in her. She had probably rushed in too soon. Naturally he would have to see the other applicants before he made a decision.

'I realize it would have been better if I had already gained my diploma,' she said at last, 'but Miss Cuttle is an excellent lecturer and she expects all of us to do well in her subject. As far as —'

'Miss Cuttle? Did you say your lecturer is Miss Cuttle?' The manager sat up. He put his pencil down and gave her his full attention.

'Y-yes, I did.'

'You're not at college up here then?'

'No, I told you I am at —'

'Yes, yes, it slipped my mind.'

You mean you didn't pay much attention, Libby thought, and wondered what sort of a manager he was and if she would like to work for someone who seemed so uninterested. He was looking at her intently now. She had no way of knowing that he was thinking of a former colleague who was managing a big creamery near London. He had two women in his laboratory trained by Miss Cuttle and he swore they were the most competent laboratory technicians he'd ever had.

'Miss Cuttle would give you a reference?'

'Oh yes. I must ask her first, of course, but I know she will.'

'What about chemical analyses? You're familiar with the centrifuge for butterfat testing and so on?' Libby assured him she was. 'You would have to train an assistant to do the sterilising of your equipment and operate the autoclave and prepare sterile rinses. Do you think you could

289

manage that? It is important to test all the milk coming into the creamery and reject any not up to standard, but it is also important that the pasteurised milk we are selling to the public is a hundred percent safe, you understand? That means regular sampling and testing and when there are any problems, and even when there are no apparent problems, I would expect sterile rinses to be taken to check the plant and pipes and keep the operators on their toes.'

'I understand,' Libby said but she felt nervous. She had never seen a creamery in operation. He seemed to read her mind.

'The new laboratory will not be ready until the end of August but I suggest you come in for a fortnight as an observer to see the milk reception and follow the processing right through pasteurising to bottling and refrigeration. When do you finish college?'

'We take our college diploma at the end of June but we have a fortnight's refresher course in August prior to taking our National Diploma in Dairying at the university in Reading. All the English diploma students go there. We all have the same oral examiners and the same written exams.'

'I see. Well, Miss Pringle, there will be other applicants to interview but Miss Cuttle's training and the fact that you live in this area are in your favour. Will you send me your references? I shall be in touch within a fortnight after the closing date.'

Libby felt the interview had gone well after

all. She sang to herself as she drove her father's car back to Langmune. She would need to save up to buy a car of her own if she got the job. Some of the shifts would be very early in the morning when she had to sample the incoming milk.

As soon as she got back to college Libby sought out Miss Cuttle and told her about her interview.

'If you give me the manager's name and address I shall be pleased to send him a reference, Libby. You're more than competent. As far as the checks on the creamery plant are concerned we have a visit arranged to a local dairy in a fortnight. You will see all that sort of thing and I shall cover it in this term's lectures. We also have a day at an abattoir booked so you will all be familiar with the tubercles which form in animals with tuberculosis. After that it is mainly revision of two good years' solid work, and of course Mr Maloney will be arranging a day of relaxation before the final examinations begin.'

'Oh? We haven't heard about that.'

'It is just for final-year diploma students – a bus trip to Blackpool, or the Lakes, or wherever your group fancies, within reason. Mr Maloney will be in charge and no doubt Miss Friar will assist him.'

Libby nodded as she wrote down the manager's name and address in her firm, neat handwriting.

Mr Maloney was the youngest lecturer at the college and he was unmarried so he had rooms in the men's hostel and in return he was supposed to act as warden. It was an open secret that he was courting Miss Friar, who was Miss Cuttle's pretty young laboratory technician. When Libby passed on this bit of news to Alice and Alma they laughed.

'They will be too wrapped up in each other to supervise us,' Alice giggled. 'Anyway we're not exactly Sunday School children any longer.'

'They will be more in need of supervision than any of us,' Alma chuckled. 'I vote we have a trip to Blackpool. We must lobby the boys.'

As it turned out the vote was split between a day in Blackpool and a day in the Lake District.

'We'll toss a coin,' Mr Maloney decided. 'Heads for Blackpool, tails for the Lakes. Right?' There was a chorus of agreement. 'It's heads. It's Blackpool. I will arrange the bus but the rest is up to you to find your own entertainment. This is meant to be a day of pleasure and relaxation before the final exams begin. Just remember we must all be back on the bus by eleven or Miss Fanshaw will eat me for breakfast.' Maloney grinned and they all nodded assent. He was only a few years older than they were and he was known to be a good sport, unlike middle-aged Miss Fanshaw. The matron ruled the girls' hostel with a rod of iron which frequently caused resentment.

Later Libby wondered whether her whole future had been decided on the toss of that coin. Surely things could never have turned out so badly if they had gone to the Lakes.

Twenty-One

On the day of the trip to Blackpool it turned out there were more men than women students in the group.

'I'd like to walk to the end of the pier first and blow away the cobwebs,' Libby grinned, stretching her lithe young body, glad to escape the confines of the bus. Some wanted to explore the tower to see what was on in the evening and to visit the aquarium, but most of the young men were eager for the thrills and spills of the pleasure beach, while a few wanted to swim in the sea and two of the girls opted to see the wax works. In the end groups of friends decided to go their separate ways but they all agreed to meet in time for an evening meal and end the day in the tower ballroom.

'I knew Hilda Aspinall wouldn't come today,' Alice said to Libby. 'She made an excuse but we all know she's stayed behind to do some more swotting.'

'I'm not missing her,' Alma grinned. 'She casts a blight on everything. She's nearly as prim as old Fanshaw.'

'I wonder if Fanny was as strait-laced when she was our age,' Libby mused.

'I think she was born that way,' Alice said darkly.

It was in the middle of the afternoon when the three friends were strolling along the promenade that someone called Libby's name. She turned round and saw Mick Butler, Billy's friend, running after them.

'I thought it was you, Libby,' he panted as he caught up. 'Whatever are you doing in Blackpool?'

'We're having a day of fun and relaxation before the finals – and I might ask you the same thing.'

'We're here on a day trip.' He waved a careless hand towards a group of other young men and women who were strolling in their direction, some of them arm in arm. 'It's the Young Farmers' Club bus trip.'

'It's a long way to come, isn't it?'

'A bit. We're supposed to be home by midnight but I expect it'll be nearer one o'clock. The driver threatened to leave us if we're not back at the bus on time,' he grinned, 'but they always say that. We'll sleep on the way home and work as usual tomorrow.'

Alice cleared her throat and Libby grinned and took the hint, introducing Mick to her two friends. Alma smiled and greeted him almost shyly but Alice winked at Mick.

'Our Libby is a bit of a dark horse after all, eh? She never told us she knew handsome young men like you.' She grinned provocatively. 'We're all meeting up for a meal then we're going to the Tower Ballroom to dance the night away – or at least the part of it before we catch our bus home.'

'Are you now? Well maybe some of us will be there too, now we know.' He looked at Libby again. 'Billy went off with a couple of others but we're meeting up later. I see why he was so keen to come to Blackpool instead of Scarborough. I suppose he knew you'd be here.'

'No he didn't,' Libby denied quickly. 'It's my turn to write. Anyway we only decided to come here on the toss of a coin. The lecturers seem to think it's a good idea to have a day away to rest our brains before we settle to the serious business of passing exams.'

'And who is this Billy that Libby has been hiding from us?' Alice asked, her eyes twinkling.

'Och we're sort of cousins. We've always known each other. He and Aunt Maggie live at the next farm to ours.'

'Is that how you see dear Billy?' Mick eyed her shrewdly, one bushy eyebrow raised.

'Of course it is.' She met Mick's eyes, warning him not to tease or exaggerate her friendship with Billy. She knew Alice would not be able to resist quizzing him if they did meet up later and then Billy might think she had made more of their friendship than he would like, especially if he was spending the day in the company of a girlfriend from Yorkshire. 'I-I'm not sure it's a good idea to meet up later...'

'Of course it is!' Mick and Alice said in

unison, and grinned at each other as though they had known each other for years instead of minutes.

Much later that evening Billy and Libby were dancing together for about the eighth time. She'd had a couple of dances with Mick and his friend and one of the lads from their own group, but Billy claimed her for one dance after another.

'We have a lot of catching up to do, Libby. I expect you've been busy studying but I miss not getting your letters every week.' She smiled up at him. He met her gaze seriously then dropped a kiss on her forehead. 'Mother said you went for an interview when you were home at Easter?'

'Oh yes, I did. I forgot to tell you they've offered me the job at the creamery when I finish my National Diploma, and I've accepted. Father is pleased.' She grinned up at him. 'I think he's expecting I'll be there to help at Langmune when it's busy.'

'Mmm, maybe we shall both end up like prodigals returning to the glen then, but—'

'Billy! Come on! That's the third time we've called you,' Mick hissed from the side of the dance floor. Billy nodded and grinned at him.

'It's past time for the bus and you know the driver said he wouldn't wait. I've got your coat. Come on, we're leaving.'

'I'll catch you up.'

'You'll need to be quick then!' Mick turned and left the ballroom, taking Billy's coat with him. Billy looked down at Libby. 'I wish we didn't have to go our separate ways right now but I'm glad Mick saw you. I've really enjoyed this evening, Libby.'

'So have I,' she smiled dreamily, 'but I wouldn't like you to miss your bus. It's a long way to walk to Yorkshire.'

'Too right it is,' he said with a sigh as the dance ended. 'I'd better run. Good night, my wee Libby.' He dropped a kiss on the corner of her mouth then sprinted away.

It was almost time to make their way to their own coach when Libby saw Billy leaning against the outer door of the ballroom looking thoroughly dejected. She went towards him.

'What's the matter?'

'The bus has left!' he said indignantly. 'They've gone without me.'

'Oh, surely not. Perhaps it's just a joke.'

'It's no joke. I sprinted all the way to where we were to meet the coach and it was just drawing away. I shouted but it gathered speed and disappeared.'

'Oh, Billy, that's awful. What will you do?'

'That's not the worst of it,' he said glumly as Alice and Alma and some of their group joined them, ready to go for their own bus. 'Mick had my coat and it has my wallet in the inside pocket with most of my money.' He drew his hand from his trouser pocket to count the loose change.

'Is that all the money you've got?' Libby asked in alarm.

'Yes. It's not even enough to pay my fare, let

alone find a bed for the night.'

'I haven't much money left in my purse,' Libby said anxiously, 'but I have some back at college. I could lend you your fare.'

'Nothing for it, Billy-boy, you'll have to come on our bus with us,' Alice said nonchalantly.

'That's no use,' Billy muttered.

'Why not? There's nothing else to do. You don't want to sleep out all night, do you? It's starting to rain. Besides nobody will notice an extra body on the bus. You can bob down behind the seat when Mr Maloney does a head count, that is if he even remembers.'

'But even if he comes on our bus, where will he sleep?' Libby asked.

'I have a sleeping bag,' Alma offered diffidently. 'I suppose we could smuggle him up to your room for the night, Libby? We could let him in the fire escape door at your end of the corridor.'

'B-but...'

'You can't leave the poor fellow out in the rain,' Alice giggled. 'That's a splendid idea, Alma, so long as he gets away in the morning before Matron wakes up. There's a workman's bus from the road end about sixish I think. If you got that into the station you would probably get a train to Yorkshire sometime before night.' Alice obviously thought it was huge joke but Libby was uneasy.

Billy frowned and chewed his lip.

'What a bloody mess,' he muttered. 'I'm really sorry, Libby. If you can lend me enough money

298

for my train fare I'll send you a cheque as soon as I get back...'

'That's OK, Billy, but Alice is right, you can't stay out in the rain all night. We shall have to be very quiet though. Matron is incredibly strict.'

'She'll be sound asleep by the time we get back,' Alice said confidently. 'Come on, or we shall be missing our bus and we don't want to draw attention to Billy. Keep in the middle of us.'

If anybody noticed Billy they paid no attention. It had been a good day away from college routine and the strain of the forthcoming exams and everyone was in high spirits, singing lustily all the way back.

The girls showed Billy the fire escape at the gable end of the building and told him to creep up and wait there until one of them unlocked the door to let him in.

Miss Fanshaw was a conscientious woman and she had waited to see the girls safely into the hostel before locking the doors securely and bidding them all a curt good night.

'It's a good thing we didn't risk smuggling Billy in the front door with us,' whispered Alma anxiously. She hurried to her room and pulled her sleeping bag from under her bed. It was Alice who went to the end of the corridor and beckoned Billy inside with a finger to her lips. She ushered him into Libby's room.

'You must go out that way in the morning. One of us will lock the door as soon as we get up. No one will ever know you've been.'

Left alone in the silence of Libby's room they looked at each other helplessly. Billy shrugged.

'I'm sorry, Libby. I never thought that damned driver would really go without me. I was really enjoying meeting up with you and catching up and dancing together and everything.' He was tempted to tell her how his heart had soared when he met her so unexpectedly but he sensed her tension and he didn't want to make her any more uneasy. He began to undo his trousers and saw her eyes widen.

'I'll sleep in my shirt and underpants. I shall be all right. I'll just slip out in the morning if you're still asleep.'

'Yes,' Libby nodded in relief. She felt deadly tired now. It had been a long day with a lot of walking and then the dancing. 'The bathrooms are all at the far end of this corridor,' she said uncertainly.

'I'm OK,' Billy grinned. 'I found a quiet corner under the fire escape.'

'Of course, it's fine for men!' Libby grimaced and grabbed her pyjamas and sponge bag and hurried along the brown linoleum of the corridor. She wished she didn't feel so uneasy. When she returned Billy was already snuggled into the sleeping bag with her cushion for his pillow. She stepped over him. He eyed her long legs beneath the thin cotton pyjamas but he bit back the admiring comment that had sprung to his lips.

'Set my alarm clock and put it underneath your pillow,' she whispered. 'I don't want you to be late but it would be awful if we wakened everybody else up at half past five.'

Libby was sound asleep when Billy pulled on his trousers and pullover the following morning. She looked so innocent and desirable with her hand cupping her flushed cheek. He was tempted to drop a kiss on her brow but instead he tiptoed to the door and let himself out. The long corridor was silent. The fire escape window was rarely opened and the hinges gave a faint creak as they had done the previous evening but he slipped through and pulled it closed behind him. He had almost reached the bottom when he heard the hinges squeak again. He looked up. There was a girl standing on the tiny platform, peering down at him. It wasn't Libby or her two friends. This one had long straight hair, so dark it looked black in the dawn light. Then he saw her features move in what he took to be a smile. She gave a thumbs-up sign. He grinned and returned the signal before he turned and jogged away down the long lane to the main road where Alice said he would catch a workmen's bus.

Hilda Aspinall had heard the girls arrive back from the day trip to Blackpool the night before. She'd heard the whispering and some hurrying to and fro before everything went silent. She could have sworn she'd heard the deeper voice of a man but she knew she must have imagined it. She was working desperately hard. She could see the headlines now and her father's pride. 'MP's daughter outshines the other students in final examinations' or something equally complimentary. Libby Pringle was the only one who

301

was likely to beat her and the annoying thing was she was two years younger because she had not stayed on at school to study advanced chemistry and biology, but she had still managed to catch up. They had one more day before the first exam and Hilda had set her alarm early to get in some studying before breakfast. So she was already awake when she heard the muffled buzz from the room next door, although Libby herself heard nothing. Even so Hilda was amazed when she heard the creak of the fire escape. There was no mistaking the figure was that of a young man and Hilda knew he must have spent the night in Libby Pringle's room. She was flabbergasted, and if she was so shocked, what would Miss Fanshaw think? Her parents had invited Matron to dinner once because her father believed in cultivating people who might be of use to him or to his family. Miss Fanshaw had been effusive in her thanks and she had been overwhelmed to find two cabinet ministers at dinner. Hilda had overheard her discussing discipline with one of them. He had approved of Miss Fanshaw's rigid authority over the young women students, or so he said.

'Since the war morals have slipped,' he declared pompously. 'We depend on people like you, Miss Fanshaw, to restore a sense of decency to our country.' If she was honest Hilda had thought both the minister and Matron were far too narrow-minded but her parents were pleased to know their daughter was safe in such a respectable establishment. So what would they say if they discovered one of her fellow students had kept a man in her room all night?

Hilda's mind buzzed. She couldn't concentrate on studying until she had decided what she could do with the information. Elizabeth Pringle had defied all of Matron's rules. The sheer audacity took Hilda's breath away, and deep down she felt a faint pang of envy. So far no personable young man had even ventured to kiss her on her cheek, let alone spend the night with her. Imagination made her shiver with excitement and it certainly coloured the version of the tale she related to Miss Fanshaw just before breakfast.

Twenty-Two

Miss Fansaw's mouth was tightly pursed, and she was outraged as she bore down upon the table where Libby and her friends were eating breakfast.

'Miss Pringle! Report to me in my room as soon as you have finished breakfast,' she commanded curtly. Without waiting for a reply her small corseted figure hurried away, anger bristling from every pore.

How dare the Pringle girl flout her rules and ruin her reputation as an upright Christian and a conscientious guardian of the young women in her care? What if Hilda Aspinall's father heard of this? The reputation of the college and her position as matron would be in ruins. She even had visions of the disgraceful episode reaching the ears of the cabinet minister and from there to the newspapers. She shuddered. She must deal severely with the girl. She must set an example so that others would not dare defy her.

Miss Fanshaw had no idea – and would not have believed – that the minister in question had a mistress in London, as well as a wife and family in his constituency. She would have been hurt and angry had she seen his rueful smile and heard him declare his sympathy for the girls who had to live by her rigid rules.

Libby could only stare in horror as she listened to Miss Fanshaw's tirade.

'Go home?' she echoed faintly. 'Today?'

'Right now! That's what I said and that's what I mean. You may pack your trunk and I will have it sent on, but you are not to go near the lecture rooms or speak to the other girls.'

'But we begin our final exams tomorrow...' Libby gasped in alarm.

'You forfeited that privilege when you flouted the rules and jeopardized the reputation of this college, Miss Pringle.'

'B-but ... What am I to tell my parents?'

'You must tell them the name of the man you invited to share your bed,' Miss Fanshaw said coldly. 'If they have any thought for your reputation they will make sure he marries you without delay.'

'M-marries me! Billy?' Indignant colour stained Libby's cheeks. 'I would rather stay single for the rest of my life than have a husband who is forced into marriage! I told you, I've known Billy all my life. We ... we're almost related. He missed his bus. We did nothing wrong, I swear on the—'

'Don't you dare blaspheme in my presence. Now go and pack. I shall arrange for a taxi to take you off these premises.'

Libby was too stunned to argue further. She felt as though she was being sucked into a whirlpool, deep and dark and bottomless. She had studied for two years. She had worked hard. Was there to be nothing at the end of it? Her new job depended on her getting her diploma. What could she tell her mother? She had always wanted her to have an education and qualifications, an opportunity that neither of her parents had been given. She felt sick as she made her way up the stairs and along the silent cheerless corridor to her room.

She had almost finished packing her trunk when there was a sharp knock on her bedroom door.

'Miss Pringle? Elizabeth? May I come in?' It was Miss Cuttle's voice. She sounded angry. She did not suffer fools gladly. Libby's heart sank even further – if that was possible.

'Come in,' Libby said. She was kneeling beside her trunk and she looked up. Miss Cuttle's face was pale with anger.

'I cannot get any sense or reason out of Miss Fanshaw. Tell me your version of what happened last night.'

Libby chewed her lip. She felt she had repeated yesterday's events half a dozen times already but Miss Fanshaw had refused to believe her. Wearily she told Miss Cuttle what had happened, leaving nothing out.

'And we did nothing wrong, Miss Cuttle, honestly. I've known Billy all my life. He would never hurt me.'

'But he has hurt you. He has compromised your reputation and I could ring that young man's neck for being so thoughtless,' she added vehemently. 'At this moment it looks as though he has ruined your whole future. I have tried to reason with Miss Fanshaw. You are almost finished here, but she is adamant. She tells me she has informed the Principal and he simply left the matter in her hands. *Her* hands,' she snapped angrily. 'We all know his mind is pre-occupied with his retirement and his wife's illness so he probably didn't understand the seriousness of your situation and its effect on your future. Libby Pringle, you are my star pupil for this year – in fact the best I've had for several years.' She pushed agitated fingers through her short hair, making it stand on end. Libby would have laughed if the situation were not so serious. As it was she felt she would never laugh again. The empty, sick feeling returned.

'M-Miss Cuttle, may I ask a favour?'

'You can ask. I doubt if I can help much.'

'If I give you a cheque, c-could you give me cash, please? I need it to travel home. I loaned my spare cash to Billy.'

'Billy!' Miss Cuttle let out an explosive breath. 'I could hang that young man. But I'll certainly give you the cash. If only that were all we needed. In fact I'll tell Miss Fanshaw she can cancel the taxi. I shall drive you to the station myself. I will leave you to finish packing your trunk for now. Be sure to take all your books with you. I want a word with Mr Donelly. He regarded you as his star student in the agricul-tural side too, you know, and Mr Mink was delighted at the way you have caught up in chemistry. There will be no use speaking to Miss Jennings. However good you are in her subject she will never disagree with Miss Fanshaw. When you have finished packing, lock your trunk and bring your hand luggage with you. Meet me at the laboratory.'

'Miss Fanshaw said I was not to go near the lecture rooms, or speak to any of the other students.' Libby's lower lip trembled for the first time. 'Not even to say g-goodbye to my friends.'

'Speaking of friends...' Miss Cuttle frowned. 'Did any of them know you had a young man in your room?'

'Oh yes. They all knew. At least, all those who went on the trip knew. Hilda Aspinall didn't go with us so she was the only one who didn't know about Billy.'

'Hilda Aspinall, the MP's daughter of course.' Miss Cuttle pursed her lips and gave a nod. 'Which is her room?'

'The end one, next door to mine.'

'So it's possible she heard?'

'We were very quiet when we came home and Billy must have been quiet when he left. Even I didn't hear him.'

'Mmm. Even so, I suspect ... Well never mind, it's too late now and there's nothing to be done about it, but certainly Miss Fanshaw would be afraid of a whiff of scandal reaching the ears of our esteemed Mr Aspinall.'

'I wouldn't mind so much if I'd done something wicked or criminal, or if Miss Fanshaw had disciplined me in some other way for allowing Billy to stay overnight, b-but I don't know how I shall tell my parents. Or what I can say to the creamery manager. I was supposed to start work there as soon as the exams are over, then I could have two weeks for the cramming fortnight before we go to Reading for the National Diploma exams.'

'Ye-es, that's difficult.' Miss Cuttle frowned thoughtfully. 'I must have a word with Mr Donelly. Next to the Principal he has most authority as the senior lecturer and farm manager. Meanwhile, although I don't encourage deceit as a rule, my advice would be to say nothing to your parents, or your prospective boss, about not taking your college finals. Wait until we see what can be worked out. Come down to the labs when you're ready to leave. Have you any idea what time the trains will be running?'

'No, but I can wait at the station,' Libby said miserably. Miss Cuttle nodded and shut the door quietly behind her. Of all the lecturers Libby had most respect for her and she knew she would be eternally grateful that the woman had taken the trouble to come and see her and hear her side of things. She had not condemned her outright. Libby shuddered at the prospect of anyone trying to influence Billy into marrying her against his will. Even if she had to confess to being banned from college she would never tell anyone he was the cause – least of all Billy himself.

When she arrived at the laboratory Miss Cuttle made her a cup of coffee and she had prepared a plate of crackers and cheese.

'I-I don't think I c-could eat anything,' Libby stammered. Shock had kept the tears at bay until now but Miss Cuttle's kindness almost caused her to break down.

'You'd better try. I telephoned the station. There isn't a train up to Carlisle until eleven thirty. You'll have to change there for Dumfries. Mr Donelly is as angry as I am about the whole affair. He has gone for a word with the Principal. He thinks your parents might have been able to appeal against Miss Fanshaw's decision but there is no time with the finals beginning tomorrow.'

Even before she finished speaking Mr Donelly returned. He shook his head in grim silence. 'If it hadn't been for that bloody MP and his daughter I think he would have agreed to let the matter drop since it's so near the end of your course anyway, Miss Pringle, but Miss Fanshaw seems to have convinced him the reputation of the college and the other students is at stake.' He pursed his lips and looked hard at Libby. 'Couldn't you just have waited until you were home again since you've known the lad so long anyway?'

'B-but...' Libby looked wide-eyed from him to Miss Cuttle and back again. It was obvious he didn't believe they had done nothing wrong. Her eyes sparked with indignation. 'I only gave him shelter for the night. I've explained all that.'

'Mmm,' Mr Donelly said dubiously. 'You're either more unworldly – aye and more modest – than I would have believed, Miss Pringle, or—'

'I believe her when she says they did nothing wrong,' Miss Cuttle interrupted firmly. 'He slept on the floor in a sleeping bag.'

'Well the damage is done now.' Paddy Donelly sighed in exasperation. 'I'm not sure how we stand for allowing you to take the National Diploma in Reading if you have not passed the college diploma but we'll get round that somehow, even if we have to tell them you were at death's door.' Libby paled but he went on gruffly. 'I'll see to all that one way or another, I give you my word. The problem is you will not be allowed back here for the fortnight of intensive revision. We advise students what they need to do, depending on the results of the college examinations. Do you think you can revise at home if we send you the relevant notes?'

'I don't think Libby needs notes. She's made a pretty good job of preparing herself for the exams so far,' Miss Cuttle interrupted.

'I shall still send them, for my subjects anyway, and for any of the other lecturers who are willing to supply them. Economics is always tricky. There's usually a question to discuss and it's important to put both sides. Now if I were you, Miss Pringle, I'd work bloody hard during this holiday and I'd aim at getting a distinction in the National.'

Libby gasped and stared at him.

'You have the ability. It would show the lot of

311

'em, including that MP and his daughter.'

'Mr Donelly is right, Libby,' Miss Cuttle advised. 'You do have the ability and there are very few students who pass the National with distinction. If you did, then that is what would be remembered – not the fact that you didn't take the college diploma. Your prospective boss would be too impressed to ask questions. You go for it, girl, and do the best you can, and then you can put all this behind you. It may seem like the end of the world to you right now, but a distinction...' She broke off and gave a crooked smile. 'Go for it.'

'Th-thank you, b-both of you. I shall do my best, my very best, now I know you have faith in me.' For the first time the two lecturers relaxed a little and smiled at her.

'Good luck then, Miss Pringle. I shall be in touch and I will let you know the arrangements for going down to Reading.' He left them alone.

'Eat up, Libby, and then we'll set off for the station.'

Libby ate to please Miss Cuttle but the food felt like sawdust in her mouth. 'I don't think Mr Donelly really believed that Billy slept on the floor and that we did nothing wrong,' she said dully.

'No, I know he didn't,' Miss Cuttle agreed. 'That's because he's a man and you are a very attractive girl. He believes it's natural for any red-blooded male to take advantage, especially when you provided him with such an opportunity. Although I think Miss Fanshaw is reacting too harshly I suspect she is afraid Miss Aspinall's father would take the same view as Mr Donelly. She is afraid of repercussions.' Libby remained silent, digesting this.

Later, hunched miserably in her seat on the train, she reflected on Miss Cuttle's remarks again. Billy had not even tried to kiss her. She was paying the price without even experiencing a hint of the passion that Mr Donelly would have regarded as normal. Billy obviously didn't see anything about her to arouse his desire. Somehow this made her even more miserable.

It was late and Libby was tired by the time she arrived at Annan station. Her stomach was churning but more with nerves than hunger. She waited dejectedly for a bus to Darlonachie, but there wasn't one. She should probably have stayed on the train as far as Dumfries and got a bus back from there. She finally managed to get a bus as far as the crossroads, two miles from the village, but it was another three miles' walk up to Langmune even after she reached Darlon-achie. If they had known she was coming her mother or father would have met her at the station, but she felt she would never be able to ask any favours of them ever again. She was glad she had only brought her suitcase.

Libby was exhausted in mind and body by the time she arrived home. Victoria knew at once that something was seriously wrong but since Libby didn't want to talk there was little she could do except try to persuade her to eat and have a good sleep. Libby didn't think she would be able to sleep peacefully with her mind in such turmoil but she had had two long and eventful days and a long walk home. She slept like a baby.

For the next few days Libby felt sick at heart. She was not used to deceit and although she avoided any direct lies she still felt bad that her parents didn't know the truth.

'However badly you have done in your final exams, Libby, it's not the end of the world,' her father said kindly. 'We know you will have done your best.'

Libby felt like bursting into tears. How could she tell them she hadn't even taken the exams? There would be no results.

'Your father is right, lassie,' Victoria said. 'There's no good fretting. You have to eat. You can't go on like this until the results come out.'

'We have to go to Reading for the national exams in August,' Libby said, trying to steer the conversation away from a date for the College Diploma results. It worked.

'You'll not be fit to go anywhere, or take any exams, if you carry on like this,' Victoria said briskly. 'It's not like you to get so depressed. You're sure there's nothing else wrong with you? You know you can always tell us, whatever it is. We're your parents. We love you, Libby, whatever has gone wrong.' Libby pushed back her chair and sped up to her room, desperately struggling to hold back her tears, longing to tell them everything.

Even Fraser treated her gently, without his usual brotherly taunts and teasing. He persuaded her to go to several of the local young farmers' events with him. He was seventeen now but he was waiting to take his driving test so it was easy to persuade Libby that he and Miriam and Grace needed her to give them a lift and she found it easier to be away from her parents' anxiety. She had lost a lot of weight and there were dark circles beneath her eyes. She preferred to be in the company of Lachie or Mimi. At only eight years old they welcomed her unconditionally.

She had received letters from her two best friends at college, Alma and Alice. Alice had included a letter forwarded from Billy. He had enclosed a cheque for the money he owed her but she had not written to him to acknowledge it. He would have realized she was back home early and would want to know why. Even a fortnight later, when she would have been due home anyway, she still didn't write to Billy. She couldn't pretend with him and she vowed she would never tell him what had happened.

The letters from Alice and Alma reflected their shock and dismay. They were angered by Miss Fanshaw's stern discipline and they blamed themselves because it had been their suggestion that Billy should stay overnight. Looking back Libby knew Mr Maloney would probably have given Billy shelter in the men's hostel if they had confided in him but it had never occurred to them at the time.

We discovered it was Hilda Aspinall who had locked the fire escape door behind Billy that morning,' Alma had written. 'She has admitted she informed Miss Fanshaw but she claims she didn't expect you would get such drastic punishment. Please do write, Libby. Shall we see you in Reading?'

None of this helped Libby. She had defied her mother's wishes and insisted on spending a year at home and two years at college and she had nothing to show at the end of it. She had not dared get in touch with her future boss at the creamery in case he withdrew his offer of a job. She was pinning all her hopes on Mr Donelly getting her in for the National Diploma examinations. Every night she spent hours going over her books, determined to keep the facts fresh in her memory.

Lying in bed together one night Andrew took Victoria in his arms. 'Do you think Libby has got herself into trouble and can't bring herself to confide in us?' he asked anxiously.

'Depends what you mean by trouble,' Victoria mused, 'but if you're asking if she's having a baby, I can set your mind at rest. She is not.'

'Ah, that's a relief,' Andrew sighed. 'I've been afraid to let her help with heavy work at the hay and so on, in case that's what was wrong.'

'I've wracked my brains and I can't think what can be wrong, unless she's fallen for someone at college and been badly let down. I can't believe

316

it's just the possibility of doing badly in her exams. She was doing so well.'

'In that case I shall set her on to work,' Andrew said. 'We can do with an extra pair of hands. At least hard work helps you sleep at night and some mornings she doesn't look as though she's slept at all.'

Victoria agreed, but she was worried herself. Libby did not go over to High Bowie as often as she used to do and she had always loved being with Mimi. Why was she so depressed?

'Libby, Willie telephoned this evening,' Victoria said to her daughter the next day. 'He wants to know if you will go over to High Bowie tomorrow afternoon. Billy has found a pony he thinks will be ideal for Mimi for the next few years. Willie has agreed to buy it and Billy is having it sent up with a lorry delivering some pedigree heifers to Scotland. Two of the heifers are to be dropped off at Home Farm.' She gave a puzzled frown. 'Billy has bought them himself and he's sending them up here, according to Willie, but he's still working at his job as under manager.'

'Did you tell Uncle Willie I would go over there, Mum?'

'Yes I did. You're finished at the hay now so you should have a bit more spare time. It's a strange thing for Billy to do though, don't you think? He's bought two expensive pedigree Friesian animals yet he'll not be here to look after them.'

'Who knows what Billy has in mind?' Libby

shrugged. She really missed Billy's cheerful letters but she couldn't bring herself to write to him while her life was in such a muddle.

'Willie says they're only three or four months in calf,' her mother went on. 'I don't know what Fergus Dunlop will say when they arrive at Home Farm.'

'Neither do I,' Andrew said. 'Fergus is a great one for traditional Ayrshires. He has no time for Friesians at all. He made that very clear when he heard we had bought half a dozen for Langmune.'

Libby left them debating and hurried to her bedroom. That morning the postman had delivered a bulging foolscap package. She had taken it to her room unseen until she could explore the contents. It would not take such a large letter if Mr Donelly was informing her he had been unable to enter her for the National Examinations. Her heart beat with hope. *Please, please give me a chance to prove I can do it,* she prayed silently. Soon she would be due to start her preliminary spell at the creamery, making herself familiar with the plant and equipment. Mr Whittaker would be sure to enquire about her results.

Twenty-Three

Libby was not the only one experiencing problems with college life. Charlotte Crainby was approaching the end of her first year and she had worked hard. She had known she had some catching up to do and in her heart she knew she was not as clever as some of the other students, but teaching was what she really wanted to do. Most of the lecturers had been extremely helpful and generous with their time but none more so than Josh Pringle.

Charlotte wished she had been honest from the beginning and told him that her real name was Crainby, but she had dreaded the jibes of those students who made the connection with the newspaper articles and her mother. Unhappily she wondered whether Mr Pringle would have been as helpful if he knew her mother had turned his parents out of the cottage where they had lived all their lives, and banned old Mr Pringle from the gardens he had tended with such love and care. Her heart felt like lead every time she thought of her mother's callous actions.

The letter arrived out of the blue. It was from the man who owned her flat. She was to be evicted at the end of the week for non-payment of rent and continually ignoring his letters. As she stood there with trembling fingers the blood drained from her face, leaving it ashen.

'There must be some mistake,' she muttered aloud. She looked at the letter again and saw the address and telephone number of the firm of solicitors who had sent it on behalf of her landlord. Shakily she gathered up some change, clutched the letter and hurried to the telephone box on the corner of the square where she lived. Eventually she was put through to the man who had sent the letter. He sounded abrupt.

'If you had replied to our earlier letters, or made an offer to pay off the amount owing, we might have negotiated. But you have left it too late, Mrs Crainby.'

'I-I am Mrs Crainby's daughter,' Charlotte stammered. 'My m-mother is a trustee for my money and she is paying the rent. There must be some mistake,' she added desperately. 'I knew nothing about this until I received the letter to evict me.'

'There is no mistake and there is no going back. You have received too many warnings already. As it is we are taking steps to take you to court for the rent owing since January.'

'January? You have received no rent since January?' Charlotte gasped.

'You must have seen the letters demanding payment.'

'No,' Charlotte said faintly. 'The landlord would send them to m-my m-mother, I suppose, or to Mr Whyte, our solicitor. He is a trustee also.'

'In that case you had better give me his name and telephone number, Miss Crainby, but the eviction still stands. There is nothing we can do about that. I must have the money owing to my client or we shall go to court.'

Charlotte gave him Mr Whyte's address and put the telephone carefully back on its cradle. She counted the change she had left then dialled her mother's number. It rang for a long time and Charlotte could imagine the bell echoing through the large house that was stuffed full of all the furniture and ornaments which had taken her mother's fancy and then been cast aside for some other frippery. At last the receiver was lifted and her mother's voice drawled down the line. Her words were slurred and Charlotte's heart sank. At Christmas her mother had promised she would stop drinking so much and pull herself together. Charlotte couldn't get any sense out of her mother, who began to laugh and then to sing. Charlotte was furious. She shouted down the telephone.

'You have never paid the rent, Mother. They are going to evict me from my flat. Don't you care?'

Her mother gave an incomprehensible reply and then began to cackle inanely. Charlotte slammed down the receiver and bit back a sob. She ran back to her flat and scraped together all the change she could find and the little book where she kept telephone numbers before returning to the telephone box. She dialled the number of Mr Whyte, since he was supposed to

321

be a joint trustee of her affairs until she was twenty-five. She demanded to speak to him urgently. When she was put through she told him what had happened.

'You are as responsible for this as my mother,' she said, trying hard to keep her voice firm. 'It is too late to prevent me being evicted, but you must see that the rent is paid without delay. I cannot bear it if they go to court and cause more horrid publicity.'

'I will call on Mrs Crainby at once.' He sounded tense and startled. 'I understood your mother intended to buy a small house or a flat for you. I raised money from the trust for that very purpose and—'

Charlotte's change ran out and the line went dead. Despondently she dropped the receiver back into place.

Charlotte had already missed her first lecture and she knew she would never be able to concentrate but what else could she do but go to the college. She would have to find other accommodation by the end of the week and it was already Tuesday. Her exams were starting in ten days.

'Miss Laine?' Charlotte had been miles away and completely lost the thread of the lecture. She had no idea what question Josh Pringle had asked her. Josh had noticed that she was even paler than usual and he knew she was not taking in anything he said. At the end of the lecture he asked her to stay behind. At first Charlotte was reluctant to tell him anything but eventually she told him about the eviction notice, then she burst into tears. Josh blinked. He wanted to take her in his arms and comfort her. Instead he offered her his clean white handkerchief.

'There must be some mistake...'

'No,' she whispered in a choked voice. 'I should have told you before. My real name is Crainby – Crainby from Darlonachie...' She couldn't look at him. She sniffed hard and blew her nose.

'I know that, Charlotte. I don't know why you assumed a different name but I guess you had your reasons and—'

'You knew?' Charlotte looked at him then. 'How? When?'

'I've known for some time. I saw your real name when I was filling in some of your reports.'

'You've never let it make a difference...' She sank on to a chair. He sat down beside her. Josh had an almost overwhelming urge to cradle the white-faced girl in his arms and protect her from whatever demons were pursuing her, but he was in a position of trust as her lecturer. She was a student and eleven years his junior. As if that were not enough she came from a wealthy family while his own parents lived in a cottage on his brother's farm. Worse even than that, his mother would never welcome a Crainby over her doorstep after Henrietta's incredible cruelty to Victoria. He sighed. Victoria was as dear to all of them as if she had been their real sister, his parents' own daughter. His mother would never forgive Henrietta Crainby. He chewed his lip.

'Charlotte, it is almost the end of term and the exams start next week. How would it do if I got you a room in the college for now? You will have plenty of time during the summer to look for another flat, if that is what you want.'

'Would you? Could you arrange that for me, even though I gave up my room?'

'I shall certainly try. It is important you pass these exams. But I can't believe your mother has forgotten to pay the rent since January. That's six months almost!'

'Obviously you don't know my m-mother,' Charlotte said bitterly. 'I telephoned her this morning. It was only nine thirty but she was drunk!' she said in disgust. 'At Christmas she promised me she would stop drinking. I should not be telling you all this. I expect you think it's disloyal, you being from such a close and loving family, b-but my m-mother doesn't love anyone except herself. She never has enough money and she blames me. I d-don't even remember my f-father but he set up a trust for me. M-mother has resented me ever since and she never says anything good about him.'

'I didn't know your father very well either, Charlotte. I was a boy at school when he died, but I do know he was well liked and respected by the people of Darlonachie.'

'Even though he had a mistress? And he had an illegitimate child. It was in all the newspapers.' She shuddered.

'I suspect your mother may have been responsible for some of the more lurid accounts,' he said gently, 'but I believe people still liked your father. I know my parents and most of the people in Darlonachie would have done anything for your grandfather, Sir William Crainby.'

'I never knew him. Mother refused to let me visit. Her resentment influenced my own opinions when I was young but now ... I think I can understand why my father needed another woman to love him. My mother has such a spiteful tongue. She doesn't love me, you know. I expect that shocks you,' she added with a note of bitterness. 'She didn't love my father either. She just wanted to live in a castle and have a title. She has told me that more than once when she's angry. And she didn't get either in the end, with my father dying so young, even before my grandfather.'

Josh wanted to smooth the hair from her brow and stroke its abundant softness where it hung over her thin shoulders. She was still far too thin and pale. Instead he stood up and moved away from her.

'First things first, Charlotte. I'll see about getting you a room in one of the student houses. Then you must concentrate on passing your exams. After that there will be time enough to sort out other problems. Now that you have told the landlord's solicitor the name of the other trustee they should be able to sort out any problems between them.'

'I suspect Mother has been too sly for Mr Whyte. He has trusted her too much.'

'This will have been a lesson to him then. I

believe he was new to the area when he took over from Mr Jenkinson?' She nodded glumly. 'He has certain responsibilities, whatever your mother may choose to tell him. He could be in serious trouble if he has not carried out his duty to you.'

'Next year I shall be twenty-five. I shall not need trustees then, but I doubt if there will be much left to control.' She grimaced. 'Mother was determined to get her hands on as much money as she could while she still had some influence. I don't care about the money but I hate being in debt and my rent not being paid, especially when I knew nothing about it. All I want is to finish my teacher training and get a job and be independent and free of my mother.' She looked up at him. 'I suppose that shocks you, Mr Pringle. I know you go back to Darlonachie regularly to see your own parents.'

'I do, but they're very loving parents and they made sacrifices and did their best for all of us. They are getting old and frail now. I like to see them as often as I can. Some day I shall buy a house in Darlonachie.'

'And I can't wait to get away,' Charlotte sighed.

Mr Whyte, the solicitor, was angry and alarmed when he realized he had been duped by Mrs Crainby. She had not bought a flat, and yet the money was gone. It made him look foolish in the eyes of the Glasgow lawyer who was demanding unpaid rent. Surely he should have been able to trust Henrietta Crainby when she was both the girl's mother and her trustee. He began to wonder how often she had persuaded him to release money from her daughter's inheritance and used it to finance her own useless life.

Henrietta had always felt in control when she was with Mr Whyte. He seemed such a mild and harmless man but as she faced him across the room now she felt nervous and alarmed. She knew she had failed in her duty as a parent and as a trustee but that was Luke's fault for leaving most of his property to Charlotte. She stared at the solicitor. Could they send her to gaol for cheating her own daughter? She poured herself another large whisky with a hand that shook.

'I think you have had enough of that,' Mr Whyte said coldly. 'If you will get me all the letters from your daughter's landlord I will sort out the trouble you have caused first of all. After that I demand to see an account of all the money you have taken from the trust and what you have done with it.'

At last Mr Whyte was taking his duties seriously. He acted swiftly to settle the debts to the landlord. Charlotte was relieved to get his letter telling her she should have no further worries from that quarter, and she settled down to her examinations. She had only one more to tackle the day a messenger came to find her and led her to the Principal's office. She stared in dismay at the sight of a policewoman and a sergeant who had arrived to tell her the terrible news.

'Is – is something wrong?' she asked as the blood drained from her face.

They were very kind. Everyone was considerate and tried to help. Charlotte felt too numb with shock and horror to cry, or to make plans, or to think rationally.

Some of her belongings were still packed after her move from the flat. It was the policewoman who helped her pack the remainder, who locked her room and helped carry her suitcases down to the front entrance. She was aware of a man drawing up beside them in a small car. He climbed out and she saw it was Mr Pringle. His face looked strained and troubled.

'She's still in shock,' the young police woman said. 'Are you sure you can manage?'

'Yes. My own family live near the same village.' Josh told her. 'I'll do the best I can. Will – will things have been?'

'Yes, everything has been attended to. There will be a couple of my colleagues waiting for your arrival.' She helped Charlotte into the little car and slammed the door shut. When she straightened up she faced Josh across the roof. 'The poor girl doesn't appear to have any family, or any close friends she can call on as far as we have been able to ascertain.'

'No...' Josh frowned, thinking. 'No, I don't think she has many relatives and she has not stayed at Darlonachie much herself in recent years.'

'I'm sure one of the policewomen will be

willing to spend time with her until she is able to take in the situation and make decisions for herself.'

'Ye-es.' Josh looked at the young woman in her smart uniform. 'I suppose you're used to dealing with these situations?'

'They are never easy and everybody reacts differently.'

'Will you stay here please? I would like to make a telephone call before we set off.' He loped away, taking the steps two at a time, and disappeared into the college buildings. Charlotte sat white-faced and silent, hunched in the passenger seat of Josh's car, her hands clenched tightly together.

Twenty-Four

It was Libby who answered Josh's call to Langmune that afternoon.

'Sorry, Uncle Josh, Mum's not at home. Did you get your new car?'

'Yes, yes I did, Libby, but that's not important now. I really need to speak to your mother, urgently. When will she be back?'

'I don't know. She went into Dumfries with Aunt Maggie. I think they have gone to the hospital. Can't I help you?'

Josh hesitated. 'Do you remember Charlotte Crainby?'

'Vaguely. She was at Darlonachie village school for a few years but she was older than me. Why?'

'I'm driving her home. She's in shock and I don't know if she has any relations or anyone who could stay with her. Libby ... her mother has committed suicide.'

'Oh no! Oh, Uncle Josh, how awful. The poor girl. Wh-what can we do?'

'I'm not sure to tell the truth, lassie.'

Josh sounded shocked and bewildered himself, Libby thought. 'I'll tell Mum as soon as she comes back and if she hasn't returned in a couple of hours I could come over and meet you at her house if that would help?'

'You're a good lassie, Libby. I would be glad of another woman there in the circumstances. And, Libby...'

'Yes?'

'Don't mention this to your granny. You know how bitter she feels about Henrietta Crainby, but I think Charlotte has probably suffered as much from her as anyone – more, probably, because she was her mother. I don't think she has any other relations. There's no one to comfort her. I must go now.'

Libby replaced the receiver and stared at it. She shuddered. Charlotte Crainby had neither mother nor father now. *I have both,* she thought, *and here I am afraid to tell them why my life has turned upside down, only now I shall have a chance to put things right.*

The large brown envelope had been from Mr Donelly. True to his word he had entered her for the national examinations at Reading. He had also enclosed notes for revision from the other lecturers and almost all of them had added their good wishes. It had cheered her tremendously. She would do her best to help Uncle Josh with Charlotte Crainby. She knew her mother had always said Uncle Josh had a tender heart if anyone was in trouble, but she could see how awkward it was when he was a lecturer and Charlotte was one of his students.

Two hours later there was still no sign of

Libby's mother returning. It had not occurred to Libby to ask how Mrs Crainby had taken her own life. Now she wondered nervously if her body would still be at the Dower House. Mrs Crainby had tried to change the name to Manton Villa but the people of Darlonachie had always known it as the Dower House and they were reluctant to change it. She wrote a note for her mother and put it on the kitchen table, then she got out her bicycle and set off for Darlonachie.

Victoria turned on to the track leading to Home Farm to drop Maggie off before going home to Langmune. Minutes later Libby reached the junction and cycled on to Darlonachie. When she read the note her daughter had left her, Victoria wished she had driven straight home first. Although Libby seemed to have improved during the past week she was still tense and on edge. How could she possibly cope with a distressed young woman who was probably suffering from shock? Josh would be there, of course, but he was a young man – a bachelor too. What could he do in such circumstances? It was only later she realized her daughter had grown into a capable woman who could make difficult decisions in an emergency.

Libby was relieved to see two police officers at the Dower House when she arrived. The young woman told her Mrs Crainby had hung herself from the banister. They suspected she had been drinking heavily beforehand. Her body had been removed and they were waiting for the arrival of Mrs Crainby's daughter. On cue Josh drove up with Charlotte. They had stopped at a roadside café on the way down. Neither of them had had anything to eat since breakfast and Josh had insisted Charlotte must drink some strong dark tea and eat at least one of the sandwiches. He had no idea what they would find at the Dower House. Afterwards Charlotte had begun to talk, haltingly at first, and Josh had listened in silence. Gradually he realized what an unhappy existence the girl had had. Once she got over the shock of her mother committing suicide he hoped her life might take a turn for the better.

Much later, when the two police officers had gone and Charlotte seemed to accept Libby's presence in her home, she telephoned Doctor Grantly. He was almost retired now and she knew Doctor Ritchie would be taking surgery. He agreed a good night's sleep would be the best thing for Charlotte, considering the ordeal of identifying her mother's body lay ahead tomorrow, and he brought the necessary medication. When he had gone Libby persuaded Charlotte to have a hot bath and get into bed. Then she made a drink of hot cocoa and carried it up, along with the two pills Doctor Grantly had left for her.

At first Charlotte just cradled the hot mug in her hands and Libby thought she would refuse to drink it. Then silent tears began to course down the girl's pale cheeks. Libby's heart ached for her.

'We're both staying with you tonight, Charlotte. We shall not leave you alone. Uncle Josh says he will sleep on the settee. I could make up

333

a bed in here if you don't want to be alone?'

'You're so kind, and I've done nothing to deserve it,' Charlotte sobbed quietly. 'I was thinking ... about the funeral. Mother had no friends. We have no family ... There will only be m-me.' She gave a convulsive shudder and Libby was afraid she would spill the hot cocoa.

'You have us, Uncle Josh and me. We'll not let you go alone. Here, take these pills, Charlotte, and drink your cocoa. Things will not seem quite so bad in the morning.' Charlotte obeyed like a child but Libby knew she would not sleep for a while and she didn't like to leave her.

'I do have one relative, I suppose,' Charlotte said slowly. 'But he will not want to know me. Who could blame him after Mother said all those horrid things to the newspapers about his mother and m-my father.'

'Billy, you mean? William Lennox?'

'You know him? But of course you must. I'd forgotten. I am the one who went away.'

'Billy is away too. He lives in Yorkshire. He will know nothing of ... of this, or of your grief.'

They were both silent for a moment, then Charlotte looked up straight into Libby's eyes. 'Grief? I don't feel any grief. I d-don't feel anything. I suppose you think that's terrible?'

'No. I think you are too shocked to know how you feel,' Libby soothed. Charlotte sighed and lay back against the pillows, her eyes closed. They were silent for some time and Libby was just thinking of creeping away when Charlotte opened her eyes.

'Libby? I would like it if you sleep in here tonight. Please.' She shivered. 'That chaise-longue converts to a bed. I ... I wish I didn't feel so ... so alone, so empty.'

'Of course I will sleep here tonight. I must telephone my parents though to let them know...'

'Of course. Parents,' Charlotte whispered, as though it was a word she didn't understand. Libby thought of all the members of her own family and how she loved them and how she had never for a moment doubted their love for her. *I'm so lucky,* she thought. They were silent for a while but Charlotte was still nowhere near sleeping.

'Charlotte...' Libby began diffidently. 'If ... if Billy did come to the funeral? I-I mean would you want him there, as ... as your brother?'

'You think he might come, if he knew?' Charlotte's eyes opened and Libby was certain there was hope in them, then her eyelids fluttered and she whispered brokenly, 'He would never come to stand at my side. Who could blame him? We were so horrible to him and none of it was his fault – or mine.'

Libby didn't answer. Her mind was buzzing. Shortly afterwards she realized Charlotte had finally gone to sleep. She crept out of the room and went to phone her mother.

Victoria was anxious about Libby staying with Charlotte but she did as she was asked and found the telephone number for Mick Butler.

'Don't worry,' Andrew said to Victoria, holding her close in bed that night. 'Josh would never ask Libby to do anything that was beyond her. He seems really concerned for the girl but you know it would never do for him to stay there alone with her and it would be cruel to leave her on her own where her mother has just died – not only died, but committed suicide.'

'I suppose you're right,' Victoria sighed, 'but Libby has been so tense. She seemed to be just getting back to normal so I don't want this to make her worse again.'

'I don't suppose it will. Ironic, isn't it, that she should be helping Henrietta Crainby's girl? I don't know what Mother will have to say to her and Josh about it.'

'Neither do I, but on the other hand your mother always helped if someone needed her. I expect Libby takes after her.'

'Maybe she does, but Mother is not the only one to lend a helping hand. How did you get on with Maggie at the hospital?'

'The doctor confirmed Doctor Ritchie's diagnosis about her heart. I don't think there's much she can do except take the pills they keep prescribing. She's supposed to rest every afternoon and avoid excitement.'

'Mmm, doesn't sound so good.' Andrew frowned in the darkness. 'I think she ought to tell Billy.'

'She says she doesn't want to put any pressure on him to come home until he's ready. Willie believes he'll be making plans to return anyway when he has finished his year's contract with that estate in Yorkshire. He doesn't think Billy would have spent his savings on buying Friesian heifers unless he intended being here to look after them when they calve.'

'That would make sense, I suppose. Strange how Billy and Libby both seem to confide in that brother o' mine.'

'Willie changed after George was killed,' Victoria said sadly. 'He was always kindly but he's more thoughtful, more considerate with people. It would break his heart if anything happened to Mary or wee Mimi.'

'I'm sure it would, but it would break mine if anything happened to you, Victoria.' Andrew's arms tightened around her. The flame of their early passion had never dimmed.

'We're so lucky to have each other,' Victoria murmured as her lips trailed a path down the warm skin of his chest.

Mick Butler's telephone number was the only one Libby had. Mrs Butler answered.

'Oh yes, love, I know who you are. We've heard such a lot about you from Billy.' She was a cheerful woman and quite ready to chatter but Libby drew a deep breath.

'I need to contact Billy urgently, Mrs Butler,' she said as patiently as she could.

'Oh, right y'are, love. I'll just get his number – but he's out with Mick. You'll not get him till after nine. There's nothing wrong with his Ma is there, lass? I know he's been a bit bothered about her lately.'

'No, it's not his mother, Mrs Butler. I ... I just need to talk to him. I want him to do a favour.'

'Oh, oh, he'll do you a favour all right lass, I'm sure he will.' Mrs Butler gave her deep chuckle.

'Well it's not for me exactly. I ... I...'

'It's all right, lass, if they call in here first I'll tell Billy to telephone.'

'I will give you my number then. I am not at home right now. Please tell him to get in touch, even if it's late. I shall be here all night.'

Libby felt nervous now she had made a move towards Billy, but she had quite forgotten about her own reasons for not wanting to talk to him.

'There's not much food in the house as far as I can see,' she said to Josh. 'I expect you could do with something to eat though.'

'I had a look round earlier,' Josh said. 'There's a side of bacon in the pantry. It looks as though it's been there a while but I expect it will be all right if we cook it well. There's nothing much else except three eggs and some mouldy bread.'

'I'll cook some bacon and make an omelette then,' Libby offered. 'There's some bottled fruit in the larder, and there's plenty of milk and butter. Somebody must have brought it.'

'Aye, Mrs McKirdle came this morning with the milk. She used to be housekeeper and cook but Mrs Crainby had flown into so many tempers she had stopped working on a regular basis. She happened to call in this morning, and that's when she found Mrs Crainby. She called the police. You know the rest.'

'Yes.' Libby shuddered. 'I'm glad Charlotte has gone to sleep. It must be terrible for her. She asked me to sleep in her room.'

'I'm very grateful to you, Libby. Your mother was the only person I could think of who might help, in spite of the way she suffered at the hands of Henrietta Crainby, but you're nearer Charlotte's age and you've been magnificent with her. You're just like your mother.'

'Uncle Josh ... It has made me realize how lucky I am with my family. I don't think Charlotte has ever had anyone to love her, not even her own mother.'

'It happens that way sometimes, lassie.'

Libby had just finished clearing away after their meal when the telephone rang. It was Billy.

'Libby! At last. It's lovely to talk to you again. I thought you'd moved to another planet.'

'Billy, I-I want to ask you a big favour.'

'I'll do anything for you, sweetheart.'

'Have you been drinking?'

'No ... we-ell, only a couple of pints. But I'm owing you, Libby.' His voice was serious now. 'I shall not...'

'Billy, this has to do with Charlotte Crainby,' Libby interrupted hastily. She had no desire to relive her last night at college. She explained what had happened to Henrietta Crainby and about Charlotte being one of Uncle Josh's students and how he had needed someone to help with Charlotte.

'And you want me to come over there for that woman's funeral!' Billy sounded as though he

339

would explode with indignation.

'No, not for Mrs Crainby's sake. It's for Charlotte. She really has no one, no one in the whole world who belongs to her – except ... except you,' she finished in a small voice.

'I don't belong to her!' Billy said hotly.

'You're her brother. You have the same father and you're luckier than she is. At least you have a mother who loves you. I don't think Henrietta Crainby ever loved anyone, not even her own daughter.'

'Libby, it's out of the question after all that stuff that was in the papers about my mother and ... and Luke Crainby.'

'He was Charlotte's father too, remember. It must have been just as bad for her. She even used another name when she went to college and when she was at the clinic in Switzerland. Did you know she has been very ill with tuberculosis?'

'Is that supposed to play on my sympathy?'

'Sympathy?' Libby snapped. 'William Crainby Lennox, the only person you feel sorry for is yourself! Just like Henrietta Crainby.'

'For God's sake, Libby, don't compare me with that ... that vixen.'

'Well don't act like her then. Anyway it would let everybody see how wrong the newspaper reports had been if they saw you two together. And did you know that your grandfather and my great-grandmother were brother and sister?'

'What? No! Are you sure? How do you know?'

'Uncle Josh explained it all tonight. My mother didn't even know who her father had been until she was grown up. He was your father's cousin and he was killed in the war. Her mother died when she was born, so she didn't have any parents. But she doesn't feel sorry for herself. She still helps other people when they need it. Anyway, you can please yourself but I'm going to the funeral with Charlotte and so is Uncle Josh. You think about it, Billy. Good night.' She didn't give Billy time to respond as she put the receiver down. Then she turned and burst into tears.

'Hey, Libby? What's the matter?' Josh came through to the hall. He pulled her into his arms and stroked her hair until she calmed down.

'I ... I wanted Billy to come to the funeral, to be with Charlotte so that she didn't feel she was so alone in the world. I don't think he'll come. I lost my temper with him.'

'I see,' Josh said slowly. 'Well it was a kind thought, Libby, but I don't suppose we can blame Billy for staying away in the circumstances. Don't be too hard on him. I think you should get to bed yourself now. There will be a lot to do tomorrow. Charlotte will need to identify the body and there will be all the formalities.' He lowered his voice although Charlotte was sound a sleep. 'I suspect Henrietta Crainby will have left a mountain of debts to sort out on top of everything else. It's just as well this is the start of the summer holiday. It will give Charlotte time to sort things out and

341

come to terms with everything.'

'Yes, I suppose so,' Libby said in a small voice. 'I'll help as much as I can but I need to get in a lot of revision for my finals next month.'

The following morning Mrs McKirdle arrived at the Dower House with a can of fresh milk and a basket of provisions, including bread and cheese and eggs.

'Constable Munro told us Miss Charlotte was staying here and that ye were both keeping her company,' she said. 'That's what I call real Christian-like after the way Mistress Crainby treated your folks, Josh Pringle.' She smiled up at Josh. 'Ah, laddie, but I mind ye as a laddie at the school, and then a handsome young fellow in the RAF and now they tell me ye're training teachers. I'll bet Polly is real proud o' ye, even though she was a wee bit disappointed when ye turned out to be another laddie instead o' the daughter she wanted.'

Libby looked curiously at her uncle. He winked.

'Well you'll no doubt have heard that Miss Crainby is a student at the same college, Mrs McKirdle? It made sense for me to bring her back when I was coming home anyway. There seems to be no one else to help so I intend to take her to see the lawyer and make the funeral arrangements when she wakes up.'

'Right then, that's a relief. While ye're out o' the house I'll make a start on cleaning through. My daughter, Jenny Kerr, has offered to lend a hand and I reckon there'll be food to prepare for the funeral?'

'Well ... I don't know about that, Mrs McKirdle.' Josh was taken aback. 'I don't think Miss Crainby is expecting many people will attend her mother's funeral and we don't even know when we shall be able to make the arrangements.'

'Och, Constable Munro said there wouldn't be any hold-ups once the lassie has identified the body. As for folk at the funeral, I reckon most o' the estate workers will be there, and the tenants – the few who are left anyway. Word gets around and ye've set an example to all o' us – forgive and forget, eh, laddie? And we all had a great liking for Master Luke and for Sir William Crainby. Their blood is in the lassie.'

To Libby's surprise Uncle Josh's face had coloured up but he nodded agreement as the garrulous woman chattered.

'Maybe I should ask Mother if she will do some baking, Mrs McKirdle, if you think there will be a lot of people at the funeral?'

'Now that would be a great idea if she would, lassie. Your mother is the best cook around these parts and I doubt if the lassie will feel like organizing anything, even if she kenned how.'

So it was agreed Libby would cycle home to Langmune while Josh took Charlotte away to see the various officials.

'I'll be back before evening, Charlotte,' Libby promised.

'Thank you, oh thank you, Libby.' Charlotte's

eyes filled with tears but she brushed them away. 'I know I shall have to get used to staying on my own, and I shall, but I would truly appreciate your company until after the funeral.'

'All right,' Libby nodded. 'We'll do that.' The look of relief on Charlotte's face was gratitude enough for Libby. As she passed through the hall on her way out she saw Mrs McKirdle glance up at the banister and shudder.

'It was good of you to come to help, Mrs McKirdle,' she said quietly. 'I'm sure Charlotte appreciates it.'

'Aye, well things are in a bit of a state. I never knew whether to stay or go these past few months. Such a temper she had when she was drunk.' She shook her grey head. 'I worked at the castle when I was a lassie, before I got married. The Crainbys were aye good to their workers, at least until she married Master Luke and took over.' She lowered her voice. 'I know it's a shock for the lassie, her mother hanging herself, but if ye ask me it's the best thing she's ever done for her. She'll be better off without her.' Libby stared at Mrs McKirdle in shocked silence. ''Tis true. She cheated Miss Charlotte any way she could and spent every penny she could get her hands on. There isna a shop frae Darlonachie to Dumfries but what she owes money.'

In spite of Mrs McKirdle's prediction Libby was surprised to find the little kirk was almost full when she arrived in the vestry with Josh and Charlotte. She had heard nothing from Billy and she bitterly regretted losing her temper with him. Deep down she didn't blame him for not coming. She knew how hurt he had been by the prejudice of the newspaper reports.

'I'm going in now,' Josh whispered. 'Chin up, Charlotte.' He squeezed her shoulder. 'You'll be fine with Libby. Wait another couple of minutes then go right to the front.' Charlotte nodded but her face was deathly pale and her teeth were chattering although the day was warm. Libby sensed rather than saw a figure behind them. Her eyes widened as Billy touched her arm. She drew in her breath and her heart raced. He looked so handsome in his dark suit and his white shirt emphasized his healthy tan.

'You came,' she breathed. He gave a solemn nod, then he took Charlotte's cold hand in his.

'Charlotte?' he said quietly, but his deep voice was firm and more assured than Libby had ever heard before. 'We'll all go in together if you agree?'

'Thank you.' Charlotte's voice was barely audible but the gratitude on her pale face was plain to see. Libby smiled at Billy.

'I'll go in and sit with Uncle Josh. You have Billy now, Charlotte.'

'We'll be right behind you.' Billy nodded. He straightened his black tie and squared his shoulders, then he drew Charlotte's hand on to his arm and, head high, he led her to the front of Darlonachie Kirk where their ancestors had worshipped and been christened, married and buried for generations past. There was an in-

345

voluntary murmur amongst the mourners at the sight of Luke Crainby's son and daughter walking side by side. Sitting behind them both Josh and Libby saw there was more than a passing resemblance in the shape of their heads and the colour of their reddish-brown hair. Libby felt she had never been as proud of Billy as he stood tall and upright beside his half-sister and his voice rang strong and true as he sang the hymns.

They were on their way back to the Dower House for refreshments when Billy said, 'My mother would have come to the funeral, Charlotte, for your sake and for your father's, she said. She's not well so I felt she was better at home.' He frowned. 'She seems worse than she was the last time I was home. What do you think, Libby?'

'Mother went with her to the hospital recently. The doctors say it is her heart. They advised her to rest and avoid stress.'

'Mmm, I thought as much.' He turned his head to look at Libby and she thought she saw a challenging gleam in his blue eyes. She raised her brows in silent query. 'You've no orders about what I should do on that front then, miss bossy boots?' There was a faint mockery in his tone and Libby didn't know whether the glint in his eyes was one of anger or humour. She suspected it was the former.

Whatever he felt, Billy did not stay long at the Dower House and the following day he returned to Yorkshire without a word of goodbye.

Twenty-Five

After the funeral Libby returned to Langmune and began preparing for her examination.

'Mr Whittaker telephoned this afternoon,' Victoria announced and Libby stiffened involuntarily.

'I suppose he wants me to start the work at the creamery?'

'No, he says there's no rush. The new building is not completed yet. They're running behind schedule. He thinks you may as well wait until the end of August. You will have taken your National Diploma by then and there'll be no need to take a break.'

'Oh, that's much better!' Libby gave a huge sigh of relief. 'Mum, there's something I should have told you when I first came home,' she began hesitantly.

'We knew there was something wrong, lassie, but we didn't know what.' Victoria put a warm hand over Libby's clenched fists and gave a reassuring squeeze. 'Don't tell us if it upsets you. We're just happy to see you getting back to normal, and we're really proud of you the way you helped Charlotte Crainby. Josh says you were wonderful, so calm and reassuring. He says you seemed to know exactly how to help her and we should be proud of you. And we are, no matter what happened at college.'

'You must have wondered why I haven't had any results about the College Diploma though...' Libby's mouth tightened at the memory of the unfairness and the humiliation.

'Well, yes, we did. But we knew you would tell us in your own time, Libby. All that matters to your father and me is your health and happiness.'

'Seeing Charlotte ... She was so desperately alone. It made me get things into perspective and realize how lucky I am to have you both, as well as Fraser and Lachie and Mimi, Granny and Grandpa Pringle too. Life has been so unfair for her, and there was me, fretting over stupid exams, or at least how to tell you and Dad what had happened. You see ... Oh, Mum, I should have told you straight away but I was so upset. They didn't allow me to sit the exams. They sent me home. I wasn't even allowed to say goodbye to my friends.' Her eyes filled with tears at her mother's horrified expression.

'Dearest child, why? Why did they ban you from the college?'

'I can't tell you the reason, Mum. It ... it concerned more than me. Please trust me. Maybe I shall be able to tell you some day, but I had done nothing wrong, I promise you. It was the matron. She didn't believe me. She just wouldn't listen.' Even now Libby's brown eyes were wide and dark with remembered shock.

348

'I do trust you, lassie, and of course I believe you. I've never known you to lie. We've been so worried about you.'

'I know, and I'm sorry. I've hated deceiving you but it seemed like the end of the world to me. Now I know there are worse things in life. I couldn't bear it if I'd had a mother like Charlotte's. Miss Cuttle believed me though, and she was angry because I couldn't take the exams. So was Mr Donelly. They have sent me loads of notes and Mr Donelly says if I get my National Diploma that's what really counts.'

Victoria pushed back her chair and pulled Libby into her arms. 'All that counts with your father and me is that you are here with us and you are well, Libby. Nothing else matters, even supposing you never pass any exams.'

'Well I mean to pass them,' Libby said, her mouth setting with determination. 'And some day I will tell you what really happened, Mum.'

Victoria patted her shoulder and smiled. 'That's my girl. But don't work too hard.'

Libby passed her examinations. There were only three students in the country who passed with distinction and she was one of them. Miss Cuttle and Mr Donelly were jubilant, as were Alice and Alma, her loyal friends.

'You'll be thinking our job here at the creamery is not good enough for you now,' Mr Whittaker teased, but he was half serious. He didn't want to lose her. He recognized in Libby a well-trained and conscientious worker. She was

349

patient and thorough with the two girls she was training as her assistants. She was firm with the farmers who supplied poor-quality milk but she understood their problems better than he did himself. She knew about milking cows and the struggle to cool milk with water which was already warm in mid summer.

'I'm quite content here, Mr Whittaker,' Libby smiled. 'I like living at home with my family and having an interesting job as well.'

Billy had not told Libby of his plans to return to Home Farm when his contract as under manager finished. He had made up his mind about certain things and he knew that letters were no use for sorting out problems. He needed to confront Libby face to face.

'I suppose you've heard the remaining farms on Darlonachie Estate are to be sold?' Josh said to Andrew and Willie after lunch at Langmune one Sunday towards the end of September. It was Josh's last free weekend before he resumed his lectures.

'Yes, we heard,' Andrew said. 'We hope to buy Throstlebrae this time. Is Charlotte Crainby very upset?'

'Not really. She was never encouraged to take an interest in the estate. Henrietta Crainby had run up tremendous debts. The solicitor told Charlotte they were her mother's debts and she didn't need to pay them out of her inheritance but that's what she intends to do.'

'Luke would have done the same,' Maggie said softly, joining the conversation for the first time. 'He was a man of honour. It seems Charlotte must have a lot of her father in her after all.'

'Yes. She's selling the Dower House too,' Josh said. 'She has asked the solicitor to invest any money that is left. When she finishes her education she will decide where she wants to live. Meanwhile she's going to rent a flat near the college.'

'Sounds sensible to me,' Victoria said, bringing in a huge trifle for desert. She loved having all the family gathered around the big table at Langmune. 'You seem to know a lot about Charlotte's affairs,' Victoria remarked and to her surprise Josh, the courageous RAF man, the assured lecturer, blushed like a schoolboy.

'Aye,' Polly butted in gruffly. 'He kens far too much about Charlotte Crainby for my liking. Just you remember, my lad, she is a Crainby, and her mother treated Victoria abominably when she was little more than a bairn, and she put your father and me oot o' oor wee hoose.'

Josh raised his eyes heavenward. He had suffered several similar lectures from his mother recently.

'Oh, Granny,' Libby said gently, putting her arm around the old woman's thin shoulders, 'Somebody has to help poor Charlotte. She has nobody to advise her, or support her.'

'Ach, lassie, you're too young to understand how wicked some folks can be, and that girl's mother was one o' the worst.'

Libby would have said more but Josh shook

his head, knowing it was useless to argue with his mother on this subject.

'Billy has been home two weekends recently and he helped Charlotte quite a bit,' Maggie said.

'I didn't know Billy had been home.' Libby felt hurt that he had not been in touch. Maybe he didn't need her company now that he had made friends with Charlotte.

'He was only here for a short time,' Maggie said, 'mainly to check up on me, I think.' She gave a wan smile. 'But he and Charlotte did go round the farms together. There's only ten left. Three of them are very small, only about twenty-five acres each. Seven of the tenants want to buy, but Throstlebrae and the other two will be for sale.'

'Lucky for some, eh?' Willie nodded at Andrew, then turned to look directly at Maggie. 'I don't suppose Billy would consider selling High Bowie to us as his sitting tenants?'

'It's not his to sell,' Maggie said without thinking, then clapped a hand to her mouth, looking beseechingly at Andrew.

'You mean you're hanging on to it, Maggie?' Willie looked disappointed.

'Are you really interested in buying?' Andrew asked his brother.

'At the right price I reckon it would be a good investment. I know I've no sons to follow on like you have, Andrew, but I think it would be a solid investment for Mimi's future. She could rent it out and have an income, or she'd have something to sell when ... well ye ken what I mean. We have to look to the future. She'll probably need it even more than your laddies.' He glanced tenderly at his nine-year-old daughter but there was sadness in his eyes. He couldn't visualize Mimi ever knowing the happiness of a loving husband and children of her own. If they could do anything to make her future secure he and Mary would do it.

'Can you afford it?' Andrew persisted.

'Not outright,' Willie admitted, 'but I expect you'll need a loan from the bank to buy Throstlebrae for Lachie, so why shouldn't we do the same?'

'Too right we shall need a loan,' Andrew said ruefully, 'but the government still seem to favour increasing home production so I reckon it's worth a gamble and a sacrifice while we have a guaranteed market for our produce – not like it was after the First War.'

'Mmm, well the same applies to us,' Willie said. 'We've taken advantage of the subsidies on lime and the ploughing grants. We've even drained the low meadow. Recently we've been thinking we could do with a shed for bullocks and another hen house, haven't we, love?' Mary nodded and looked apologetically at Maggie. 'We're not complaining. We don't expect a landlord to make such improvements, but if the farm was ours that's what we'd do.'

'I know exactly how you feel,' Maggie smiled. 'The first thing Billy intends to do when he comes home is to build a bull pen with a safety

353

gate. Fortunately he and Fergus seem to get along very well together now they're getting to know each other better, but Fergus still thinks a pen just for a bull is a waste of money. So I know everybody has different ideas.'

'Well!' Andrew grinned and looked at Victoria. 'If that's how you and Mary feel, Willie, I think it's time you became landowners as well.'

'It's all very well for you to say that, Andrew, but we don't want to move to one of the other farms. We like being at High Bowie, even if a lot of folk would think it's a bit isolated.'

'I was not suggesting you move. Listen, Willie, before we knew you and Mary were getting married, or that you wanted to farm on your own, I'd already agreed to buy High Bowie from Maggie. She needed to sell. I thought you would be happier shepherding at High Bowie than milking cows at Langmune so...'

'You mean you own High Bowie?' Willie was staring at his elder brother and he was not pleased. 'You're our landlord?'

'We,' Andrew corrected. 'Victoria and I do everything together.'

'And you've treated us as a charity case all these years!' Willie said bitterly. 'And we never knew. We paid the rent to Maggie.' He turned accusing blue eyes on Maggie.

'When we realized you'd planned to rent a farm together,' Victoria said quietly, 'it seemed the right thing to do. We had borrowed the money anyway. You paid us a rent instead of us having to buy sheep and pay you to look after them, so it suited everyone. We kept the land in the family and we used your rent to pay back our loan.'

'Now, Willie lad.' Joe Pringle spoke for the first time, his voice low but firm – he was still head of his family. 'Andrew and Victoria did what they thought best. Somebody else would have bought High Bowie if they hadn't. So don't get on your high horse.' His eyes twinkled at Polly. 'It's bad enough when your mother gets on hers.'

'Joe Pringle!' Polly spluttered, but she saw him wink and nodded her head, adding her support.

'Your father's right, Willie. Grab the chance to buy your own farm while it's being offered. I expect it would suit Andrew and Victoria to sell High Bowie just now, when they want to buy Throstlebrae.'

'Yes, it would.' Victoria looked at Mary. 'It would allow us to offer a bit better price and we'd be more likely to get it.'

'Will you give us time to talk it over on our own?' Mary suggested calmly. She knew it was what Willie had dreamed of and she could make him realize Mimi's future was far more important than pride if they were alone together. Besides, he ought to be pleased Andrew had wanted to help them get started on the farming ladder. Lily, her own sister, had always grabbed everything and given nothing.

'Aye, take as much time as you like,' Andrew said. 'If you pay us what we paid Maggie plus

355

the interest we've paid the bank, I reckon that would be a fair price all round.' Willie scowled, considering. He had always been proud and independent.

Ten days later they all recalled the conversation round the table at Langmune, but it was not the buying or selling of farms which were imprinted on their minds – it was Billy Lennox's plan to build a bull pen as his first priority at Home Farm.

Twenty-Six

At the end of a satisfying day at the creamery Libby felt content, almost happy, as she drove home in her little blue Austin car. Just before she reached the fork in the track which led to Home Farm and on to High Bowie a figure seemed to peel itself from the fence along the top of the grassy bank. He slithered down to the road and she drew to a smooth halt.

'Billy! I thought you were not due home for good for another week?' She frowned, noticing how white and shattered he looked. She switched off the engine and climbed out of the car to stand beside him. He gripped her hands tightly and they sat down together on the grassy bank. 'What's wrong? What is it, Billy? Tell me.'

'Fergus Dunlop,' he said in a low voice. 'Oh God, Libby. He's dead. He was killed early this morning. The bull, it ... it turned on him. He was on his own in the shed. He couldn't get away. Nobody to help him...' The words tumbled out in a torrent. 'Dear God, if only I had insisted we build a pen when I first realized Fergus took such risks...' He pushed a hand through his hair.

'Who...? How did you hear?'

'Derek heard the bull roaring when he came

357

out of the byre to carry the milk units to the dairy. He said he was roaring and pawing – you know the way they do when they're angry or upset. He didn't see Fergus at first. He was almost buried in the straw in a far corner of the shed. Then he ran to the house and told mother of course. She phoned for the vet. He came and shot the bull but mother had insisted on going out to see what she could do for Fergus. It was too late to do anything by the time they got to him.' Billy buried his face in his hands, his shoulders hunched.

'Oh, Billy, you can't blame yourself...'

'Well I do!' he shouted. 'I do blame myself. I knew Fergus believed he could handle any animal on his own, including the bloody bull. That's not all either. God knows I came as soon as I could when Derek phoned me but Mother had collapsed with the shock. She's in hospital.'

'Oh no! Oh, Billy, how awful.' Libby put her arms round his shoulders and held him tight.

'I was on my way to tell your mother, b-but I couldn't face her.' His words were muffled as she held him against her. 'I decided to wait for you. Will you tell her what's happened, Libby? Mother is not allowed visitors. They let me see her briefly but she's heavily sedated.'

'It'll be a wonder if they haven't heard already, knowing what the grapevine is like. No one can blame you, Billy. You weren't even there.'

'No, and I see now I should have been,' he said bitterly. He raised his head and looked her in the eye. 'It was almost on this very spot where wee Sylvie was killed with the tank. Do you remember that day, Libby? I can still hear Milly screaming at me, telling me that was my fault too.'

'Milly was half crazy. She didn't mean it, Billy. You must forget about all that.'

'I can't forget. I expect Fergus's wife blames me, just as Milly did.'

'Have you seen her?'

'Briefly. Your Doctor Ritchie was with her. She was too distressed to say anything. He said I should wait until tomorrow to talk to her. He ... he seems quite a nice fellow.'

'He is. Come on, Billy, get in the car. You're coming home with me. You look shattered.'

He shook his head. 'I've got to get back to Home Farm.' He shuddered at the prospect.

'Come on, get in here.' Libby tugged at his arm. 'You need a cup of strong tea. When did you last eat?'

'Eat? Breakfast I suppose...'

'And you need something inside you. Get into my car.'

'Bossy wee bugger,' he muttered, but he obeyed.

Maggie Lennox survived but she was very frail and the doctors insisted she should go to a convalescent home until her condition was more stable. Privately they told Billy she might never be fit to return to the farm.

Fergus Dunlop's widow was a sensible and

capable young woman but her immediate worry was her home and her two children. The cottage had been tied to Fergus's job. She had a son, Robbie, who was almost sixteen and keen to work on the farm. He had helped his father during holidays and weekends. She also had a daughter, Fiona, who was thirteen and doing well at school. Julie Dunlop knew Fiona was already upset and she dreaded the effects a change of home and school would have.

Billy suggested Julie and her family should stay in the farm cottage and Robbie would work at Home Farm when he left school. He asked Julie if she would work in the house at Home Farm for a few hours each week and do some cooking and washing, until his mother was well enough to make decisions herself. Julie was relieved.

'It gives us all time to get used to the change,' she said to Billy. 'And the money will be useful.' Billy nodded. He still felt he could have prevented her husband's death if he had taken command of Home Farm sooner. He felt responsible for his mother too, even though the doctors insisted that any kind of shock would have affected her badly due to her heart condition.

Libby couldn't help feeling a little hurt as weeks passed into months. Billy had sought her out when his defences were down and he had needed comfort but ever since it was as though he had regretted showing his need of her. He was subdued and withdrawn whenever they met.

There was a barrier between them which had never been there before and which she found impossible to penetrate. Looking back she wondered if the barrier had always been there and she had been too wrapped up in her own problems to notice it. Had he resented her interference over Henrietta Crainby's funeral? She had rather commanded him to attend, and yet he and Charlotte seemed to be on friendly terms. According to Uncle Josh, Charlotte had even stayed at Home Farm for a weekend.

Maybe the awkwardness had developed before the funeral, when she had severed her contact with Billy. He would have asked about her exams and her results. It had been easier to stop writing to him than to deceive him, especially while her future had seemed bleak and uncertain. Underneath his confident air she knew better than anyone how sensitive Billy could be. He had proved that again when he recalled wee Sylvie's death, and again in the way he had befriended Charlotte when she needed him most.

Perhaps the time had come to clear the air and tell him what had happened at college. She had been too shocked to think clearly about anything, but she had never blamed Billy. It had seemed liked the end of the world – her world anyway – at the time. Miss Fanshaw's first priority would always be guarding the reputation of the college. Surely no one else would have suggested forcing a young man to marry, not now, not since the war, when men and women had been forced into all sorts of strange situations together. Even if her reputation had been blemished it had been as much her fault as Billy's and in the end her future had not been ruined forever by sleeping in the same room. The bleak black abyss she had imagined had not materialized. She had gained her National Diploma after all, and she had got her job in the laboratory.

It was time she explained all this to Billy. There was no need for him to feel responsible for her; certainly not to the point of marriage to someone he did not want. It seemed quite ridiculous now, even though it had seemed so serious at the time. So Libby reasoned to herself and planned what she would say to Billy, but she could not deny a yearning deep within her. Billy was obviously not the least bit attracted to her as a woman. She was an old friend and nothing more.

Twenty-Seven

Victoria and Maggie talked easily together of times past as they sat in front of the window of the convalescent home.

'I feel I'm ready to leave here now,' Maggie said, 'but I can't make up my mind what to do. I get so short of breath, even without climbing stairs to my bedroom. Home Farm is a lovely house but it is too large and not convenient for someone like me.'

'I know what you mean, Maggie,' Victoria said gently. 'Would you consider making a downstairs bedroom?'

'I could, but Billy is managing very well with Julie Dunlop. She is a nice young woman and she comes in here once a week to see me and brings my clean washing. She's always pleasant and she doesn't blame Billy for Fergus's death. He blames himself.'

'I know,' Victoria nodded. 'Can I make a suggestion, Maggie?' she asked tentatively.

'Of course you can, Victoria.' Maggie smiled warmly. 'You've been the best friend I ever had, especially since Luke died.'

'Mmm, it was Luke I was thinking of. You know he left Ivy Cottage to my brother Mark? Mark and Catriona never married and she has

363

never been back to Darlonachie since his death, so I've sort of taken it over. There was a family of evacuees in it all through the war and for a while after. Miss Phipps rented it for four and sixpence a week after she had to give up her sewing shop.' Victoria smiled reminiscently. 'She was always kind to me when I was young. It's four months since she died and I've been wondering what to do about the cottage. I know it's very small but it could be quite cosy if it was freshly painted and a couple of new carpets and curtains put in. I'm sure Andrew will agree if I make the small back bedroom into a bathroom. It would be an improvement and I hope it will be Libby's some day.'

'You're offering it to me?' Maggie looked at Victoria, her eyes brightening. 'I think I would like that. It would be so convenient for the grocer and the butcher, and even for the doctor's surgery,' she added with a wry grimace. 'Seriously, Victoria, it would be ideal.'

'That's fine then. We'll need time to get it sorted and decorated. I'll have a word with Andrew. He'll get things going. Meanwhile I wondered if you would like to come to Langmune for Christmas, either for the day, or if you feel like staying you can have the little sitting room where Miss Traill used to sleep.'

'Ah, Victoria, you're a good friend to me,' Maggie said huskily. 'I've been wondering about Christmas. Billy was asking what I wanted to do. He doesn't want me to get over tired but his friend, Mick Butler, wants to come to

Home Farm on Boxing Day and stay until the New Year. If I come to Langmune it would be an ideal solution, if you're sure?'

'Of course I'm sure.'

'In that case I shall tell Billy to go ahead. I think he feels he should ask Charlotte to spend Christmas at Home Farm too. Now that she's sold the Dower House she has nowhere else to stay in Darlonachie and he thought it might be a bit lonely for her on her own at the flat.'

'Billy is a considerate laddie,' Victoria said warmly. 'I'm glad he's managing to bury the past and all the bitterness Henrietta caused. None of it was his fault, or Charlotte's, but they have both paid for her jealousy and spite.'

'As you did too, Victoria,' Maggie said quietly. 'We all did,'

'Yes,' Victoria smiled, 'but you and I can both be thankful Luke Crainby was such a true friend and an honourable man. We're lucky.'

When Billy heard his mother's plans to move to Ivy Cottage he was relieved to know she felt up to leaving the convalescent home, but pride wouldn't allow him to leave all the preparations to the Pringles. The new bathroom was installed before Christmas and as soon as Mick arrived on Boxing Day he announced that he had some decorating to do.

'I'll help with the painting,' Charlotte offered promptly, 'but I'm no good at hanging wallpaper.'

'I'll come too then,' Mick grinned. 'Will Libby be there?'

365

'How should I know?' Billy scowled.

'You could phone and ask her?'

'I shall leave that to you since you're so keen to have her there.'

'OK, I'll do that,' Mick said cheerfully. 'All's fair in love and war and you're not making much progress. I thought you'd have had a ring on the lass's finger by now,' he said in his blunt Yorkshire way. 'All the letters you used to write to her...' He shook his head and gave a despairing sigh.

'If you mean a wedding ring she made it quite plain she didn't want to marry me,' he snapped. 'Maybe you'll have better luck, though I wouldn't count on it. She's a child of the heather and I don't think she'll leave Darlonachie, even for the Butler acres.'

'No need to get nasty, Billy boy,' Mick grinned, then he sobered. 'Did you ask her to marry you then?'

'I didn't have to. She'd already told her friend Alice that it was the last thing she wanted.'

Charlotte had listened to this exchange, part banter between two good friends, part serious.

'That doesn't sound like Libby,' she said thoughtfully. 'Are you sure this girl Alice was not wanting you herself?'

'Living with your mother has made you cynical, Charlotte,' Billy said. 'Why would Alice want me?

'Mmm...' Charlotte pretended to consider this. 'You're quite a handsome fellow, at least when you're not scowling. And you can be very considerate and kind,' she added seriously, holding his gaze, 'and Libby certainly knows that and values such qualities in people. I expect she told her friends.'

'I've only seen Alice once, and she certainly doesn't know me. Anyway, Libby stopped writing after we had that day in Blackpool.'

'Ah, I remember now. That was the night you missed the bus home,' Mick chuckled, 'and you spent the night with Libby. You must have misbehaved, old boy, and probably frightened the girl with your ardour.'

'I didn't do anything!' Billy said indignantly, even though he knew by the glint in Mick's eyes he was only teasing. 'Not that I wasn't tempted,' he muttered. 'Oh, come on, let's get down to the cottage and see what we shall need to decorate it.'

The banter between the two boys was a revelation to Charlotte. She had been a lonely only child and most of her school days had been spent with girls. In the end Mick persuaded her to telephone Libby and ask if she would join them at the cottage. Charlotte didn't miss the expectant look in Billy's eyes in spite of his feigned lack of interest.

'Libby has to work between Christmas and New Year,' she reported. 'She says the cows don't stop milking, and people still expect their milk on the doorstep, so someone has to keep a check on things at the creamery too.' Mick looked disappointed. 'But she says she'll join us when she is free, and in the evenings,' Charlotte added with a teasing grin. 'You'll have to make do with that.'

When Josh heard about the work at Ivy Cottage he decided to offer his services. Polly was not pleased. She guessed Charlotte Crainby would be helping too while she was staying at Home Farm. Billy welcomed Josh's help. None of them had hung wallpaper before but Josh had watched his mother and he was precise about the measuring and methodical in his work. After one or two mistakes he got into the way of it. Billy's first priority was always the work at Home Farm and Mick usually stayed to help him, so there were times when Charlotte and Josh were alone together at the cottage. Although he always referred to her as Miss Laine when they were at college and, as her lecturer, she addressed him as Mr Pringle, when they were alone he called her Lottie. She was pleased he had remembered she had liked the people at the Swiss Clinic calling her that. She had been shy about calling him Josh at first but gradually she did as he asked. She felt at ease in his company and she told him things she had never imagined discussing with anyone. She never noticed the eleven years difference in their age, but Josh was increasingly aware of it, especially when he listened to Mick and Billy teasing her and the way they all laughed together – so young and carefree, he thought. None of them had experienced war, with its destruction and death, or the way it made a man intensely aware of the precious things in life – the sound of laughter, a kind word or a thoughtful gesture, the swish of silken hair against his cheek. That was a delightful sensation he had only recently discovered. Even if there were no other obstacles Josh knew his mother would never accept a daughter of Henrietta Crainby into her family. He would not upset her without good reason. He was aware that both his parents were growing increasingly frail. There was nothing he could do anyway until Charlotte finished her college training, but still his mind went round in circles, and always with Charlotte at the centre.

They all wanted to get the cottage finished before Hogmanay so Libby stopped off on her way home from work to lend a hand with painting on the Saturday afternoon. She was surprised to find only Billy there.

'Mick and Charlotte have gone into Dumfries for another tin of paint and Mick wanted to get some beer to celebrate his first Scottish New Year.' Billy smiled wryly. 'I'm not sure what he's expecting.'

'If we get this finished in time maybe we can all celebrate. What about Uncle Josh? Where is he?'

'He has finished all the papering but he intended to lend a hand with the windows. Your Granny Pringle had other plans for him today though.'

'I can imagine,' Libby grinned. 'I'm afraid Granny doesn't like the idea of us spending too much time with Charlotte. She can't seem to accept that she's a completely different sort of person to her mother.' She sighed. 'I suppose when people get old it's not so easy to forgive and forget. Come and have a sandwich and some coffee. I haven't had my lunch yet.'

'No, neither have I,' Billy said on a note of surprise. 'Have you plenty?'

'Yes, I stopped and bought a loaf and butter on my way home. It's just cheese or corned beef though.'

'That'll do fine. I'm ravenous now I've thought about food.' He grinned at her in the old familiar way and her heart did a somersault. They ate in companionable silence.

'I think my mother will like living here,' Billy said. 'It was good of your parents to suggest it.'

'We wouldn't have had the cottage if it hadn't been for your father. He left it to Uncle Mark. Mother has taken it over since he was killed in the war but she says she doesn't feel it should really belong to her. I think your father would be pleased to know your mother is here. Mum says he loved her very much.'

'Too much, some would say. He gave her a bastard.' The bitterness in Billy's tone was obvious.

'Oh, Billy.' Libby reached out and laid her hand over his clenched fist. 'No one thinks about that. You're you.'

'Yes, I am. Me...' He looked at her oddly, opened his mouth to speak and snapped it shut again. Libby sighed.

'You remember the night you missed the bus back from Blackpool, Billy?'

'As though I could forget it.'

'Matron discovered you spent the night in my room. She ... she...'

'She had you banned from college. I know.'

She jerked her hand but he turned his swiftly and grasped it tightly, holding her prisoner.

'How ... how do you know that? I never told anyone, not even Mum.'

'I wondered when you would get around to telling me,' Billy said tightly, 'or if you ever would. I sent you the cheque, remember? My address was on the back of the envelope. Your friend Alma wrote to say it had arrived but she was posting it on to you. She told me what had happened and she said they blamed themselves, her and Alice, because it had been their idea I should stay the night. I knew then I should have refused. It was my thoughtlessness. We were all afraid your future would be ruined when you weren't permitted to take the exams.'

'B-but I asked them not tell you.' Libby's face was pale.

'I know.' Billy nodded grimly. 'By the time they received your letter they had already spill-ed the beans so they felt more guilty than ever. Alice wrote to ask me not to let on I knew. She also added that I was not to worry. Because...' His words became clipped and angry. 'Although Miss Fanshaw believed I should be compelled to marry you, I was quite safe because you had said it was the last thing on earth you would consider.' His grip had tightened painfully now. 'Did you say that, Libby? Did you?'

371

'Let me go, Billy, you're hurting me.'

'Did you say that?' he demanded harshly. 'Tell me.'

'Of course I did. I would never, ever want you – or any other man – to be compelled to marry me against your will. Let me go!'

'But how do you know it would have been against my will?' Without warning he moved swiftly round the table without releasing her hand. He pulled her to her feet and held her tightly against his chest. 'Have you any idea how tempted I was to make wild and passionate love to you that morning before I left? Have you, Libby?'

'N-no ... I w-was asleep...'

'Yes, you were.' He smiled then and his face softened. 'And you looked so innocent and so desirable, Libby Pringle.' His voice was deep and husky now. 'But I would never want to take you against your will...' He lowered his head and his mouth sought hers, gently at first, but as her lips parted his kiss deepened urgently. 'Would it be against your will, Libby? Would it?' His lips were on hers, finding his answer as she responded to his kisses with a fire to match his own.

'We got the paint and we—' Mick halted abruptly in the doorway.

'I ... we didn't hear the car return...' Billy said gruffly.

'Obviously!' Mick was grinning unrepentantly. Libby's face was flushed but her eyes were shining. Mick called over his shoulder, 'I think we have to go away and come back later, Charlotte...'

'Don't be a silly bugger,' Billy muttered, but his eyes were tender when he looked into Libby's. He couldn't stop smiling as his fingers gently smoothed her tousled hair. Mick began to sing one of the latest songs. ' "*Que sera, sera...*" '

Libby was helping her mother tidy away the remains of the festive season and gathering the Christmas cards together. 'We seem to have had more cards this year,' she said.

'Yes, I think people are spending more money now the war and the rationing is behind us, but I hardly had time to look at them all properly. Keep any aside if they contain messages.'

'I will,' Libby said. 'There's a bit in the one from Catriona in Edinburgh, did you see it? She says she has been ill. There's a photo attached as well.'

'I remember glancing through it,' Victoria said absently. 'She doesn't usually write anything except their names. She didn't say what had been wrong with her, did she?'

'No, only that she has spent some time in hospital.' Libby was studying the photograph of the three children, a dark-haired boy who looked vaguely familiar and two younger fair-haired girls. She set it aside with the few cards her mother would read at her leisure. 'That boy in the photo looks just like Fraser,' she said before her thoughts turned to Billy and all thoughts of the little Edinburgh family were forgotten, at least for the present.

It had been the best Hogmanay she could remember. Billy had driven the four of them into Dumfries where he had booked a special dinner at the King's Arms Hotel. He had said it was to celebrate finishing the cottage and to thank them for their help, but Libby knew from the look in his eyes that they had more to celebrate than decorating. They had waited at the Mid-Steeple until midnight struck. Suddenly everyone was singing Auld Lang Syne and kissing everyone else with choruses of 'Happy New Year'.

'I think ours will be an extra-special year, Libby,' Billy whispered. She just had time to nod before he seized her in his arms and claimed her mouth in a lingering kiss.

'Hey, none of that here!' Mick Butler teased. 'Let me kiss the lass. Happy New Year, Libby! I really think it's going to be.' He lowered his voice. 'You'll make sure he asks me to be best man at the wedding, won't you?'

'You're jumping ahead of yourself, Mick Butler,' Libby laughed and gave him a gentle punch in the ribs.

They sang Auld Lang Syne in the car on the way home, then, because Mick didn't know all the words, he gave them a rendering of 'Ilkley Moor b'aht 'at'.

Charlotte was glad Billy had invited her to spend Christmas at Home Farm. It had been the happiest she could remember and she told him so. She was disappointed when Josh declined to join them for Hogmanay.

'I think I should spend it with my parents while I can,' he said. 'Who can tell what another year might bring.' She understood – indeed she envied him the warmth of his close family circle.

In the weeks that followed Billy was busy moving the pieces of smaller furniture his mother had chosen to move from Home Farm to Ivy Cottage, and buying the extras she would require. He knew how much she would miss the warmth and convenience of her Aga cooker, and had asked Victoria if he could install a miniature version as a surprise. It fitted nicely into the cottage kitchen and it would ensure she always had some warmth. Maggie was delighted. Billy couldn't remember her hugging him so tightly since he was a small boy. He was glad he had come home, back to the glen and the people he loved. They more than made up for the gossip and scandal that had gone before.

A fortnight later Libby told him Fraser was to sing in the Young Farmer's concert.

'He's a bit nervous so he wants me to go and support him.' She grinned. 'He just wants to be sure there's someone there to clap.'

'We'll both go. Shall we take Mimi and Lachie with us? They're nine now, old enough to enjoy it. We could go on the Friday night, then it wouldn't matter if they're late for bed.'

'All right, if you're sure you don't want to go to the dance afterwards?' Billy guessed Libby was a bit disappointed they wouldn't be going dancing but he had other plans.

Lachie and Mimi were excited. Billy collected them early to get good seats in the hall so the two children could see everything.

'What was all that whispering about? Were you giving Fraser some of your expert advice?' Libby chuckled.

'Och, that was just man talk,' Billy teased.

The first half of the concert went very well and Libby was surprised to hear her young brother singing. They were all amateurs and enjoyed the fun of putting on a concert but he was better than she had expected and she was proud of him. So it was a surprise when the compere approached Billy towards the end of the interval.

'Fraser must have a bit of a sore throat. He says he is losing his voice. We wondered if you would fill in for us and sing the couple of songs he was supposed to do. Here they are...' He handed Billy a sheet of paper. 'You can substitute the first one with "Old MacDonald" if you like, then the youngsters can join in.'

'Oh yes, Billy, please do,' Mimi chirruped.

'All right,' Billy grinned. 'I'll sing the first song for you two and the second one for Libby.'

'What is the second one?' Libby glanced at the sheet of paper. 'It's "I Remember the Red River Valley". Yes, I like that sort of music. It's funny though, Fraser didn't complain about a sore throat and he sounded fine to me in the first half.'

It was getting towards the end of the concert

when Billy received the signal to go backstage and he crept away. Mimi and Lachie snuggled in on either side of Libby. They were getting tired now but they were eager to join in Billy's song. It seemed everyone else was enjoying Old MacDonald's animals too, judging by the noise.

When the hall grew quiet again Billy made an announcement. 'Now I have a song of my own I would like to sing for a very special person.' There were a few whistles and cat calls but Billy went on calmly. 'You know the tune to "Red River Valley", so listen to the words.' He waited while the pianist played the opening bars, then his deep melodious voice filled the hall:

'In this glen there's a girl I desire
For her nature so tender and kind,
Her sweet smile lights my heart with a fire
And I can't get her out of my mind.

May I sit by your side 'cause I love you?
Please tell me you'll soon be my bride
And dear Libby I'll always be true...
If we can go through our life side by side.'

The hall erupted with whistles and cat calls. Libby's cheeks were hot and she tried to hide her face against Mimi's soft hair. Billy jumped off the front of the stage and came hurrying back to her. He lifted Mimi from her seat and sat her on his knee.

'Will you, Libby? Will you marry me?' he asked, his voice low and urgent. In the dim light

377

Libby glimpsed uncertainty in his blue eyes. She nodded.

'What does she say?' someone called.

'Say yes! Say yes!' came a chorus from the audience.

'Kiss her! Give the lassie a kiss!'

Billy stood up, still holding Mimi in his arms. 'The answer is YES!'

There were more cheers and whistles and calls. 'Kiss her! A kiss! A kiss!'

'We'll save that for later,' Billy grinned widely.

Libby was barely aware of the rousing finale to the concert but she did see Fraser joining in the singing with gusto and grinning all over his face as he caught her eye.

Mimi and Lachie were very tired as they snuggled up in the back of Billy's car. He held the passenger door open for Libby, but he dropped a kiss at the side of her mouth before she got in.

'For a minute or two I was really worried after I'd made such a public proposal, Libby. I was afraid I had spread my dreams under your feet and that you were about to trample on them.'

'I'd never do that, Billy,' Libby said softly. 'I love you too much.'

'And I love you more than life itself,' he said huskily. 'What a time to choose for such declarations with two wee ear-wiggers in the back.' Libby glanced behind.

'They're both asleep already, but they really enjoyed the concert and they were excited about

378

being out so late.'

'I hope your parents don't disapprove, Libby? Perhaps we should have asked them first?'

'I wouldn't be surprised if they've guessed,' Libby smiled, 'but I know they will approve.'

'Mmm, but we'd better go and tell them as soon as we've taken Mimi home, especially after making such a public announcement. I must have been mad!'

'It was lovely, and so unlike you, Billy.'

Andrew and Victoria assured Billy of their approval. Later, snuggled in their big bed at Langmune, Andrew turned to Victoria with a note of wonder. 'I can't believe our wee lassie has got to this stage already. It seems no time since we stood at the top of the hill and watched Billy playing in the garden at High Bowie, and wondered what sort of world it would be for them, with a war just beginning. Where have the years gone?'

'I suppose they've flown so fast because we have been so busy, and so happy together.'

'Yes, we have, haven't we?' Andrew began to caress her smooth skin. To him Victoria would always be the girl he had loved for as long as he could remember. In the darkness his mouth smiled against hers. 'I wonder what the young folk would think if they could see us now...'

'We're not that old! Anyway, love isn't just for the young,' Victoria murmured softly. 'It's like good cheese and wine – it gets better and better...'

* * *

Elizabeth Anna Pringle and William Crainby Lennox were married in Darlonachie village kirk on a beautiful day at the end of September. Mick Butler was best man and Libby's friends Alice and Alma were bridesmaids while Mimi was the happiest flower girl in the world. Her lame leg was hidden by the long pale blue dress which Polly had sewn with loving care. Mimi's wide smile, sparkling blue eyes and fair curls won many hearts that day. Libby had also invited Charlotte to be a bridesmaid but she had tactfully declined.

'I do appreciate being asked, Libby,' she said with a smile, 'but I think it might upset your grandmother if I had such a prominent role at your wedding. I would love to come as a guest though, if I may? I shall be able to mingle and lose myself in the happy throng.' She didn't add the words which were uppermost in her mind: *and see your uncle Josh and maybe even dance with him.*

Billy walked down the aisle with his new bride on his arm and as the church bells pealed he stood on the steps of the little kirk and kissed his wife. Together they looked on the upturned laughing faces and heard the many good wishes. He was thankful he had seen sense at last and returned to his roots, to the hills and glens where his ancestors had lived and loved. He had his mother's blessing and she had assured him he and Libby would have had his father's too. And there was nothing that could have made him more content.

CL 16

St
0

HISTORY FROM
OBJECTS

The
Victorians

Angela Royston

WAYLAND

First published in 2010 by Wayland
Copyright © Wayland 2010

First published in paperback in 2012

Wayland, 338 Euston Road, London NW1 3BH
Wayland, Level 17/207 Kent Street, Sydney, NSW 2000

British Library Cataloguing in Publication Data
Royston, Angela.
The Victorians. — (History from objects)
1. Material culture—Great Britain—History—19th
century—Juvenile literature. 2. Great Britain—History—
Victoria, 1837-1901—Juvenile literature.
I. Title II. Series
941'.081-dc22

ISBN: 978 0 7502 6764 9

Produced for Wayland by Calcium
Design: Paul Myerscough
Editor: Sarah Eason
Editor for Wayland: Camilla Lloyd
Picture research: Maria Joannou
Consultant: John Malam

Printed in China

Pic credits: Alamy Images: The London Art Archive 21r, Corbis: Alinari Archives 11r, Hulton-Deutsch
Collection 10; Istockphoto: Noriko London 20, 27b, Nicoolay 11l; Shutterstock: Jacqueline Abromeit 21l, Jeff
Banke 7t, Mikhail Pogosov 4, 17b, 18t; Wayland Picture Library: 3, 5, 6, 7b, 8, 9t, 9b, 12, 13t, 13b, 14, 15t,
15b, 16, 18b, 19, 22t, 22b, 23, 24, 25t, 25b, 26t, 26c, 26b, 27t; Wikimedia Commons: University College
London Digital Collection 17t.

Cover photograph: Wayland Picture Library

Wayland is a division of Hachette Children's Books, an Hachette UK company.

www.hachette.co.uk